FATED: BLOOD AND REDEMPTION

BAAL'S HEART
BOOK THREE

BEY DECKARD

BEY
DECKARD
BOOKS

CONTENTS

AUTHOR'S NOTE

To F who has been there so often for me.
For our many tête-à-têtes about fate and the plague of coincidences that
follow me everywhere I go, I want to say thanks, big guy, for not making
me feel fucking insane.

Let's go grab a beer.

CONTENT WARNINGS

abuse, murder, dubcon, rape (non-detailed), and a lot of rough sex
and general pirate shenanigans.

SOUNDTRACK

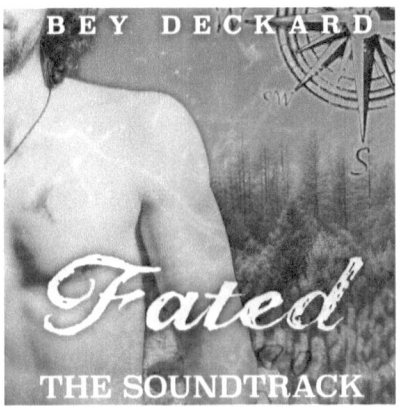

https://geni.us/FatedOST

PROLOGUE

The slave breathed through his mouth slowly, nose not yet numb to the fresh pile of excrement someone had deposited right in front of him earlier. Naked except for the slave collar and harness that never came off, his whole body ached from the uncomfortable position he was in. The ground was cold and slimy under his knees, and his back throbbed from the way he was bent forward, neck and wrists secured in the wooden stocks. He shifted slightly and winced as his movements caused a sharp lance of pain through his bowels. Someone had penetrated him with something the previous day. Probably a branch, judging by how rough it had been. He'd been blind with agony.

Now it was mostly a constant, dull ache, but he dreaded the thought of taking a shit.

The slave opened his eyes and was relieved to see that the little town square was almost empty. That was good. When the men from the mining town were on their own, they mostly left him alone; the abuse came when there were a few of them together, and it was always worse when they had been drinking. The slave figured he'd been pissed on by every man in town. And probably every dog. He winced at the thought. His own bladder was full, but he held it even though eventually he'd be kneeling in his own piss puddle again.

With another painful shift, the slave closed his eyes. He wished that they'd just killed him when they found him covered in his master's blood.

*B*linking slowly, the slave raised his head at the sound of someone approaching on the wooden planks that served as walkways in the town square. He must have fallen asleep again. It was amazing what someone could suffer through and still get some bloody sleep. He eyed the men approaching as he licked rainwater off his lips.

The one on the left, the one who had put him in the stocks nearly a week earlier, was his master's brother-in-law Lester. He didn't recognize the other.

The stranger was tall, and as he walked with long strides, the hard soles of his black leather boots thudded loudly on the warped, wet wood. As they got closer, the slave could see that the man wore a greatcoat that covered him from chin to ankle, and atop his head was a wide black hat with a curved brim. The only hint of colour he saw was a bright-red silk scarf that peeped above the coat's collar when the stranger turned his head to speak to Lester. The men stopped next to the slave, and as he craned his head up to see the two of them, the rain blurred his vision some-what. Or, he thought, maybe it was the lack of food finally getting to him.

Squinting, the slave silently studied the stranger. He was a middle-aged man with a tanned, angular face, a fine, thin nose, and an upper lip that was bowed like a gull's wings. He had a foreign look to him that was confirmed by the strange accent he spoke with after he had circled the slave a few times.

"He's damaged," the man said quietly, "on top of being obviously half-starved and subjected to the elements."

"What of it?" growled Lester. "I ain't lowerin' the price, if that's what yer after, Captain. Yer gettin' him fer a song as it is. He's as strong as a bloody bull, I can guarantee at least that."

"Regardless of what you get for him, you're making a profit," pointed out the tall man, a wrinkle appearing on his smooth brow. "You told me you were going to have him put down."

"Three silver. Take it or bloody leave it," muttered Lester.

The slave made himself look directly into the stranger's dark, deep-set eyes and was surprised by what he saw there. No disgust, no scorn, and nothing resembling pity. Just quiet self-possession. The tall man's eyes widened slightly after a moment.

"I will give you four if you arrange for his transport to my ship," said the stranger as he turned away and lifted a small, red velvet pouch from his coat pocket.

Lester swore under his breath. After a few seconds he nodded.

"Fine. But, I'm bloody done with this devil. He's yer trouble now," he growled and accepted the coins. Lester handed the keys over to the stranger and turned to go arrange for a wagon.

The slave ground his teeth together. He had just been sold for less than the price of a barrel of beer. He scowled at the stranger in the coat. The man was probably a pervert. The slave had seen his kind before. All perfumed and proper and dainty manners until they had him chained to the bed. His heart jumped quick in his chest as he prepared to bolt as soon as the stocks were open. However, the tall man stared at him a moment longer, a small smile playing over his lips.

"There is nowhere to run," he said softly. "It would be a miracle if you could even get to your feet on your own."

The slave bared his teeth and clenched his hands into hard fists.

The stranger chuckled and slipped the key into the lock. The mechanism clicked.

With a roar, the slave forced himself up and ran, his legs pure fire as he tried to make his escape. However, he got no further than a half-dozen paces before something cool and strong curled around his neck and jerked him backwards. He landed on his back in the thick mud and began to writhe, trying to regain the breath that had been knocked from him. The stranger stooped over the slave, pulling free the whip from around his neck.

"Impressive," was all the man said before relieving the slave of consciousness with the weighted whip handle.

The slave awoke to find himself lying on worn boards in a small jail cell. Painfully, he got to his knees and looked around. The room where the cell was housed entirely made of wood. There were odd, little round windows on one side that showed grey sky beyond. As the slave was contemplating the strange room with the curved wooden wall, the floor beneath him moved, and he was momentarily unbalanced, falling forward onto his hands. Beneath his palms, the planks were worn smooth, and there was an unmistakable bloodstain that darkened the wood in a broad, uneven shape. He frowned and pushed himself back up again. A ship. What's more, the stranger had said *his* ship. What could a ship's captain want with him?

The slave reached forward and used the bars to haul himself slowly to his feet. The pain in his ass throbbed with every heartbeat, and he wondered if he was permanently damaged. When the ship rocked again, the slave shifted his weight with the motion and felt a grin crease his face. Despite his discomfort, he felt a little excited. He'd never been on a boat before. Not even a small one.

The door opened and three men descended the steps into the small room. The captain had shed his greatcoat and stood wearing a loose blood-red shirt cinched tight over his torso by a glossy black vest covered in raised shapes.

Brocade. Just like the cushions in father's study.

The slave shook his head hard to rid himself of the prim little voice in his head. It had been a long time since last he heard it speak, and it brought with it a deep ache in his chest.

"Is he mad?" asked a deep voice.

The slave looked up. The man to the captain's right had the darkest skin he had ever seen. He stood with his arms crossed over his chest as he appraised him, his black eyes narrowed. The hair that fell from his scalp was corded into long, thin, matted braids that were several shades lighter than the gaunt face they framed. When the man turned to look at the captain, the slave saw that there were carved beads chased with silver that hung on a few of his locks.

Mad?

"No, Peter. Just ill-used, I think," said the captain. He then said something in a tongue the slave didn't understand, and the men with him nodded.

"I'm going to unlock this door. Again, there is nowhere to run to, and I doubt you can swim," said the captain to the slave; his dark eyes had the same amused glint they'd held before as he reached forward and placed a key in the lock.

As soon as it had turned, the slave pushed open the door and rushed forward. Hands grabbed at him, but he fought free, landing at least a few solid punches before he was able to break for the stairs. Up he ran, then out onto the deck of a large ship. He didn't slow. Men stopped what they were doing to stare at him, naked and wild and running for his life. When he reached the front of the ship, he saw that that captain had spoken the truth. They were in the middle of the harbour; the only way to shore was to swim. Then he would be free.

The slave looked behind him and saw that they would be on him in a few seconds. Without another thought, he stepped up onto the side of the ship and jumped overboard.

Instantly, he knew he was in trouble—he couldn't keep afloat. Thrashing his arms around and kicking wildly in a panic, the slave tried to keep his head above water, but again and again he sank below the surface, choking and spluttering. Finally he was lost in a murky, green world, his lungs burning as he fought to find the way back up... But which way was up? He felt the edges of his mind get blurry.

A hand closed over the slave's wrist, and another circled his waist. He struggled weakly in the man's grasp, but he was barely holding onto consciousness. Then something tightened over his chest, and he was quickly hauled up and out of the water. He swung in midair, rising slowly as he coughed out the water in his lungs. Beneath him, he thought he could see the dark-skinned man swimming in place.

When at last he reached the side of the ship, he was grabbed by his harness and dumped onto the deck like a bloody fish. Before he could turn to get to his knees, the captain planted a boot in the middle of his chest and held him down while the others put shackles on his wrists. The man was laughing and shaking his head.

The slave would kill this bloody captain, just like he had his last master. Then who would be fucking laughing?

The slave sat in his little cage, his arms wrapped around his knees with his eyes half-closed. He'd been brought to this new prison the previous day, an iron cage bolted into the side of the captain's quarters. He could tell it was new; the iron smelled freshly forged, and the well-worn wood of the floor and wall was brightly scored in places. A cage built especially for him. Seemed like he was to be kept as an object for sport after all.

Though the slave had drunk down the whole pitcher of water, he couldn't bring himself to touch the food he had been given. He was terrified of what would happen if he did. That morning, he had finally sat down on the pot to take a shit, and he had gone faint from the pain of it. When he made himself look, there was nearly as much blood as stool. The pain continued to twist inside him with every movement.

Despite his injuries, he'd made the best of his time. The slave had worked free one of the metal rings on the small barrel inside the cage and had bent it in his hands until the metal gave and snapped. Then, he'd folded the piece over itself again and stomped it flat beneath his heel. The new edge of the metal had cut into him, and his foot still bled, but he thought it had been worth the effort. Though the weapon wasn't particularly sharp, with enough desperate force it would pass easily between a man's ribs.

Desperation was all he had left.

The door to the room opened, and the captain walked in, the thump of his boots on wood muffled once he reached the thick carpet in front of the cage.

"Will you try to run again, I wonder?" asked the captain softly with a twist of his lips. His dark eyes were once again creased in amusement.

The slave didn't respond. He just pushed himself up onto one knee and bowed his head slightly, as if in deference. He would attack the man as soon as the door was open.

The captain unlocked the cage, but instead of stepping into it like the slave had expected, he took a step back. The slave frowned. It would be harder to stab a man who was on his guard. However, he got to his feet with a grunt and, weak from pain and lack of food, he took an unsteady step forward.

The captain's eyes darted to the slave's hand, spotting the makeshift blade.

"Ah, so you're going to kill me? Is that it?" said the older man with a smile.

The slave growled at him and tightened his fist on the folded metal, preparing to slash out with it with his next step.

"I admire your tenacity. Any other man in your position, with the extent of your injuries and malnourishment, would have given up by now. I have to say that I am amazed you're able to stand at all," said the captain.

With a quick step forward, the slave lashed out, but the captain moved gracefully out of the way with a small laugh. Frustrated, he lurched forward again, but once more the man avoided his blade. He held it out, hand shaking with the effort of keeping his arm up. Teeth clenched, he steeled himself to try once more before he collapsed, but then the captain took a half step forward so that the folded metal rested against his breast.

"You don't have the strength, Tom," said the man in a gentle voice.

Tom?

There was rushing noise that blocked everything out for a few heartbeats, but when the blade fell from his nerveless fingers, he heard it bounce from the carpet to the wooden planks. The slave let himself fall slowly to his knees, his mouth dry and his heart slamming against his ribs. He stared up at the captain in agony.

"That's what it says on your papers," said the captain with a tilt of his head. "Your name is Tom."

1

CAPTAIN BLACK

And when the day arrives, I'll become the sky, and
I'll become the sea, and the sea will come to kiss
me, for I am going home. Nothing can stop
me now.

— TRENT REZNOR

WEEK ONE

Captain Black stood on the quarterdeck, arms crossed over his chest, surveying the noisy crowd below. Over half of those assembled were crew hopefuls, and he was glad for their presence. The *Heart's* numbers had dropped dangerously low on the journey to Ereme'ia Balor, and they desperately needed to replenish their crew if they were going to make the journey home. Scanning the crowd, Jon was happy to see a few of the tall, bronze-skinned fisherfolk. Having them come on account would most likely be a great help, as they were already sailors. If they were anything at all like the hardworking Polas, it would take a minimum of effort to get them integrated into the crew.

Already thinking like a captain, thought Jon with a smile.

On top of the aspiring pirates, they had also taken on a number of passengers. Anxious to leave these lands and memories behind, some of these ex-citizens and slaves of Balor would travel all the way to Madierus to help repopulate the island. A life of peace and freedom under a fair ruler was understandably appealing after the horrors that they had been subjected to.

"Shit," murmured Tom at his side.

Jon frowned and followed the first mate's line of sight. Near the back of the crowd stood a number of burly men sporting the same winding black tattoos as Tom. One of them had his arm in a sling.

"That's the fucker whose arm I broke," grumbled the first mate.

Jon looked over at Tom. He lounged almost indolently forward over the black and red railing, forearms crossed and elbows resting on the painted wood as he watched the group of men. However, Jon knew that the first mate was anything but relaxed. Tom's green-blue eyes were narrowed in suspicion, and the lines of his jaw were tense. From one large, callused hand dangled the glossy, brown loops of a whip, and Tom's knuckles whitened as he shifted his grip; the first mate had carefully repaired, oiled, and rebraided his trophy from the mines, and he'd learned quickly how to use it.

"You think they're here to make trouble?" asked Jon quietly. He glanced again at the ex-slaves and frowned.

"Let's bloody hope they're not," said Tom grimly.

Jon nodded. If there was anything they could do without, it was more trouble. With a sigh, he turned his eyes back to the current crew of *Baal's Heart* and tried not to cringe at what he saw there. Save for Cook and two or three others, the pirates stared up at Jon with expressions ranging from disbelief to unveiled contempt as they muttered amongst themselves. They weren't happy that Baltsaros's "cabin boy" was now their captain, and Jon didn't blame them. Normally, the crew elected a captain, but these weren't normal circumstances.

"Shall we get this over with?" asked Jon, dropping his hands to the railing.

Tom nodded and headed to the staircase.

"We will be taking on twenty-five men and women as crew. No more, no less," shouted Jon, leaning forward to stare down at the assembly. "Those who have experience as sailors or have relevant skills will be chosen first. Understand that you will be leaving your old life behind you. Slave or master, you are all equals under these sails. If you take issue with that fact, do not even think of joining my crew—"

"Fackin' 'ell, this ain't yer bloody crew!" yelled someone from below. Jon couldn't tell who it was, but Tom's whip picked out the man for him a heartbeat later; following a loud crack, a line of red appeared on the grizzled pirate's cheek a finger's width from his eye. With a howl, the man clutched at his face, blood leaking from between his fingers as he fell back into the crowd.

"The next fucker who opens his bloody mouth will lose his bloody eye," growled Tom from his place on the stairs. He stared at the crowd as he coiled the whip in his hands. "When the fuckin' captain is speakin', ye bloody well listen. That goes for all of ye, Jack Tar and landlubber alike. I don't care who the fuck ye think ye are!"

"I will speak to you all individually before asking you to make your mark," continued Jon as if there had been no interruption. "Aboard my ship"—he looked pointedly at the scowling pirates— "there will be *zero* tolerance for treachery or rabble-rousing. If you can't obey the simple articles we have, leave immediately. This will be the only warning I will give." He locked eyes with each known troublemaker in turn, waiting for them to begrudge him a nod before moving on to the next. The crowd grew so quiet and tense that all he could hear was the water chuckling against the hull. Ceara, standing up on a crate near the back, gave him a quick thumbs-up of encouragement when he spotted her. He furrowed his brow and nodded after a heartbeat, turning his eyes back to the men and women below. He clenched his teeth hard but then let out a sigh.

Ceara. A snake among jackals.

This should be interesting.

He straightened and clapped his hands hard together once, though he already held the rapt attention of all aboard.

"Good. Now that *that* is out of the way, it's time to get acquainted," Jon smiled warmly. "Welcome to *Baal's Heart!*" He gestured to Nathaniel who stood at the base of the steps holding a sheaf of pages tacked to a small board—the middle-aged mapmaker had been chosen for this task due to the quality of his penmanship. "Those who are passengers, please line up in an orderly fashion so Nathaniel can get your details. Don't expect this to be a pleasure cruise, however. You will all be assigned duties for the duration of the trip."

A few of the passengers, obviously ex-citizens, looked dismayed by the news.

"What about them who can pay?" piped up a very short, portly man in maroon silks. In his arms, he held a lumpy bundle. Jon frowned. Passengers weren't the same as crew and thus wouldn't share in the plunder, should there be any; the "no prey, no pay" model wouldn't benefit them. As such it was potential for glaring inequality between rich passengers who could pay for others to do their chores and those who had nothing but the clothes on their back. He rubbed the collar of his coat between thumb and forefinger as he thought.

What would Baltsaros do? he wondered. However, it was doubtful that asking Baltsaros would accomplish anything. The captain's mental state had deteriorated further since they had put him in the cage, but neither Tom nor Jon thought letting him out was a good idea. Not with that happened the other night.

*J*on stared at the ceiling above the bed, sleepless with worry. The moon was so bright that it shone through the stained-glass windows and made pale patterns on the smooth boards overhead. With his brain churning in the relentless grind of worry, Jon's eyes tracked the ghostly shapes as they slid back and forth across the ceiling with the ship's gentle rocking. Though he couldn't hear his footfalls, the occasional creak of wood told him that Tom was above on the quarterdeck, probably pacing as he smoked. Tom's bluff, dismissive confidence in regard to Baltsaros's recovery didn't fool Jon for a second; the first mate was just as stressed as he was about the captain's injuries.

Jon rubbed his face, bleary and tense, and looked over at the man lying beside him on the bed. He was startled to see that he was awake. Tiny pinpricks of light were reflected in Baltsaros's dark eyes as he watched Jon silently.

"I'm sorry, did I wake you?" whispered Jon.

A deep crease appeared between Baltsaros's brows. After a moment, he shook his head slowly.

"Are you in pain?" Jon said, turning onto his side. Another headshake. "Thirsty? No?" He sighed and reached out to check the man's forehead for fever. He felt powerless and frustrated in the face of Baltsaros's suffering.

At his touch, Baltsaros's brow smoothed out, and he reached up to place his fingers against the back of Jon's hand.

Jon smiled at the contact, but his heart sank at the dry heat that burned beneath his palm—he was getting worse. "We'll get home to Madierus as soon as we can... I'm sure Abetha will be able to help you somehow."

"Yes. It will be all right," Baltsaros rasped, encircling Jon's wrist with his long fingers.

Jon nodded quickly, made suddenly uneasy by the glittering gaze of the sick man. It was as if the only signs of life in his face were the coal-black eyes that watched him without expression.

Baltsaros pulled Jon's hand away from his forehead and pressed a soft kiss to the inside of his wrist before letting go. His lips were hot and parched, and Jon felt another pang of concern.

"Come here," whispered Baltsaros. "I want to hold you in my arms. It will make me feel better like nothing else can."

Something felt... *off*. However, Jon brushed aside the feeling and moved closer to him, placing his head on the man's shoulder. Gingerly, he curled his arm around Baltsaros's waist, bracing himself and trying not to put too much weight on the man beneath him. The position would quickly get uncomfortable, but he didn't want to hurt him. A little sacrifice.

Baltsaros's fingers came up to stroke his cheek, his jaw, down the bridge of his nose; when his fingertips brushed Jon's bottom lip, Jon let out a little sigh.

"You're such a soft creature," murmured Baltsaros.

Jon frowned, none too happy to be called "soft". He was not the weak thing he had once been. However, he forced himself to let the words run off of him like droplets down a duck's glossy back. It was meant as a compliment, a way for Baltsaros to say how much he liked touching Jon. Nothing more. It should make him happy.

Then why do I feel like running?

The thought had barely touched his mind before Baltsaros's hand closed over his mouth, his thumb and forefinger painfully pinching Jon's nose shut as he rolled over on top of him. He froze for half an instant before he tried to push the man off, but Baltsaros wrapped his other hand around Jon's throat and *squeezed.* Panic flooded Jon's brain as he fought to free himself. For a man who was so wounded, Baltsaros bore down distressingly hard on Jon as he crushed his windpipe, slowly robbing him of breath. Nothing Jon did shifted his iron grip—not his nails clawing into flesh nor his feet battering at Baltsaros's shins as he struggled desperately. It was like Baltsaros was made of senseless clay. A deadly golem.

"*Min haeken,*" murmured Baltsaros. "Stop struggling. Give in, my soft little thing. Give up. Hush now, Jon. It will only be a moment longer. Give in. That's it, my love... You don't need to suffer life any longer. Let me take this pain from you. I will never be able to hurt you again... Trust me, Jon. Trust me..." His voice continued to coo and whisper in Jon's ear as he fought for his life. His vision swam with amorphous shapes that fled down a narrowing tunnel of darkness. With his last surge of strength, Jon reached up and beat against the headboard with his fist, nerveless to the carved figures that dug into his knuckles with every strike.

There was a strange, warm feeling in Jon's chest, and the world went crazy with bright colours right before the blackness overtook him.

*J*on gasped, clawing at his throat with one hand while the other pushed at the figure above him. The cool air seared his lungs, and he felt tears run down the sides of his face as he fought to free himself.

"Jon! Jon, it's me," said the man straddling his waist as he grabbed Jon's hand.

"Tom? Wha—" Jon was momentarily overcome by a coughing fit.

Tom quickly helped Jon to sit up, his brow wrinkled in concern. The first mate then lurched to his feet and splashed some water into a cup, returning with it to the bed where Jon sat.

After taking a few sips, Jon tried again.

"What happened? My fucking throat..." he said hoarsely. "Where's Baltsaros? He tried to kill me."

"Aye. Bloody good thing I heard ye bangin', lad," said Tom, glancing at the cage across the room. In it, Jon could see a figure huddled on the narrow cot, rocking slowly. The first mate's fingers touched his neck softly, and Jon turned to look at Tom. The big man was trying to hide his fear, but Jon could almost see it like a cold mist in the air between them.

"This'll hurt ye for a bit, but he ain't done ye real harm," said

Tom in a choked voice as he delicately prodded at Jon's bruised throat. With a sudden realization that the first mate had breathed life back into him, Jon hiccupped a sob and leaned forward until his forehead rested against Tom's collarbone. He closed his eyes. The first mate's arms came around him, and he both heard and felt Tom's long, shuddering sigh.

"What are we goin' to do, love?"

"I don't know. I just… don't know."

~

"All personal wealth will be stored in my quarters until we reach our destination," Jon said to the crowd of passengers. There was a surge of voices raised in dismay, but Jon held up his hands, pushing back the tide of objections. "It is not optional. You will simply have to suffer through a taste of equality while aboard."

"Equally poor!" someone shouted.

Jon shook his head with a laugh.

"As far as I am concerned, the lot of you are getting free passage; you will have somewhere to sleep, and we shall feed you. If that is poverty, then maybe you should reassess your decision to sail with us." He smiled. "The discussion is *closed*. We sail in three hours. Stay or go; it is up to you. I don't care. However, you will not sail with full purses."

Jon turned away, his heart beating nervously against his ribs. *Show no fear.* He took a deep breath and tried to relax into the role.

"You mates," he shouted at those who wished to join the crew, "line up smartly against the gunwale, if you will. Tom will get to you in a moment." He watched the men and women move to obey him. Some lined up quickly, desperate to show how eager they were to become pirates. Others walked almost nonchalantly to the side of the ship, believing that eagerness wouldn't work in their favour, and Jon smiled at the ridiculous display of indifference. However, when he saw Ceara jump down from her crate and join the hopefuls, he felt a lick of disquiet again. He had agreed to take Ah'puch's ex-spymaster as far as the southern peninsula as a passenger. There had been no talk of her joining the crew.

With a frown, he looked away. Despite all the help she had given them, Jon knew that she was loyal to one person and one person alone: herself. They needed her, and it worried him that their lives depended on someone he couldn't trust.

We'll cross that bridge when we get to it, I suppose, he thought, rubbing his hand across his forehead. After a thought, he turned to the first mate.

"Tom," he said quietly, "can you assign a taskmaster to watch over the passengers? Someone you trust. I don't want any shenanigans, got it?"

"Aye, Cap'n," said the first mate with a grin. The husky sound of Tom's voice and the way his sea-green eyes twinkled mischievously at Jon brought a hot flush to his face. The first mate was getting a kick out of Jon being captain. No doubt the minute the two of them were alone, Tom would show him a different version of the fealty Jon was looking for in the crew. The thought made his cheeks even warmer, and he let out a slightly awkward laugh.

"Stop thinking about your cock, Tom, and see to my orders like a good boy, hm?" he said, trying to sound playful.

Tom's eyes darkened, and his grin widened as he scratched his chest.

"It ain't *my* cock I was thinkin' about," said the first mate with a wink. However, he quickly went down the rest of the steps and started yelling orders at the crew along with a rolling, abuse-laden stream of curses. Jon smiled wide.

It was good to be home.

2

SKELETONS IN THE CLOSET

$\mathcal{T}$om let out a grunt as he lifted the heavy coil of rope onto his shoulder. With all the added bodies, they needed to free up space so that everyone had somewhere to sleep —those sleeping abovedeck for the time being would only be able to do so as long as the weather held out. That morning Tom thought he could smell rain on the horizon, so had pressganged some muscle into helping him clear out the starboard bunkroom.

For as long as he had been on board, it had been used as a storage room, and that made it a big, tedious job. The room was piled high with all number of ship's supplies: spare rope, barrels that badly needed to see a cooper for repair, piles of old sailcloth, crates full of odds and ends.

He dumped the rope outside the door for one of the others to take and turned back to grab a pair of boards leaning against one of the bunks. With a surprised huff of breath, he skipped a step back and dropped the boards when he saw what lay behind them. Chuckling sheepishly when he realized what it was, Tom scratched the back of his neck and leaned forward to take a closer look at the larger-than-life wooden skeleton that lay on the sagging bunk mattress.

"Well, hello there, matey," he said with a grin. "Yer a gruesome fella, aint'cha?" He reached out to wipe some of the thick dust off its skull. The skeleton's mouth was open in a soundless scream, and its body was bound with a rusted length of chain. Most of the paint had worn off the old ship's figurehead—leaving it a stained and mottled thing of mismatched wood—but the carving itself was incredibly lifelike.

Bloody deathlike is more like it, thought Tom in amusement. He wondered who had made it and whether it had once graced the front of *Baal's Heart*. Maybe it was just plunder from another ship? He gave it a soft pat on the clavicle.

"If ye sit tight like a good skelly, maybe I'll bring ye out to see the light o' day an' fix ye up with the best view on the ol' tub. Aye? Hm? All right then," laughed Tom, taking up the wooden boards again.

When the light dimmed behind him, Tom turned quickly. Standing in the doorway was the big tattooed fucker that he'd fought at the inn, Saban. The ex-slave had his arm in a sling, which made him about as useful as teats on a nun for most of the work that needed to be done. Worse was the fact that Saban had neither his numbers nor letters; they'd only taken him on because he'd had experience working on a boat before he'd turned bouncer.

He will be useful; bones knit in time, Jon had said.

Aye, but what about grudges?

Tom eyed Saban warily. Even with his busted arm, the Balorian ex-slave was a match for the first mate if it came to violence; at the inn, it had been Saban's sledgehammer fist that had downed Tom like a sack of wet meat in the end.

"Peace, friend," said Saban quietly. His baritone was as smooth as river rocks compared to Tom's gravel. "I did not come aboard for revenge."

"Friend, aye?" muttered Tom with a sidelong glance at the

taller man as he walked past him. After handing off the boards, he turned and appraised Saban. "What d'ye want then, mate? I'm busy." There was something about the way the other man stood —emanating a quiet, self-possessed power despite his injury— that made Tom's pulse tick up a notch. He felt strangely intimidated.

And just a wee bit horny. With an inward chuckle, Tom crossed his arms and tried to shoo away the stray thought that had him wondering what it would be like to have that hard, smooth body bent over his.

"I had never seen a slave stand up and fight the way you did," said Saban with a soft smile. "There is such fire in you. Even if in reality you had not been a slave for some time, I can't imagine that your head bowed as swiftly as ours to a master."

Tom grunted and dipped his chin slightly, made uncomfortable by the praise. He leaned down to pick up a big bundle of what seemed to be old clothes and threw it out the door.

Saban watched Tom silently as he worked. After a few moments the ex-slave spoke again.

"I wanted to thank you personally… and pledge brotherhood to you for what you did for us," said the broad-shouldered Balorian.

"Didn't do nothin', mate," growled Tom. He glanced up and met Saban's eyes; they shifted between green and brown in the rays of late-day sunshine that spilled into the dusty room. Saban stared back at Tom, his expression of calm confidence unchanged. With a sigh, Tom scrubbed a hand over his shorn hair and lifted the other shoulder in a shrug. "Listen… Honest to fuckin' gods, Saban, I didn't do nothin'. Was all a bloody coincidence. I only had the mates spreadin' tales of mutiny in the mines to cause confusion… never meant to start up a bloody rebellion. I had no idea Jon was also spreadin' rumours and that the redheaded bitch would spread 'em further. We weren't out to save anyone but the captain, understand? I ain't no hero. Go find some other mate to be yer brother, aye?"

Saban just smiled wider and nodded solemnly before turning to leave. Tom had a feeling that his words had little effect.

"Why do you have *such* a hard time accepting thanks or praise when, as soon as you're in your cups, you make everyone keenly aware of just how much of an important man you are?" said a nearby voice, full of amusement.

Tom grimaced and turned his head to the woman sitting cross-legged on a dusty bunk. The way she managed to appear as if out of thin air made him feel embarrassingly uneasy.

"What do *you* want?" he mumbled, gathering up an armload of sailcloth.

"He is quite the handsome one, isn't he?" Ceara said. "With that smooth, dark skin and those gorgeous eyes of his. I wonder how tall he is." The slight woman tapped her bottom lip, a little wrinkle appearing between her brows.

"Don't know. Didn't notice," grumbled Tom, almost tripping on a loose board as he turned away. "Now get yer skinny ass gone if ye don't have somethin' of bloody use to me."

"Don't be so tetchy, sweetheart. This 'redheaded bitch' was simply sent here to tell you that Captain Black wants you in his quarters," said Ceara with an amused twitch of her lips as she stood. As she passed him, Ceara gave Tom a quick little pat on the backside and was gone.

Tom clenched his jaw and balled his fists, taking a few slow breaths to tamp down his annoyance.

Tetchy indeed.

om ducked through the door of the captain's quarters and saw that Baltsaros was out of his cage. The older man sat at one end of the long mahogany table, a bowl and mirror in front of him as he shaved carefully with a sharp blade. Jon sat at the opposite end, poring over a map he held stretched out between his hands. As Tom strode into the room, he saw that Jon had a long, unsheathed knife across his knees. The young captain wasn't taking any chances with Baltsaros, and Tom was glad for it.

The first mate leaned his discovery up against the back wall and stood back, admiring it.

"What in hells is that?" said Jon, looking up, his blue eyes wide.

"It's the old figurehead for the ship," said Baltsaros quietly as he stared at the wooden skeleton. There was a deep crease in his forehead. "Where did you find it?"

"It was in the bunkroom we're clearin'," Tom replied with a frown. Though Baltsaros had sounded annoyed, he just nodded, smiled, and resumed shaving.

"Why is it so... grotesque? I thought that the ship was called *God's Hammer* not *Hell's Minion*," said Jon, grinning.

Tom chuckled and reached out to mime pinching the skeleton on its cheek.

"Don't let Jonny-boy here make fun of ye, matey," he said in kind voice. "I think yer just fine." Tom turned to look at Baltsaros and saw that he was staring hard at him with eyes like pitch. In the blink of an eye, his sharp-planed face creased into an amused grin. However, when Baltsaros looked back down at the mirror he held, his expression went dark once more.

Tom straightened his shoulders and tried to ignore the pulse of worry that suddenly soured his stomach. He hated Baltsaros's constantly shifting moods. The captain he had worked and fought with was lost somewhere in this strange husk of a man. Tom wanted nothing more than to shake the bloody hells out of him until his senses came back, but he knew that it was a fool's thought. It felt like the separation was driving him mad; it was bloody depressing that the last time he and the captain had even touched was when Tom had had to wrench a knife from Balt-saros's hand a few days earlier.

"I have to go see Nathaniel. This map needs to be updated with the one from Polas's ship," said Jon. He had his eyes on Baltsaros as he spoke, a tense expression on his youthful face.

Tom knew that Jon was even more sensitive to the chaos that

whirled through the captain like a maelstrom. It made him furious that Baltsaros had put them through all of this. At least when he had been killing folks and eating bits of them, he had been in control of himself the rest of the time. And what was this bullshit jealousy he was feeling over the fact that Baltsaros had tried to kill Jon numerous times now but hadn't *once* tried to kill him? What kind of stupid did you have to be to—

"Tom?" Jon's voice cut into Tom's thoughts, and he looked up. "Can I leave you here with him?"

"Aye," replied Tom, pulling out a chair for himself. The first mate was tense. Unhappy. Bloody miserable even. He smiled wide at Jon. "Dont'cha worry, love."

Jon's eyes narrowed, and he pressed his lips together. Tom knew he wasn't fooled for one second. When Jon came around the table and put his arms around Tom for a quick embrace, he murmured in his ear:

"We'll make this right. Don't *you* worry."

Tom let out a slow sigh, nodding again, but grinned in surprise when Jon took his earlobe between his teeth and bit softly. Jon's breath was warm against the side of Tom's neck for a moment longer, and then he was gone.

Tom let his smile fall.

"What's the matter?" asked Baltsaros, patting his starkly planed face with a soft cloth. His eyes were clear again, his mind once more his own.

But for how long?

Tom just scowled at the man's question and shook his head.

"What is it?" pressed the older man, a note of concern in his voice.

Tom scrubbed a hand over his face, closed his eyes, and took a deep breath.

"Tired of jerkin' off," he finally muttered. He risked a glance at Baltsaros and hunched his shoulders in embarrassment and annoyance at the man's grin.

"Feeling neglected?" asked Baltsaros, laughing.

"It's not funny," mumbled Tom, balling his fists under the table. He heard the captain sigh and then the muffled scraping sound of chair legs against the wool carpet. He stared down at the tabletop as Baltsaros came around and put his hands gently on his shoulders.

"You're right. I'm sorry, my tomcat. It's not funny," said Baltsaros quietly. "Has Jon not been...?" His words sounded odd, as though he was forcing himself to say them.

"Not with you sittin' there half-mad in yer fuckin' cage. It ain't right..." growled Tom, his jaw tense. He closed his eyes and chewed on the inside of his cheek. Baltsaros's fingers had tightened their hold, and the first mate could feel a faint tremor in the man's hands. "It's more'n that, Da," he said softly. "Not just the fuckin'... I... just miss... *you*. I bloody want ye to get well, ye know?" Tom looked over his shoulder at Baltsaros; the older man's eyes were vague as he stared off to the side.

Tom frowned, but just as he was about to speak up again, even though he could barely breathe for the tightness in his chest, Baltsaros suddenly dropped his hands and took a step back. The tall man's chiselled face contorted in anger as he stared at Tom.

"Who are you? How did you get on my ship?" growled Baltsaros in his native tongue.

Suddenly, all the worry and horror of the past few weeks came to a head inside Tom; fury crashed through him as he lurched to his feet, and he grabbed Baltsaros's collar in one callused fist, yanking him forward roughly.

"Ye know who I bloody am," he said hoarsely, catching Baltsaros's wrist in his other hand when he began to struggle. "Ye know ye did this to yer fuckin' self, aye? This is yer godsdamned fault, Da. We could'a left—me, you, an' Jon—but *no*... Ye had to go an' get yer bloody head scrambled, didnt'cha? And ye did it without a single, fucking, bloody thought about what would happen to—" Tom's voice broke and he couldn't finish the words.

Without a thought about what would happen to me if I lost you.

Blood sang in his ears as his heart battered his ribcage, and he tightened his grip. When he saw Baltsaros's eyes widen in fear, Tom let out a low groan.

Da didn't fear.

"Why are you afraid?" Tom shouted into his face, made angrier by the fact that Baltsaros flinched. "Just stop it. Please fuckin' stop it, Da! Please... Come back to me."

The captain's brows came down in confusion over eyes that couldn't see Tom for who he was. It was bloody hopeless.

Panting through clenched teeth, Tom dragged Baltsaros across the room and threw him into the cage. He slammed the door shut and, without a backwards glance, stalked out of the room.

A deckhand ran up to him with a bucket and brush, obviously intending to ask him something. Tom's hard fist connected with the young man's jaw, knocking him senseless with one blow. Blind to the shocked faces around him, the first mate simply stepped over the prone body and walked away.

~

*B*altsaros looked up when he heard a soft sound from across the room.

"You," he breathed in dismay. "How did you get back on board?"

The other didn't reply.

"You came here to gloat, didn't you?" said Baltsaros, sneering as he got to his feet. He held onto the bars, his knuckles whitening. "I should have cut you into tiny pieces instead of just sinking you in that barrel. *I should have cut your fucking heart out.*" He pressed his forehead to the bars, angered by the silence.

"I wanted you to *suffer.* I wanted you to *feel* yourself dying slowly. I don't know how you managed to escape, but you're not getting this ship back, Romas. You'll have to kill me first," he growled.

"Baltsaros?"

He turned his head. Jon's dark eyebrows were pinched over his storm-grey eyes as he stared at him.

"Are you ok?" asked Jon, approaching the cage.

Baltsaros glanced back at his uncle, but the light had shifted, and he saw that the man had somehow hidden himself in the skeletal figurehead. *I'll be watching you,* he thought.

Twisting his features into what he felt was a pleasant smile, Baltsaros turned to Jon.

"Yes, Jon. I'm perfectly fine," he replied.

3

HOPE AGAINST ALL HOPE

Hope is the pillar that holds up the world. Hope is
the dream of a waking man.

— PLINY THE ELDER

WEEK THREE

Jon washed his hands and face with cold water from
the ewer and sighed when he looked at himself in the
mirror. He was scruffy and his curls were a wild
scribble around his head from being whipped up by strong winds.
He looked more like a madman than a captain. He frowned at the
thought and turned to the cage bolted into the side of the large
stateroom.

Baltsaros was asleep and, though he was covered in a warm
blanket, his bare feet dangled off the end of the cot. With a small
smile, Jon walked over and reached through the bars to tug the
blanket into place; it was getting cooler the further north they

went, and he hoped that it wouldn't get as cold as the first pass through the black mountain range had been or else they would run short on fuel for the potbellied stoves and braziers.

Ceara should have warned me.

He frowned and looked over at the great map at the back of the room. He was starting to have his doubts as to whether the ex-spymaster really knew as much as she claimed she did. She was frustratingly vague on details about their destination, claiming that she was keeping that information to herself because she felt it was her only leverage. She had depended on such tactics in the emperor's court, and Jon had tried—with little success—to get it through her thick skull that he wasn't the type to just throw someone overboard when they outlived some bit of usefulness. He just hoped she knew what she was doing.

Jon extinguished the candle before tugging his shirt up over his head. Instantly, the skin of his chest prickled, and his nipples turned into hard little sensitive points. Once he'd kicked off his boots, he undid his pants and stepped out of them, leaving his clothes on the floor to crawl onto the low, wide bed. The sheets were chilly against Jon's bare skin, and he shivered as he burrowed further under the covers.

As he closed his eyes, he wondered whether Tom would stay out all night yet again.

❧

*T*om bounced on the balls of his feet and brought his fists up. Wrapped around his hands were thick strips of unbleached hempen cloth, bloody now for the damage he had wrought.

"C'mon, poppet," he taunted his opponent. "Ye said ye would down me in less than three punches. What are we up to now, mate?" Grinning lopsidedly because of the swelling on the right side of his face, Tom danced around the man, jabbing at the air playfully. Laz had hit him perhaps a dozen times, each strike an

FATED: BLOOD AND REDEMPTION

explosion of pain that pumped sweet adrenaline into his system. He was high as a kite and everything was fucking grand.

It was almost enough to take his mind off things.

Laz threw a punch at his face, and Tom ducked with a low laugh at the last second, catching the ex-slave with a hard blow to the kidney as he fell past the first mate. The tall man crashed to the boards with a groan of pain; breath whistling past swollen lips, he panted for a moment before climbing unsteadily to his feet. The small crowd shouted and laughed their encouragement as Tom hopped back when Laz lunged for him. Unfortunately, Tom wasn't quick enough this time and was barrelled back into a crate by the lanky ex-slave. His head hit the edge of it, and the pain momentarily stunned him. White-hot stars flashed in his vision as his heart raced, and he fought against the faintness that loomed. With a growl, he shook his head, sending drops of blood and sweat into the audience and tried to free himself from Laz's bear hug, toppling both of them over onto the deck where they began grappling at each other, each trying to gain the upper hand. With Laz on top of him, Tom managed to loop his legs around the other man's waist and he squeezed, but Laz reared back and head-butted him hard in the nose. Overwhelmed with pain, Tom nearly went limp, but he forced himself to wrap his arms around the taller man's neck and hook his ankles together. He hung onto the ex-slave with all his might as Laz bucked like a trapped badger. Tom crushed his thighs together, letting out a pained grunt when he was punched in the ear. Tom felt the bloom of excruciating pain, but it didn't matter… He knew he had won; he was simply stronger than the ex-slave. He tightened his hold on Laz's neck, slowly cutting off his air and blood supply while his legs squeezed the breath out of him.

"Give up, matey," panted Tom. "Yer bloody beat."

Laz wheezed in his ear, the blows to Tom's head getting weaker and weaker with every punch. Finally the lanky Balorian let out a strangled groan and strained hard against Tom before he finally went still. Tom loosened his grip and pushed the insen-

31

sate man off of him, staggering painfully to his feet. His ears were ringing. He spat a bloody gob onto the deck and looked around.

"All righty, who's next?" he slurred. When no one stepped forward, he lurched a step and pointed at a husky, dark-haired man he only vaguely recognized. "You. C'mon."

However, the man just shook his head and quickly turned to go. As the crowd began to trickle awkwardly away—a couple men dragging Laz behind them—Tom swayed slightly as he glared. Harris clapped him on the shoulder.

"Tom, ye beat the shit outta four lads t'night. I think ye can call it a night… Save some for 'nother day?" said the bearded pirate. " 'Sides, yer lookin' a little cockeyed, matey. Why don't ye git yerself t' bed?"

With a scowl, Tom pulled away from Harris.

"Fuck off," he growled.

Harris shook his head before he too left.

Alone in the dim, golden nimbus cast by the lantern, Tom lowered himself down onto a squat crate with a groan and looked at his hands. His fists throbbed tight against the strips of material, and he let out a long, frustrated sigh. He knew he had one more fight in him. Tom needed that last bit of violence so that when he staggered back to his little room belowdeck, he would be asleep before he closed his eyes.

At the soft sound of footfalls, Tom lifted his head. Saban stared down at him, his hazel eyes wide with sympathy. Without a word, the big Balorian sank down in front of Tom and slowly began unwinding his bindings one-handed. The first mate just watched him, too surprised to react.

Saban's long fingers easily took apart the bloody hemp cloth, and he let out a low whistle at the first mate's bruised and bloody knuckles. Then he started on Tom's other hand. When he spoke, his voice was low and gentle.

"Who are you really fighting?"

Tom frowned. He lifted his freed hand to his nose to gingerly wiggle the bridge of it. It hurt but didn't seem to be broken. Eyes closed, he leaned his aching head back against the mast.

"No one," he muttered.

"Then, what are you trying to prove?"

"Why the fuck d'ye care?" Tom grunted. He cracked his eyes open and met Saban's oddly soulful gaze. The big ex-slave had the same kind of good looks that were carved onto statues of gods and princes. The only thing that marred his beauty was a pale scar that ran down one dusky cheek and puckered up the corner of his lip slightly. It wasn't even ugly. It just gave him a sort of wistful grin. Saban pulled away the last of the bindings, and Tom winced as the material stuck to the drying blood on his split knuckles. He grimaced and flexed his fist.

"Why shouldn't I?" asked Saban, smiling as he reached up to grab Tom's chin and tilt his head in the lantern light. Saban's dark brows came down slowly as he appraised the damage.

"That bad, aye?" said Tom with a chuckle, but both the words and laugh came out sounding stiff. His pulse was stuttering; the Balorian's fingers had been so gentle on his hands, and as they slid along his jaw, Tom felt a small ache in his chest that had absolutely nothing to do with his wounds.

"Nah, I've seen you take worse," said Saban, the corners of his eyes crinkling in amusement.

Tom let himself be pulled forward slightly so that the ex-slave could take a look at his ear. Saban cupped the side of his head softly and peered at the wound there. He was so close that Tom could see that he had a tiny mole at the corner of one eye.

Without thinking, he turned his head to press his lips to the other man's in an open-mouthed kiss. However, Tom felt Saban immediately stiffen, and the first mate felt a heart-stopping flood of embarrassment as he was pushed back. With a fiery flush burning his face, Tom tried to get to his feet. However, Saban held onto his wrist, his brown-green eyes unreadable.

"Listen," choked Tom, "I didn't mean to... I thought ye..."

"It's all right," Saban replied after a moment. "Really. It's all right. Just… a misunderstanding. It's fine. Really." He released Tom's arm and stood, brushing off his knees.

Tom looked down and rubbed his face.

What the hells was I thinking?

Saban sat down on the crate next to him, his shoulder almost touching Tom's.

"Tom, you smell like you've been drinking all day, and you look like you've barely slept. Plus, you're probably punch-drunk from those last few blows. You were reacting to my kindness… nothing more," said Saban in his velvety baritone. "Forget it happened. I already have."

Tom clenched his teeth, ignoring the pain in his jaw.

"It was stupid," he muttered. His mind skittered away from the thought of Jon.

It didn't really happen. Not really.

He turned and stared into the inky darkness off the port side, breathing deep to clear his mind. After a thought, he dug a finger into his mouth and pushed at a back tooth to see if it was loose. When Tom spared a glance at Saban, he saw that he was staring off in the other direction; the first mate furrowed his brow, confused.

"Why are ye bein' nice if ye aren't lookin' to…" Tom trailed off awkwardly.

Saban turned, his eyes wide.

"Is that the only reason you think I'd be kind to you? No, I have no desire for men as lovers; but I am kind to those I desire in *friendship*," said the man with a smile. "And you are nearly impossible to befriend, you know that? Every single one of my attempts has been rebuffed in one way or another."

Tom grunted and spat pink onto the worn wood between his feet, mulling over Saban's words. It was true. The broad-shouldered Balorian had approached him a few more times since the day in the bunkroom, and Tom had sent him away each time with terse words, made uncomfortable by what he had thought were advances of a more carnal nature. He felt like a bloody idiot.

"Aye. Sorry," he finally said, nodding to himself. Tom pushed himself to standing without looking again at Saban. "Talk to me again when I ain't half-dead. I'll have... friendlier words for ye next time."

He walked away, but when he reached the trap door to belowdecks, he decided not to descend to his room after all. The tiny space had seen far too much of him lately. It had seen too many nights of his self-pity.

No, he needed Jon.

~

*J*on lay awake, restive and worried. Baltsaros had cried out in his sleep like he did most nights since his rescue, and he had startled Jon from his slumber. Alone in the cold stateroom, Jon wondered where the first mate was. Was he fighting? Drinking? Passed out and at the mercy of some unsavoury characters? Ever since Tom had finally confessed to Jon that two men had nearly molested him when he was too drunk to defend himself, he found himself thinking a lot about the big man's safety.

I can take care of myself, Tom had said with a surly scowl.

"But you didn't," whispered Jon into the dark. "The captain had to save you."

Jon threw back the blanket, but just as he was about to get out of bed to go find the wayward first mate, the door to the captain's quarters opened and shut quietly. A shadow crossed the room on silent feet.

"Tom?" he whispered.

"Aye," replied the first mate.

Jon moved over and turned onto his side, waiting for Tom to join him. When the mattress sank down under Tom's bulk, Jon pulled the blanket up over the both of them. The first mate stank of whiskey and blood.

"Are you ok?" asked Jon in a hushed voice. Tom remained

silent, and Jon frowned, feeling out with a blind hand for the man next to him. He encountered Tom's warm skin and felt him let out a slow exhale.

"I'm a bloody fool," muttered Tom. "Yer gonna hate this… but I have to tell you. I kissed someone, Jon."

Jon's hand froze and his mouth went dry. He thought about Ceara with her flame-red ringlets, sapphire eyes, and cupid's-bow lips.

"Oh?" he said faintly.

Tom's hand closed over his and squeezed.

"I'm tellin' ye because I want ye to know there ain't no secrets I'll keep from ye. And I know ye'd wanna know. And I swear to fuckin' gods that it won't happen again, love," replied the big man. Jon felt the rumble of Tom's voice through his fingertips. "It was a mistake. A misunderstandin'… honest."

Jon licked his lips and swallowed; he was irritated and hurt, but Tom had told him and that counted for something. He had to trust.

"Ok," he whispered. He must have sounded skeptical because Tom let out a low sound that was part groan, part sigh, and he pulled Jon onto him.

"It was bloody stupid of me," said Tom, curling his rough fingers around the back of Jon's neck when he settled against his shoulder. "I'm sorry. Really, really, fuckin' sorry."

Jon nodded and ran his hand softly over the first mate's furry chest. Putting the kiss out of his mind, he instead concentrated on the fact that he was really glad Tom was there with him. Though the weeks at sea had gone by in a blur, Tom's absences had been strongly felt. The first mate always claimed that he slept belowdecks so that he didn't wake Jon up when he came in late, but it was blatantly obvious that Tom was having a hard time facing Baltsaros and had turned to drink and violence to drown out his feelings. Because of that, they hadn't spent nearly enough time together; Jon was sick of sleeping alone, and something had to be done about it.

With that in mind, he slid his hand slowly down Tom's stomach, but the first mate grabbed his wrist to stop him.

"Jon," breathed Tom. However, he didn't resist when Jon pulled his wrist free and brushed his fingers lightly over Tom's soft cock. "What if he wakes?" The first mate's voice was hoarse. "Stop it."

"So he wakes up. What of it?" replied Jon. Tom began to harden under Jon's fingers, and he traced the flared edge of his cockhead with a fingertip. The first mate sighed, but Jon couldn't tell if it was from pleasure or frustration. "*I* had to listen to you two fuck before, remember? I'm sure he'll live through it."

"Not what I mean..." muttered Tom.

"Then what is it?" Jon turned his wrist so he could encircle Tom's cock with his hand. He squeezed and felt the first mate's throbbing pulse against his palm.

Tom tensed and let out a soft groan.

"Hells, he might be lucid enough to join us—if he's up for it. Or, if he isn't, he might not even know what's going on," Jon pointed out.

Tom shifted slightly beneath him.

"What?"

"Don't talk about Da like that," replied Tom tersely.

"Like what?"

"With bloody disrespect."

Jon's forehead wrinkled.

"You think that acknowledging Baltsaros's mental state is some sort of disrespect? You can't even stand being in the same room as him most of the time. Don't you feel that *that* is disrespect?" asked Jon, incredulous. The big man stayed silent. "It's the reality, Tom, and you're going to have to face it and quit being so fucking touchy." Jon pulled his hand away. "He needs you. *I* need you."

"Love, he ain't even sure who the fuck I am half the time," murmured Tom. Another long pause. "What if he never gets better?"

"Then he never gets better. But I very much doubt that," said Jon with a sigh.

"I'm just so… bloody pissed at him," said Tom.

"I know." Jon tilted his head up to kiss Tom's jaw. He tasted blood on his lips.

"And I'm pissed that I'm pissed, ye understand?"

"Yes, I do," whispered Jon. He reached for Tom's cock again and began to stroke it slowly. However, it was obvious from the way it stayed only half-hard that the first mate might be too drunk or tired for anything more to happen.

"And I just fuckin' *hurt*. All the time." The first mate's voice was faint.

"I know," repeated Jon. And he did. There was a raw wound inside of him that bled every time he let himself think about Baltsaros. It took everything he had to cover it up. They had to make it to Madierus. He had to believe that Abetha could somehow help. So… He had to go on. And so did Tom.

"No more fighting," said Jon to fill up the silence.

"What? None?" Tom sounded so dismayed that Jon finally smiled.

"How are we going to sail this ship when you beat up all my sailors?" Jon laughed softly.

"How 'bout I beat them only a little?" Jon could tell Tom was grinning, and suddenly, in the midst of all the pain, everything was all right again.

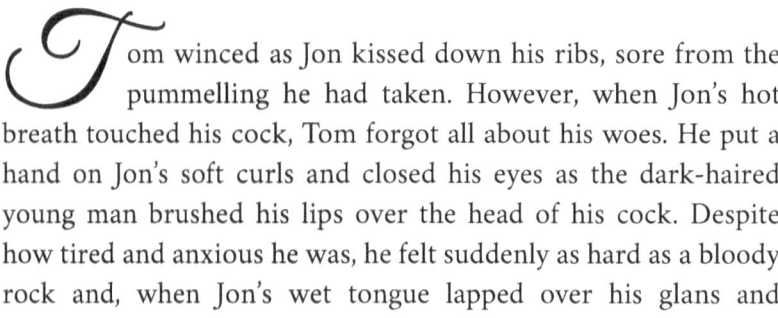

om winced as Jon kissed down his ribs, sore from the pummelling he had taken. However, when Jon's hot breath touched his cock, Tom forgot all about his woes. He put a hand on Jon's soft curls and closed his eyes as the dark-haired young man brushed his lips over the head of his cock. Despite how tired and anxious he was, he felt suddenly as hard as a bloody rock and, when Jon's wet tongue lapped over his glans and stopped to tease into his slit, he couldn't hold back the groan that burst from him.

"That's more like it," said Jon, chuckling.

Tom thought of the pathetic one-handed sessions in his sad little room and shut his eyes, pushing down on Jon's head to coax him to continue. He let out a shuddering sigh as Jon closed his lips over him and sucked softly, his velvet-rough tongue stroking the underside of his cockhead. Shifting his hips slowly, Tom surprised himself with a little, needy moan. He hadn't cum in a few days; he wasn't sure how long he'd last. As if reading his mind, Jon took his mouth away, though his fist remained tight around the root of Tom's cock.

"Tell me when you're close," whispered Jon.

"Mmhm," said Tom, then let out a sharp exhale when Jon's hot mouth covered him again.

Alternating between bathing Tom's cockhead with his soft, wet tongue and deep-throating his thick length until Tom thought he could feel Jon's lips touch his groin, Jon brought him quickly to the point where he was moaning with every breath. His cock was slippery with Jon's saliva, and spit ran down to where his skin was tight over his tender balls. He quickly put out a hand to stop Jon when he felt a hint of the sweet, exquisite pulse start deep inside him.

"Close," he gasped, using all of his self-control not to spill right there and then.

Jon released him, and Tom frowned as he tried to slow his breathing; his cock bobbed up from his belly as he panted softly, and the keen edge of his passion slowly dulled as he waited for Jon to continue. It felt like forever before Jon moved again, but when he did, it wasn't to resume sucking Tom's cock. Jon crawled up and over Tom's body until he was straddling the first mate's chest.

"I'm going to fuck your mouth, and you're not to touch yourself," warned Jon. Tom grinned wide in surprise. He'd been expecting a quick suck and fuck, but it seemed Jon was in the mood for something better. He opened his mouth obediently when the cock touched his lips, but when Jon's hands slid under his head to hold it up, Tom was barely given a chance to take in a breath before Jon pushed his length into him, bumping the back of his throat.

Tom choked and tears sprang to his eyes, but Jon pulled back before he gagged.

"That's a good boy," murmured Jon. Tom's heart pounded in his ears as he let out a small groan around the cock in his mouth. It leaked salty precum onto his tongue, and Tom felt his own still-hard erection stir against him, aching for contact. "I can't decide what I'd like more," said Jon almost conversationally. "Do I cum down your throat or do I fuck your ass instead?"

Tom's brow wrinkled and he made another soft sound. When Jon talked about fucking, it always drove him crazy. With his cock so hard he thought the skin would split, he felt utterly frantic with need. Tom was dying to touch himself, but instead he reached up to grab Jon's hips to pull him forward again; relaxing his throat, he lost himself in the feeling of Jon's cock sliding between his lips in short, trembling little thrusts. Jon soon began to let out shuddering breaths, but he stopped suddenly with a low moan. After climbing awkwardly off Tom, Jon lay down next to him and pulled at his arm.

"I want you on top of me," whispered Jon. "Come here."

Tom immediately moved to obey. Straddling Jon's narrow hips, he reached back, grasped Jon's spit-wet cock in his fist, and positioned the head of it against his pucker. Jon's hand closed over Tom's cock as the first mate eased himself down into the stretch, taking in all of Jon's length as he settled.

"Fuck that feels good," Jon said, his voice a little shaky. "Tom, you're not to cum. Not until I say so."

Tom nodded and began to move—forward to fuck his own length through Jon's fist, and back to slide the cock deeper inside him. He was covered in sweat despite the chilly room, and it ran cool down his chest. The sky had started to lighten outside the portholes, and Tom realized he could make out Jon's face. Mouth open and eyes closed tight, the young captain's head was flung back as Tom rode him slowly. Seeing Jon's naked abandon almost tipped him over the edge; Tom had to fight for a moment to control himself.

Thankfully, Jon opened his eyes with a quiet, raw sound right then.

"Cum for me," he said. He curled his other hand around Tom's balls and stroked him faster. The first mate didn't need any more prompting.

Pleasure uncoiled quickly inside him, and he let out a low growl a heartbeat later at the heady, almost agonizing release, thick cum erupting from his sensitive cock and onto Jon's chest and belly. Each breathless pulse sent another jet, and he panted and grunted with the force of his orgasm. Beneath him, Jon bucked up, his eyes clenched tight again, teeth bared as he came deep inside Tom, his hands squeezing the first mate's cock almost painfully as he rode out the ecstasy that thundered through him. Then, with a last shuddering sigh, Jon went still, his chest heaving and skin slick.

Tom chuckled and wiped the sweat from his eyes, his mind hazy and vague from glorious relief. Jon's blissful grin made him feel softly emotional, and he leaned down to kiss him lightly.

"Thank you," murmured Jon. "I needed that."

"Aye," said Tom happily. He was wonderfully sated and really fucking exhausted. Everything actually felt all right for once. Tomorrow was a new day, and he would face it with a new hope.

However, sleep's siren call had him in its clutches and pulled at him like a jealous mistress. With a grimace he lifted himself off Jon and leaned over the side of the bed to grab Jon's discarded shirt to use as a makeshift cloth to clean up. When he sat back up, he was startled to meet Baltsaros's silent gaze across the room. The older man stared openly at him, and Tom clenched his jaw, his heart sinking and his good mood all but forgotten.

A deep wrinkle appeared on Baltsaros's brow. He turned away

and pulled the blanket over his shoulder, but Tom hadn't missed the glimmer of wetness in those dark eyes.

He frowned and turned back to Jon, wiping at his chest with the wrinkled shirt.

"You ok?" asked Jon, his blue eyes only half-open.

"Sure, love," muttered Tom and forced a smile. "Just bloody tired is all."

When he finally settled down next to Jon a few minutes later, he curled his arm around the slighter man's waist and pressed his face against the side of his neck. Hope. Hope and trust. That's what Jon was to him. He just had to hold on to him and everything would be all right. It had to be.

4

MENDING CRACKS

*T*om whistled cheerfully as he carefully carved another sliver from the peg he was making. The top bolt in one of the foremast's horn cleats had rusted in two, and he hadn't been able to find another one in the ship's stores. Instead, he was whittling a small piece of hardwood into what he hoped would be a fair replacement. He turned the cleat so the holes met up and tried to push the peg through. It was still too wide, so he shaved another small piece off.

"You seem to be in a good mood this morning," said Saban as he walked up. The ex-slave held a little pot of warmed tar in his big hand. Tom nodded in greeting. He watched Saban kneel down and pour a little of the tar onto an exposed rope wedged between the worn boards to shore up the weatherproofing.

He *was* in a good mood; the previous night's fucking had been followed up with a little head in the empty galley that morning, and he felt like a new man. Tom couldn't wait to get Jon behind closed doors again so he could repay the favour. He grinned and resumed shaping his wooden bolt as Saban worked next to him. He appreciated the Balorian's quiet company; Tom had been worried whether friendship had meant a whole lot of jawing, but

Saban seemed to be happy with silence. The first mate found his calm nature oddly comforting. Something about the big man reminded him of Beard—a sort of gentle giant until the hells broke loose, and he became a godsdamned, living battering ram.

Tom pushed the peg into the hole again and was happy when it was a tight fit. He worked it into the hole as far as he could with his hand before he turned his long knife around and started hammering at it with the bone handle. Slowly but surely, the makeshift bolt sank into the mast.

When he heard a sharp intake of breath, he turned and saw that Saban was curled forward, his torso trembling. Slowly the man lifted his head, and Tom was astonished by the change that had taken over him. Saban's normally dusky face had gone ashen, and his eyes bulged.

"What is it?" asked Tom, confused.

Saban licked his lips and blinked rapidly. Panting, he rocked slightly as he held his broken arm against his chest. Tom frowned; it looked like he was on the verge of collapse. He got to his knees and put a hand on the ex-slave's shoulder.

"Saban?"

"It's ok. I just knocked my arm," Saban replied hoarsely, but the skin beneath Tom's palm was covered in sweat and gooseflesh.

The first mate felt a pang of alarm; Saban should have been well on the mend by now. He gently pushed the man's hand away from his arm and pulled aside the material of the sling. What he saw beneath made him grimace. About halfway up Saban's forearm, the skin was swollen and purplish around a prominent bump.

"Fuck, I'm sorry, mate," said Tom, looking up into Saban's pain-reddened eyes.

Saban let out a short laugh.

"No, you're not. You broke it fair and square," he replied faintly. "It'll be fine. Just give me a minute."

"It ain't healin' right," muttered Tom. He touched Saban's arm gently and was dismayed by how hot it was. He'd seen bad breaks before; this one wasn't getting better on its own. The ends of the bones weren't aligned properly, and the arm had no protection. He just hoped...

"Come on, mate," he said, bracing Saban under his good arm with his shoulder.

Saban let out a groan as he got to his feet, and he leaned heavily on Tom a moment, obviously feeling faint.

"Where are we going?" he mumbled. Sweat was beaded on his upper lip.

"To see Da."

⁓

*B*altsaros peered across the room. It was a godsdamned sculpture. Just wood. There was no sign of his uncle because his *uncle couldn't possibly be on the ship*. He tried to focus on that fact and make it stick. Not his uncle. Just a carving. When Jon had caught him talking to the screaming skeleton again, he had asked Baltsaros if he wanted it taken away. He had said no, wanting to use it to help train his mind.

Romas is dead. You stuffed him in a barrel weighed down with cannonballs and threw him into the deepest waters you could find.

Even if his fanatical uncle *had* managed to escape the barrel, he would have died from divers' disease at that depth. Romas had been fat and old, and the water frigid—three factors that always seemed to contribute to deep-water fatalities. Baltsaros figured the man's odds of survival would have been slim.

Scratching at his jaw, he was startled to feel the thick stubble there; time was still passing strangely. Wearily, he sat back down on the cot and looked over at the books piled up on the small barrel he used as a side table. Those he had read when he was younger he could still remember, but the ones he had read in the past year were gone from memory. Same with his recent diaries—it was as if a stranger had penned them. Baltsaros was utterly frustrated. At times he felt a glimmer, a mere hint of what was there before, but his mind seemed full of holes. Just that morning he had woken up thinking that Tom was dead but couldn't remember why he would have thought that.

He picked up one of the leather-bound books with his family crest embossed on the cover and flipped back to an entry that said simply in his own elegant handwriting:

Bad storm. Eight men lost. Tom?

*A*ll following entries after it were the usual observations about weather patterns, the ship, the crew—here and there something about Jon specifically—but nothing about Tom until the very end where he had noted that the first mate had come back. That was it. The next book was spotty in its records; Jon had said that the weather had turned so cold that the ink had frozen in the inkwells, and he had been unable to write. Again, the memories were there somewhere in his mind. He could feel them. He just had to find them.

The door to the stateroom opened and in came Tom supporting a tall, dark-skinned man who had one arm in a sling. The stranger had tattoos down one side of his body, and Baltsaros frowned.

The same as... Tom's? he thought in confusion. Sure enough, the first mate's torso was also covered in markings. When had that happened?

Tom fixed him with a steady, narrow-eyed appraisal as he helped the man to sit.

"I'm all right, Tom," he said quietly, lifting his chin a little. He couldn't remember the last time he had seen the first mate.

Not true, whispered the throaty little voice inside him, and his mind was flooded with an image of Tom straddling Jon across the room, his body moving in a sinuous, smooth motion as he rode the panting, straining, dark-haired man on the bed. He remembered the way the sweat on the first mate's muscled thighs had caught the early-morning light. Baltsaros felt a soft pulse of emotion, and it wasn't particularly pleasant. He ground his teeth together and stood, reaching for the bars.

Tom came across the room and stood outside the cage. His brows were low, shadowing his eyes so they were dark like the ocean's depths. His sun-bronzed skin bore new marks—healing bruises and new shiny scars—and the creases in his face were more prominent. His tomcat seemed older and more serious. Staring at him silently, Tom rubbed his thumb along the side of his jaw; it was a tic that Baltsaros knew so well.

All of a sudden, a memory bobbed to the surface of his fog-shrouded mind. Tom tied to the mast as the captain's whip kissed his back. At first there was no context to the fragment, but as Tom watched him warily through the bars, a portion of the last year's events spread through Baltsaros like blood in water. It was faint and felt almost like it had been lived by another man, but it was there.

"Da?"

Tom's gravelly voice touched a raw nerve inside him, and he closed his eyes, breathing slowly while he tried to piece himself hastily back together. Tom needed him. Baltsaros had to force his damaged mind to find the old channels of familiarity, the ones that Ah'puch's machine had tried to obliterate. A man lost in his own brain, he had to dive into open wounds and strange waters to find his way through the burnt labyrinth. He opened his eyes gave a little smile.

"Apologies, Tom," he said softly. "What do you need?"

Tom looked a touch relieved at his words, his broad shoulders lowering slightly from their tense upward slant. He pulled the iron key from somewhere in his shortened trousers and jammed it into the lock.

"This mate's Saban," he replied as he yanked open the cage

door. "His arm's busted. Weeks past, now. Still ain't healin' right. Can ye take a look at it?"

Baltsaros nodded and stepped past Tom.

"Saban, can I see your arm please?" he asked gently. The tall stranger looked up at him with a pained expression. Suspicion clouded his dark eyes, and he glanced over at Tom.

"You keep your father in a cell?" asked the man in accented but fluent Common.

Baltsaros lifted his eyes and met Tom's.

The first mate paused for only a second before his face creased in a smile.

"He's a bloody, fuckin' lunatic," said the burly pirate, crossing his arms. "But, he's been settin' bones since before ye were whelped, mate. Trust him."

Baltsaros stared at him, aghast at being called a lunatic. He'd have the first mate over a barrel and ploughed with no relief for the sheer impertinence of his words. Then he blinked at the first mate's widening grin, Tom's words coming back to him through the haze: *I just miss you.*

Indeed.

He quickly lowered his gaze to the wounded man to try to intercept the jumble of emotions that rushed to batter at his impaired brain. But it was good. Something deep inside him felt a little more familiar.

With careful hands, Baltsaros quickly divested Saban of his sling and laid his arm on the table. It was a compound fracture—closed thankfully. The last thing the man needed was an infection settling into his wound. He prodded gently along its edge while Tom did something behind him. It was somewhat hard to tell with the swelling, but it felt like an oblique break with only slight luxation. It was relatively good news for the future of the man's arm as it would most likely lay straight if Baltsaros was successful in setting it. A tight splint would be enough to hold it. The bad news was that the bones had had plenty of time to knit together and the length of the raw edges pressed together would mean rebreaking it was going to be more difficult. The first mate handed Saban a mug full of rum and pulled up a chair to watch Baltsaros.

"So?" asked Tom. He sounded strangely invested, and it made Baltsaros wonder if there was something between the two young men. Did Jon know?

He pushed a little harder along the edge of the break and heard Saban try to hold back a grunt of pain.

"Son, you better down that rum and more," he said kindly, looking up into the man's eyes. They were a blend of greens and browns, a beautiful complement to his dusky-skinned, aristocratic face. "I don't understand why no one reset your arm—"

"I was a slave, sir," replied the man, his deep voice slightly hoarse. "My master, that dog-fucking imbecile, decided that teaching me a lesson was more important. How he thought I was going to serve him properly after that..." Saban shook his head and took another deep swallow of dark rum.

"It's over, mate," growled Tom. "He's rottin' in the pits of the black hells."

Yes, definitely something between them, judging by the first mate's vitriol.

"I have to rebreak your arm. Do you understand?" Baltsaros said. "It's going to hurt. But it's the only way. I'll do my best to set it straight, and then it should mend properly."

Saban nodded quickly, his face greyish.

"Tom, I need you to get a few things and then help him onto the floor. You're going to have to hold him down and keep him from jerking away."

Tom stood and left the room quickly to get a leather belt, some wood, and some strips of cotton or silk.

Baltsaros watched Saban down the rest of the rum, and he went to go get the bottle. As he sat down and refilled Saban's mug, pouring himself a small measure in the process, he realized something. This was the first time he could remember being free without Jon or Tom's presence. At least, he *thought* so. Smiling thinly to himself, he drank down a little rum and studied Saban.

Tall, undoubtedly strong, handsome, and there was obvious, keen intelligence in his hazel eyes.

"You're not his father," said Saban, wincing as he sat back more comfortably.

Baltsaros shook his head with another smile.

"And I would say, judging by how quickly he hopped to obey you, that he's used to following your orders," continued the ex-slave.

This time Baltsaros chuckled.

"Yes, he is. Though not always well, he does obey me."

"So *you* are the captain that he went to rescue, not Captain Black." Saban looked at him curiously.

"You're very observant. Your intelligence, I take it, was entirely wasted in your previous duties?" Baltsaros asked.

"Entirely," agreed Saban, his smile rueful. There was an interesting, quiet power to the man that Baltsaros found soothing.

"Well, once you're healed, I'll try to find something to use your skills on," he replied. He touched a spilled drop of rum with his forefinger and traced a circle on the tabletop with it. "However," he said, choosing his words carefully, "whatever your *arrangement* is, I want you to understand that Tom belongs to me. And to Jon. Don't have any aspirations of coming between us."

Saban raised his brows.

"Tom is a friend. Nothing more," said the tall Balorian softly.

"Tom's not one for friends," replied the captain with a frown.

Saban shrugged and then leaned towards him, a thoughtful expression on his face.

"Sir, are you genuinely suffering from some malady of the mind?" he asked. The question, though off-putting, was spoken without a trace of prejudice.

"Yes," admitted Baltsaros. "Temporary, I'm sure."

"I think I am beginning to understand why Tom fights now. He's worried for you." Saban's face was slightly flushed with drink, but he seemed far from inebriated. "What form does it take?" he asked with interest.

Baltsaros thought for few seconds before answering.

"Loss of memory, but not all memory—only from the last year or so," he said. "I have, ah... turns where I am not myself during which time have no control over my violent actions nor do I have any subsequent recollection. Why? Do you know of such things?"

"My father suffered from something we call *dementia*," said Saban quietly. He said the word in Balorian, but it was similar to one they used in the north to describe those who had lost their mental faculties. "I took care of him and was able to affect positive changes in him. Perhaps, as repayment for treating me, you'd let me try some of the same things with you that helped to ease my father's mind."

"I'm afraid my actions are probably not on the same level as your father's," replied Baltsaros, intrigued. "What makes you think you can help me?"

"He killed my mother."

A long silence passed between them. Saban's eyes shifted from brown to green with a subtle movement of his head, and Baltsaros was reminded of the deep, ancient forests of the mainlands. Calm. Still.

Finally, he nodded.

⁓

Tom walked into the room and put his armful down on the table. Without a word, he quickly helped Saban down onto the thick, hand-knotted silk rug while Baltsaros picked through the pile of wood pieces. The older man chose three narrow slats that Tom had pilfered from Nathaniel's map-framing supplies and placed them next to a length of garnet-coloured silk that Baltsaros probably recognized as an old shirt of his. The first mate grinned reassuringly at the big Balorian.

"All righty, mate," he said, holding up the leather belt. "You're goin' to bite down on this. It's gonna hurt, but yer a big boy, and I think ye'll be fine," Tom told Saban, placing the belt between his teeth. He'd had enough bones set to know that it wasn't as painful as you'd think; fear and expectation were the worst parts. "I'm gonna kneel on yer shoulder a bit so ye don't jerk, but try not to move, savvy? I have no bloody problem knockin' ye out with a punch, ducky."

Saban chuckled with the leather belt clenched between his teeth and nodded once.

Tom glanced up at Baltsaros and saw that the older man's deep-brown eyes were on him. He didn't look like he was about to launch into his bloodthirsty god bit, nor did he look vague and scared. No, Da looked confident, thankful… and fond. Tom ducked his head and adjusted his hold on Saban's shoulder to hide the heat that rose in his face.

"Ok," said Baltsaros quietly, placing one hand under the Balorian's wrist and the other on his upper forearm. "Take a deep breath."

5

THE BURDEN OF TRUST

*T*om took a step back and rolled his shoulder, pushing into sore muscles with his fingers as he craned his head to the side. A whole morning spent sanding and carving was starting to wear on him. Maybe it was time to call it quits. He squinted at the ship's figurehead, lashed for the moment to the mast, and nodded to himself. It was starting to look pretty decent. Once he was done fixing it up, he'd paint it; black for the contours, red for the eyes... But they had no white paint. That part would have to wait until they made port somewhere.

"Not bad," said a deep voice.

Tom turned to Saban with a smile. Over the course of the last week, a real friendship had begun to grow between the two of them, and he was bloody glad for it. Saban seemed to know exactly when Tom needed him to keep his mouth shut and when he needed some good-natured ribbing. In return, Tom had found himself confiding in the man. They were just little things, but it surprised him that he felt he could trust Saban at all with his words. There was such a deep well of understanding and patience in those hazel eyes.

Tom realized he was staring and looked back at the wooden skeleton with a shrug.

"Ahh, mate. I ain't got Da's skills, that's for bloody sure. But... aye... not bad."

"I think it'll make a fine addition to the ship," said Saban.

Tom nodded and leaned down to pick up his knife. Jarrod had given the bone-handled dagger back to him as a parting gift before they had set sail; the cheeky, stub-fingered young man had claimed that he had too many knives anyway, but Tom had seen the gesture for what it was. He smiled and tested the edge. It was dulled from use.

"Can I have the key?"

Tom nodded distractedly, digging around in the deep pouch sewn into his trousers for the iron key. He stood and handed it over to the big Balorian. Saban had definitely proven his worth when it came to Baltsaros; he had been spending all his free time with the captain, doing gods knew what, but it was definitely helping Baltsaros to regain control of himself.

"Tell Da that we're gettin' close to the mountain range. He might be up t' seein' it with his own eyes, aye?" said Tom, sliding the knife into its sheath at his belt. "Take advantage of the good weather an' all too." Though the wind still brought with it a chill, the sun shone bright in a cloudless sky.

Saban nodded with a smile and turned to go. Tom watched him walk away, admiring the hard muscles of his shoulders and calves. He couldn't wait until the Balorian's arm healed completely; Saban had promised to show him a new way of fighting, and Tom was looking forward to it.

He pocketed the good bits that were left of the sandpaper, lest they be blown overboard, and made his way to the trapdoor. As he descended the narrow stairs quickly, Tom was assailed by the smell of burnt hair, and he wrinkled his nose, scouting around for the cause. After a second, a loud popping noise came from the biggest of the bunkrooms followed by a long string of curses. Tom frowned and walked to the room. Fingers wrapped around the handle of his knife, he pushed the door open slowly. Smoke drifted out of the crack, an acrid smudge that immediately coated his throat and caused him to choke.

"What in bloody hells is goin' on in here?" he growled when his coughing subsided, peering into the gloom.

Nathaniel waved his arms through the smoke with an embarrassed grin, and Tom saw that Malik was stooped next to one of the small electricity generators they had taken from Ereme'ia Balor. When the dark-haired shipwright looked up, Tom saw that he was missing his eyebrows. The first mate barked out a laugh and stepped into the room.

"We are trying to enter a new age of technology," said Nathaniel, coughing. "But we can't get the blasted thing to work. Uh, careful where you step!"

Tom stopped and saw that the ground was littered with broken glass.

"What in Bal's name is that stench?" Ceara peered into the room, her hand over her mouth and nose. "Please tell me you're not cooking dog in here."

Next to her was the small, mousy slave girl from the emperor's palace, Bettie. Tom furrowed his brow. Maybe *mousy* wasn't the right word, at least not anymore. The time spent in the sun and wind had transformed the young woman somewhat. She had some colour in her cheeks, and her hair looked a mite more bronze than the dull brown it had been. She looked... nicer. Happier.

"Oh no!" said Bettie and stepped forward, nimbly avoiding the broken glass. She went down on her knees next to Malik and reached for the machine.

"Miss, you'd better not... touch..." said Nathaniel quickly but trailed off in amazement as Bettie confidently flipped a few toggles and turned a small knob.

"There. You had the levels all wrong for these! No wonder

you've been blowing bulbs," she said with a nod. Tom almost laughed at the looks on the men's faces, but then he realized he probably looked just as astonished. He grinned.

Bettie glanced around, suddenly aware of all the eyes on her. Colour rose in her face like pink blooms. She definitely blushed pretty.

"How did you? What…" started Malik, wiping at the smoke stains on his face. He pointed quickly at the middle-aged cartographer. "Turn the crank."

Nathaniel immediately started winding the leather-covered handle at the back of the machine, and the shipwright lifted a nervous hand up to his eyes, the other arm shielding Bettie.

The bulb on the floor next to Malik started to glow and Tom took a step back, but when a few seconds went by with nothing exploding, he let out an amazed chuckle.

"Well, I'll be damned!" said the surly, dark-haired Malik. He cracked a smile and turned to the young woman next to him. Tom couldn't help but notice how his eyes widened at Bettie. Malik opened his mouth to speak, but nothing came out.

"I am Nathaniel," broke in the cartographer after a second of awkward silence. "Nate, if you'd like. This is Malik. I don't believe we've had the pleasure of your acquaintance." Nathaniel's eyes were creased at the corners as he sketched a bow to the kneeling ex-slave girl. Tom smiled and joined Ceara at the door.

"Huh, I knew that she handled changing the bulbs, but I had no idea how much she had picked up from the engineers. Interesting," murmured Ceara. "You know, I assumed that those two were… together."

Tom shrugged. So had he. However, the way both men looked at Bettie as she used Nathaniel's chalk to sketch out something about the machine on the floor spoke volumes.

Should be interesting.

He figured that the machine was in good hands and turned to go. If they managed to get the generator working via wind power and bulbs placed around the front of the ship, the long pass through the rift in the mountains wouldn't be so fucking gloomy.

"Tom," Ceara said, grasping his arm.

He stopped and frowned at the redheaded woman.

"What d'ye want, wench?"

Ceara's lip curved in amusement at what had become almost a term of endearment.

"I think we have a problem on board," she said quietly, her expression sobering as she lead him away from the door. "I think someone's been... ah... taking liberties with some of the female passengers. No one wants to talk about it, but I overheard something distressing this morning." Ceara's wide blue eyes searched his. He knew that she was having a hard time acclimatising to this new life. Gaining the trust of some of the ex-slaves was proving to be difficult; not everyone believed that she had been helping in their cause while spying for the emperor. For someone who had built her life on filching information, Tom was sure that it was a bit of a hit to the ol' self-esteem to have to rely on her own ears for the inside scoop.

"Why the fuck are ye tellin' me, love?" he asked. "The captain's the one who deals with the—"

"I'm not sure I want to bring it to Jon just yet. Bal knows, he seems to have enough on his plate at the moment. Plus, well... I have no idea who it is."

Tom's mind went immediately to Laz. After all, the man was a known rapist. However, the first mate had personally promised Laz that if he got any ideas about continuing his behaviour, Tom would tie one end of a rope to the ex-slave's cock and the other end to a cannonball and let fly. Laz had turned white as milk before assuring him that he was a changed man. But maybe it was a case of a badger not being able to change its stripes. What could he do? Threaten him again?

"Fuck," muttered Tom. "Can't ye just tell them girls to—" He saw the warning in Ceara's eyes and cut his words short. "Fine. I'll bloody look into it. But ye gotta give me more 'n that, dove."

"I think it's one of the rich passengers. The girl mentioned *dokschas* in exchange for her silence," said the petite woman, her gloved hand plucking at the high collar of her dress.

"Ah! See, now ye might be mistakin'. Might be a case of ol' fashion whorin'. Ain't nothin' wrong with that," he pointed out, hopeful for a quick resolution.

"Tom, she was crying."

He pressed his lips together and scratched the back of his head. He nodded.

"Ye keepin' safe?" he asked gruffly after a thought.

Ceara did nothing more than twist her wrist and a small dagger appeared in her hand. With a dark smile, the knife disappeared and she turned to go.

"I'll let you know if I hear or see anything else," she said over her shoulder as she walked away.

Tom grinned, not knowing whether he'd feel sorry for or envious of the man who could make the fiery woman's heart go pitter-patter.

~

*J*on flipped through the sketches Ceara had handed over. They all showed the same thing: the black mountain range.

"I don't see it," he finally said, looking up at her.

"I didn't expect you to," she said with a smile. The sun had brought out more freckles on her snub nose, making her seem younger. Jon realized he had no idea how old she actually was. Ceara winked at him and plucked the drawings from his hand. She rifled through them, sorting them.

"See this mark here?" she asked, pointing to a small smear in the corner.

Jon nodded.

"This is one," she said. Then she held up the next drawing. "This... is two."

Sure enough, there were two small smears.

"Place one and two on top of each other and hold them up to the light... What do you see?" she handed over the sheets of paper.

Jon frowned and lifted them up. There, in the middle of the drawing, where the lines met up, was a symbol. It looked familiar. He reached down next to him for the water-filled compass they had taken from Polas's boat. Sure enough, on the silver cylinder floating inside, was the same symbol on one end. He glanced up and saw that Ceara was watching him with obvious amusement.

"Well, you're no dummy, that's for sure," she said, flashing a white-toothed smile. She gave him two more sheets, one with three smudges and the other with four. Jon aligned them and held them up to the sun. There, in the midst of all the lines, was another symbol. He grinned. The symbol matched one of the ones on the brass ring around the compass's base.

"That's really clever!" he said with a laugh. "Did you design this?"

"I did."

Jon turned the globe in his hands and looked at the four feet that held up the device.

"So, if this part of the base points towards the rising sun... That's what this sun symbol means, right? I'm guessing we will know the correct path when these two symbols line up. Am I getting that right?"

Ceara simply nodded and turned towards the mountain range looming in the distance. Her fiery ringlets danced in the cool wind.

Jon put the sheets of paper down on the bench and weighted them down with the ocean compass.

"Why did you finally decide to give me these, Ceara?"

The ex-spymaster said nothing for a long moment. When she turned back, her eyes were wide and scared. Jon frowned.

"Trust for trust. You'll trust me if I trust you, right?" Ceara said softly, her lips barely moving. He was still angry with her for kissing Tom, but he could see she had completely dropped her guard; it was naked fear he was staring at. He instinctively reached for her shoulder.

When she flinched at his touch, he nearly pulled his hand away, but she quickly grabbed it and curled her fingers over his with a little squeeze.

"What is it?" he asked.

She laughed a little shakily, and he felt her tremble. He frowned and pulled her into his arms, her tiny frame held rigid for a moment before she sagged against him.

"I... may have exaggerated a little when I said that I knew there was no truth to the stories of what lies beyond the mountains," she whispered.

"Ceara, don't be foolish. There is no truth," he said, rubbing her back slowly in a way that he hoped soothed her.

"A lifetime of belief is hard to give up," she replied, her voice muffled by his greatcoat.

"Trust me," he said with a grim smile. "There are no monsters on the other side." *The only true monster I know is right here with us.* He felt Ceara nod against him and take a slow breath. He closed his eyes briefly and tightened his jaw. Why was he always the one offering solace these days?

When Ceara pulled away, her eyes were red-rimmed but dry. She quickly straightened her cloak and brushed her hair out of her face, squaring her shoulders. The walls were back up. However, when she smiled a little sheepishly, he realized that she had given him a tiny window to see through.

Trust for trust.

Jon thought back to the way she had bared herself to him before, showing him the secret scars beneath her clothes.

"Sorry," she muttered, her cheeks rosy. "Moment of weakness. But... Thank you."

"Thank *you* for trusting me with these," Jon said, gesturing to the coded drawings.

Ceara nodded again.

"Listen, I am sorry that I've been... terse with you," he continued. "Why don't we start over? Ok? Show me I can trust you, Ceara."

"I can try," she said, her cheeks dimpling with a grin.

"And… I'm willing to forgive you and Tom. But I don't want it to happen again."

Ceara's eyebrows shot up; immediately, Jon felt stupid for bringing it up.

"Tom… and I?"

"Yeah," he said, his face hot. However, he frowned when she continued to look at him in confusion. "The kiss?" he prompted, but he was rewarded with a slow shake of her head.

"I have no idea what in the name of Bal and his unholy minions you are talking about, Jon Black," she said.

"You don't?" he asked faintly, but it was blatantly obvious to him that she was telling the truth.

She shook her head again.

"But… Who else could it be?" Jon said in dismay.

Ceara shrugged.

"Shouldn't that be a question for Tom?"

Jon let out a humourless laugh and ran a hand over the tangled mess of his curls.

"I suppose it is. I just thought asking him would sound… peevish. I'm trying to be less sensitive, I guess," he said.

"And you just figured it *had* to be me?"

When he nodded, Ceara surprised him by punching him in the shoulder. He recoiled with a sharp cry and then laughed, rubbing what would undoubtedly turn into a bruise. For such a slight woman, she packed one hell of a wallop. He wondered what Katherine would make of her.

The ex-spymaster smiled serenely and sat down on the bench, arranging her skirts as she gazed up at him with wide, limpid blue eyes. When she hadn't said anything after a few moments, he scowled at her.

"What?" he asked, suspicious.

"I may be wrong," said Ceara lightly as she crossed one knee over the other, "but it seems to me like you're a man who needs to get a few things off his chest; don't take this the wrong way, but you look like shit, Jon. If you like… If you can *trust* me, I can be the person to listen to you. I can offer my advice, if you want it. And, I promise not to breathe a word of anything you say to me. I swear on my life."

Jon felt a small swell of gratitude that was quickly shredded into lace by doubt, and he turned away to look again at the looming mountains they were approaching. It *was* tempting to tell Ceara everything. Just to have someone to talk to. He could tell her about his persistent lack of confidence when it came to his relationship with Baltsaros and Tom. How he felt like he was holding them to ridiculous values that they didn't believe in… but that he had no idea how to change that about himself. About how deeply, yet differently, he felt for both men. About his strange dreams. About his fears and doubts over Baltsaros's recovery.

About Baltsaros's bloody appetites and penchant for outright murder? whispered the little voice inside him.

No. Never about that, he thought. Jon just couldn't trust her with that information, and far too much of what he could say otherwise was tainted by those secrets.

He turned back to her.

"You *are* wrong, Ceara. I'm fine," he said with a wan smile. But when she narrowed her eyes at him, he felt an impatient spark of anger quickly turn to flame and he glowered at her, suddenly sick to death of having his fortitude questioned. "I just don't need you meddling into my affairs. Now get out of my sight."

Ceara gaped at him for a half second before her features reclaimed their usual expression of artful scorn. She stood and shook her head.

"I'm going to give you one piece of advice, sweetheart," she said, tugging her cloak around her as she started down the quarterdeck stairs. "Stop being such a godsdamned prick. It doesn't suit you."

6

MEASURE FOR MEASURE

Eye for eye, tooth for tooth, hand for hand, foot for
foot...

— KING JAMES BIBLE, EXODUS 21:24

*T*om had briefly considered using Bettie as bait to find
out who the molester in their midst was. However,
planning the ridiculous ploy had worsened his hangover, so he
had decided to take a good measure of hair-of-the-dog to remedy
the situation.

He belched and put down the mug, wiping his mouth with the
back of his hand and feeling on the edge of squiffy. He wasn't a
spy. Meeting problems head-on had always been his strong suit.
Hells, his underhanded attempt at landing Jon in the Portsmouth
jail had nearly cost him everything, hadn't it? No, this dog's breakfast didn't warrant fucking tippy-toeing around like some cloaked
weasel.

Tom slid off the crate, grabbed the lantern, and headed to the
trapdoor.

On reaching the smaller of the bunkrooms, the one designated for women passengers, Tom pushed the door open with such force that it banged hard against the wall. There was a small, surprised shriek, and several women sat up and goggled at him in the dark. It was well past midnight, but he figured that meant they were all in one place.

Tom lifted the lantern high so he could see all their faces.

"I'm gonna ask ye ladies a question, and I bloody expect to be answered," he growled. "Who's the scoundrel been doin' some unwanted rootin' of yer cunts for pay?"

The room was utterly silent. A few of the women shared looks. Others simply stared at him in sleepy confusion. Tom frowned, realizing that perhaps his meaning has been lost. He hung the lantern on the hook next to the door, and speaking in what he thought was pretty decent Balorian while thrusting his finger into the hole made by the thumb and forefinger of the other hand, he repeated himself.

"Who's been fuckin' ye and givin' ye coin to quiet yer tongues?"

This time he figured everyone got his meaning; a few of the women smirked at the rude gesture, and he let himself grin a little. When no one responded after a few moments, Tom let out a frustrated sigh.

"Listen, lassies, ol' Tom is just tryin' to do right by ye," he implored. "I don't want anyone on this ol' tub gettin' done to 'em what's them don't ask for, savvy? Tell me, an' I'll see yer troubles gone." He figured the man had probably threatened that more pain would come to them through his mates should any of them squawk, but he didn't have time for this shite.

Tom pulled his long dagger out from the sheath nestled in his lower back and held it up. Eyes widened nervously at the sight.

"I'll just keep askin' the same fuckin' question, loveys. Every time I get no reply, someone's gettin' a haircut," he growled. It was a ridiculous threat, but he hoped at least one of them was vain enough to care about it. He scowled, looking around for someone fitting. To his right was a woman who looked like she had either been moneyed or a well-kept slave; her dark braid hung thick and glossy over her shoulder. "Let's start with *you*, darlin'."

Immediately the woman sat up straight in bed.

"You wouldn't *dare* lay a hand on me!" she spat. She glared down at him from her bunk like he was nothing but a turd, even lifting her nose a little to get away from the stench.

Tom sighed. Aye... rich.

"You can't just come in here... It's the middle of the night!" she continued, stoking her affront. "And you certainly can't threaten us into talking about such a... such a... *sensitive* matter!"

"S'all right, Samma. I am wanting to see the fat pig pay," said a small voice to Tom's left.

He peered into the gloom and saw a sandy-haired woman sitting in one of the lower bunks. She swung her legs over the side of the bed and leaned forward into the light, looking up at him with tired eyes. The woman had the faded remains of a bruise on one side of her face, and her coarse nightgown did nothing to hide how pathetically thin she was.

"He is named Punga," she said with obvious loathing. "I am of the hoping your sharp blade will be of cutting off more than his hair."

He grinned.

*P*leased with himself, Tom made his way back to the night air above, happy to have taken care of at least half of that little problem. Ceara'd be off his back now.

He rubbed a hand over the top of his head, brow furrowed in thought as he made his way to the gunwale to drain his bladder before heading to bed. He felt like it was a good thing that he had done. Something to be proud about. Taking coin for a little bit of sport was nothing to look sideways at, but when it came to not wanting the sport to begin with? Tom shook his head as he stuffed his cock back in his pants and then thumped back down onto the planks. Memories of a small room and a creaking, stinking bed came back to him. Worse even was when you weren't the one taking the coin… just sold off as a warm hole. With a sigh, Tom reached down and grabbed the lantern, thinking again about how much he would love to see his master's brother-in-law pay for what he did. It had been Lester's idea, after all, to make money off Tom on nights when he wasn't fighting in the cages. The fat bastard was probably still laughing as he collected money off the back of some other poor sod.

Yeah, he was glad that Punga would be stopped.

Tom extinguished the lantern, suddenly feeling lower than he had in days. The thought of curling up with Jon was nice, but what he really needed, really ached for right then was the man who had freed him from the black hells with a few bits of silver.

~

*B*altsaros heard the door open and lifted his head. In the centre of the long table, the candle was drowning itself slowly in wax, and in its dim light he saw Tom enter the room. Jon snored quietly in the low, wide bed, oblivious to the first mate's return. Baltsaros placed his head back on the pillow and watched as Tom made his way towards the bed. However, after staring down at Jon for what felt like a long time, the burly pirate turned around and made his way to the cage on silent feet. The first mate peered down at him and Baltsaros decided to keep pretending sleep—the last thing he wanted was a late night exchange that could turn ugly because of his cracked mind. Tom waited a moment longer and then grabbed the back of one of the chairs to drag it closer to the cage.

With a deep sigh, Tom settled back in the seat and crossed his arms, obviously having decided to watch over Baltsaros's sleep. However, almost immediately the first mate's head began to nod. After a few minutes the candle finally expired, and the resulting puff of smoke drifted pale in the moonlight. Baltsaros smiled; he could barely make out Tom sprawled backwards in the wooden chair, sound asleep with his arms dangling to either side.

The first mate would be sore in the morning; Baltsaros knew from first-hand experience what spending the night in those chairs felt like.

~

*C*aptain Baltsaros cleared the maps and books off the long table and stepped quickly to help Peter heave the unconscious slave onto the mahogany surface.

"Shit," gasped the first mate. "He's a heavy one, isn't he?"

The captain nodded distractedly and turned to the armoire to get his surgical tools.

"Turn him onto his stomach, please," he said, picking out a few jars of salve and a small bottle of refined oil before grabbing the small box containing his scalpels, forceps, and needles. "And tie his wrists to the center legs. There's no telling how long the laudanum will last."

"Aye, aye, Captain," said his first mate with a nod. "I'm amazed you got him to take it at all."

Baltsaros shrugged, depositing the items on the table as he watched Peter bind Tom. To be honest, he was somewhat amazed too. He'd fully expected to have to wrestle the burly slave to the ground to rid him of his pathetic little weapon and then force-feed him the sedative; the boy was completely wild, and the captain needed to take a close look at his injuries. However, when Baltsaros had spoken his name, it was as if he had thrown seawater onto flame. Tom had gone limp and wide-eyed, collapsing in front of him in an almost catatonic state. It had been nothing then to hold a cup of water laced heavily with laudanum to his lips.

Baltsaros wondered how long it had been since the boy had heard his given name.

"Sweet mother of lords, will you look at this?" murmured Peter. "What have you brought aboard?"

Reaching out, the captain touched young man's back. The dive into the harbour the previous day had relieved the slave of his patina of mud and filth, and Baltsaros could clearly see that what he had mistaken for clumped dirt was flesh marred by layers and layers of healed whip marks—a horrifying landscape of punishment that started at his shoulders and tapered off below his buttocks. In addition, the skin beneath the captain's palm was hot; a fever seemed to have set in.

"I don't know yet," he confessed. He tapped the leather harness. "Here, help me get this off of him."

It was immediately obvious that they would have to cut the harness off; the buckles were rusted shut and caked thick with grime. Thankfully, the leather was rotted and came apart easily with the use of sharp blades. When the harness fell away, it left behind thick calluses and fainter scars beneath it.

"I've seen overworked beasts with marks like this... never a man," said the first mate, his dark eyes wide. He reached out and touched the dark ridges on the boy's back.

Baltsaros stroked the stubble of his cheek, wondering what his silver had purchased.

*W*hen he had been told of a rebellious slave killing his masters, his interest had been piqued. It wasn't often that one heard such things; the mainland mining towns that still used slave labour had been doing it for generations and had slavery down to an art. That a man had not only escaped but had also managed to get past the guards and into his master's very bedroom was impressive indeed. Then, when it had been mentioned that the slave was being sold off for pocket change, the captain had decided to take a look.

On arriving at the town square, he had been dismayed by what he had found. Naked and filthy, a young man, barely out of boyhood, knelt bleeding in the mud with his head and wrists secured in the stocks. The scene was utterly pathetic, but the captain had no desire to nurse a beaten, cringing creature back to health. Baltsaros had almost turned to leave right then, but the slave had lifted his head and met his gaze with eyes the same colour as the water off the white beaches of Madierus. The captain had expected to see defeat, fear, and despondency, but all he saw was determination and a fierce will. Those eyes are what had moved his hand to his purse.

The captain looked up at Peter and smiled at the first mate.

"Leave us," he said.

"Aye, Captain," replied Peter, his eyes darting to the slave boy lying face down on the long table. "I'll be above if you need me. Just shout."

Baltsaros watched him leave and waited until the door was closed before he looked down at Tom again. The boy was impressively muscled, and Baltsaros recalled what the man who sold him had said: Tom had worked in the mines hauling stone before he had been put in the cage to fight for money. The man had also said something about having to keep Tom separate from other slaves due to a penchant for violence. The captain placed a hand on the boy's warm calf, the muscle hard and defined against his palm. Then, with a grunt of effort, he forced the boy's legs apart as far as he could and set to work.

After carefully washing his hands, Baltsaros poured a little white alcohol on them before he reached for the thick oil he liked to use as lubricant. When he'd first inspected the slave in the stocks, he had noticed dried blood along the inside of his thighs; he suspected he knew why by the way the boy's walk was slightly crouched as if movement caused him pain.

Baltsaros rubbed the boy's anus with oil and gently slipped two fingers inside him. Sure enough, there was an object lodged in the lining of his rectum. Feeling around its edges, he thought he could grab it with the narrowest set of forceps.

Moments later, when he held the long, bloody splinter of wood in his palm, Baltsaros felt the first honest swell of anger over the boy's treatment.

*W*ith Tom drugged anew and sleeping easily on his side in the cage, Baltsaros leaned across the table and stared hard at his first mate.

"Take Calum and Wraith with you into town as soon as the sun sets. Find me the man I spoke to earlier today; he goes by the name of Lester. Bring him to me, and make sure no one sees you. Do you understand?" he said quietly.

Peter's eyes took on a guarded cast, but he nodded without hesitation.

"It will be done, Captain."

~

*B*altsaros smiled again as Tom shifted in his sleep on the uncomfortable chair. Lester had lasted nearly four hours before he had succumbed to his injuries, the least of which was caused by a long splinter of rough wood. Afterwards, Baltsaros had pulled a chair up to the cage, exactly where Tom now slumbered, and had spent the night watching over the boy, too fired up from blood to sleep and full of ideas on how to win the young slave's trust.

The memory suddenly made him sit back slowly against the bars and furrow his brow. He had never told Tom about what had happened that night; it had never occurred to him to do so, and Baltsaros wondered why that was. Would telling Tom that he had killed the man for what he had done have changed the timbre of their relationship from the beginning? Sorrow coloured his thoughts, and he sighed softly to himself. Why had it taken over five years and another feverish, ill-used boy in his cage to show him Tom's true worth?

He rubbed at his chest as if he could make the tight ache disappear. With Saban's help he had begun to get himself under control, but it was a far cry from the iron hold he'd had on his emotions before. They now soared and churned inside him at every moment, his pulse skipping like a drunken madman as it tried to keep up with the tumult that drove the sleep from his mind and plunged him into a torrent of self-doubt and fear. Even when he seemed like his old self, it was a sham; he couldn't find the well of peace that had always cooled the fury in the past.

However, the semblance of control was better than naught.

Tom muttered in his sleep, something crass and nearly unintelligible. With a soft chuckle, Baltsaros stood and put his hand on the lock, intent on getting the big brute back to bed so he wouldn't be in a sour mood in the morning; when Baltsaros realized what he was doing, he pulled his hand away from the lock, staring at it in dismay, and took a step back.

It was the last thing he needed to remember, given his predicament.

7

THE RIFT

$\mathcal{T}$om whistled a little shanty he had learned from Calum as he made his way down from the main topgallant mast. They'd been beating to windward all morning and had finally arrived at the mouth of what Ceara called simply "The Rift". According to the ex-spymaster, the strong headwind that moaned through the slit in the mountain range would change direction with the setting of the sun—something about cooling air and warmer waters beyond the narrow fjord that would shift the wind eastward. To Tom it sounded a little hogwashy, but it was true that he'd seen it happen in other places, only not as violent a turnabout as the woman claimed this one to be. For the moment, however, they were anchored as they prepared for the journey through.

Tom peered around below him as he climbed down and saw that Malik and Bettie were still fiddling with the rack of bulbs they had mounted on the bowsprit. He was glad that they'd brought the outlandish things aboard; with bright lights shining before them, they would easily be able to navigate through the forked channels.

Forked like a dozen devils' wicked tongues.

Looking up at the towering black cliffs to each side of the *Heart*, he could barely see the birds that were wheeling high above the ship. There was no mist here to shroud the stupefying size of the mountains they'd sail through, and Tom had never felt so *small* in his entire life. He'd been studying the diagrams that Ceara had brought with her because he would be at the helm tonight, and it honestly made him more than a little bloody nervous; if he missed a quick course change, it could mean anything from being becalmed in a blind alley to being dashed against submerged rocks. A dubious fucking honour indeed.

He jumped down and landed easily on the deck. That was later though. He had to look into his little side project first.

Taking the portside stairs two at a time, Tom pulled the blade from his belt before he reached the low door to the brig. He pushed it open and went down the last few steps into the pitch darkness beyond. There was a muffled groan straight ahead, and Tom grinned. Reaching up, he scraped his knife against the wall until it encountered brass. He then flipped the latch on the blacked-out porthole cover and swung it open, letting a little light and air into the dank, stuffy room.

"There, lovey. Ain't that a little better? Awww... Who's the fucker who let ye stew in the black all night, aye?" he laughed, walking towards the bars set into the back of the small room. Hanging upside-down from one of the beams above was a fat little man, stripped naked and trussed up like a pig; the lass had wanted to see the *pig* pay, after all.

Tom unlocked the door and stepped in, prodding with his knife at the fat that bulged out between the hempen ropes. With a squeal, the man writhed, trying to get away from the sharp blade, but Tom just chuckled to himself and kept poking at him until the man swung back and forth, turning in a slow circle. The stench of urine was ripe in the room, and Tom noted with some amusement that the wood was wet below the man's head.

"Gah, ye stink, Punga," he said, sneering. "How d'ye like pissin' on yer own face? Ye like that?"

The fat, little rich man just let out a low, pathetic moan behind the gag Tom had put on him.

"Now are ye gonna finger yer mates to me and make gods-damned sure they ain't gonna stand so much as in the same breeze as them girls, or do ye wanna spend another night down here, pissin' up yer nose?" he asked, pushing Punga again with his knife.

With another squeak, the fat man nodded quickly, his bulging red eyes pleading with Tom.

The first mate smiled and began sawing at the rope above. Just before it gave, he kicked the hanging man in the shoulder so he wouldn't land on his head. With a frown Tom wondered why he bothered sparing Punga the bruised skull when no one else had done the same for him.

~

Jon stared hard at the four men lined up on the deck and then glanced over at Tom. The first mate sat on the gunwale fishing pieces of conserved pear out of a jar with his knife, slurping them down and licking his fingers as he watched Jon pace back and forth. They had less than an hour before the sun went down; meting out punishment was the last thing Jon wanted to do. Irritated, he walked past the men again.

He glanced up at the quarterdeck and saw that Ceara also watched him, her blue eyes unreadable with the sun behind her. This was the first real discipline he'd had to dish out since taking on the title of captain. He felt like everyone was judging him. Eyes closed, he squeezed the bridge of his nose and thought for a few seconds.

"All right," he said, straightening his shoulders. He glared at Punga. "You're the ringleader and the one responsible," he said. "Ten lashes and a fortnight in the brig. The rest of you lose your bunks for a week just for agreeing to intimidate other passengers." His eyes darted to Tom and saw that the first mate's eyebrows were high. He looked skeptical.

Were ten lashes not enough? Should he have said twenty? Jon gritted his teeth. What was the proper punishment for this sort of thing? He wished Tom hadn't put him on the spot like this.

"Ten lashes? You mean you will have me whipped? For seeking out a little companionship? She was a slave, Captain. They're used to this sort of thing!" blurted out the fat man. He clutched at Jon's arm.

Jon pulled his arm away and took a step back. On Punga's face was a look of pure incomprehension. The fact that there was not a shred of remorse or even understanding of what he was being punished for finally pushed Jon's mood over into true anger. He balled his fists and, resisting the urge to shout, began to speak in a low, furious voice.

"Not only did you *disobey* my direct command to give up all personal wealth during your time aboard, but you *assaulted* a fellow passen—"

"Assaulted?" spluttered Punga. "Listen, I don't know about that. A little misunderstanding. Heh heh. For certain! But... that your beast had me hung upside down in the dark like a fucking slave. Isn't that punishment enough? Lords of Summer, you can't expect to have women on board your ship without knowing they'll provoke the appetites of..."

Jon's blood felt hotter, and his mouth tasted sour as he listened to the shit pouring out of Punga's mouth.

Degenerates who held ignorant beliefs, Jon. Little lives that would only serve to pollute others. Baltsaros's words.

"Tom. Throw him overboard," he growled. "I don't have room for trash on my ship."

Punga's eyes bulged with terror, and he took a step back, his mouth opening and closing like a dying fish's. Jon's gaze darted to Tom; he saw that the first mate stared at him with deep creases in his forehead and ocean eyes narrowed in concern.

Oh for fuck's sake, Tom, he thought in annoyance and locked eyes with him.

Do it.

With a tight nod that spoke volumes about his disapproval, Tom grabbed the man by his tunic and bent his knees. The first mate grunted as he hoisted the struggling little fat man and tossed him over the gunwale. Punga let out a strangled yell as he flew headfirst over the edge into the dark water below with a loud splash.

Jon turned to the other men to ask if there was anyone else dissatisfied with their punishment when a scream rent the air. Heart in his throat, he jumped to the side of the ship and looked over. When he saw the great, slimy black shapes churning the water red where Punga had been a moment earlier, the blood froze in his veins.

More screams and yells erupted as passengers and crew alike witnessed the creatures writhing in their feeding frenzy. Tom's hand on his shoulder broke Jon from his horrified trance, and he looked up at the first mate. He was sure that the shock on the big man's face was mirrored by his own.

"Weigh anchor. Now. The current should be enough... Now, go do it," he said hurriedly, but something stopped Tom before he took a step—a shower of small rocks clattered to the deck from above, and they both looked up in time to see a large chunk come loose from the cliff wall and crash into the water only feet from the boat. Jon realized that the creatures weren't their only problem.

Face bleak, he looked around; it was complete chaos along the deck as men and women ran around with nowhere to go, the sounds of their panic echoing and amplified by the high cliff walls to either side. As he watched, another piece of the cliffside broke free and slid into the water. Jon realized he had to get them quiet, but he remembered Ceara's fear about the myths of the mountains. There would be no pacifying them now. He turned back to Tom.

"Belay that last order. Get everyone below, Tom. Lock them in the bunkrooms. Place good, strong men with them," he yelled above the growing din. "We need to get this panic under control!"

"What the fuck are they?" shouted Tom, his face grim.

"Sharks? Sea serpents? I don't want to find out. But we have to shut everyone up or they'll bring down the mountain on our heads. Anyone panicking goes below, no exception."

Tom nodded quickly and turned to go, but before he could, Jon grabbed his arm.

"I meant to pull him back on board. I swear to gods, Tom, I didn't mean for him to die."

Tom's eyes softened, and he gave Jon's hand a quick squeeze before he pulled away to start rounding up passengers.

Jon watched him go, unsettled by the blatant doubt he had seen flash over the first mate's face.

~

It took nearly a quarter hour to get the frightened Balorians secured away belowdecks. Once he was pretty sure there would be no more bloody excitement, Tom sent a few men to stand by the capstan; the wind had shifted, and the ship strained to be on its way. As he mounted the steps to the quarterdeck, he kept his eyes on Jon. The serious young man was looking over the charts at the bench; he would be helping the first mate to navigate the narrow channels once they were on their way.

Tom gave Jon a faint smile as he took his place behind the ship's wheel. Pitching the bastard overboard wasn't what was bothering him; the man's life or death hadn't concerned him in the least... though being ripped apart by those *things* sure made for a good tale to tell. No, it was the way that Jon's voice had taken on the same cold, precise tones that so often fell from Baltsaros's lips. Even his accent had changed a little. Tom shook his head and tightened his hands on the handles without a word.

"You're worried about me," said Jon softly.

Frowning, the first mate nodded, keeping his eyes forward.

"Don't be worried about me, Tom," said the young captain.

Chewing the inside of his cheek for a second, Tom nodded again.

"We ready?" he asked gruffly. He looked over at Jon and saw that he was staring at him with an odd expression on his face.

"I'm not turning into him," said Jon. "If that's what you're worried about."

Tom shrugged and turned the wheel a little back and forth, impatient to get going.

"Ye bloody sounded just like him, Jon."

When Jon reached for him, he wasn't expecting the sudden, sharp pain in his scalp as his fingers snarled a wicked handful of Tom's hair and tugged his head back. Jon brought his face close, his storm-grey eyes furious.

"You wanted me to be captain, so I am being captain. It is not easy for me, but I am fucking doing it the only way I know how," Jon growled through clenched teeth. "If you don't like it, you can go fuck yourself. And... What makes you think you can go behind my back and string up passengers without my say-so?"

Tom opened his mouth to speak, but Jon's hand tightened its hold, and he let out a pained grunt instead.

"The issue should have been brought to me first. Me. The *captain*. Isn't that how it works on this fucking ship? No. Instead you go around terrorizing people and then suddenly come dump the problem in my lap with no warning, putting me on the gods-damned spot to figure out what sort of punishment fits the crime. I had no idea what to say... Shit, how do you think that makes me look in front of the crew? Half of them still see me as some kind of fucking bed warmer for you and Baltsaros."

Jon gave Tom's head a little shake, and he winced.

"You need to work *with* me, Tom. Not against me. Gods-dammit, you know Punga could have sat, not *hung*, in the brig for another day or two, and we could have taken care of things *together*. And, for hell's sake, you ass, of *course* I was going to pull him out of the water. I saw that look on your face, Tom. I'm not a godsdamned killer. I've killed three men now, and I'm pretty damned sure it's not going to become a hobby. I don't want to see you doubt me like that again. *Understand?*" He let go of Tom and stood glaring him.

Tom rubbed the back of his head.

"Yes, Cap'n," he said sedately with a small nod. Then Tom let the grin he'd been holding back curve his lips and cocked his head. "Feel better?"

Jon's face creased into a sheepish smile, and he chuckled, nodding.

"Much," he confessed. "Gods, I am not cut out for this shit."

Tom shook his head.

"Naw, love. I think yer doin' just fine. Yer bloody right, ye know. I should stop worryin' about you so much, and I should'a come to ye the second that red-haired witch came to see me."

"Ceara came to you?" Jon heaved a sigh and raked both his hands through his mess of curls. "Argh! Fuck. Ok. I'll take care of her too. If she's trying to win me over, she sure as hells is taking the wrong path. I can't stand the idea that people would take things like this into their own hands rather than bother me. Bother me, for fuck's sake. I know I'm stressed as fuck, but bloody hells, how else am I going to learn?"

Tom grinned wider at Jon's increased use of profanity.

Jon furrowed his brow and leaned forward, his blue eyes dark in the dying sunlight as he studied Tom for a long moment. When he finally spoke, his voice was low and intimate.

"What? You think this is amusing? Just so you know, if you get us through these mountains in one piece, I plan on using you so thoroughly that the only words left to you will be *please* and *more*."

The first mate blinked, taken by a sudden pulse of heat when his heart kicked up in surprise. He laughed and Jon smiled back a little wolfishly.

"Aye, aye, sir," Tom said and eagerly grabbed the ship's wheel again.

· · ·

*W*ith men positioned at the bow and along both sides of the ship, holding oars and long boat hooks to push away from the rocks should they get too close, Jon hollered down the orders to wind the capstan so they could be off. As soon as the anchor lifted from the seabed, the *Heart* moved forward, driven by the strong wind and current.

Hands tight on the wheel's handles, Tom took a deep breath and said a stupid little prayer under his voice, hoping for the best. As they passed between the black cliffs, it felt like being entombed. The high walls to either side of the ship blocked out most of the sky, leaving only a narrow, dark-blue ribbon above them. The lights at the front of the ship, though shining brighter than any lantern could have, seemed swallowed by the dark; Tom could see next to nothing.

Beneath his feet, the ship barely moved, so still was the water they sailed through. However, he could almost feel the pull of the strong undercurrent, as they were pushed further and further into a silent world hedged in by the massive cliffs. Next to him, Jon shuffled through a few pages, seemingly unaffected by the oppressive gloom around them.

"I wish there was a better sense of scale," Jon muttered to himself as he held a diagram up to the lantern he'd placed on the bench.

"What's Ceara say?" asked Tom.

"Hasn't actually been through this before. Just knows about it... or at least knew where all these maps were kept. Gah... What in hells does this one even mean?" Jon furrowed his brow and peered closer at the page in his hand.

Tom shrugged and tried to brush off his jitters. When he looked to the side, at first he saw absolutely nothing, but when something glittered and his eyes quickly refocused, he realized the walls were a lot bloody closer than he'd assumed. He squinted at the shimmer and was startled when he realized they were eyes: thousands of little, shining eyes watching him silently from nooks and crannies in the mountainside. Even though he knew they were birds or small, harmless critters, they gave him the heebie-jeebies.

"Port! Port!"

Tom easily heard the call from the bow before it was relayed back to the quarterdeck, the night was so quiet around them.

"That's the first fork," said Jon, holding up a page. "About thirty degrees before we can straighten out again."

Nodding, Tom spun the wheel while the men pulled the braces to turn the yards slightly. The ship reacted quickly, like she too was in a hurry to be out of the narrow passes.

"Good. Ok, we go back starboard for a while after this. Then there is a section where—hang on..." Jon flipped through some more drawings. "Yeah. There's a section where it'll be a really tight squeeze. The ships coming through here are not as wide as *Baal's Heart*, but we should make it."

Tom tightened his jaw at the use of the word *should* but just gave another curt nod, staring off into the black hells. It would take them the entire night to get through the rift in the mountain range. If he made an error and they found themselves still between the walls at sunup when the wind would die out, it would mean having to spend the entire next day anchored in the squeeze, waiting until the wind turned their way again.

Narrowing his eyes, Tom gritted his teeth and prepared for the next turn. There was no fucking way they were going to spend a whole day trapped in the black mountains.

*N*early ten hours later, dead on his feet and shoulders aching from what felt like a thousand turns of the ship's wheel, Tom watched the grey skies lighten over the water with a smile. They had made it through the rift without a single mishap and, bugger it all, it actually felt a little like a letdown. All night, the crew had acted as a tight unit, helping him to get through the winding forks easily. Even Ceara had been a help deciphering the maps in the end and had made sure deckhands brought Jon and him a little grub and drink to brighten the gloom somewhat.

With a yawn that threatened to dislocate his jaw, Tom scratched at his chest and looked over at Jon who sat drinking a mug of warmed, sweet wine.

"Piece o' cake," said the first mate with a grin.

Jon nodded and smiled tiredly.

"Piece of cake," he agreed.

Tom felt a few cool drops pepper his face and squinted at the clouds. It was a light drizzle for now, but it looked like the sky would open up and they'd get soaked. As if to confirm his suspicions, lightning flashed bright right then.

He called out for the men to pack up the bulbs and stow the electricity machines belowdeck before they got too wet. Then Harris could take over, and he and Jon could finally go rest their weary heads. Tom sank to his knees in front of the bench and placed his hands on Jon's thighs, smiling up at the tired young captain.

Jon let out a soft sigh and reached for Tom; his palm, heated from the mug, was warm against the first mate's cheek.

"I know I keep saying it, but I *need* you," Jon murmured with a small frown. "But, I don't need your fucking worry. I need *guidance*. I need you by my side... Just like you were this whole night."

"Aye, love," rumbled Tom. "I'm here now."

~

ever leave my side again. Words spoken by Baltsaros a million years earlier when hope had been a new and shining thing. Jon suddenly felt old. He closed his eyes for a moment, burying his thoughts. When he opened them again, he saw that Tom was just watching him quietly, his blue-green eyes somewhat sleepy and red-rimmed... completely guileless. Jon stroked Tom's rain-wet cheek with his thumb and then trailed his fingertips along a scar that followed the line of his brow bone and bisected his sandy-blond eyebrow. He'd never asked where Tom had gotten the scar but thought he was probably better off not knowing. Jon had stopped asking about the marks that ran the length of Tom's body when he realized that most of them came with a story of abuse that soured his stomach. The fact that they were always delivered with a wry smirk and a show of indifference made Jon feel even worse. The things that Tom had been through... He couldn't even imagine it.

"What's the sad look, love?" asked Tom, moving his hands up Jon's thighs to clasp him around the waist.

The big man stared up at him, and Jon thought again just how remarkable it was that Tom was *his*. His to share, of course, but still. He shook his head and smiled, taking hold of the first mate's head to pull him up for a kiss.

However, the moment was shattered when Ceara came running up the stairs, a look of worry on her freckled face. Tom scowled at the interruption, pulling away from Jon.

"Bloody hells, what the fuck is it now?"

8

THE DEVIL YOU KNOW

*B*altsaros woke with a groan, blinking away dreams he didn't understand. The light was dim, and the floor beneath him rocked as if the waves were chopped up by a strong wind. Shakily, he got to his feet and looked out of the porthole. The sky was dark with ominous clouds, and the glass was speckled with rain or seawater.

Baltsaros glanced around the empty room and frowned; he was thirsty but his cup was empty. Curling his hands around the cold iron bars, he stared at the icebox for a long moment. There was a pitcher of water in there. Cold water to soothe his parched throat. Baltsaros sighed and looked at the door to the stateroom. He'd promised himself he wouldn't but...

His fingers found the small catch, and he pressed down on it while pushing up on the other corner of the lock where there was a second, tiny button. There was a click, and the door swung easily on its oiled hinges. Having orchestrated his own mutiny, Baltsaros had thought it wise to put something into the design of the cage should he find himself made the occupant. He was, at least for the moment, thankful his memory of the lock's fail-safe had returned.

Baltsaros slipped out of the cage and quickly opened the icebox, pouring himself a cup of cold water. He was on his second glass when suddenly he was pitched against the table by an especially jarring wave. The metal cup fell from his hand, and it bounced to the floor, rolling away. Unbalanced, he grasped the sides of the table.

Have to get back to the cage, he thought. The cold water sat strangely in his gut, making him a little nauseous. There was a low laugh and Baltsaros looked up. Ah'puch grinned at him from the shadows, the handle of Jon's knife sticking out from his chest.

Oh gods, not now.

"You're dead," choked Baltsaros, his fingers curled into claws on the wood as he leaned forward over the table. "Go back to the black hells!"

"Do you really think that soft little creature you keep in your bed could have killed me? Do you really think that?" laughed the emperor. His face was pale as the moon, drained of blood. Blood that was now on Jon's hands.

"Oh... Of course he could, don't be stupid," hissed the beast as he stepped out from the dark. "When we're done with him, he won't be able to stop killing and killing and killing again. You'll have ruined him, Baltsaros. Doesn't innocence taste good?"

"No," he whispered. He had to find Jon. Protect him somehow. Warn him. Baltsaros felt hot bile in his throat and nearly gagged.

"Well, what are you going to do then?" asked the beast with a rasping chuckle. It wrapped its hand around the dagger in Ah'puch's chest and yanked on it. Fresh blood poured down the man's shirt and over the carpet. The floor yawed beneath Baltsaros's feet, and he clung to the table like a man drowning.

"Oh ho... But you'll have to get to him before I do," said the beast and licked the blood from the knife with its long tongue. *Hungry.* The emperor looked on with a crazed, gory smile.

"Oh my, We think that may be a good idea," agreed Ah'puch. "We think you need to get to Jon. To kill him. Kill him, Baltsaros. *Kill him* before he kills you."

No. No, that's not right, thought Baltsaros; his hand scrabbled over the surface of the table, closing over the dagger that lay there. *No. I need to kill Jon before I destroy who he is.*

Yes, that was much better.

Baltsaros stumbled across the empty room and grasped the door. He opened it a crack and looked beyond. When he saw that there was no one close by, he left quickly.

The deck rocked beneath his feet, but Baltsaros had regained his footing. Shivering from the cold wind and rain, he peered up the stairs and thought he saw the silhouette of two men on the quarterdeck. If Tom was up there, sinking a dagger into Jon would prove to be difficult. He would simply have to kill them both… But something was nagging at him.

He felt nauseous again and blinked rainwater out of his eyes.

What am I doing? He looked at the dagger in his hand. In the murky light, he could see that rain was washing away the blood on it. Blood from where? His hands were covered in it.

Out of the corner of his eye, he saw movement, but when he turned, he saw it was only a swaying, dark lantern. A second later, lightning crackled across the sky and was reflected in the four panes of glass of the lantern. *Four lights.* Baltsaros moaned and stepped backwards, his mind closing in on itself. Escape. He needed to escape.

"No more," he whimpered. "I can't take any more pain. Please."

Four lights above his head, the cold metal table beneath his body.

In a panic, he turned and ran, pushing men out of his way.

Have to get belowdecks, he thought. *Have to get away from… Ah'puch? Romas?*

The fact that he did not know terrified him.

He reached the trapdoor and hauled it open, stumbling down the narrow, steep stairs into the dark passageway below. He turned and in another flash of lightning saw *it.* The machine.

Pain.

Pain.

Pain.

Electricity like hot knives burning into his skin, into his brain. Chasing him like a beast in his own mind, pulling shriek after shriek from him as it worked to rob him of all coherent thought and destroy his body. The nausea crested in Baltsaros again, and he retched, staggering backwards in the dark. He had to get away.

Cries. Darkness. More lightning. Blood.

He waved the dagger in front of him, trying to fend off the monsters real or imagined that crowded him into a corner. His back against the wall, Baltsaros howled his pain.

"I don't want to kill!" he shouted. "Please don't make me do it!"

Red hands, red feet, sharpened teeth, and fists that beat. How they laughed...

Like an egg cracking and spilling its yolk, Baltsaros's mind suddenly let free the memories it had kept locked away for so long. With a low moan, he felt himself collapse, the dagger clattering to the floor as the truth of his past came back to him.

~

*T*om held his hand out to stop anyone from coming forward. He glanced over at Jon and saw that he had gone down on one knee to examine Baltsaros. They'd followed Ceara down and discovered the captain muttering to himself and waving a bloody dagger as he paced frantically back and forth in the galley. Then, with a cry that chilled Tom's blood, the fight had gone out of the older man, and he had fallen down in a heap.

Baltsaros sat staring at his hands, oblivious to the crowd that had formed around him.

"Get the fuck out of here, ye cunts!" Tom yelled. "And close the bloody door!"

In embarrassed silence, the crew filed quickly out of the room, leaving Jon and Tom with the stricken man. Everyone would now know the damnable truth of Baltsaros's condition. Jon rose slowly to his feet and put his hand on Tom's shoulder.

"I'll keep everyone away," said Jon. "And I'll get the Balorians abovedeck to see with their own eyes that we haven't sailed into the afterworld." He chuckled, but there was no humour in it. "I have captain-y things to do."

"What about Da?" asked Tom.

"I think the less people the better. And... well... He doesn't trust himself around me. I'm starting to realize that he probably never has," said Jon a little sadly with a shrug. "Just... I don't know... Watch him. He trusts you, Tom." He squeezed Tom's shoulder and furrowed his brow. "Or... Do you think you can't handle him? Do you need me to send Saban down?"

Tom shook his head.

"Naw, love. Yer right. I'll be fine with Da. I'll get him back to his cage as soon as I can."

Jon nodded tiredly, and Tom watched him go, closing the door behind him.

Looking down at Baltsaros, he saw that there was more blood on the man than before. With a frown, he swiped a few of Cook's clean towels and sank down cross-legged in front of the captain. He started tearing the white cloth into strips as Baltsaros watched him quietly.

"It's my blood, isn't it?" he asked.

"Aye, it's yer fuckin' blood, ye daft bugger," grunted Tom. "Where the fuck did ye get the knife, Da? Who let you out of the cage?"

Baltsaros smiled, but it didn't reach his eyes.

"I let myself out. That cage was meant to hold others, not me. As for the knife? I... think someone may have left it on the table. I honestly can't tell you."

Tom reached for Baltsaros's arm and turned it. There were slices along the inside of it, right over the scar that he had made with Jon. With a shake of his head, the first mate set to work bandaging up the mess as best as he could; thankfully, it didn't look like stitches were needed. He glanced up and saw that Baltsaros's dark eyes were on him, but there was no hint of insanity in them. Just sadness.

"Da, what happened?" he asked gently as he tucked in the edge of the towel.

Baltsaros took his arm back and smiled appreciatively at Tom's handiwork.

"You've got skilled hands," said Baltsaros. He then leaned back against the wall and rubbed his face, like a man weary beyond words.

Tom picked the dagger up off the floor and stared at it. He recognized it as the dagger he had given Jon. Noticing something on the handle, he frowned; there were three notches carved into the wood, one of them fresh.

Bloody hells, Jon, he thought, the small knot in his gut tightening. *And ye wonder why I worry...*

Wrinkling his brow, he looked back up at Baltsaros, but he had closed his eyes and seemed lost in thought. As Tom waited for him to break the silence, he took up a piece of towel and began to wipe the blade clean.

~

*B*altsaros opened his eyes and saw that the room had lightened. It looked like the rainstorm had passed and had been replaced by a weak afternoon sun shining through the portholes. When he shifted, his arm throbbed and he grimaced. For once, he could clearly remember everything that had happened.

Sitting on the floor with his back against the freestanding counter was Tom, turning something over in his hands as he whistled low to himself. When he felt Baltsaros watching him, Tom looked up, the amusement in his green-blue eyes barely hiding his concern.

"Ye fell asleep," accused the first mate with a cheeky grin. It looked forced.

Baltsaros smiled.

"I'm sorry I fell asleep on you, Tom."

"Look," said the first mate, holding up the turnip he had been carving. "It's a cock."

Baltsaros laughed and shook his head. Sure enough, the turnip looked like a very squat, erect penis, complete with a suggestion of testicles at its base. It was utterly ludicrous, but so comfortingly Tom. The first mate smiled wide, looking a little more relaxed. However, when he put the turnip down, his face grew serious. On hands and knees, he approached Baltsaros and settled closer.

With a groan, Baltsaros pulled himself away from the wall to stretch his shoulders. However, despite being sore from sleeping against the wall, seated on the hard floor of the galley, he felt more rested than he had for the past month. It was good.

"How long was I out?" he asked.

" 'Bout an hour or so," replied the first mate. "D'ye feel like talkin' to me now?"

Baltsaros shook his head slowly.

"I don't know," he admitted. "I've remembered something, but it's a little too... raw to talk about. I'm not even letting myself think about it too much for fear that I'll be spun into another episode like the one that landed me here to make a complete spectacle of myself in front of the crew." It was the truth. Even letting himself brush the edges of these new memories brought a sense of deep dread unlike anything he had ever felt. The memory was back, but he could not yet use it.

"Though, I think I understand the danger facing Jon now," he continued. Tom's brows pinched together in concern, and Baltsaros watched the first mate's eyes grow wary.

"Jon was right. I've been holding on to a... belief that I am naturally morally corrupt. A killer by accident of birth," he said slowly. The words felt odd to say. "Something *evil* as he put it."

Tom snorted, but Baltsaros shook his head.

"I'm being serious, Tom. I... know now where it stems from."

"Is it about *red hands*?" the burly pirate asked quietly.

Baltsaros winced and took a deep breath, looking away. Too much pain.

"Sorry, Da," said Tom, reaching out to clasp his uninjured arm.

Baltsaros sighed at the warmth of his touch and placed his hand over Tom's rough one, patting it.

"However, Jon was obviously wrong in his assurance that I would not try to kill him again," Baltsaros continued. He couldn't remember trying to suffocate Jon, but the bruises around the younger man's neck had haunted him for days. "Seems I keep trying for him because, for some reason, my subconscious has decided that killing Jon is preferable to killing his innocence."

"Subconss...?" Tom's frown deepened.

"Ah... There's no word for it in Common, I'm afraid. In the north we use it to mean the part of us that brings us dreams. Thoughts hidden from ourselves that speak truths. Understand?"

"Aye," mumbled Tom. "So, we're to continue keepin' ye from killin' Jon? Ye know, the lad's not near as innocent as yer damn head thinks he is, Da." The first mate looked exhausted as he pulled his hand away to scrub at his face.

"Yes, I'm aware. I'm trying to keep that in mind," said Baltsaros. He frowned at Tom as the first mate blinked his reddened eyes, knuckling the corner of one as he sighed softly. "What's wrong with you? You look like you've been up all night."

Tom let out a laugh and clapped his hands to his knees, leaning forward with a weak grin.

"Aye, that I have. Bloody dog-tired. Shall we get ye back to yer cage so I can get some shut-eye? Oh hells..." Tom's forehead creased as he climbed to his feet and helped Baltsaros to stand. "Keepin' ye in there ain't gonna work, is it?"

Baltsaros shook his head with a smile.

"I'm afraid not," he replied. "But I'm sure you and Jon can come up with something to keep this 'daft bugger' from killing anyone or cutting himself up again."

Tom winced, and Baltsaros reached out to smack his cheek playfully.

"But, you ever call me *daft* again, or any variation thereof, I will dedicate myself to reacquainting you with the definition of *obedience*. Have I made myself clear?"

With a wry grin, Tom ducked his chin.

"Aye, Da," he replied. "Gods, I've missed ye."

Baltsaros chuckled. There was still a long road to recovery ahead, but he felt something he hadn't felt in a long time: hope.

9

NO REST FOR THE WICKED

The voyage of discovery is not in seeking new land-
scapes but in having new eyes.

— MARCEL PROUST

*T*om squinted in disbelief at the tiny catches on the iron
lock and shook his head.

"Yer fuckin' tellin' me that I sat like a bloody dog in this godsdamned thing for six bloody months—"

"Five," Baltsaros corrected him.

"Five bloody months and I could'a let myself out at any time?"
He looked over at the bed where Jon was busy with Baltsaros.
Since they couldn't keep him in the cage any longer, and Punga's
cronies occupied the brig, Jon had suggested that they just tie
Baltsaros up; the captain had laughed and offered up his wrists
with an amused twist of his lips.

Tom grinned at the look of concentration on Jon's face and let
out an exaggerated sigh.

"Fuckin' hells, lovey," he chided, walking up to the bed. "When
are ye gonna learn how to tie a bloody half-decent knot?"

"Hey, it's not that bad," said Jon, but when he went to tighten the knot he had made, it fell apart. "Ok. Maybe it is. What did I do wrong?"

Baltsaros smiled patiently and settled back more comfortably on the bed; he almost seemed like his old self.

"Here, let me." Tom took the tangled hempen rope from Jon and climbed up onto the soft mattress. Doubling the length over in his hands, he quickly wove a clove hitch on a bight around Baltsaros's wrist, careful to avoid the bandaged cuts. As Tom reached for his other arm, he saw that Baltsaros watched him closely.

Tom started to feel strangely shy with the man's dark eyes on him, and he realized it had been a long time since he and the captain had been so close; it was almost overwhelmingly intimate. Fumbling the rope, he dropped the loose end on the older man's chest.

"Sorry," he mumbled, keeping his eyes on his task.

"Don't tell me that you're suddenly unable to knot a rope too?" said Baltsaros, clearly amused.

Tom just scowled, but he'd been bound so often by the man that tying him up in return felt absolutely foreign. It was making his fingers clumsy.

It was also making him bloody horny; by the time Tom had finished tying up Baltsaros's arms, his pulse was thrumming in his ears, and he felt hot and tense.

When he glanced up, he saw that Baltsaros looked subtly amused. There was something else in his gaze too: lust. Then, when Baltsaros let out a small noise and shifted slightly, closing his eyes, Tom looked over in surprise and saw that Jon had lifted up the bound man's shirt and was stroking down the line of his pelvis with his fingertips, teasing at the waistband of his pants. Trust Jon to grasp the mood of the captain before he did.

As he watched, Jon leaned forward and kissed Baltsaros's hip bone, eliciting another quiet sound from the man. But, when Jon raised his blue-grey eyes to Tom's, he looked a tad unsure, as if he were waiting for the first mate to do something.

"Tom? Come here." Baltsaros's voice was quiet, and Tom turned to look at him. All exhaustion was gone from his system and his cock, already primed from embarrassed arousal, started pressing against the material of his pants. However, Tom faltered a moment with an exaggerated grin built on nerves; he hadn't felt this awkward since that first time.

~

*T*om paced the dark corridor. His ire had brought him right to the captain's chambers but had sputtered out somewhat, leaving him unable to open the door. As he made another pass in front of the rooms, Tom shook his head and muttered to himself as he rubbed a hand over his shaggy, dirty-blond hair.

"Fuckin' Abetha and her fuckin' bloody uppity fuckin'..." he said, trying to rekindle the outrage that had brought him to Balt-saros's door in the dead of night. He swivelled on his heel to come back about and, fists clenched, he bowed his head and rested it against the dark wood of the door.

It was the way Abetha always *looked* at him, like he was the scum of the world. The way she constantly corrected his speech. And what about the utter and total lack of remorse over his ten fucking years as a slave? She was his bloody *mother*, the cold cunt. That they—her and his yellow-belly of a father—had given up on him after so little effort. Shit, all those long nights... poor little boy crying and praying himself to sleep... just wanting to go *home*.

Tom let out a slow breath, the anger in his belly growing.

And then, since his father had stretched his own neck like the bloody coward he was, the fucking captain had married his "poor", widowed mother. That was a fucking laugh. Tom pressed his palms to the wood and smiled a bitter smile. Well, that wasn't going so shit hot, was it? Tom had bloody made sure of it. The little birds that whispered into Abetha's ear about the captain's conquests and appetites had been costly, but it was working. Baltsaros now slept alone.

Lying in bed earlier, restless and brimming with rancorous feelings, Tom had thought about how, if he beguiled his way into the captain's bed and won him over with lust, the sham of a marriage would be over.

Then why couldn't he bring himself to open the door?

After pushing away from it, he resumed pacing. He had never seduced someone before. Had never wanted to. Sex held almost zero appeal for him.

But, there *had* been those dreams. Tom stroked the hollow of his stubbled cheek as he glanced at the door. Nothing concrete, nothing too specific. Baltsaros's long legs coming towards him... the way the black leather hugged the muscles of his thighs and the bulge between them. The hint of a wicked, dark smile. Tom was only ever partially clothed in the dreams and when the captain's large hands reached for him, he felt *good*. Good enough that he would often wake with a mess to deal with. The thought made him grin a little. The captain *was* an attractive man—that was a fact. Tall, muscular, and broad-shouldered, he was like a handsome storybook hero come to life. Except this hero's dark eyes sometimes betrayed the cold savagery he was capable of, even if his lips lied with their graceful smile. And yet... There were the incredible kindnesses he had bestowed on Tom: saving him, fixing him up, making him whole again, and giving him purpose.

Straightening his shoulders, Tom decided that if he didn't do it now, he'd never be able to.

The door opened quietly on its hinges, and Tom made his way across the darkened room and through the second door within. Beyond, he could make out the large four-poster bed and hear Baltsaros breathing deep in slumber. Tom tugged his shirt up and over his head, pausing to undo and kick off his pants before he circled to the side of the bed, his heart hammering. Quiet as a snake, he slipped under the cool covers and heard the captain stir in his sleep. Slowly, Tom reached for him. When his hand encountered bare skin, he nearly pulled away. He hadn't expected the captain to sleep naked.

That makes it easier, don't it? he thought. He slid further down the mattress and under the sheets, moving closer. The captain was on his side facing him, and it took Tom no time to find his cock. When he lifted the soft thing and sucked gently it into his mouth, he felt Baltsaros start awake. Doubt flared up in Tom for a heart-stopping second; what if the captain rejected him? He had only heard from others that Baltsaros liked men as well as women... But what if they were wrong? However, when the captain's hand found the back of Tom's head and didn't pause before pressing into him harder with a groan, he relaxed a little; he knew there was no mistaking him for a woman.

As the heavy organ in his mouth began to stiffen against his tongue, he tightened his lips near the root of it. When he reached up to grab the captain's hip, the man's skin was soft and sleep-warm against Tom's hand. Eyes closed, Tom thought he could do this. It wasn't so bad. The captain smelled clean yet musky, and the way his fingers stroked his head and neck felt... nice. Still, he wondered how long it would take to get him off.

Baltsaros's cock was big but, Tom thought with a sardonic, inward smile, nothing he couldn't handle. He started moving with more purpose, letting the muscles of his throat relax so he could take in more of the hard length. What he got in response was a deep groan, and he pulled himself closer, wrapping his arm around the captain's waist as the man thrust himself against Tom. Soon, between the cock in his mouth and the smothering blankets, Tom started to feel a little lightheaded. He stretched his arm up to push aside the covers but was startled when the captain suddenly grabbed him by the hair and pulled his head back. Tom clutched at Baltsaros's hand, but the captain wouldn't release him. The blanket was lifted away.

"What are you doing in my bed, Tom?" asked Baltsaros, staring down at him, his features barely visible in the gloom of the bedchamber. However, there was a smile in his voice. "And sucking me off with such consummate skill, I might add…"

Before Tom could reply, Baltsaros rolled over on top of him and, straddling his neck, he forced his cock back into Tom's mouth and further down his throat for a few thrusts. This wasn't turning out the way Tom had planned. Nausea began to rise in his gut; he felt the tiniest flutter of panic at being trapped but kept himself from biting down.

What a fucking stupid bloody idea, he thought, realizing that he'd have to shove the captain off and scupper whatever good will that had grown between them. *Forget being part of the bloody crew now.* Tom knew he had lost the upper hand. He couldn't stomach the thought of slaving under another man again, and this was no different, not a fucking bit different from any other time.

Then, all of a sudden, it was.

With a small moan, the captain pulled his cock from Tom's mouth and crawled backwards, pushing Tom's thighs apart and covering his body with his own. Burying his face in the side of Tom's neck, he bit gently and then brushed his lips softly against his skin. Tom closed his eyes and frowned at the resulting shiver.

"Ah, you gorgeous brute…" murmured Baltsaros, his voice a warm purr in Tom's ear. "You have no idea how ridiculously tempting you are, do you?" He chuckled and closed his hand loosely around Tom's throat. Using his thumb, he pushed Tom's jaw up, opening his neck to more bites… harder this time. "I don't normally fuck my crew—business should never bunk with pleasure—but I cannot lie and say that I haven't thought about you naked and willing in my bed." The captain kissed the rim of his ear, making the hair on Tom's neck prickle before he moved his tongue to the soft area below it. "Often, I must confess."

Tom let out a shaky exhale. The words and the focused attention to sensitive skin made him feel really strange. Like in his dreams.

Shivering again in the captain's grasp, he furrowed his brow and brought his hands up to clasp Baltsaros's waist. With surprise, Tom realized he was getting hard against the older man's belly.

Baltsaros's teeth closed on his neck again, this time with some real pain, but it felt good. Experimentally, Tom let out a shy little noise to show the captain he was enjoying himself, and Baltsaros laughed huskily against the side of his neck before biting again with more force. When it sent a jolt of pleasure straight to his groin, Tom groaned and shifted his hips slightly, eager for some friction on his stiff cock.

The captain pulled back, going up on one elbow to scrutinise him for a moment.

"What I do?" Tom asked warily, eyes narrowed. Suddenly nervous and exposed, he thought about ending whatever this was and telling the captain to piss off and go fuck some other wretched thing. Tom would then go drink himself sick on his mother's too-sweet wine and try to find his own way off this fucking island. However, when the older man stroked back Tom's hair and then slid his thumb along the side of his neck, he felt his breath catch in his throat.

With a little tilt of his head, the captain shifted his hand and pressed his thumb hard into the spot right below the corner of Tom's jaw. The pain was sharp and immediate, and Tom let out a grunt of surprise, but the pressure stopped only a few moments later. Baltsaros ducked his head to lick at the area instead; his tongue felt soft against his skin and left cool traces behind.

A helpless whimper escaped Tom's lips at the sensation, and he tightened his hold on the captain. His cock was a fucking iron bar trapped between them.

"Didn't that hurt?" asked Baltsaros.

Hurt? Tom blinked. Yes... but... He just shook his head, not trusting himself to explain what he was feeling.

"Interesting," mused Baltsaros.

Closing his eyes, Tom felt confused and slightly embarrassed by his body's reaction. However, when Baltsaros found Tom's nipple and pinched it hard, the noise that came from deep in his chest sounded raw, needy. Then the captain bit at it with sharp teeth, and Tom couldn't help but let out a full-throated groan of pleasure.

"You like that?" asked the captain.

Tom's nipple throbbed. Eyes still tightly closed, he nodded quickly, trembling.

"I want to hear you say it." Baltsaros's voice was quiet, confident.

Startled, Tom opened his eyes. *Say it?* He felt a rush of heat in his face. When the captain lifted himself off Tom a moment later and reached down past his cock to grab his balls in a long-fingered hand, Tom's heart began to race.

"Say it, Tom," purred the captain. Tom let out another hitched breath and then a low moan as Baltsaros squeezed his sack, sending more pain and pleasure coursing through him.

How could he say it? The pain became intense, and he nearly yelled out. He had spent the last decade being forced to do things against his will; he wasn't about to submit to something he didn't want to do.

But that's it, isn't it? The realization made him groan, shaking him with more than the physical agony inflicted on him. The fucking truth was that he *wanted* to do it.

"Yes," he finally choked out. "Aye. Yes." The pressure on his balls decreased for half a heartbeat before Baltsaros squeezed again.

"Yes, what?"

Tom bucked up from the bed, his eyes clenched tight and heart like a crazed animal trying to burst from his chest.

"Yes!" he cried out. "Yes, I like it!"

"There we go," chuckled Baltsaros, easing up on his brutal hold. "Just like that. That wasn't so bad, was it?" Tom panted and strained up against the captain as the older man began to stroke his cock slowly with a sure hand. He was lost in the sensation. Tom had never felt this sort of desire before; it was overwhelming.

"Yes, you're perfectly exquisite. A handsome tomcat just begging for a firm hand to tame you, hm?" murmured the captain. "Oh, my boy, I think we will have a lot of fun, you and I."

~

om stretched himself out next to Baltsaros as the captain closed his eyes and let out a soft sigh; Jon had undone the laces of his black pants and was kissing his way across newly exposed skin.

The first mate couldn't help but notice how much Baltsaros had aged since he had first rescued him; the creases at the corners of his eyes were now deeply etched and the lines next to his mouth more pronounced. It was to the former that Tom bestowed his first light kiss as he leaned over, the skin soft and thin against his lips. Baltsaros sighed, submitting to the gentle treatment, and Tom smiled wider. Older, but no less handsome. He moved further down, kissing the man's sharp cheekbone, and then continued along the curve of his strong jaw. Baltsaros's stubble was rough on his lips, and Tom let his tongue slide over the short bristles as he pressed his kisses into his skin. When he made his way to Baltsaros's neck, he smiled again; Baltsaros lifted his chin, leaning into him with a low, pleased growl, his pulse strong and fast against Tom's mouth.

When Jon made a small noise and Baltsaros's breath hitched in his chest, Tom pulled away and looked over. The dark-haired young man held Baltsaros's hard cock in his hand, but his brow was knotted as he stared at it, motionless. It was obvious why—though healed, Baltsaros's length was crisscrossed in shiny, taut pink scars from the abuse he had suffered.

"Shit, Da," said Tom, scowling.

"Does it hurt?" asked Jon quietly.

Baltsaros's laugh rang out, startling the first mate.

"No. No... not really. But, Jon, even if it did," Baltsaros replied with a grin, "I'd never forgive you if you stopped." He lifted his torso a little, looping his bound wrists up over Tom's head to pull him back down again.

"I was enjoying that," murmured Baltsaros, his face serious and dark gaze locked on Tom. "Kiss me again."

Tom felt a tightness in his ribs that spread up his sides and crept up his neck as he stared back. Heart thudding in his chest, he leaned in and pressed his lips to the corner of Baltsaros's mouth. He was startled when Baltsaros turned his head and captured Tom's mouth fully.

All timidity left Tom as he opened his mouth to the kiss; breathing into it, he curled his hands under Baltsaros's head, the long strands of his hair snagging on his rough fingers in his fervour to deepen the kiss. Baltsaros groaned into his mouth and Tom quested out with his tongue; finding his eagerness matched, he let out a small sound of his own. They didn't often kiss this way, and it made him feel both wanted and desperate for more at once. However, when Baltsaros tensed, he quickly pulled back, breathless. Tom saw that he had an almost pained expression on his face and turned to see that Jon was slowly running his tongue along the scarred skin of his cock.

Baltsaros let out a shaky breath.

"The scarring makes me more sensitive than I'm used to," he said with a tight smile. "Pair that with the fact that I haven't ejaculated in a very long time. Ahh…" Baltsaros closed his eyes, his body trembling. Panting a few short breaths, he lifted his head and looked past Tom to where Jon had begun to slide his hand along his shaft while his mouth worked the head of his cock. "Well, I'm afraid it won't take much."

"That's fine, Da," said Tom with a grin and shifted his hand so he could run a thumb along the older man's cheek. "Just relax and let Jon make ye cum. Then, we're all gonna sleep right here like old times, and in the mornin' we'll do it again. If yer up to it."

Baltsaros let out a chuckle that ended on a low, needy gasp. In reply, he just nodded his head.

Tom leaned in to kiss him again, slowly and deeply until the body beneath him shuddered. When Baltsaros came, he turned his head to cry out, but his arms held Tom against him, possessive and thankful.

*T*om lay on his side watching Baltsaros sleep. Jon was passed out, curled up against the older man's other side, completely dead to the world. Blearily, the first mate rubbed his face. He hadn't slept in a long time, but he couldn't let himself doze off now. He didn't want to wake to find Baltsaros strangling Jon in his sleep, no matter how sane the captain had seemed earlier. He reached out and touched the back of Baltsaros's hand, testing to make sure that the binds were not too tight. Tom figured he'd lie there just a little while longer, until he couldn't keep his eyes open anymore, and then would ask Saban to watch over them while they slept. That or he and Jon could take turns. Tom let out a yawn that creaked his jaw and turned onto his back. After sliding a hand beneath the waistband of his pants, he scratched lazily at his balls and pinched the loose skin of his limp cock; even his pecker was too exhausted to perk up. Stroking it softly, he wondered whether trying to wake it up was worth it.

There was a rapid knock at the door, and he sat up with a groan, annoyed at the disturbance. He quickly draped a small throw over Baltsaros and Jon and padded to the door. When he opened it quietly, he was surprised to see one of the younger deckhands, flushed and wide-eyed with excitement on the other side.

"Ship," panted the boy. "Ship off port bow. Two sails, but all-a bristlin' with guns like a bleedin' hell's warship and flyin' the cross n' crown. They seen us, sir. Comin' right for us, almighty."

Tom clenched his jaw in frustration; it didn't look like he'd get rest any time soon.

"Aye," he grumbled. "Go feed the bloody chase guns. And the portside sixteeners. Run like a devil's after ye, lad. I'll be deckside in a jiff."

He turned back and saw that Jon watched him sleepily from the bed, a worried expression on his face.

"What is it?" he asked, his voice hoarse.

"Just our fuckin' luck, ducky," growled Tom. "It's the royal bloody navy."

10

PLUNDER

Through his binoculars, Jon watched the ship—what Tom had called a *ketch*—coming towards them. He lowered the double spyglass and looked over at Tom. The first mate stood with him at the bow, glowering like a storm cloud as he chewed on the end of his slender cigar.

"We can't come about?" he asked with a frown.

Tom shook his head and then passed his hand over his eyes tiredly.

"Nay," said the first mate. "Fuckers'll be on us before we can run. If they catch the same wind, we're beat for sure. They're smaller and faster than us, love."

Jon's heart felt like it was lodged in his throat.

"So your solution is that we face them head-on?" he replied. "I thought we were outgunned."

"Aye, that we are," said Tom with a scowl but didn't offer anything else. When he saw Jon's bleak stare, his green-blue eyes narrowed coolly at him.

"Ye got a better fuckin' plan, Jon?" he growled, smoke trickling from his nostrils.

"No! I don't! You know I don't have a fucking clue about sea battles. I've never been in one, only read about them."

"Then keep yer bloody mouth shut n' leave me to it."

Jon stared at the first mate, offended and hurt at once. He felt completely useless, and Tom was being unnecessarily harsh. His stomach churned as he wondered for the hundredth time why they had made him captain if he was just going to be a puppet.

"It's almost sundown," he said. "Isn't there some kind of gentleman's agreement about not fighting after dark?"

Tom just laughed harshly and turned away.

"Brace round portside, ye lazy bastards. Put yer bleedin' backs into it and haul, lads!" he bellowed to the men pulling at the rigging.

Jon threw up his hands.

"Fine," he said a little angrily. "I'll stay out of your fucking way. I'm sure there's something I can do elsewhere."

Without a backwards glance, he made his way sternward, weaving through the bustling crew as they prepared for the coming battle. As he avoided a pair of men playfully swinging cutlasses at each other, he shook his head. He couldn't understand why the hells anyone was laughing or joking. Were they so eager to wind up at the bottom of the sea? Jon might not have that much experience, but it didn't take a genius to see that the odds were definitely not in their favour. On top of the fact that they were no match for the heavily armed ketch, the Devil's Isles modifications still encumbered the *Heart*, making her unwieldy. The navy couldn't have picked a worse time.

Why in the hells are they out here anyway?

Jon yanked open the door and then ducked quickly as something came flying towards his head. The golden tureen bounced against the wooden frame and landed with a clang on the wooden planks. Wild-eyed and dishevelled, Baltsaros paced at one end of the long table while Saban stood slightly crouched at the other.

"What in hells is going on?" asked Jon, frowning at the dented dish that rocked a few more times slowly on its side. When he and

Tom had left Saban to watch over Baltsaros earlier, the man had been asleep still. From the looks of it, he had been wrong in assuming that the worst of the captain's episodes were over. It was hard to believe that the lunatic across the room was the same man who had laughed and kissed him in breathless thanks less than an hour earlier.

"I don't know what set him off this time," said Saban, his deep voice quiet. "I was just sitting here, and suddenly he started shouting about being attacked."

Baltsaros muttered to himself, shaking his head like a dog with ear ticks before he turned around to dig through the armoire.

"Well, he got that right," replied Jon, watching the captain. "By Tom's estimates, the navy will be on us shortly after sunset."

Saban blinked.

"That's… soon. Isn't there anything we can do to evade them?" asked the Balorian. "What should I be doing?"

Jon knew that Saban was anxious to show his worth as a sailor; the broken arm, though mending well, was a source of frustration for the ex-slave.

"Tom's got everything under control. Supposedly. We're to keep barrelling towards them like fools and then rake them with cannon and pistol fire as we swing back into the—Watch out!" Jon pulled Saban to the side as Baltsaros lunged at them with one of his small surgical knives. Saban quickly grabbed Baltsaros's arm and twisted his wrist. The older man panted, letting out a small grunt of pain as Saban wrenched it further around, and Jon reached out and grabbed the knife before it dropped to the carpet. He held it in front of Baltsaros's face, his heart breaking at the utter madness that seemed to crackle around the man like a lightning storm.

"Saban, go into the third drawer of the armoire and look for a blue velvet bag full of a yellowish powder. And get the rope from the bed," said Jon soberly.

"What are you planning on doing?"

"We're going to sedate him, and if we make it out of this alive, we're going to *keep* him sedated until we get to Madierus."

*J*on mounted the quarterdeck stairs and approached Tom. The first mate leaned forward against the wheel, his eyes focused on the ketch coming towards them in the grey murk of dusk. They'd soon be in firing range of the naval vessel. Jon felt almost high from lack of sleep and fear, like it was all happening to someone else. He could see the flurry of activity below as the men rolled and heaped cannonballs and grenadoes on the deck while others loaded rifles and pistols.

"Sorry I bit yer head off before," said Tom quietly after a moment. "Just fuckin' tired and pissed is all. After all we been through, it don't seem fair for us to be holed through by the bloody navy." He lifted a flask to his lips and took a long pull before passing it over to Jon.

Jon accepted it with a nod.

"S'ok," he said, taking a small sip of the rum before handing it back. "You know what you're doing."

"What I'd like to know is why the fuck they're out here at all," spat Tom. "We're in the middle of bloody nowhere! What sorta fuckin' business do the king's bilge rats have all the fuckin' way out here?"

Jon blinked. *Business.*

Jon's pulse sped up, and he grabbed Tom by the shoulders, pressing a hard kiss to the first mate's lips.

"Don't let anyone ever say you don't have a way with words," he said with an excited grin.

Tom stared at him like he had gone completely insane.

"*Business*, Tom," laughed Jon. "Business! Gods, I hope I'm right. Really... It's the only thing that makes sense!"

"What in hells are ye yammerin' about?"

"I don't think they're going to fire on us," said Jon quickly. "Why would they be out here? No one comes out this far because there is no way through the mountains. Or, that anyone *knows* of, right? What if it's the king who's been in business with Ah'puch?"

Tom's ocean eyes widened, and Jon could see that the wheels were turning.

"Aye... No one'd think of attackin' the navy for a belly full o' gold. Shit, Jon... Bloody hells, ye could be right." The first mate frowned and looked out over the preparations below.

An idea took hold of Jon.

"How many men to sail the ketch? Minimum, I mean."

Tom thought a moment, his brow creased. He shrugged a shoulder.

"Ten. What are ye thinkin'?"

"What if we didn't fire on them... but *took* the ship instead? Pretend that we're the ship they're meant to meet with and wait until they're close enough to use grapple hooks to board her?" asked Jon.

"Why in hells for?"

"So we can use it to send Baltsaros to Madierus while we go drop some of our passengers off at the southern peninsula," he replied. "He's really not good, Tom." Jon told him what had taken place belowdecks with Saban.

Pain flashed across the first mate's face before he turned away, craning his head to look up at Baltsaros's family shield flying on the ship's flag.

"Well... I just hope you're bloody right," muttered the big man. He nodded to himself. "With the sun at our backs, they might'n have made out our colours. Take the helm, lovey. I'll get us sorted in two flicks of a lamb's tail." Tom made for the stairs, shouting over his shoulder. "And if ye got a juju, kiss it and ask it for some luck. I think we're bloody owed some."

*J*on smiled broadly, feeling completely exposed as he held the lantern over his head and waved at the navy ketch. However, his gamble that the king was using the navy to do his dirty work had paid off. Instead of firing on them as they came into range, the smaller ship had simply swivelled its main mast and swung about in the wind so that the *Heart* would come up beside her.

"Ahoy!" he yelled out over the darkened waters that separated the two ships. "Ahoy there!"

"Ahoy!" came the reply after a moment. "Where's Captain Roki? What is this ship?" The man's voice had a reedy quality to it, and his tone was suspicious. Jon imagined he could hear the hammers being pulled back on muskets pointed at his head.

"The captain's sick!" he shouted back, accenting his Common with the slight rasping sounds and cadence of Balorian. "I am the first mate!" He didn't have to convince the man, just stall long enough that the strong swimmers who had dived overboard made it to the other ship. They would climb aboard and begin picking off the crew so that the grapple hooks would find their marks and not be cut loose.

The other man was silent for a long time. When he finally yelled back, Jon almost groaned.

"What is the name of Roki's daughter?"

Jon's nerves were shot. He was going to get them all killed.

"I'm sorry? Please again? I did not hear you!" he shouted helplessly across the water, exaggerating his accent further. When the man repeated his question, Jon tilted his head. He could barely see the ship's captain, but there was something in his voice. *Something like a man lying.*

"Are you forgetful? Roki has no daughter!" he hollered. There was another long pause during which Jon worried over whether he had blown it.

"All right, all right! Same deal as before then? I'll send my men over as soo—Hey!"

Jon watched the man's lantern bounce off the side of the ship before splashing into the water below. Next to Jon, Harris spun his grapple hook in a wide circle before letting it fly with a grunt, and a moment later there was an audible thud of metal against wood as it landed aboard the ketch. When Harris hauled on the line and found resistance, he let out a little whoop. Quickly, the others followed suit and began the task of hauling the two ships together. Grinning wide, Tom jogged up with the captain's long scimitar in his belt.

"Let's go get us some navy scum, boys!"

~

*T*om clung to the shrouds for a second, judging the distance. The sea was calm so the ships were tight and cosy, and Tom doubted anyone would wind up in the drink this time. Above them, the sky had cleared and the gibbous moon shone bright.

Bloody nice night for some plunder. He grinned to himself as he leapt across and landed nimbly to the other ship's deck. Two men grappled at each other near him, and he had to step backwards to avoid them.

"Scotty! Aft!" he barked. "Rémi and Harris! Below… See what we got here." He heard a grunt behind him and turned quickly to see a naval officer collapse with a gushing bloody hole in his throat. Tom smiled up at the tall, white-haired man holding the fishing spear—Tuli or Tuvi, he could never tell the twins apart— and ducked his head in thanks before moving on to see what they were up against.

The ketch had been shored up and modified to hold what seemed like twice the number of guns than she was meant to. The crew quarters, always tiny on a ship this size, must have been reduced even more, making Tom feel almost sorry for the men who had to live in such cramped quarters. He snarled and leapt forward, swinging his sword to take the hand off a man who had stepped out of the dark pointing a pistol. *Almos*t sorry. The naval officer let out a shriek, and his flintlock bounced to the boards, letting off its shot with a deafening bang. The upside to the diminished crew quarters, Tom knew, was a diminished crew. He figured they numbered no more than twenty. This would be duck soup for the pirates.

Tom let out a yell when fire suddenly exploded in his face. Blinded, he lashed out with his sword, trying to cut his assailant in two. A boot kicked him in the ribs and he grunted, swinging around. All he could make out were bright blooms in the blackness, and his eyes streamed and smarted. However, when the boot hit his side again, he lunged and caught the man around the waist. The move sent the both of them flying, and they glanced off the mast, landing on the wooden planks where Tom used his weight to pin the man beneath him. His hand closed on his attacker's throat, and he squeezed hard, pawing at his eyes with his free hand. When his vision cleared a little, he saw that the gasping, struggling man's face was growing dark.

"Ye bloody hit me in the head with a lantern?" he growled, still blinking rapidly. The man's eyes bulged, and he scratched hard at Tom's hand as he tried to free himself. With a frown, Tom reached behind him for his long dagger and released the man's throat only to slit it a second later.

*J*on looked away with his jaw clenched tight when Tom reported that all the naval officers had been killed and tossed overboard. It was hard to tell what was going through his mind, but to his credit, he didn't object. Tom had reasoned that they couldn't take navy men on as prisoners and that leaving them in a dinghy just meant they would die slow deaths; even by sail, it would take over two weeks to get to the closest island. Tom had heard stories of men surviving a long time aboard rowboats far from shore, but they'd mostly been stories about cannibalism. A quick, clean death was better.

"What did you find on board?" asked Jon after a moment, obviously eager to get off the subject of the men's fates.

Tom grinned wide.

"Nothin' as shiny or gold as what we already have, but lovely things all the same," he replied and handed Jon an inventory of the plunder. The hold of the ketch had been chock-full of silks, steel and iron pots, spices, and swords. However, none of those things were as valuable as the barrels of wine and beer that Tom had ordered brought aboard the *Heart*. That was treasure indeed.

With treasure in mind, Tom dug into the pouch in his trousers and pulled out something else he had found while rooting through the ketch's hold. Feeling a little silly, he handed it to Jon.

Jon looked curiously at the piece of blue silk, his brow furrowed.

"What is it?"

Tom laughed and rubbed a hand over his mouth, lifting his shoulders in a shrug.

"It's just a scarf. I thought it'd look nice at yer collar," muttered Tom, embarrassed. The wisp of blue had reminded him of Jon's eyes so he had pocketed it. "Ye don't have to wear it. Forget it." He reached for the scarf, but Jon pulled back and smiled.

"Thank you. It's just unexpected, that's all. It's beautiful, Tom. Really."

Tom scratched the back of his neck and nodded, his face hot.

Jon watched him for a moment before holding out the piece of silk.

"Actually," he said with a smirk. "Can you put it on me? You know how I am with knots."

Tom took the soft piece of grey-blue silk and looped it around the back of Jon's neck, carefully tying it over itself like a cravat in the front and tucking the loose ends beneath Jon's black shirt. After giving him a quick, chaste kiss on the cheek, Tom stepped back and smiled sheepishly.

"There. Ye look like a right lord," he said. Jon's seal-brown curls framed his face and continued in a tumble over his shoulders, nearly as dark as his shirt. The scarf that peeped out from the open collar really did bring out the blue in his eyes, and Tom was glad that he had given it to him.

"*Sweet* is definitely not the word I would have chosen to

describe you when we met," laughed Jon, fingering the silk at his throat.

Tom scowled, but really it was just an act.

"Who d'ye want to send with Da?" he asked before Jon had the chance to say something completely ridiculous.

"Saban definitely. And Ceara—I want to be rid of her. Pick ten men to go with them, but make sure not to gut us too much. The ketch has superior guns. They won't need our best men."

Tom nodded.

"Of course, Captain," he said with small smile.

"We'll part ways at daybreak," continued Jon, running a hand through his curls. "Shit, I am starting to forget what sleep feels like. You know what? I'm going to admit defeat right now and just crawl into bed."

With a laugh, Tom grabbed Jon's arm and pulled him towards the door.

"Ye'll do no such thing, lovey," he said. "We just pulled off a pretty bit o' piracy. Let's go open one of them barrels and have a drink or five with the lads. Show 'em the captain's proud of 'em, aye?"

Sighing as Tom led them out of their quarters, Jon nodded tiredly but didn't resist.

11

STRAIGHT AND NARROW

The jealous are troublesome to others, but a torment
to themselves.

— WILLIAM PENN

*J*on laughed until he got a stitch in his side and tears rolled down his cheeks. The story wasn't even that funny—just something stupid about a near-sighted man mistaking a horse for his wife—but Jon was so exhausted and near-drunk that he couldn't stop himself long enough to take a breath.

Then a pair of warm lips touched the side of his neck, and his laughter turned into a gasp. Tom's deep voice spoke softly in his ear.

"If there was a good bloody time to take a powder, here's yer chance." The first mate's breath tickled the little hairs at his nape, and Jon shivered when Tom's mouth brushed the rim of his ear. He was struck with an almost overwhelming urge to be alone with Tom.

Wiping his eyes, he rose quickly from his crate and ducked

through the crowd, following the first mate through the dark. When they reached the door of the stateroom, Jon grabbed Tom's wrist and turned him, backing him against the wood so he could kiss him hard. The big man moaned softly when Jon's hand closed over the bulge in his pants, but he pulled away from the kiss with a laugh.

"I thought ye were tired, lad?" asked Tom with a wide grin.

"Mmmhmm. I am," replied Jon with a little squeeze that made the first mate wince. "But I want to fuck you first. Then we sleep like the dead. Sound good? Fuck, that sounds good to me."

Tom just nodded, eyes crinkling at the corners as he cupped Jon's face in his big, scarred hands.

"What ye say t' gettin' indoors before ye have me on my knees fer all t' see, love?"

Jon grinned and stepped back, releasing the first mate so he could open the door to their quarters. He dragged Tom inside and, walking a little unsteadily, propelled him towards the bed with one hand while he worked on the opening of his trousers with the other. After turning around so he could sit against the box holding the feather mattress, he pulled his cock out of his pants and began to stroke it.

"Down," he gestured impatiently. "Get down. I want your lips around my cock."

Without a word, Tom dropped to his knees and grabbed Jon's hips, opening his mouth to take in his length quickly. The first mate's tongue flicked underneath the sensitive head, working its way along the edge of the foreskin as Jon squeezed his shaft.

"Take it deep," he murmured after a moment, moving his hand away. "And look at me while you do it."

He stroked Tom's hair almost distractedly, looking down into his gorgeous blue-green eyes as he gorged himself on Jon's cock, his lips brushing the thatch of curly dark hair at the root of it. Tom's mouth felt so great on him; he wrapped his hands around the back of the first mate's head to keep him in place while he shifted his hips a little. It always amazed him how well Tom could do this. In the same position, he was usually forcing himself to relax, tears in his eyes and just waiting for that moment where he could finally surrender to it. Tom, on the other hand, could deep-throat him without a hint of a struggle, submitting willingly to Jon's sometimes cruel treatment.

The thought of Tom struggling sent a strong surge into his cock, and he pulled back with a groan, rubbing the head of it against the first mate's lips.

When a floorboard squeaked, Jon's heart stuttered and he looked towards the sound, startled.

Across the darkened room stood Saban looking incredibly embarrassed.

"I am so very sorry. I came in here earlier to check in on Balt-saros and fell asleep at the table. I was just trying to leave so you didn't see me. I am so, so sorry. I didn't mean to interrupt. I had perhaps too much to drink. I should be going to my bunk," stammered Saban.

Jon stared at him. Normally he'd be in an agony of shame, but something about the man's words conflicted with the way he held himself. Almost like he'd been standing there for a while.

Feeling reckless with the wine singing in his blood, Jon smiled wide at Saban.

"Did you want to join in?" he asked, his tone less teasing than he had intended. It was only as he said it that he realized that the idea actually appealed to him. A lot. Maybe he was getting over his archaic, prudish ways? "You can if you want. Why don't you come here?"

Tom's head swung around, and he looked up at Jon with a wrinkle between his brows.

"No. No, thank you," replied Saban in a choked voice. "I'm not... ah... uh..."

Jon had never seen the big Balorian so flustered before.

When he glanced down at the first mate again, he saw that he was shaking his head slowly. Jon frowned and stroked the side of Tom's face. There was something in Tom's expression that stilled his fingers. His fevered high beginning to ebb, Jon looked from Tom to Saban.

"Oh." Understanding dawned on Jon when he met the tall man's hazel eyes.

Guilt.

It was stupidly obvious. Why hadn't he seen it before? Jon's anger bubbled up, coupled with the deep feeling of betrayal he hadn't yet been able to shake over Tom's indiscretion. The two men were so often together... and Saban was so arresting with his handsome face and his broad-shouldered, sculpted body. Why *wouldn't* Tom want to kiss him?

He let out a small, harsh laugh and shook his head, letting his gaze drop to Tom; the muscles in the first mate's jaw bulged and he shrugged. Feeling like a fool, Jon clenched fists and shut his eyes before he made anything worse. The door of the stateroom opened and closed a moment later as Saban left.

When Tom came up to sit next to him on the bed, Jon heaved a sigh and leaned against his muscled shoulder. Why was he still filled with bitterness about a stupid kiss—something Tom had confessed to and apologized for? It was such a small thing.

"I'm sorry," Jon said faintly. "Ceara was right. I should have asked you who it was you kissed. If I had known, I would have never suggested... with Saban... Agh!" He scrubbed a hand over his face, growing angrier with himself. "I'm sorry I'm such a godsdamned immature *child*. Why can't I just get over this... this *stupid* blinkered way of thinking? Why does my stupid heart feel like it's going to break just thinking about you with someone else? I don't even know why I tried to get Saban to... What was I thinking? I'm not like you. I would have just regretted it." He was weary beyond reason, brittle and bordering on hysterical. Jon knew he would start to laugh any second, and then he would cry.

"Ahh, Jonny... love," rumbled Tom, wrapping his arm around Jon's back. With his other hand he patted Jon's chest, right over his heart. "Ye do all of yer thinkin' with this... and not so much with *this.*" The first mate rested his hand on Jon's flaccid cock. "It ain't a bad thing. Just a thing."

Jon chuckled softly at Tom's logic.

"Yer laughin', but if ye change or not, I don't rightly care. As long as yer happy, I'm happy. Aye?" said Tom, fondling Jon's cock teasingly. "I'll suck almost any's cock ye order me to, but only when yer there and only if ye *really* want me to."

"Well… I'll keep that in mind," Jon replied with a soft smile and then let out a little groan, moving Tom's hand away. "I've completely fucked up for tonight, and all I want to do is sleep and forget everything. Can we do that? Is that ok?" He peered across the room to where Baltsaros slumbered on in his drugged sleep.

Tom just nodded and set to work ridding himself of his pants before sliding naked beneath the covers; lying on his back, he watched Jon undress. When Jon joined Tom, he lay on his stomach, half on the first mate. Tom curled his arms around him, and they lay there entwined, skin against skin, soft and warm. It was both comforting and sensual; when Tom stroked down his back and cupped his buttock and squeezed, Jon gave a sigh of pleasure. He was debating trying to rekindle the earlier mood when Tom's gravelly voice woke against his ear.

"Wouldn't have worked anyways," said the first mate. "Saban's as straight as a bloody pin."

Jon frowned.

"I'm not so sure about that," he replied, thinking again about what it was that had bothered him about the man's stance. "He was facing away from the door, not trying to get out. I think he was watching us and just him shifting his weight caused the board to squeak." Tom's hand stopped in its caress, and Jon suddenly wished he hadn't said anything. However, when the first mate began snoring quietly a few moments later, Jon wondered if Tom had heard him at all.

*B*leary from too little sleep, Tom leaned against the rigging and supervised the exchange of supplies. They had decided that half of the gold would go to Madierus with the ketch, while the lion's share of foodstuffs would come with them. Baltsaros was already safely aboard and sleeping peacefully in the tiny captain's quarters and once they were done loading and unloading, they would part ways.

In the wan light of dawn, Tom caught himself staring at Saban again as the big man stretched up to grab a bundle, and he looked away. He thought about what Jon had said about Saban watching them. Jon had to be mistaken. But if he wasn't... Tom turned to watch the tall Balorian lift another sack over his shoulder. When he saw Tom's eyes him, Saban looked embarrassed before averting his gaze. The first mate took another drag from his cigar just to have something to distract him from the nervousness squeezing his guts to jelly.

Truth was, the thought of being made to service Saban had wildly excited him. However, his knowledge of the man's tastes had just made the whole thing bloody uncomfortable, and he'd been glad that nothing had happened. But... If Jon was right about Saban...

Tom blew out a plume of smoke and sent the stub of his cigar flying over the gunwale. That line of thinking was pure rubbish, and he'd better get his head on straight; Saban was his mate and that was that.

Jaw clenched tight, Tom jumped to the deck to help the boys haul up a particularly unwieldy bundle. Damn Jon. In just a few words, he had turned Saban from a safe fantasy to a... what? A possibility? Damn Jon to *hells* for planting the seed in his head. Shit, he figured that Jon would fly right off the handle even *knowing* that he sometimes jacked off thinking about the handsome Balorian.

When Tom leaned over the side to grab the last of the grapple hooks that had held the boats together, his eyes met Saban's again.

Instead of looking away this time, a tiny wrinkle appeared on the man's brow, and he pressed his lips together. Tom stared into that green-brown gaze for a moment before nodding.

"Safe journey," he muttered. When Saban nodded back, Tom turned on his heel, anxious to get back to Jon. He was glad the big Balorian was leaving; it meant he wouldn't have to go out of his way to avoid him.

12

WELL KEPT

Good things come to those who wait.

— ENGLISH PROVERB

*J*on stretched out, his tendons popping as he let out a long groan. When he rubbed his eyes and sat up, he was dismayed to see that the light outside was far too bright for it to be daybreak. He slid off the bed in alarm when he noticed the empty cage and began digging through the pile of clothes on the floor, looking for a pair of pants. The door opened as he was jumping on one leg, trying to pull up a pair of half-inside-out trousers. Glaring at Tom, he grabbed the side of the table as he tried to untangle the pant leg.

"Is he gone? Lords of the black hells, please tell me he is not gone," he growled, dreading the answer.

Tom looked surprised and stopped in his tracks, a steaming cup of coffee in each hand. It was obvious by his expression that Baltsaros was indeed on his way to Madierus.

"Shit, Tom… *Why didn't you wake me up?*" He stopped wrestling with the pants and stood half-naked, clutching the material to his hip.

Creases appeared on the first mate's forehead, and he slowly put the mugs down on the table.

"Tried," he replied. "Ye said to leave ye."

What Jon felt was panic, and it crushed his lungs. He'd missed Baltsaros's departure.

"He was drugged, lad. Wouldn'a mattered. Not like he'd notice if ye was there or not."

"That's not what matters, you idiot. Fuck..." Jon let the pants fall and wrapped his arms around himself. "You should have tried *harder*. Tom, what if I never see him again? The least you could have done is given me a chance to say goodbye! How long have we been sailing? Can we come about to catch up with them?"

Tom shook his head.

"The sun's past the yardarm," he replied. "Hours gone, love."

"Fuck fuck fuck fuck!"

"Two n' a bit weeks to the peninsula, five more south to Madierus. We'll see Da in two months. What are ye goin' on about?" said the first mate, taking Jon's shoulders in his hands.

"What if we get attacked? What if there's another big storm? What if they sink?" Jon whispered.

With a little shake of his head, Tom furrowed his brow at him.

"Listen," said the first mate quietly. "If I knew ye'd be this sore, I would'a tried harder to wake ye. But yer talking bloody nonsense. Aint'cha tired of worrying yer damned head over things ye got no control over? Jon, if ye die, how're you gonna feel bad about not sayin' what I figure is a useless goodbye to Da? Ye'll be dead. Now, there's all manner of ways Da could perish outside our reach, ye know that right? Aye, they could sink. Or they could get to Madierus all dandy and throw bloody *soirees* every single fuckin' night, and Da could choke on a bloody fish bone and die right before we make shore."

Jon frowned at him.

"That's not making me feel any better."

"Ye made the right choice... *We* made the right choice. Da wasn't gettin' any better with our half-arsed doctorin'. We were bloody shooting into the brown on our own, and ye were right to strike sails and send him off. He'll get to help faster; it ain't healthy for a man to be sleepin' on the toxy powder fer two months, love." Tom sighed and squeezed Jon's shoulders. "I'm just sayin' ye gotta stop worryin'... Whatever happens, happens, and there's no point in thinkin' of future tears now. Aye?"

Jon shrugged. He wished he could be as jaded as Tom was to the possibility of tragedy. Then he realized something and smiled a little.

"We always seem to be telling the other not to worry," he pointed out.

With a twist of his lips, Tom rubbed the side of his thumb against his dark-blond stubble.

"Aye. Too much worryin' on board," he grinned. "Worryin' ain't good for a man's soul."

Jon tilted his head at Tom.

"I don't know why, but it surprises me that you believe in souls, given your complete disregard for anything sacred," he said.

"Who says I'm disregardin'?" replied Tom. His ocean eyes narrowed in amusement as he slid his hands down over Jon's naked hips before dropping down to his knees and nuzzling against his soft cock.

"I've got a burnin' need to kneel and pray right now."

Jon laughed and pushed Tom's head away.

"You and Baltsaros," he chided. "You can't solve everything with sex."

The big man just shook off Jon's hand and licked delicately at his cock before looking up at him wide-eyed.

"I can try," he said, smiling. He face grew serious, and he leaned forward to bathe Jon's stiffening cock with his tongue softly, tugging gently at his foreskin using only his lips. He glanced up again. "Jon, do ye remember the last time we weren't interrupted or too tired to fuck? When was the last time ye had me on my knees for a good ploughin'? Yer cock balls-deep in my hole, fuckin' me hard and rough..."

Jon let out a huff of breath at Tom's words, his brow pinched. He felt almost bad thinking about it, but the fact that Baltsaros was not there felt a little... *freeing*. His cock bobbed higher with every rapid pulse of his heart, fed by the look in Tom's eyes.

"Aye, that's better," breathed Tom before curling his hand around Jon's shaft to suck the head of it between his lips. He bobbed his head a few times, his tongue running along the bottom of Jon's cockhead every time he pulled back.

Jon closed his eyes and took Tom's head between his hands, giving in to the sensation. When Tom brought up his other hand to cup and fondle his balls gently, Jon gave a soft sound and tightened his hold, plunging his length faster into the hot, wet tunnel of Tom's mouth. His knees started to feel a bit weak as he was brought closer by the first mate's skilled tongue and hands, and he slowed his pace, holding Tom and his eagerness back. He felt a trickle of sweat run down his chest and was panting when he finally pushed Tom away roughly.

"On the bed," he said, pointing.

Tom rose to his feet a little unsteadily and dropped his pants before climbing onto the bed. He quickly got onto his hands and knees and looked over his shoulder, waiting for Jon.

"Spread your knees more," said Jon. "The way I like."

Without a word, Tom lay his head down on the bed before he widened his legs further.

Jon loved seeing Tom this way, completely exposed. It brought out urges in him that other positions didn't. He felt little to no tenderness... only a desire to feel the mouth of Tom's pucker open over the head of his cock before he shoved his whole length roughly into his oiled hole. He grabbed the bottle they kept handy and poured a little of the pale oil into his palm. Stroking himself, he watched Tom's cock sway in time with the big man's breathing for a moment before he tipped the slender bottle above Tom's furry crack and let a slow trickle out. Tom's sphincter contracted when the cold oil touched it, and Jon reached out to smear it, sliding a finger into him. The hot, slick walls hugged him up to his knuckle and, hand on his own cock, Jon searched and quickly found Tom's sweet spot to begin rubbing it in a slow circle.

Muffled by the bed, Tom's low whimper made Jon smile.

"You like that?" he asked, his oiled finger stroking the dimpled little nut inside Tom. When Tom didn't answer, he pulled his finger out and delivered a hard slap to the back of the first mate's thigh.

The groan that came from Tom had nothing but pleasure in it, and Jon laughed to himself over the strange conundrum of how he was supposed to punish someone who enjoyed being punished a little too much. He slipped his finger back inside Tom and continued to jerk himself slowly, watching the first mate's cock drip a clear string onto the coverlet. He had an idea.

"You'd love to touch your cock, wouldn't you?" he murmured. "Or have me touch it?"

"Aye," came the reply.

"Well... You can forget about that," he said with a smirk. Tom stopped pushing back against Jon and stayed still. "No one is touching your cock today. At all. That's your punishment for not waking me up."

Tom lifted his head and twisted to the side, staring at Jon with his face flushed.

"That's damn cruel," he said, obviously not believing him.

Jon stopped fingering him and dealt him a few stinging slaps before thumbing him open to continue the slow tease. His own cock was throbbing in his fist, the length of it slick with more than just oil.

"Yes, it is," agreed Jon. "But that's the way it's going to be."

With a deep furrow in his brow, Tom thought.

"Please?" he said after a moment.

"You can say please a thousand times, and I won't relent. Not this time."

"Ye can't be bloody serio—"

"Keep talking, and I'll make it tomorrow too," growled Jon.

When Tom turned his head away with a small sound, Jon stroked his reddened ass cheek and slid his thumb over the slick, sensitive opening.

"Just think about how good it'll feel when you *do* cum," he murmured, pushing a finger back inside Tom. The first mate moved against Jon, and he let out an appreciative noise.

"Yeah, it'll feel really nice when I let that fat cock of yours spill," continued Jon, exciting himself even more. His cock was leaking over his knuckles, and he moved closer to rub it against Tom's ass. He pulled his finger to the side, stretching Tom open a little and let out a slow breath at the sight. Experimentally, he began to push his cockhead against Tom's hole without moving his finger away and groaned when the edge of his glans squeezed passed the constricted entrance.

Tom made a faint sound, something that sounded a little pained, but he didn't move away. Instead, he shifted his hips eagerly, inviting Jon to slide his cock deeper.

Jon's breathing was hoarse as he pushed harder, so tight against the finger shoved inside Tom.

"Fuck!" He squeezed the base of his cock quickly to stop himself but let out a strangled groan as he realized he was too late and going to cum right then and there. Jon shifted his hands quickly to Tom's hips and pounded into the first mate, crying out and then grunting with the force of his release as he came hard inside Tom.

~

Tom let out his own cry with Jon's orgasm. When he was told he wasn't going be allowed to cum, Tom's first honest reaction had been annoyance. However, he had stifled it and forced himself to concentrate on what Jon was doing to him instead; in the end, the rush he felt at Jon's climax filled him with an intense pleasure and when they collapsed together, he breathed as hard as if he had cum too. Jon pulled out with a small gasp, and Tom lay there a moment, groggy and oddly happy with himself. So he wasn't going to cum... It wasn't the end of the world. After all, Baltsaros had made him wait numerous times before. Jon was just normally a little kinder. It was an interesting change, but he wasn't convinced that Jon would actually go through with his promise.

Tom shrugged to himself and turned over onto his back, watching Jon as the slight, dark-haired man made his way across the room to clean up at the basin. When Jon came back and handed him a cup of water, Tom accepted it with a small smile and sat up to down it in two gulps, very aware of the tenderness of his slowly softening cock and the dull aching need in his balls. However, as Tom waited for Jon to say that he had changed his mind, Jon walked over to the cupboard, pulled out a fresh pair of pants and a shirt, and began to get dressed. Tom folded his hands behind his head and leaned back against the headboard with a resigned smirk.

Bastard, he thought fondly.

When Jon saw him watching, he smiled. This time he definitely looked proud of himself.

"Lordin' yer satisfaction over me, lad?" Tom asked, eyebrows high.

Jon's smile widened before he turned to grab the shirt from the back of the chair.

Though hard work aboard the ship had changed Jon's body, packing sleek muscle onto his slight frame, he still retained his slender, lithe youthfulness. In the shifting light, the damp cherub curls, though nearly black and not gold, did nothing to squelch that image of unsullied boyhood. However, the illusion was shattered when Jon tilted his head and Tom saw the dark stubble of his cheeks; even more so when Jon reached for him with a bold hand to pinch his nipple and then pet the fur of his chest like he was a dog.

"Aw, poor Tommy-boy. You'll keep," Jon assured him. "Get

some sleep now if you want, but I need you up by mid afternoon. We still have that issue with those assholes in the brig. I want to make sure they're not going to try to take some kind of revenge over their mate's death. We need to put our heads together and come up with something to keep this sort of thing from happening. We have two weeks aboard with these... Tom, you're not listening to me, are you?"

Tom shrugged a little. He looked down at his cock; it had visibly plumped up a bit and lay straight and half-hard on his belly.

"Is it because I said 'put our heads together'?" said Jon, grinning.

Tom grinned back.

"You're incorrigible," said Jon, rolling his eyes before he made his way to the door. "Mid afternoon! Be up!"

Tom watched Jon leave and let his smile drop, wondering how he would get any sleep at all without taking care of his cock or without letting his thoughts wander to the worries over Baltsaros's journey that hung like black clouds at back of his mind.

13

FORTUNE'S TELLING

Fate leads him who follows it, and drags him who
resist.

— PLUTARCH

*J*on stared up at the *Jewel*. It looked like the marble
finish had cracked on the east side of the building
and was being repaired; he could see crumbling red
brick between the posts of the scaffolding. As Jon watched, a
pallet was hoisted up a wooden crane powered by three long-
eared donkeys and lowered to the roof of the second floor.

"I wonder what happened?" he mused.

The first mate finished tying the rowboat's mooring line to the
bollard and straightened, putting his hands on his hips.

"Old buildin'," he said with a shrug. "Cheap materials."

Jon nodded and followed Tom off the floating dock and up the
path leading to the brothel. He remembered how awestruck he
had been the first time he had seen it and laughed a little at
himself. After everything he had witnessed in the past months, the
Jewel just looked a little dingy. It was nothing but a red brick

building fronted by an elaborate façade to make it look like a fairy-tale castle. Even the "guards" at the front didn't look as grand as they once had to him; as they passed between the huge doors, Jon saw that the uniform of the man closest to him had been patched, and there were sweat marks under his arms.

Curling his lip in distaste, he mentioned it to Tom after the first mate had ordered something at the bar.

"Look at you, mister fancy world traveller," said Tom, sliding a small glass towards Jon. He chuckled. "All snooty and lookin' down yer nose…"

Jon made a face at him, then peered at the murky green liquid suspiciously. Despite how vile it looked, he lifted it up and touched the rim of the glass to the first mate's before he brought it to his lips. His nose told him only a split-second before he tasted it that the liquid would burn, and burn it did. It tasted like nothing he had ever had before; pungent and rotten, it seared his throat all the way down and set fire to his chest. Jon choked and coughed, tears streaming down his face as Tom downed his and smiled serenely. When he could swallow without gagging again, Jon wiped his face and glared at the first mate.

"What in the black hells was that?" he rasped.

"It's called *Dragon's Milk*," laughed Tom, collecting Jon's glass. "And don't ask me how it's made… Ye don't wanna know, love. Another?"

"Ugh. No. Never," Jon said with a grimace and watched Tom pour himself another shot before tossing it back without so much as a lip-twitch. His tongue felt burned, and his mouth tasted like stagnant harbour water. "You think you're so tough, drinking fucking poison. Hey… Wait… Don't tell me you made me drink that shit because I haven't let you touch your cock in three days."

Tom grinned wide and lifted his hand palm up. *What can I say?*

"What if I make it four?"

"Ye wouldn't…"

"Try me, big guy," Jon said, smiling. It had become a new facet of their play, one that he knew they both enjoyed. While Tom claimed that it was honest-to-gods, horrible punishment for him, it didn't explain why he was going along with it so willingly. It's not like Jon had anything to keep Tom from jerking off anytime that he so wished. He just... obeyed.

Tom capped the bottle of Dragon's Milk and passed it back to the man behind the bar, asking a few questions in a language Jon didn't recognize. With a nod of his head, Tom turned back to Jon with a frown.

"Can I leave ye here, lovey?" he asked. "Got somethin' I'd like to take care of. Be back before ye miss me, aye?"

Tom winked and slapped some coins down on the glossy wood before making his way around the side of the bar and through the door there.

When the bartender pointed to a clean, empty glass with a raised eyebrow, Jon asked for something to wash the horrible taste from his mouth. With a smile, the man pulled a pint of pale beer and set it in front of Jon with a flourish before pouring himself a small glass of amber liquid and picking up the book he had set down on their arrival.

"Cheers," said Jon, but the man didn't hear him. Turning, Jon leaned back against the bar and looked around while he sipped his beer. It was the slowest period of the day, Tom had explained. It was post-breakfast so the late- or overnight clients had left with their "pipes cleaned", as Tom had put it, but it was too early for the afternoon crowd. Theoretically, the only reason they were there was to kill some time; they had dropped off their passengers earlier that morning and were only waiting for some supplies and mail to be loaded onto the *Heart* before they made their way south to Madierus.

Across the room, a pretty girl in an almost see-through purple dress smiled at him, and Jon smiled back. He knew that she might only be interested in him for the gold in his purse, but a small part of Jon hoped it was because he cut a pretty dashing figure.

The first mate had tamed Jon's hair into a tight, braided queue that had made his scalp ache at first until some of his ringlets had worked themselves loose, and during the three-week trip to the southern peninsula, the beard he was trying to grow had filled in enough that he no longer had patchy parts. It was barely more than thick, black stubble, but he thought it made him look slightly dangerous, which he liked. His pants were new, bought the previous day up the coast at a small town that specialised in textiles. They were black and made of a heavy, soft material that clung to him like a second skin. His loose white shirt was freshly bleached, and at his neck he wore Tom's gift; he knew that the blue silk made his eyes seem a brighter hue. He had even polished his boots to a shine that morning. Tom had laughed and called him a strutting peacock when he saw him all dressed up, but the approval and admiration in his gorgeous eyes had made Jon's cheeks hot.

Grinning to himself, Jon glanced again at the prostitute in purple and took a swallow of beer. As he lounged against the bar trying to recreate the sort of charming disinterest that Baltsaros seemed to so effortlessly project, he was startled when something hard whacked the side of his leg.

"Buy me a beer and I'll read your fortune," croaked a tiny old woman with a cane and an ill-fitting wig.

"Um. Ok?" replied Jon. A little flustered, he began digging around for some coins. When the beer had been poured, he carried it to a small table for the woman. However, when Jon turned to go back to the bar, she hooked his arm with the crook of her cane and pointed to the seat across from her.

"Oh. No… That's all right," he said kindly. "You can have the beer. It's on me. No need for fortunes or anything. I don't believe in that sort of thing."

"Then whatever I have to say won't make any difference, and you can just laugh to yourself over the foolishness of an old woman," she said with a smile that showed off her lack of teeth. However, there was something in her rheumy eyes that made Jon feel a little guilty about not being more charitable, so he let out a silent sigh and sank down into the hard-backed seat, wishing he had brought his beer with him. To go get it now just seemed rude at this point.

The woman pushed her beer towards Jon with a tilt of her head.

"Go on, son," she said in a voice as weathered as her skin. "I don't much like the taste of it."

"Then… Why did you want me to buy it for you?" he asked, perplexed, but the woman was busy shuffling some dog-eared cards in front of her and didn't reply. With a frown, he picked up the pint glass and took a long swallow, watching as she took forever to move the cards around the table with no rhyme or reason. He wondered what the hells was taking Tom so long.

Finally, when the cards were arranged in a crooked semicircle, the old woman sat back in her chair and peered at Jon.

"Well. Go on," she coaxed, waving a gnarled finger at him. "Pick."

Jon furrowed his brow and looked down at the mess of cards. When he glanced up at the old lady, she was watching him so closely that his skin prickled in discomfort.

"How many?" he asked and then cleared his throat because his voice sounded odd. "How do I choose?"

"Doesn't matter!" said the woman, laughing. "You don't believe in this anyway, do you, son?"

With an impatient sigh, Jon reached out and held his hand over the cards, intent on just selecting a few at random quickly so he could get it over with. He tapped three and sat back.

The old woman put her crooked finger on each of the cards, pushing them away from the rest before sweeping the pile to the side. Slowly, she turned over the three cards.

"Ahhhhhhh…" she said, nodding her head. "Yes, yes. I see." When she didn't offer anything else, Jon felt himself growing annoyed.

"So? What do you see?"

"Don't rush an old woman, Jon," she scolded him. "Drink your beer like a good boy."

Jon felt a cold flood of unease.

"How do you know my name?" he asked quietly.

The woman squinted at him shrewdly.

"Do I? Aren't you all johns? This is a whorehouse, isn't it?" she said and cackled like it was the best joke she'd ever told.

He laughed along with her a little hesitantly; there was something about her that made him think she was not nearly as batty as she made herself out to be. Jon started to wonder if Tom had put him up to this.

"The Moon," said the old lady, pushing the card towards Jon. On the card was a picture of a boy with a moon for a face sitting in a pool of water. He had one eye opened, and the other closed, and in his hand he held a crayfish. "The Moon represents dreams and intuition. The inner self. This little crawdad here is all the strange things that can crawl up out of the pool of the mind. One eye open for visions. One eye closed for dreams. Do you have strange dreams, Jon?"

Jon swallowed, mesmerised by the movement of her finger over the worn card. There could be no mistaking her use of his name this time. He could hear his pulse like muffled drumbeat in his ears, and he nodded slowly as he thought of his dreams that often seemed weighted with portent.

"The Tapestry..." said the woman, sliding the next card towards Jon. On it was a blue, three-sided tapestry with three yellow stars in the middle, a clawed animal holding each corner. *A three-sided tapestry.* Just like the one in his daydream the day they had come for Tom.

Then, to his alarm, he realized that the three animals were a thickly maned lion, a large cat, and a wolf. Mouth dry, Jon looked up at the old seer in alarm. The wild cat and lion from his dreams —Tom and Baltsaros.

"This has to be a joke," he whispered. "Tom set you up to this, didn't he?" He had told Tom about the dreams, but there was no way that Tom knew about Jon's family crest—the one that was woven into the moth-eaten cloth that used to hang above the small breakfast table in his castle home. *A wolf.*

The old woman sucked on the corner of her toothless mouth for a moment before continuing.

"The Tapestry represents the warp of Fate and weft of Time working to weave together different aspects of your life to create a strong bond. The three corners are birth, life, and death—there cannot be one without the other two. But see here? There is a tear on one side... one that will have to be mended. Once you do, you will stop looking at your feet and realize that looking to the stars is a better means of finding your way. But, is this a joke? Could be. Could be that this tapestry here is just to keep you from the cold. What do I know? But three... oh three. *Three* is a magic number. Did you know that, Jon?"

The woman grinned to herself and pushed back on the ratty wig perched atop her head.

Jon blinked and was startled when he found himself staring at a stunningly beautiful young woman smiling like an imp at him from across the table. Her eyes were a soft, warm brown framed by dark gold lashes, and they crinkled at Jon in amusement as he stared agape at her. Her full, rosy lips made a playful pout, and she swept her thick, autumn-honey hair back over her shoulder.

"Shall I continue?" she asked with a wink.

Though Jon didn't answer, she slid the next card towards him. This one looked older and smaller than the rest, like it had come from a different set of cards altogether. The only thing on it was a blue whirlpool, crudely drawn. The young woman's finger circled the painted water as she spoke. Jon's vision began to swim, and he clutched at the table to keep from slipping out of his chair.

"The Whirlpool. Swirling and dragging all towards it, pulling everything closer and closer, round and round. You are the epicentre. Events in your life, often unrelated, coming together *just so*. Tell me, Jon... Are there things in your life you cannot explain? Do fluke and fortuity court you like lovers?

The question sent a chill down his back, and Jon started to feel nauseous. The Devil's Isles and Tom's tattoos. The blood rituals and Baltsaros's desires. So many other little coincidences that seemed to follow Jon wherever he went. He couldn't pull his eyes away from the woman's finger stroking the flaking paint around the black abyss of the whirlpool's centre. He felt as if he were falling headfirst into it.

"Jon?" A hand clasped his shoulder, and he started, breaking out of his trance. Tom smiled down at him. "There ye are."

Jon swallowed and stared up at Tom, speechless. The first mate frowned, and there was a touch of worry in the lines of his face.

"Now, Granny, have ye been fillin' the boy's head with yer bloody foolishness?" he asked with a shake of his head.

When Jon turned to the woman across the table, he saw that she was once again a toothless old woman with skin like long-crumpled paper and eyes that were clouded and heavy-lidded with age.

Beaming up at Tom, the woman flapped a hand like a gnarled claw at him.

"Oh, Tommy, my love," she said with a fond sigh. "Were I a century younger, I would put you over my knee for such impudence... But we all know you would like that far too much! Ha!" The old woman chortled to herself, rocking back in her chair. The wig slipped further, showing more of her patchy, wisp-covered scalp.

Tom chuckled.

"Oh yer still a great beauty, darlin'," said the first mate with a waggish smile, "with men singin' songs of your loveliness from shore to shore!"

"Hush now, you silly thing. We both know that no matter how buxom or lovely I once was, you'd have never given me the time of day if there was a bonny lad in the room!"

Jon's heart had slowed a little, but he felt dazed as he watched the exchange.

Tom just laughed with the old woman before grabbing Jon's arm.

"Up, lad," he said, pulling Jon out of his chair. "Quick as wink! We gotta be runnin'…. There's an escape to be made! So long, Granny. May ye bloody outlive us all."

"Escape from what?" asked Jon as he spared a glance back at the old woman. Her smile was sly and eyes canny as she watched them depart.

When he looked over at Tom, he saw that the first mate had an old jute bag slung over his shoulder. Jon thought he heard the clink of bottles within.

"Well," replied the big man, opening the door for Jon, "some might take exception to me takin' a few things. Figure it's only fair considerin' I never collected the last of my wages…" He grinned wide and headed down the path at a brisk pace with Jon following.

Jon waited until Tom was settled between the oars before pushing the dinghy away from the dock. He was confused and nervous about what had just happened. It felt like he had just woken from a dream and couldn't remember all the details.

Tom watched him as he rowed.

"I gotta say, love, it was a damn sight eerie seein' ye starin' at the empty table, still as a statue an' bug-eyed like ye were seein' visions."

Jon started.

"What do you mean *empty*? There weren't any cards? Oh *fuck*," he breathed, feeling lightheaded.

Tom burst out laughing.

"Ye can be a damned gullible fool, love," he said, shaking his head at Jon. "No, Jon. I was just takin' the piss outta ye. Lords tell me, ye didn't take any of that ol' biddy's nonsense serious, did ye?"

"She said some very… relevant things. I don't know." Jon fiddled with his shirt cuff, embarrassed. "Enough that I thought you'd put her up to it."

"Me? Naw. Listen, she's just some ol' tramp lady who's been swindlin' folks out of coin since back in the days when the *Jewel* was just a four-room hump shack. They just keep 'er around for the tourists, mainly," replied Tom. Sweat beaded on his sun-bronzed brow from the exertion of pulling the oars. "I got no bloody idea how she makes any coin, seein' as she never charges for a 'bad' readin'."

Jon stared at Tom, wondering if he was just teasing him again.

"What? Didn't ye give her any money?" asked the first mate with a smirk.

"No... I didn't."

"Oh," replied Tom, sobering a little. It had obviously just dawned on him that Jon was honestly rattled. He glanced over his shoulder at the *Heart*, anchored just outside the narrow, manmade harbour. When he turned back to Jon, he smiled reassuringly. "It ain't anythin'. Trust me. Forget what she said."

Nodding, Jon tried to brush off the feeling of dread that had taken hold of him. She was obviously good at reading body language, and Jon could very well have led the woman's whole performance, feeding her information just by his reaction to her words. He was reminded of the far-travellers that came to the maidens' faire every spring and the way that they would prey on easy marks; he had witnessed with his own eyes how an old man with tarot cards had fished and obtained cues from the woman he was doing the reading for. It must have been the same with the old woman at the *Jewel*.

"What's on my family crest?" he asked Tom.

The first mate flashed a white smile as he put away the oars and then stood to grab the line dangling from the *Heart*.

"Easy," replied Tom with a wink. "A wee mouse with dewy eyes holdin' a lovely little flower, all precious and fuckin' innocent like."

Laughing, Jon stood.

"Fine!" he said, throwing up his hands. "I'm a gullible twit."

His anxiety over the strange card reading began to retreat even further into distance as he helped the first mate prepare to hoist the dinghy up the side of the pirate ship.

14

AT LONG LAST

release • n. *relief or deliverance from sorrow, suffering, or trouble.*

O nce the supplies were stowed and they were on their way, Tom dragged Jon to their quarters and emptied the contents of the bag onto the bed. He grinned at the look on Jon's face and climbed onto the mattress to sit against the headboard, pleased with himself.

Tom had been pissed as hells when the new manager had denied his request for his final wages. Not that he really needed the money, seeing as he was a rich man with a king's ransom of gold, but it was the *principle* of the thing. However, instead of punching the fucker—as was his first instinct—Tom simply walked away and swiped a set of keys from the holder in the hallway on his way out. After a visit to one of the liquor closets, he'd ducked into his favourite of the specialty playrooms to grab a few items.

On the bed lay the spoils of his plunder.

Jon grabbed the four bottles of whiskey and lined them up on the table before picking up the flogger with a raised eyebrow at Tom.

"We have one of these."

The first mate shrugged with a smile.

"This one's better. And ye can never have too many!"

With a little laugh, Jon set it down next to the shackles Tom had also taken. He then picked up a leather box and shook it with a jingle before undoing the little clasp on one side. His eyes darted to Tom's in bewildered surprise.

"What are these?" he asked, holding up a smooth metal ring.

Tom scratched at his jaw and grinned wider. He knew that the box contained more metal rings of different sizes as well as a few leather ones.

"Cock rings."

Jon stared at the ring in his hand, his brow furrowed in confusion.

"How do they work?" he asked after a moment.

"Ye know when Da ties your cock up tight? Right behind yer balls...?"

Understanding dawned on Jon's face, and he reddened a little, nodding. He dropped the ring back into the box and frowned.

"There's one with a bunch of little bells on it in here."

Tom laughed, sliding one hand into his trousers. He was already too hard to put one of the rings on, but that was ok. He used the tips of his fingers to softly tease the head of his cock.

"I just grabbed the box. Fucked if I know," he said. He almost regretted not taking one of the leather masks fitted with a wide O at the mouth. Watching Jon blush as he looked through the sex paraphernalia was both amusing and more than a little arousing.

Jon put aside the rings and picked up a small wooden box. When he saw the sticks of *char* in it, he just chuckled and shook his head. The last thing on the bed he lifted with a smirk on his face.

"Sort of big, isn't it?" he said, turning the smooth wooden phallus around in his hands.

Tom squeezed his cock and gave him a crooked smile. Jon glanced at the first mate's crotch, only just registering that he was playing with himself without permission.

"Aren't you afraid I'm just going to leave you high and dry again? Hm?" asked Jon with a little head tilt.

Moving his hand down to his aching balls, Tom dipped his chin and sobered.

"Aye. But I don't really care, love."

Jon stared at him for a long moment.

"Take off your pants," he said.

Tom sat up and quickly rid himself of his trousers. His cock jerked by itself as he shifted up on his knees, and he wrapped his hand around the base of it with a smile. However, Jon shook his head when Tom reached for him.

"Hands off your cock, Tom," said Jon, his blue-grey eyes amused. His expression darkened as he watched Tom. "Lie on your back, hands behind your head."

After he lay down, Tom closed his eyes and waited. After a moment, he thought he heard the soft sounds of Jon undressing. Jon joined him on the bed, and Tom let out a small sigh as his cool palm stroked him from stomach to thigh, avoiding his cock altogether. While it was frustrating, it did feel nice, and when Jon leaned down to kiss the curve of his pelvis, Tom groaned quietly in encouragement. Jon's beard scratched softly against his belly, and Tom opened his eyes to watch, shifting his hips eagerly.

"Bring your knees up," murmured Jon against his skin.

Tom did as he was told, opening his legs and pulling his knees up to bare himself. Jon cupped Tom's sack and squeezed, tugging it playfully. Tom crushed his eyes shut; while it looked like his cock wasn't going to get any love, Jon *did* know how to treat his balls.

However, he gave a little grunt of surprise when something cold touched him a moment later. Tom lifted his head and saw that Jon had the large wooden cock in his hands, a serious expression on his face. Tom licked his lips and took a deep breath; he'd stolen the overlarge dildo on a lark, not really expecting to have it used on him.

To be honest, he really wasn't sure how he felt about it. He put his head back on the pillow and stared at the boards above.

Without a word, Jon rubbed the fake cock over Tom's hole as he poured oil on him and then began fingering him to get him ready. Tom knew he could say no. Jon would stop and then maybe they'd just fuck normal-like instead, but Tom's cock was rock hard, and he had to admit to himself that he was actually excited about being fucked by something so big. Jon's fingers stopped moving, and Tom raised his head again.

Looking at Jon, he saw that the dark-eyed lust had been replaced with a question.

Is this ok?

In response, Tom grinned—embarrassed that Jon had picked up on his nervousness—and nodded. He lay back again, hands cradling his head and closed his eyes, breathing deep to relax himself.

Jon began working on him carefully and slowly. His finger was joined by a second, and he added more oil as he slid them in and out of Tom with teasing strokes of his prostate. Almost all his jitters gone about the big dildo, Tom moved his hips in time to Jon's finger fucking. It felt so good. He pulled his hands out from under his head to curl them behind his knees, holding onto his legs to give Jon better access to his ass. Jon laughed softly, slipping his fingers out to knead Tom's balls for a moment. Then the head of the dildo touched him again and Tom tensed.

Jon paused, just squeezing at Tom's sack before stroking behind his balls and along his inner thighs gently until Tom had taken another deep breath or two. There was no hurry in his caress; it dawned on Tom then that Jon would take all the time in the world if he needed it.

Tom clenched his teeth against the tightness in his lungs and forced himself to breathe deep again. Though Jon didn't know the extent of the abuse he had suffered—and never would, if Tom had his way—the way he was so attentive reinforced one thing over and over to Tom: no matter how much pain Jon could inflict, he would never *hurt* him.

Jon pushing the wooden phallus against his puckered opening brought Tom out of his reverie, and he made a small, slightly shaky sound. Jon's hand stroked the back of his thigh, his palm now warm and slippery with oil. The pressure increased and Tom felt himself begin to open up. He winced as the stretch bordered on painful for a moment, but it was more out of nerves than any real discomfort.

"Fuck, Tom," breathed Jon. "I am so *fucking* hard right now... watching this... doing this to you. I never thought..."

Tom let out a groan at Jon's words, his arousal rekindling again as he realized that the wooden cock sliding into his ass was not going to be the uncomfortable challenge that he had assumed it would be. Since the thing didn't actually have a head, being smooth and widening only slightly near the base, he knew he could take it.

Tom heard Jon take a shuddering breath and, hearing the rapid sound of skin on skin, came to the conclusion that Jon was jerking himself off as he fucked Tom's ass with the dildo. Tom's cock twitched against his stomach in response, almost painfully stiff and so sensitive that when he breathed and it moved against his belly hair, it sent little jolts of pleasure through him.

He lifted his head to look at Jon and saw that he was flushed; his eyes had taken on the glazed, rapt look of profound arousal as he stroked himself quickly. Then Jon began pulling the phallus almost all the way out and pushing it back in, slick and hard into Tom's body.

"Oh gods," murmured Jon. "I think I'm going to cum just looking at you."

Tom arched his head back on the pillow, his breath short and his heart thundering. He let out a gasp a moment later when the dildo left his ass and he heard Jon's strangled cry as he sent a jet of cum right against Tom's throbbing pucker. A second volley followed and then Jon pushed his slick cock inside Tom, fucking him quick and hard with a few deep thrusts as he rode out the tail of his climax.

Tom felt frantic and desperately aroused when Jon pulled out with a satisfied growl.

"Wow, sorry…" he said, panting. "I meant to draw that out more but…" He let out a breathless laugh. "Well, I guess it was a little too much for me."

It was hard not to feel disappointed. Jon obviously meant for him to "keep" another night. Tom started to lower his legs, but Jon stopped him with a hand, shaking his head as he caught his breath.

"I didn't mean I was done with you," he said with a smirk.

The first mate watched as Jon uncorked the little bottle of oil and poured some into his palm. He then stroked over Tom's asshole and into him, taking up the dildo a second later to begin working it into him again.

Tom was getting to the point where he was getting tense and frustrated, and if Jon wasn't going to let him touch his fucking cock, he'd rather just end their play right there. He was about to tell Jon exactly that when the smooth tip of the dildo prodded right into his prostate and sent a distinct burst of pleasure through him. A little startled at the sensation, Tom let out a soft sound.

Eyes closed, Tom furrowed his brow as Jon began to thrust the wooden cock quick and shallow into him, deliberately rubbing it over and over again at the sensitive point. It started off as a small, albeit pleasurable thing, but then he began gasping as an insistent, heady feeling began building inside him, like a bubble swelling with every pass of the dildo.

Tom whimpered. It was nearly intangible and sweetly agonizing at once—a growing pressure spreading warmth through his groin that would recede a little and elude him as the wooden cock moved away. He was only just aware of Jon whispers of encouragement as he began to moan louder and louder.

Drenched in sweat, Tom dug his fingers into the backs of his own thighs almost painfully. He was nearly there. So close. He was almost beside himself. *So. Fucking. Close.* It was insanity.

Then, deep inside him, the bubble finally burst and unleashed a rushing, wild tide that tore through his body. What came from his throat was nothing short of a yell; Tom arched his back and shuddered as his cock jerked, sending a thick jet of cum onto his chest. Powerful and violent, the waves surging inside him didn't crash to the shore; one would swell up only to be taken over by another and another, sharpening the intensity of the torrent that shook him. He was completely unable to stop the sounds pouring from him as he came harder than he ever had before. All at once, it was too much.

"Out," he gasped. "Out. Please *out out, out.*"

Jon pulled the wooden phallus out of him, and Tom turned to his side, curling into a ball as the pulsing, pounding surf finally began to recede. Hand around the base of his cock, clutching at himself so he didn't shake to pieces, Tom realized that his face was covered in tears and he was bawling his eyes out.

Jon curled up behind Tom and put his arm around him, murmuring soft things against his neck as he shuddered and wept. He didn't even know why he was crying... just that he was, and it felt like his heart was both breaking and flying at the same time.

"Sorry," he said and began to laugh, but a tremor shook him just then, and he went back to sobbing like a babe.

"It's ok," whispered Jon. "Don't be sorry. It's all right. I'd never judge you for crying, Tom. I love you. Cry as long as you need to. I'm right here. It's ok."

Tom cried until his tears dried up and then lay quiet on the pillow, just thinking. It was the second time something like this had happened to him, though it hadn't been *quite* so intense last time. He thought about the night that he snuck into Baltsaros's bed and how the captain had held onto him as he was beset by an inexplicable swell of emotion. Tom buried his face in the wet pillow, trying not to set off another bout of tears. A little embarrassed, he tightened his hand around Jon's, sighing when Jon kissed the nape of his neck.

"Five more bloody weeks," he muttered, thinking about much he missed Baltsaros.

"Yes, five weeks," replied Jon, with a small bite to his shoulder. "It'll go by fast. I'll make sure of it." His body was soft and warm against Tom's back, and when he nestled closer, Tom smiled.

"Aye, I can believe ye will, love," he said, wincing as the shift made him aware that he was a little sore. Moving his arm to get more comfortable, he encountered a cooling puddle on the pillow and grimaced. "Jon, we made a mess." Between their cum and the copious amounts of oil Jon had used, the sheets were completely soiled.

"Mmhmm," came the sleepy reply. "We'll clean up later."

Tom chuckled, sliding the wet pillow out from under his head and pushing it off the bed. He thought about the piles of discarded clothes on the floor and the dirty dishes they'd left on the table that morning. Baltsaros would be appalled at the pigsty they'd turned his cabin into.

Jon's mind must have followed the same path because he nuzzled against the back of Tom's neck with a little sigh.

"Like y'said... five weeks. S'nuff time... clean. Hm?" mumbled Jon.

Even though it was only barely past midday, Tom felt Jon twitch against him as he fell asleep. The first mate was also completely exhausted, like he had just fought a brutal fight and won. He closed his eyes and sleep claimed him almost immediately.

15

HOME, SWEET HOME

With a grunt, Jon pulled on the rope, helping to haul the buntline as the men above worked to quickly furl the sails and tie them.

"Heave!" he yelled. "Heave, lads!"

When the sails were finally secured, he stepped back and smiled up at Tom. The first mate climbed down the rigging quickly and jumped to the deck next to Jon. He could almost feel the excitement radiating off the big man as they watched the hidden lagoon of Madierus get closer. They had made exceptional time; the trip had taken them only four weeks thanks to an unusually strong late-summer wind. The crew was exhausted, but their supplies had lasted well, and nothing unusual had happened during the journey south. Tuli clapped Jon on the shoulder, and he turned.

"It is beautiful!" exclaimed the tall ex-fisherman, his bright blue eyes wide. "Is there a... magic we should create for the arriving?"

Jon laughed and shook his head. No matter how many times he had reassured the newest members of the crew, they still had a hard time accepting that there were no set rituals to follow aboard. He didn't blame them; a lifetime of following a strict regimen of rites and sacrifices wasn't something so easily shrugged off. He smiled to himself as the lanky, white-haired man wandered away to the capstan. The men from the fishing clans were probably the worst, but superstition seemed to run rampant in sailors as a rule, no matter where they hailed from. As if to emphasise this fact, Jon saw one of the older northerners kiss a medallion he wore around his neck as he watched the harbour come into view.

"We bloody made it," murmured Tom.

Nodding, Jon saw that the land bridge they had concocted to keep invaders from entering the harbour had been shored up. It looked less like a bunch of floating bundles and more like a permanent addition. As the *Heart* approached, a man ran along the narrow strip of land and bent low to fiddle with something on a small boulder. A piece of the land bridge began to swing outward, and Jon saw that there were men on the other side pulling on a rope.

The man at the edge of the manmade strip of land pulled off his hat and began to wave it at the ship. When a woman's voice drifted over the water, Jon felt his face stretch into a wide smile and the fever of excitement he'd been keeping at bay finally took hold. He ran to the side of the ship and skipped up onto the gunwale to hang off the shrouds and yell back at Katherine, waving like a complete fool.

"Ahoy!" he laughed, giddy at seeing his friend.

"Ahoy yourself!" cried Katherine with a whoop, and she began running back along the land bridge to meet them at the beach.

Once they were past the opening, Tom glanced over at Jon, his brow wrinkled and his blue-green eyes wide. He'd never seen the first mate look so nervous before, and it resonated inside him.

Baltsaros.

Were they coming home to a madman?

Jaw clenched tight, Jon looked back over the clear turquoise water to the white beach and saw a group of people waiting for them in the shade of the almond trees.

"Ye got this?" asked Tom, his face tense.

Jon frowned.

"What? Why? Where are you going? We can't lower the boats yet, we haven't—"

"Don't need one," replied the first mate, and he took off at sprint without waiting for Jon's response. In amazement, Jon watched the big man clamber nimbly up the bowsprit and then dive headfirst off the front of the ship. Jon jogged to the bow and peered over the gunwale.

"Impatient ass," he said, smiling to himself as he watched Tom swim away from them. Glancing around, he saw that the crew's eyes were on him. He scowled.

"Well, what the fuck are we waiting for? Let's get that anchor down so we can get our asses to the beach. I don't know about you, but I'd like to feel a little sand underfoot!" he yelled.

A loud cheer went up and Jon grinned wide.

～

Tom turned his head to the side and sucked in a lungful of air as he propelled himself forward with long strokes, cutting through the water easily. The water was cooler than his skin, but not by much, and it stretched in front of him—a bright, clear blue against a sandy bottom dotted here and there with dark smudges that could be rocks or fish.

Tom was a powerful swimmer; he'd made sure of that after the long-ago blunder of jumping off the ship without knowing how to stay afloat. He'd been out further than this before, way past the mouth of the lagoon, especially in those early days when swimming had been a form of escape. Anything to get away from the fury that baked his bones every time he bore witness to his mother's scorn. Getting so worked up about it was stupid, he knew. But if she had done anything... *any* bloody thing at all to make him feel welcome, then she wouldn't be the one bearing the brunt of his bitterness for what had been done to him.

He took another deep breath and was startled when his hand hit sand. Tom stopped and reached down, steadying himself and letting his legs drop so he could kneel in the long, shallow stretch of water. Scanning the beach, he saw with dismay that there was no sign of Baltsaros. Kat nodded at him when their eyes met, and his little sister beamed at him with Jon's giant mutt panting at her side, but there was only a coldly appraising look from the woman who had given birth to him. He shook some water off as he staggered to his feet, surprised by the depth of anger that spiked him.

Forcing an impudent grin onto his face, he walked through the thigh-deep water and up onto the hot sand, stopping short of the shade.

"Well, well… Ain't this the poorest piss of a welcomin' party?" he said with a wink, avoiding his mother's gaze. "A man comes back from the bloody dead and not a mug o' beer on the lot of ye!" Kat rolled her eyes and the dog came padding towards him. He patted its gigantic, furry head and then smiled at his sister.

Tom got down on one knee and held out his arms to Eloise. The little girl had grown at least a hand since he'd last seen her.

"Come 'ere, my wee love," he said with honest warmth. His sister smiled shyly at him. "Aww… C'mon my poppet." This time she approached him and submitted to a rough hug with a little giggle. "Wait 'til ye see what I got for ye," he whispered to her, thinking of the golden tiara he had found among the golden loot from Balor. He squeezed her thin arms and pecked a kiss on her cheek before standing.

Brushing sand off his wet knees, he looked up and met his mother's eyes. They widened at him.

"Where the fuck is he?" he asked, his words barely a growl.

"He's in his tower," Abetha said after a moment, her pale hands clutched in front of her. How in hells a woman living on a tropical island remained so bloody white was beyond him. For some reason it made him even angrier.

Without a word he pushed past her and headed up the crumbling steps that led to the cobbled street above. The stones burned the soles of his feet when he got to the top, and he took off at a quick jog that would get him to the castle in no time. He had intended to wait for Jon, but between Baltsaros's absence and the presence of his mother, he felt on edge. Tom just needed to see... with his own eyes...

One breath for every three beats of his bare feet on the narrow road brought him to the castle gate in only a few minutes. He went past the koi pond and down the covered, arched walkway to a set of wooden doors that led to the tower stairs. Taking them two at a time, he made his way to the second floor and down the little hallway. Tom was surprised to see Saban seated in a chair right outside Baltsaros's bedchamber with a book of children's fairy tales open in his lap.

Saban looked up, startled. A slow smile spread across his face, and he quickly rose to his feet.

"Tom! You made it!" said the big man, clapping Tom on the shoulder. For a moment, it was like old times as he threw an arm around Saban's neck to slap his back in greeting; but, when Saban's big hand touched his side, the awkwardness came back in a rush, and Tom took a clumsy step back. Saban's eyes narrowed, looking both puzzled and a little crestfallen at his reaction.

Scratching the side of his thumb against his stubble, Tom glanced down at the book in Saban's hand. It was only then that he remembered that the ex-slave had only begun to learn his letters when they parted.

"When did you arrive?"

"Just now," Tom replied. "Wait... Didn'tcha hear we were spotted?"

Saban shook his head.

"No. I've been on watch all morning and came straight here from my quarters downstairs," he replied.

"Ah. Have they got ye in the old closet of a servant's room then?"

"Yes," replied Saban with a laugh. "I don't mind. Really. I'm close to Baltsaros in case he wants me."

Jealousy suddenly flared up in Tom like a hooded green snake at the thought of the handsome ex-slave in Baltsaros's bed, and he clenched his fists. Saban shook his head at Tom's reaction.

"I'm a glorified nurse. Nothing else. Relax," he assured him, and Tom let out a grunt, feeling both foolish and anxious. He was getting as bad as Jon. As Tom forced his shoulders down, he stared at the big wooden door behind Saban with a scowl.

"Really, Tom, I get it," said Saban softly. "He told me about what happened with Jon and what you went through. We... actually talked about it a whole lot."

"Yer not makin' me a whole lot happier 'bout it," muttered Tom, not thrilled to have his past aired like dirty laundry.

"And I told you... I'm not like *that*."

Tom turned to Saban and met his hazel eyes; he couldn't help but think of what Jon had said. However, all he saw before him was a man who was trying to comfort him and who was honestly glad to see him. He reached out to clasp Saban's forearm again.

"Sorry," he grumbled. "Four weeks can take the wind out of a mate's sails." He turned back to the door. "He ain't privy to us arrivin' then?"

"No. Like I said, I've been here all morning. So has he. He rarely leaves his quarters. Abetha and I have been trying to keep his days stress free. I'm sure she didn't tell us of your arrival because she wanted to make sure both you and Jon were aboard and alive first. Jon *is* here, right?"

"Aye," replied the first mate and took a step towards the door. "I need to see Da."

"That might not be a good idea." Saban's hand closed over his shoulder, but Tom shrugged it off. Keeping Baltsaros from excitement... It made bloody sense. But he didn't care.

Tom reached behind him and pulled the long knife out of his sheath. He looked at Saban with a menacing smile.

"I bloody need to see Da," he repeated. "Don't make me slit yer fuckin' throat, lad."

A flash of something crossed the big Balorian's face. Tom had seen it before… a second before he had been knocked senseless by Saban at the inn. He braced himself, dagger tight in his scarred fist, but Saban just smiled with a shake of his head and lifted his hands in supplication before stepping away from the door.

Tom yanked it open.

For a moment he was surprised by how bright the room was. He didn't know what he had been expecting… a darkened sickroom? His da stretched out in bed? Maybe tied to the posts with some heavy chains. Instead, what he was greeted with was a rather startled-looking Baltsaros who glanced up at him from behind a messy desk, a book in one hand and a quill in the other.

"Tom!"

The first mate quickly shut the door as Baltsaros rose to his feet, his eyes wide. For a second, all he could do was stare. The captain looked well. His hair was much shorter, falling only just past his cheekbones, and the dark circles under his eyes had vanished. Baltsaros looked younger, refreshed; he stepped out from behind his desk and smiled.

"Of course they wouldn't want to tell me," he said, shaking his head ruefully. "Welcome to my life. Do you have any idea what it's like to be nursed back to health by a brute with the strength of three men and a woman with a mind like a hedge maze?"

Tom stood rooted to the spot. He realized that he was clenching his teeth and took a quick breath through his nostrils.

"It's not the most pleasant thing in the world, though they do mean well, I suppose," laughed Baltsaros. He motioned to the plush, wing-backed chair. "Sit! Please."

After weeks of nervous anticipation, this was not what Tom had expected. Half of him was giddy with relief at finding the captain not only alive but also with both oars in the water, and the other half was weirdly reluctant to move from his place near the doorway. He wanted to press himself into Baltsaros's embrace, but the man's how-do-you-do had only stretched to offering him a comfortable fucking seat.

"I love ye and bloody missed ye, Da," he blurted out, all of his rehearsed words flying from his mind in favour of bluntness.

Baltsaros froze. He tilted his head, his dark-brown eyes on Tom's. All the first mate could see at first was confusion.

What am I doing? he thought in dismay. *Jon is right... I'm a stupid hasty fool. There's a time for everything and now's the wrong fucking time.*

However, Baltsaros took him in his arms a moment later with an audible sigh.

Tom sagged against the captain and buried his face in his collar. Baltsaros smelled like the imported eastern perfume he liked to wear—sandalwood, cardamom, woodsmoke—and his own soft musk beneath that. *This* was home. Tom's hands scrabbled over Baltsaros's back for a better hold, pressing them together. His heart thundered in his ears, and he felt like a hundred thousand miles were peeled from his past.

Baltsaros let out a small, hoarse laugh.

"You're crushing me, my tomcat," he said with an exaggerated wheeze.

Tom didn't care. He tightened his grasp like he was holding on to a rope above a bottomless pit. When Baltsaros held him tighter and he pressed his cheek to Tom's hair, the first mate ground his teeth together. Tom knew they had made the right choice to send the older man away, made obvious by his apparent recovery. But...

"I also fuckin' hate ye a little," he growled against Baltsaros's pale linen shirt.

Da's long fingers stroked the short hair at his nape, and Tom let out a heavy breath.

"Is it strange that I'm glad for both?" asked Baltsaros after a moment, his touch soothing.

Tom laughed. Before it became awkward, he pulled away. Tom

scrubbed at his face and then sniffed a few times to get a hold of himself. He curled his lip.

"Well... I'm glad yer alive," he said, forgoing the offered chair and straddling the cushioned stool in front of it instead. He looked around at the familiar surroundings before bowing his head and rubbing both hands over his cropped hair. When he looked up again, he saw that Baltsaros had leaned back against the big desk and crossed his arms.

"Where's Jon?" asked the captain.

"He'll be here soon enough, Da," replied Tom with a crooked grin. "Can ye blame me fer wantin' ye to meself for a titch?"

Baltsaros chuckled and the crows' feet at the corners of his eyes deepened. He pointed to the cut-crystal glass decanter of something honey coloured, and Tom nodded, feeling a little nostalgic about this tradition of sharing a drink in the captain's sitting room. After pouring a few fingers into two tumblers, Baltsaros handed one to Tom and walked past him to sit in the comfortable chair he had earlier offered. Tom turned the ottoman around, the wooden legs scraping on the marble floor, and faced the captain. He lifted his glass.

"Strong winds and merciful fuckin' seas," said the first mate soberly.

Baltsaros raised his own drink and repeated the time-honoured toast of sailors before touching his glass to Tom's.

After downing the liquor, Tom held the glass out to Baltsaros with a wide grin.

With an amused shake of his head, the older man poured another liberal measure of the fine rum and watched the first mate knock it back with a smile.

Tom frowned and looked at the wide-open leaded-glass window. He could hear the clop of horse hoofs on the cobble-stones. Jon would want to come see them but—and it made Tom feel like an asshole even thinking it—after nearly seven weeks, he needed to be far away from Jon's bleeding heart.

When he glanced at Baltsaros, he saw that he was being

watched with an almost pained expression, and he felt a lance of worry spear him. He eyed Baltsaros warily.

"Get that look off your face, Tom," said Baltsaros reproachfully before taking a small sip from his tumbler. "I was just thinking to myself that I missed you very much."

Nodding, Tom scratched his neck. Though they touched him, the words sounded weird coming from Baltsaros.

The silence that followed was uncomfortable, and Tom realized he'd gotten used to Jon's constant need to talk everything out. He smiled to himself.

"Ye had no troubles?" he asked after a moment.

Baltsaros shook his head and leaned forward to fill Tom's glass again.

"We ran into a squall a week into our trip, but the ketch handles storms better than the *Heart*. We got blown off course but not by much, and we didn't lose anyone. Ceara has proven herself to be quite the competent sailor. I'm glad you and Jon decided to send her with me."

Tom just nodded, thinking about how she had been sent away by Jon to rid themselves of her.

"I have to say that I was not very happy when I awoke aboard the *Saber*. However, when I finally came to my senses, I understood why you did it."

"Saber?"

Baltsaros chuckled.

"*Black's Saber*. Not my idea. The boys named it after Jon," he replied. "I'm sure he'll be thrilled about that. I had to name my own ship after myself."

Baltsaros turned his head and his eyes went slightly vague for a moment.

"You should go," he said abruptly. "I feel... not... well."

"Ye seem fine," said Tom, alarmed.

"Am I fine? I don't think so. My memory is still spotty... When things do come back to me, it's as when circulation comes back to a numb limb. Saying that it's unpleasant is an understatement."

Baltsaros turned back to Tom and smiled sadly.

"See, the day I named *Baal's Heart*... It was the day we lost you. I just remembered that now. I also now remember not under-standing why Jon was so broken-hearted over your death," he said, turning the crystal tumbler in his hands. There was a deep crease between his brows, and Tom was dismayed by the tremor he saw go through him. "I'm not happy about being reminded how foolish I was in that regard. Not realizing your worth was the most idiotic thing I've ever done. Argh!"

Baltsaros lurched to his feet and startled Tom by throwing the glass against the wall. It shattered and sent shards flying. The door opened and Saban poked his head around.

"Everything all right?"

"It's ok, Saban," said Tom, standing up.

"You should go, Tom," growled Baltsaros.

"I'm stayin' put. It's bloody time I muck in. Saban, mate, go to Jon. Don't tell 'im that Da's off his nut, but let 'im know that I'm takin' the night, aye?"

Saban's eyes darted between Tom and Baltsaros, and he slowly nodded. Before Saban turned to leave, Tom grabbed his arm.

"Jon'll be sore, but tell 'im not to fret. Savvy?"

With another nod, the big Balorian left and closed the door quietly behind him. Tom slid the bolt home so they wouldn't be disturbed.

"You have no idea what this is like," whispered Baltsaros behind him. "Tom, I am better and I am worse. Just when I think I can control myself, I remember things and it drives away every-thing but these... *feelings*. There's a maelstrom in my head."

"Use me," said Tom, turning.

Baltsaros's eyes went flinty for second before they widened in something that looked like fear.

"I can't."

"Use me, Da," repeated the first mate, taking a step closer. Balt-saros's nostrils quivered and he reached for Tom's shoulders, digging his fingers in painfully.

"I *can't*," breathed Baltsaros. "I can't control it. I can't take the chance."

"Bloody quit yer 'can't' bullshit, Da. Yer not a bloody coward and yer not a weak man, for hells' sake. *Use me.* I can take it. We'll get ye sorted out... Are ye still havin' turns as a madman?"

Baltsaros shook his head once.

"Not often," he replied softly.

"All righty," said the first mate with a grim smile, "if all ye are is pissed, then take it out on my hide, old man."

"Tom," warned Baltsaros.

"Don't tell me ye've gone all soft on me, ye daft fucker."

Baltsaros bared his teeth and pushed Tom away. The first mate fell back against the corner of the desk and landed hard on the floor. One of his hands came down on a piece of broken glass and when he lifted it, he saw it was bleeding. He slowly got to his feet, his eyes on Baltsaros. With a growl, he lunged forward at a crouch and barrelled into the taller man at waist height, sending them both crashing against the footstool and onto the carpeted marble floor. Baltsaros let out an enraged yell as he flipped Tom over onto his back and punched him square in the jaw.

Pain exploded in Tom's face, but he just bucked up hard and dislodged Baltsaros, grabbing him by the shirt to shove him head-first into the wall. He climbed again to his feet, breathing hard and ready for more, and watched Baltsaros pull himself to standing by using the arm of the wide, wingback chair.

Glaring at Tom, his chest heaving, Baltsaros took a step forward. There was a bloody handprint on his linen shirt, and his hair had fallen over his eyes; he looked furious... and, to Tom's relief, just the tiniest bit amused. Tom didn't normally fight back so hard.

"I'm stronger 'n ye, Da. And ye've obviously been sittin' on yer arse too godsdamned long," taunted the first mate with a wry grin. He brought up his fists. This was exactly opposite of what Abetha and Saban would want, but he didn't care. Tom wanted to see if he could spark some kind of reaction out of the captain that wasn't immediately overshadowed by that bloody fear he kept seeing.

When Baltsaros came at him with a roar, Tom was ready for him.

~

Jon stepped out of the jolly boat, and as he turned around to grab the rope from Harris, he heard a thundering clatter behind him. Before he had a chance to react, something slammed into him, and he fell back on the sun-bleached boards, nearly rolling off the edge of it as he fought to free himself.

"Brutus!" he shouted with a laugh, pushing the mastiff's muzzle away from his face. "Stop it! Ouch... ouch! Watch it! Hey, buddy, yes I missed you too. Agghh! Stop it!"

He was trying to wiggle out from under the overexcited dog when there came a shrill whistle. Right away, Brutus stopped trying to lick the skin from Jon's face and jumped off, trotting back down the pier. Jon sat up, wiping dog slobber off with the hem of his black tunic. He could see Eloise dancing around the giant mastiff on the beach, and he grinned to himself. When Jon turned, he was startled to see that some of the passengers on the jolly boat were staring at him in shock.

"My dog," he said by way of explanation. Though from the looks of it, Brutus was more than happy to obey Eloise better than he had ever obeyed Jon. Maybe it was time to stop thinking of him as *his* dog. But Brutus was really the only link left of his old life; the dog had been his constant companion and only real source of happiness for a time. Jon let out a sigh and got to his feet.

As he was helping people out of the boat, Katherine approached with a broad smile on her tanned face.

"Jon."

"Katherine," he replied with a grin. When she continued just to stare at him, he frowned.

"What?"

"Jon... I don't know if you know this... but there's some sort of terrible growth on your face," she said, pointing to his chin with a smirk.

In mock indignation, Jon stroked his short, well-groomed beard.

"You're just jealous because you can't grow one."

Katherine barked out a single harsh laugh and shook her head at him.

"No, I'm just amazed because I didn't think you could grow one, kiddo."

Then Jon noticed something and laughed.

"What in the black hells? Lords, that thing is going to give me nightmares."

Katherine lifted her arm and appraised the hook that was attached to her stump. It was shaped out of dull grey metal, scored and dinged in places, and looked like it had been repurposed from something used to torture people with.

"Sexy, ain't it?" she said with a wink.

"Oh yeah. I'm getting hard just lookin' at it," he drawled.

Katherine blinked at him before grinning wide again. She pulled Jon into a quick, firm hug.

"Missed you, cabin boy."

"Missed you too," he replied. "And it's *captain*. Show some bloody respect."

"So I heard. How's that treating you?"

"Pretty great, actually. How's the farming life?"

Katherine made a tragic face and tugged on her braid.

"Not cut out for it," she said. "Fucking hate it. And"—Katherine glanced around—"Maya is driving me up the fucking wall, Jon. Not cut out for happy home life either, it seems."

Jon handed her a bag that she could sling over her shoulder, and he picked up a sack of his and Tom's clothes.

"What are you going to do, then?" he asked, as they began to walk down the pier.

"Ask for my spot back on the crew," replied Katherine with a little shrug.

"Like that's going to happen. Kat... You've got a hook for a hand. You're going to be as useful as tits on a nun, as Tom would say. How are you going to hoist a rope? Or load a pistol?" he said teasingly. But when he saw her smile fade some, he bumped his shoulder against hers. "Hey... I was kidding. We'll figure it out. I'm sure Baltsaros will find a place for you."

"What? Not you, *Captain* Black?" Kat grinned at Jon and jammed her rather squashed-looking straw hat back on her head.

"Well. No. When Baltsaros is back to health, he'll want his ship back." Not *if*... when. Jon had to believe he'd recover.

The sun shone down bright, and Jon shaded his eyes to glance back at the ragtag group that was following them. Madierus had gained eleven new citizens, soon to be twelve since one of the women was heavily pregnant. They were mostly ex-slaves and poor folk. The rich passengers had all disembarked at the southern peninsula. He turned back to Katherine.

"First thing we need to do is get these folks settled. I'm going to need your help with that." When Katherine nodded, he continued. "We picked up some tents and cots on the way here so we'd have temporary shelter for them at the very least. However, we're going to have to build at least three more structures, I believe, to accommodate everyone."

"Four."

"Ok, four. We also bought some basic materials and brought back window glass. It's all coming in on the next jolly boat. See Hitch for the full inventory. I also need for someone to show our new immigrants around and get them acquainted with laws and customs here. Most speak decent enough Common, and the ones that don't are still able to make their needs known. Talk to Nathaniel, and he'll give you the passenger manifest," said Jon. He stepped onto the sand and let out a little sigh at the soft heat between his toes. "Another thing—I'd like everyone to be made welcome, so I figure we should have some sort of welcoming celebration. Tom says it'll be the full moon in three days, so we'll hold it then. These folks are a little on the superstitious side, so it doesn't hurt to have the party made more meaningful by the moon. Or something. Just feels right. Though, skip using the word "blessing" or any permutation of that. And definitely no human sacrifice."

He chuckled to himself but saw that Katherine just stared at him wide-eyed.

"I'm not going to get into all the details, but the place we went to was wholly driven by human sacri—"

"Yeah, we heard," said Katherine, waving his explanation away.

Jon frowned. She seemed amazed at something.

"Kat? What is it then? Why are you looking at me like that?"

"It's just… You're different, Jon," she replied. Grinning away the seriousness after a pause, she leaned back to appraise him with a glint in her eye. "I got it! Your balls finally dropped!"

"Oh, fuck you!" He laughed and punched her playfully in the shoulder. Then he took a deep breath and straightened his spine.

"Come on," he said. "We're keeping the queen waiting."

~

Tom grunted and struggled hard against his bonds as he lay facedown on the mattress with his arms tied behind his back and his pants down around his knees. Baltsaros had finally managed to pin him, and, using the silk curtains that had been torn from the bed in their struggles, he had trussed Tom up tight.

With an aching jaw and his ribs sore from the fight, Tom breathed heavily through bared teeth as the adrenaline coursed through him, lighting his blood and giving him that dizzying high he always chased after. Growling, he tried to twist his arms apart but was rewarded with another hard crack of the riding crop to the back of his thigh. Tom clenched his jaw against the pain that lanced through him, setting his skin on fire.

Baltsaros chuckled and struck Tom again, this time across his ass, and the first mate let out a sharp gasp. A few more cutting blows, and Tom finally cried out, eyes shut tight and face pressed against the bloodstained sheet. Bracing himself, he waited for Baltsaros to hit him again.

"Please," he choked when nothing happened. "Da, please?"

"Please what, Tom? Please hit you again? Please *stop* hitting you? Or please fuck you?" laughed Baltsaros, stroking the tender flesh of Tom's backside with the crop. "You don't even know, do you?"

Tom moaned and turned his head. His cock was so bloody hard beneath him. Getting fucked *did* sound good to him... but...

"That's what I find so absolutely fascinating about you," said Baltsaros as he ran the tip of the crop along Tom's crack before striking him again across his thighs, forcing another strangled cry out of him. "And so marvellous. It's all mixed up in your head... You get lost in this, and then I find you, don't I? At the very edges of your pain, I pull you back."

The switch came down again, slicing into the back of Tom's biceps this time, and he yelled out.

"Please, Da," he said, panting.

"That very first night. Right in this bed... I spent a long time wondering why I didn't turn you away," murmured Baltsaros, placing his cool hand on Tom's burning thigh. "But then I asked you to join me again the next night. And the next. I was stupid not to realize that you *meant* something to me."

This time, Baltsaros slapped him with his bare hand. Less painful. More personal. Possessive. Tom's breath whistled from his lungs, and his senses were screaming at him.

"Please, Da," he whispered.

Laughing, Baltsaros slid his arm under Tom's hips and helped him to kneel so that he was presented, ass up. A few more slaps tore a soft sob out of Tom, and then there was pause where he could hear Baltsaros fumbling with his clothing.

Tom groaned loud as Baltsaros's cock breached him. Thick and hard, Baltsaros pounded into him without mercy, his big hands locked around Tom's hips to drive himself deep. The first mate began to grunt in time to the relentless fucking, the noises forced out of him by the brutal thrusts.

The loud slapping of Baltsaros's thighs against him was a frenzied thing, and each slam into his body coupled pain and pleasure in Tom. Panting, he closed his eyes tight as he felt the sweet warmth grow. Then Baltsaros growled and buried his cock to the hilt inside him; Tom's hands came free, and he realized that Baltsaros had cut his bonds. He quickly went up on one fist as the man resumed fucking him at a frenetic pace and began to stroke himself with the other hand, his torn palm stinging from the friction. His balls were tight, and every time Baltsaros's big cock opened him up, he came closer to spilling. He cried out softly, skirting the edge again, swollen and needy.

In response, Baltsaros leaned into his thrusts, letting out a long groan, and Tom couldn't hold back anymore. He let out a loud grunt and came hard, each pulse a deep burst of pleasure that radiated through him and left him shaking, weak, and empty in the end.

In a daze, he collapsed flat on the bed when Baltsaros finally released him, his pulse loud in his ears and a warm, buzzing feeling in his limbs.

"That wasn't prudent," muttered Baltsaros as he settled next to Tom.

"Mm? Fuck off."

Baltsaros let out a surprised laugh and kissed Tom's shoulder.

"I said it wasn't prudent. I didn't say I didn't enjoy it, Tom," he pointed out. "That being said... I feel... good. Normal." His fingers traced the welts on Tom's backside, and the first mate let out a huff of breath. "How did you know I wasn't going to really hurt you?"

Frowning, Tom lifted his head and looked over at Baltsaros.

"Didn't. But what's a bit o' my blood when it gives ye peace, Da?"

"Ah."

Tom grinned and then winced at the pain in his face.

"You know you're crazy?" Baltsaros said fondly.

"Naw," said the first mate and moved so that he could lie on his side with his head in Baltsaros's lap. The captain stroked his fingertips along the line of Tom's jaw and then skimmed the rim of his ear. It tickled, but Tom liked this new aspect of Baltsaros... where he was softer after fucking. Before Jon, there had only been a handful of times where Baltsaros was so... Tom frowned and searched for a fitting word.

Kind? Could a dyed-in-the-wool killer—if that's what the man still was—be kind?

He reached up and touched the bruise on his da's jaw gently and made a face.

"Sorry."

Baltsaros caught Tom's hand in his and when he saw the cut on his palm, he kissed it quickly and looked away. He blinked rapidly, but not before the first mate saw the glimmer of wetness in his eyes. Tom pulled his hand away, unnerved by the captain's reaction.

When he noticed Tom's scrutiny, Baltsaros swiped at his eyes tiredly and let out a long exhale.

"See? I'm not all right," he said with an apologetic smile. "According to Abetha, I should be talking all these emotions out and finding out what triggers them. She thinks it's healthy and crucial to my recovery. I think she's foolish, but then again, I've been stuck here as a virtual prisoner. It makes me irrational, I'm afraid. Besides, you don't want to hear what I have to say."

"Who says?" asked Tom, wrinkling his brow.

"You've never been one for talk," said Baltsaros. He then shook his head. "Sometimes I think... well, that things were simpler before..."

Before Jon.

The words hung unspoken in the air.

Tom curled down the corners of his mouth and shook his head.

"Simpler ain't better."

Baltsaros laughed and nodded a few times, stroking Tom's short hair.

"True," he murmured.

Tom closed his eyes, giving in to the soft caresses. It was a nice complement to his aches elsewhere. He thought of something.

"I sent Saban to keep the lad away… but… Should I go fetch him?" Tom looked up at Baltsaros, not knowing whether he would be disappointed if the man said yes. However, Baltsaros shook his head after a thought.

"No. Not yet. Stay with me tonight. Jon can keep until morning."

Tom closed his eyes again and smirked at Baltsaros's choice of words. It was true, though. Jon would be ticked off, sure, but he was leagues away from the boy who had made mountains out of every fucking molehill. He'd get over it. Tom let out a little happy groan when Baltsaros's fingers slid down his neck, scratching softly at his chest before pinching his pierced nipple.

"I'm glad you're here, my tomcat."

"Mmm," he agreed, arching a stretch of his back as if he were really a giant cat. "Do that 'gain but harder."

Baltsaros chuckled and obliged.

16

TROUBLE IN PARADISE

*J*on stared at Saban, letting the words sink in. The tall ex-slave regarded him quietly, sympathy in his green-brown eyes.

"He doesn't want to see me," Jon said tersely.

Saban's shapely brows pinched together.

"I don't think it has to do with *want*, Captain."

"No, I get it. Tom and Baltsaros are going to hole up for the night and call for me in the morning like a bloody servant," snapped Jon. But, when Saban opened his mouth to reply, Jon lifted a hand to stop him.

"I'm sorry," he said with a sigh and let his shoulders slump. "You're just the messenger. Don't mind me." Jon massaged his temples, eyes closed, and tried not to feel the anger by telling himself that it wasn't betrayal. If Tom thought he should stay away, he probably had a very good reason. The first mate's instincts were good, and the truth of the matter was that he had known Baltsaros for far longer than Jon had. It just stung. He looked up and saw that Abetha watched him with guarded eyes. There was compassion there and warmth... and bitterness. At first he thought the last was aimed at him, but as he stared at her, she swallowed, lifting her chin a little, and he understood.

"Thank you, Saban. Let me know if anything changes?" he said awkwardly, still feeling a little uncomfortable speaking to the ex-slave after what had happened. Saban just nodded slowly.

Jon took a step towards the queen, and Abetha raised an eyebrow at him.

"Both of us left in the lurch, hm?" he smiled sympathetically. He then tilted his head at her. "Your Majesty, why do you let Tom believe you care so little? Why not let him into your pain? He has no idea…"

Abetha's eyes turned cold, and as her nostrils flared slightly, Jon realized that he'd crossed a line in assuming that he could speak to her as a friend—especially about something so personal.

Drawing herself up, the icy queen averted her gaze and focused on a spot over his shoulder.

"I had Cook make up some beefsteak pies with stuffed quail and greens. We dine in an hour. I'll have Pesha show you to your room," she said in reserved tones.

"No, thank you, Your Majesty," he replied politely. Baltsaros was right about the pigheadedness of mother and son. Suddenly his exile didn't seem so cutting, compared to the river of tears he saw behind the stately queen's luminous eyes. "I'll pop down to the *Grog Blossom* and catch up with old friends. If you'll excuse me, that is."

Abetha just gave a prim little nod and turned, dismissing them. Jon felt bad for a moment, wondering if he should stay after all and keep company with the sad queen during the meal. However, Saban gave him a quiet, reassuring smile.

"Go see your friends, Jon," he said, eschewing Jon's title for the first time. "The queen and I have things to discuss anyway."

Jon realized then that Saban was also aware of the queen's feelings, and he pressed his lips together with a nod. Though there was still jealousy in his heart over what had happened with Tom, he knew he was indebted to Saban.

"Thank you," he replied, putting extra warmth in his voice. "You're a good man. I'm glad for your presence."

At Saban's skeptical brow lift, Jon let out a genuine laugh.

"Ok… mostly glad," he admitted. "I'm working on it, but we are allies. I promise you that. Maybe friends one day." He put out his hand and when Saban took it, Jon shook it with a heartfelt squeeze, truly believing his words.

*J*on pushed open the doors of the *Blossom* and smiled wide when he saw that it looked exactly as it had when he left. The place was full, and he had to push his way through a group of deckhands to get to the bar. Standing on a stool with her back to him, Maya was lighting one of the coloured lanterns against the growing dusk.

"I heard that the beer here was pretty good," he said loudly.

Maya started and turned around, shaking the burning taper in her hand.

"Gods and goddesses! Jon!" she exclaimed, jumping down. She quickly ducked beneath the bar and hugged him tight with a soft little laugh. Then she pulled back and stared up him, clucking her tongue. "Just look at you. You were comely before, but I'd have to call you downright handsome now. I love the beard! You look so dashing!" Her big blue eyes crinkled at him fondly.

"Oh, babe, don't tell him that. Now he'll want to keep that god-awful face fungus," laughed Katherine, appearing with two mugs of ale in her good hand. Jon took one and downed half of it in a way that would make Tom proud.

Maya snapped her fingers and pointed at someone in the crowd. A young, gangly lad with bright-orange hair nodded and passed under the bar, taking his place at the pumps.

"Send a pitcher out back," she told him. "And have Wenz bring us three trenchers of chowder when it's ready."

Jon let himself be led to the patio where Maya good-naturedly ousted a pair of carpenters to free up one of the tables for them.

He sat down and looked out over the water where the *Heart* was still being unloaded.

"Wasn't expecting you here until tomorrow at the earliest, Jon," said Maya reaching for his arm. "What happened?"

Jon wrinkled his nose as he stared down into his near-empty mug and shook his head.

"He just wasn't ready to see me," he replied. "It's ok though. I'm not sore. I waited nearly two months to see him. Another night is not going to kill me."

"Where's Tom?" asked Katherine.

"Where do you think?" he replied with a short laugh.

"Ah. Poor honey," said Maya with a little pat to his bare forearm.

Jon looked up and saw that both of them were staring at him with pity. Instead of making him angry though, it just made him feel sheepish, and he shrugged, chuckling to himself.

"I'm a big boy," he said and drank down the rest of his beer just as the ginger youth set down a pitcher and third mug in front of them. Jon smiled. "Like I said: I'll live. Stop staring at me like that." He poured himself another beer and served Maya and Katherine.

"So! Tell me everything that's happened while I've been gone," he said after another deep swallow.

*T*he chowder was good, but he barely tasted it. He'd had too much to drink and his senses were a bit hazy. It was pitch-dark beyond the tavern, but if Jon leaned forward in his seat, he could just see the lights of the castle nestled against the mountainside.

During the *Heart's* trip to the southern peninsula, Madierus had known a strange outbreak of something that had claimed three lives. However, four babies had been born, so Katherine had quipped that it hadn't been all bad. They'd also seen a drier summer than usual, which explained the ex-pirate's frustration at being a farmer. Jon had laughed and teased her about it, but that had led to a bickering fight between the two women that had seen Maya storm off in the end, claiming that she needed to take a look at the stores in the cellar. Katherine had just shaken her head and poured another round of drinks before launching into a tirade of what felt like every single argument the married couple had had since his departure.

Finally, Katherine's ranting wound down, and she let out a long sigh.

"Well... How is everything with you?" she asked, peering at Jon.

"S'ok," he slurred a little with a shrug.

"I mean... like, *everything*?" Katherine said with an exaggeratedly shrewd look. The tall woman was definitely as drunk as Jon, and he smiled at her expression.

"You mean between me n' Tom?" he replied, taking another sip.

"Yeah. You know I don't get it. Fucker's not good enough for you."

"That's not true," he said with a scowl.

"Oh, s'everything is rainbows and fucking kittens with you two?"

After another long look at the castle, Jon heaved a sigh of his own.

"No," he admitted. "Not really."

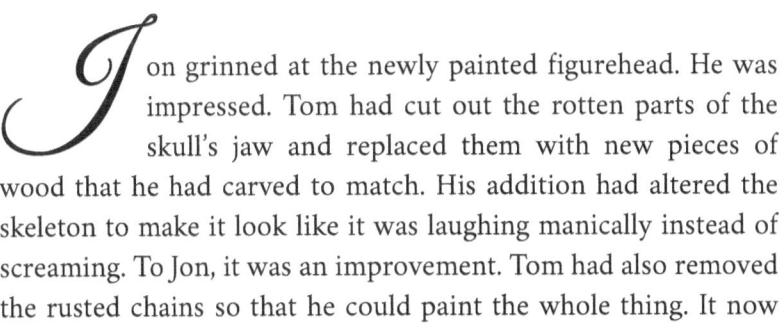

$\mathcal{J}$on grinned at the newly painted figurehead. He was impressed. Tom had cut out the rotten parts of the skull's jaw and replaced them with new pieces of wood that he had carved to match. His addition had altered the skeleton to make it look like it was laughing manically instead of screaming. To Jon, it was an improvement. Tom had also removed the rusted chains so that he could paint the whole thing. It now just looked like it was clutching its bony chest instead of being bound.

"I think you should leave the chains off," said Jon, squinting. "I've got an idea. Why not paint a heart in red between the fingers here? Would certainly hold with the name of the ship, right?"

The first mate's brow wrinkled, and he nodded slowly.

"Aye," he agreed. "Just hopin' Da won't take offense at the fact that the skelly looks barmy, seein' as if it's *Baal's* heart, then…"

With a laugh, Jon nodded, but it was fitting. The ship had always had a madman at the helm… The thought sobered him. He watched Tom take up the red paint and begin to trace out the shape of a heart between the figurehead's bony fingers. However, he smiled to himself again as the first mate's tongue poked out of the corner of his mouth with his concentration. Jon stepped forward and slowly stroked Tom from shoulder to hip. In response, Tom let out a little growly sound and ceased his painting.

"Do ye want me to join ye somewheres, love?" asked the first mate.

"Yes," replied Jon, reaching around to grab the bulge at the front of Tom's shortened pants.

"Is it gonna be like last time?"

Jon stopped fondling the first mate.

"What does that mean?"

"Ye've been—" said Tom a little hesitantly, "—soft a lot. Just wanted to know if that's what yer gonna be like."

Jon pulled away and frowned.

"I have not. What are you talking about?"

Tom turned to him and smiled crookedly.

"No… Not yer pecker, lovey. Just the way ye've *been*."

Jon thought about the last few times Tom and he had been together. Shared passions, slow build-up, breathless afterwards and sated. He stared at the first mate.

"This is because I don't feel the need to beat the shit out of you every time we fuck?" he said, incredulous. "I'm sorry that bothers you so much."

Tom's jaw worked for a second, and Jon was sure he was going to say something, but instead he turned and went back to his painting.

"I just need to be in the right frame of mind," Jon said. "We talked about it."

Tom let out a grunt with a little nod, but he didn't turn again.

"I can't be like that all the time," continued Jon.

This time Tom didn't reply.

"If that's what you really want though, I suppose I could try to..." Jon said faintly.

Turning to face him, the first mate looked exasperated.

"All I needed was a bloody *yes* or *no*, Jon," Tom replied. "Just wanted to fuckin' know if I was gonna be coddled or cocked hard. That's it. *Yes* or *no*. We'd fuck all the same... Just wantin' to know."

"Tom... If I'm not doing it for you, I'm sorry. Shit, I wouldn't mind it if you took the lead sometimes, but I haven't complained, have I?" Jon pointed out. "If you just told me what you wanted, then maybe I could—"

His fists balled, Tom stared at Jon.

"*Yes* or bloody *no*. That was it, Jon. Stop yer fuckin' yammerin'. I don't rightly care."

"You obviously do," whispered Jon, dismayed by the first mate's reaction.

Tom narrowed his blue-green eyes at Jon for a moment and then resumed his work on the figurehead like Jon wasn't standing there.

The first mate was right. Jon hadn't been very commanding with Tom, and he couldn't remember the last time they'd done anything but just fuck and fall asleep together. He realized that he had misunderstood just how much violence was a part of Tom's make-up; he had assumed—wrongly, it seemed—that Tom was happy for the reprieve from Baltsaros's sadism. The taciturn first mate didn't exactly make his needs known. In fact, Tom rarely wanted to talk about anything; it was more than a little frustrating.

After watching him for a couple of minutes, Jon spoke up.

"Yes," he ventured quietly.

Tom side-eyed him.

"Yes, it was going to be like last time."

After capping the pot of red paint, Tom then dropped his paintbrush in the jar of turpentine and started towards their quarters without a word.

However, the exchange had soured Jon's mood, and he no longer felt particularly into it, knowing the first mate's dissatisfaction. But, that was part of the problem: was Tom really dissatisfied or was Jon just projecting his own biases? It was so hard to tell. If he asked, Tom would shrug and say that Jon was putting words in his mouth and that just because he mentioned something, didn't mean that there was more to it than that.

Confused and a little tense, Jon followed Tom anyway.

～

Katherine banged on the table, laughing as Jon finished giving a not too explicit account of some of the problems Tom and he had faced in the long weeks alone with each other.

"Sounds like the honeymoon is over!" she chortled. The ex-pirate then rocked back in her chair and beer slopped over the edge of her glass as she tried to take a drink from it.

Maya, having rejoined them, glared at her wife.

"Jon… Those *are* valid complaints," said Maya, taking away Katherine's mug of beer.

"Hey!"

"For all that you dislike Tom, you two are pretty similar in some respects," said the pretty tavern owner, her blue eyes snapping at Katherine.

The pirate blinked slowly at her wife in confusion.

"Wha? What I do?"

Jon stood unsteadily, realizing that he'd set off another round of bickering, and decided to call it a night.

"Forget I said anything," he mumbled. "Going home... Ha! *Home*. Fuckin' home? As if that's home." He held tight to the side of the table to stop himself from swaying.

"Jon, you should probably stay here. The little room upstairs is empty."

Screwing up his eyes at Maya, Jon shook his head. His vision was a little doubled, but it wasn't too bad. Sleeping in that bed upstairs would only remind him of the night he had spent with Baltsaros there, and he was already feeling like a sad sack.

"Nah. I'm good," Jon said, patting her shoulder. "See ya tomorrow, Maya. Have good night, hm? And Kat?" He grinned drunkenly.

"Yeah?"

"Fuck you."

*J*on barely registered the walk home except for getting turned around after taking a piss against a fan palm. It had taken him a few minutes to realize he was going downhill instead of up, and he had nearly fallen down onto the beach when he tried to correct his course. After staggering up the long walkway, he steered way clear of the fishpond in case he tripped and fell in, and then he quietly opened the side door.

With a mumbled curse, Jon stopped at the foot of the stairs. He couldn't go up to Baltsaros's room; he wasn't wanted.

Don't be such a bloody baby. Jon scowled at the first mate's voice in his head.

Leaning against the stone wall, he peered down the dark corridor. In his haste to get away from the castle, he'd neglected to find out where his own room was. Where was he going to sleep? Then he recalled seeing a sitting room somewhere nearby and started to make his way down the hallway, his hand trailing over the stones to steady himself; Jon figured he could sleep on a chair if he found one.

However, when he reached the room, Jon realized that Abetha would probably have his hide if he dirtied any of her chairs; he didn't want to chance it. Jon turned when he heard a noise behind him and smiled when he saw it was just Brutus.

"Hey, boy," he whispered. "Come to spend a li'l time with me?" The big dog sat down on his haunches and tilted his blocky head at Jon, a glimmer of slobber on his jowls. Jon took a step towards Brutus and knocked his leg against a small stool. With a pained, muted groan, he rubbed his shin. When he turned to replace the dainty piece of furniture, he saw glass doors and remembered that this room led out to a small terrace with *chaises longues* and parasols.

"Good 'nuff, eh, Brutus?" he said with a wry grin.

*A*fter he'd stretched out on one of the wicker couches, Jon looked up at the twinkling stars and sighed. At least he wouldn't freeze—the night was balmy. Brutus turned around three times, settling down on the ground next to the chair, and Jon put a hand on the dog's head just like old times. He closed his eyes and shifted on the hard surface until he was as comfortable as he'd get. Before long, the sounds of the surf and the whistling frogs lulled him to sleep.

Jon stared up at the sky. There were pale-green lights that danced in the deep blue-black expanse, painting a path across it. His feet were cold and when he looked down, he saw snow. At first he thought he was on the deck of the Heart, *but the silhouette of sails were actually mountains, and the snow beneath his feet covered frozen soil, not boards. He took a step forward, glancing up at the night sky again. This time he could see stars. They blazed like electric lanterns above his head. There was a*

keening behind him, and he saw that the black lion held the back of the tawny wildcat's neck in its teeth. With fascination he watched the lion mount the cat, thrusting quickly as blood ran from where its fangs had punctured skin. Jon found himself getting aroused. When he walked forward to join them, Jon realized he was on a path between two large mounds, and that he was freezing. His bare foot touched ice, and he looked down to see that there was a frozen whirlpool in front of him. In the center was a heart carved out of ice. It began to beat, and Jon felt a pressure in his chest. He looked down and saw that his chest was made of clear ice and that there was no heart within. He called out to the animals, to his protectors, but they were too involved in their mating to pay attention to him. Across the whirlpool, a boy with a moon for a face had one eye open and one eye closed. He smiled at Jon.

"Are you awake, Jon? Or are you sleeping?"

~

*J*on blinked awake and stared up at the man standing over him. Saban smiled, the scar at the corner of his mouth dimpling.

"Are you awake, Jon?" asked the big man in his smooth baritone.

Jon licked his lips and squinted. The sun was just coming over the trees, and for a moment he had no idea where he was. His head felt like there was a cannonball in it, and his mouth was pasty and foul. Jon knuckled his eyes and then swallowed against the nausea that assailed him when he sat up. A shiver went through him, and he wrapped his arms around himself, realizing that he was slightly damp from sleeping out of doors. Only broken pieces of the previous night came back to him, and Jon hoped he hadn't made a complete fool of himself.

"Late night?" asked Saban, looking amused. In one hand he held a cup, and when Jon's brain finally registered the smell of coffee, he pointed to it.

"Mine?"

Saban nodded, handing the mug over to Jon, and watched him down some of the bitter black liquid.

As it hit his stomach, it churned; Jon quickly pulled the cup away from his lips and clenched his jaw. Salty saliva pooled in his mouth as he sat with his eyes shut, fighting against the urge to be sick.

"Do you want me to bring you some bread?" asked Saban. When Jon shook his head, Saban added: "It's fresh baked and will sop up some of that alcohol you still have floating around in your guts."

"Ok. Yes," whispered Jon.

He cracked an eye when the turmoil subdued somewhat in his belly and looked around. Brutus was nowhere to be seen. He had probably gone back to his mistress's side once Jon passed out in sodden slumber. The dew sparkled on the short spring grass, and Jon shivered again, wishing he had asked Saban for a blanket.

The broad-shouldered Balorian returned a few minutes later with a small basket containing half a loaf of dark bread. After handing it to Jon with an amused grin, he dragged one of the smaller wicker chairs closer and sat down, legs stretched out in front of him.

"Another beautiful day in paradise," rumbled the big man as he closed his eyes and turned to face the warm rays of sun. "If you had told me one day that I not only would be a free man, but one who lived on an island such as this, I would never have believed it. I would have probably told you that you were a prime candidate for a sacrifice, spreading such preposterous tales."

Jon nodded as he chewed slowly. The bread was unbelievably good. He waited a few moments after swallowing to make sure that it wasn't going to come right back up and took another bite. Saban turned his hazel eyes again to Jon and watched him silently.

"I was wondering... Do I owe you an apology, Jon?" Saban asked in a soft voice.

With a frown, Jon tore another piece off the loaf and ate it. Tom had been very clear that it had been he that had kissed Saban, not the other way around, and that Saban had pushed him away immediately. Jon thought about the Balorian watching Tom pleasure him in the dark of the captain's quarters, and he felt himself redden, both from the embarrassment of being seen and from the stupidity he had uttered.

"I feel like I owe *you* one," he admitted, meeting Saban's eyes.

With a chuckle, the big man shook his head.

"No apologies then. A new page."

Jon returned the friendly smile and then nodded. After a few more mouthfuls of bread, he gestured to the nearly empty basket.

"You were right. My stomach is better, thank you. I need more coffee, but it looks like I'm going to live," he said. Though his head was pounding, the warming sun was drying his clothes and he was beginning to feel more human.

"Good," said Saban. He stood and took the basket from Jon. "Because the captain wants to see you."

Jon's heart dropped off a cliff at the words and his pulse felt light and airy. Dizzy, he laughed to himself and rubbed at his face with numb hands.

"Shit," Jon muttered.

He rose to his feet unsteadily and mumbled a thanks to Saban before turning to leave.

The ex-slave touched his shoulder, and he looked up.

"Don't look so worried, Jon," said Saban with a quiet smile. "He spoke often about you with warmth. I'm sure that hasn't changed."

*a*fter smoothing back his wet hair and tugging down his fresh tunic, Jon opened the door to Baltsaros's rooms. When he saw the upturned furniture and blood on the floor of the empty sitting room, he felt worry lick his heart. He crossed the space in a few quick strides and yanked open the door to the bedchamber, afraid of what might be on the other side.

In the large room beyond, chairs had been tipped over—one of them missing a leg—and it looked like a chunk of plaster from the wall had exploded on the rucked-up carpet. The big four-poster bed was in shambles; the coloured silk hangings were torn, half of them on the floor, and there were big bloodstains on the sheets. However, sitting serenely in the midst of the disaster was Baltsaros, reading a bound book and drinking from a delicate, pale-blue porcelain cup. Next to him, face down and only half-covered with the sheet was Tom, fast asleep with one brawny, tattooed arm dangling over the side of the bed. There were two heavy tomes open on his broad back. It seemed that the first mate was being used as a makeshift bookstand by Baltsaros.

The scene was so preposterous in its domestic tranquility in comparison to the surrounding destruction that Jon let out a laugh. Tom twitched and shifted slightly in his sleep, and Jon saw that his muscled buttocks were striped with fresh welts that continued down the back of his legs.

When Jon took another step into the room, Baltsaros hastily put down his coffee and got out of bed. Wearing only a blood-red silk dressing gown, Baltsaros crushed Jon into his embrace. With a startled laugh, Jon hugged the tall man back and then smiled up at him when he pulled away.

"I have *missed* you, my love," said Baltsaros, giving Jon's shoulders a hard squeeze.

Obviously not enough to see me right away, said the bitter little voice in Jon's head. He felt his smile slip a notch, but he pressed himself back against Baltsaros and closed his eyes.

"Missed you too," he mumbled. The robe was slippery-soft against him as he cleaved to Baltsaros's strong body a moment longer. When they finally broke the embrace, Baltsaros's eyes searched Jon's face, his eyebrows high.

"You look sick, Jon. Are you all right?"

Jon knew that he was probably pale, and just then a tiny tremor went through him. The second cup of coffee was sitting badly in his gut, and he felt weak and shaky.

"Had drinks with Kat and Maya last night," he admitted,

wiping at the sheen of perspiration on his forehead. "Many, *many* drinks."

Gaze narrowed in amusement, Baltsaros shook his head. He reached for the hem of Jon's tunic to pull it up, and Jon automatically lifted his arms to let himself be undressed. Baltsaros's eyes were clear, and he seemed self-assured. Jon felt his hope swell; maybe things would be better now.

"What happened to the room?" he asked, glancing around. Jon shivered when a warm breeze came in through the window, and he realized just how awful he felt.

"Tom was helping me work through something," Baltsaros replied, dropping the shirt next to an upended table.

When Baltsaros reached for Jon's belt, Jon stopped him.

"I feel like shit," he whispered.

With a chuckle, Baltsaros moved Jon's hand away and resumed.

"I'm not expecting anything," he replied with a soft smile.

Baltsaros's expression was serious but tender as he undid Jon's belt. His light-brown hair had been cut shorter; it concealed his eyes as he leaned forward and Jon could see how threaded it was with white. When Baltsaros saw him watching, the graceful curve of his lips spread into a grin and he tilted his head. Despite his throbbing headache and the green nausea that kept sloshing through him, Jon found himself grinning back shyly and wished again that he hadn't gone to excess the evening before. His pants fell to the floor, and when Baltsaros moved to hold him again, Jon let out a nervous little laugh. It had been nearly two months since they'd really had a moment like this—three, if Jon counted the trip from the other side of the black mountain range while Baltsaros struggled so hard with the effects of his ordeal. Held confidently in strong arms, a steady heartbeat against his skin... Hells, if the floor had been rocking gently beneath his feet, Jon would have thought himself back aboard the *Heart* before all of the madness had started. But was it truly over? Not if the state of the bedchamber was anything to go by.

Baltsaros's voice broke through his thoughts.

"Tom said that you've been doing a praiseworthy job, and that I should consider making you quartermaster once we set sail again."

Jon pulled back and frowned up at Baltsaros.

"He did?"

Nodding, Baltsaros touched Jon's cheek, his warm brown eyes on his beard. Jon could tell he approved of it.

"I had the impression that I was beginning to annoy the fuck out of him," said Jon, turning his eyes to the slumbering first mate.

Baltsaros laughed and led Jon towards the bed.

"Yes. Maybe a little," he said as he took the books off Tom's back to pile them on the bedside table. "But he also sounds more deeply devoted to you than ever."

Jon climbed onto the mattress, looking askance at all the bloody handprints on the white sheets as he crawled in next to Tom. Baltsaros undid his robe to let it fall from his shoulders before he gathered it up and draped it at the foot of the bed. In addition to the healed burn marks from the electrodes on his torso, there were bruises and scratches that he had obviously sustained during his tussle with the first mate.

"He does?" asked Jon.

"Tom?" replied Baltsaros as he slid under the covers and settled next to Jon. "Of course he does. Your need for constant reassurance hasn't changed, I see." Despite the teasing words, Baltsaros's tone was fond.

At the sound of his name, Tom turned over and threw his arm around Jon's waist, dragging him closer so that the first mate's mostly limp cock nuzzled up warm between his cheeks.

"Mmm?" Tom burrowed his face into Jon's shoulder and promptly fell back to sleep.

Baltsaros stretched to his full length with a quiet groan and turned to smile at Jon.

"And, before you ask: No, I am not 'cured'. I'm still unable to gather my thoughts at times, and when it comes to regulating my reactions, I'm still doing poorly. However, Abetha believes that the worst is over and I truly, honestly think that you are in no danger from me. As long as we keep things… sedate. Now," Baltsaros reached out and stroked Jon's curls, "why don't you try to sleep. You'll feel better. We have all the time in the world to talk."

Tom's heat felt good against his back, and when Baltsaros moved closer to him, Jon curled his arm around his hip, let out a long sigh, and closed his eyes.

17

BLOOD AND PROMISES

Happiness or satisfaction consists only in the enjoyment of those objects which are by nature suited
to our several particular appetites, passions, and
affections.

— JOSEPH BUTLER

*B*altsaros watched his boys sleeping entwined on the soft feather mattress and smiled to himself. After tightening the sash around his waist, he smoothed the tunic over his hips and left the bedchamber. The door closed silently behind him, and Baltsaros looked around at the shambles that his sitting room had been turned into. With a crooked grin, he stooped to put right the ottoman; Tom had been correct to provoke him the previous day. Instead of being launched into lunacy by the fight, Baltsaros had been *right there* the whole time, in control and aroused and... happy. As he picked up the stack of letters that had been swept to the floor, he frowned in thought.

His adult life had mostly been one of contentment—a calm, clear sea of satisfied self-possession, marred only occasionally by ripples of annoyance. Those sources of irritation had, for the most part, been easily dispatched, thus returning his mood to a placid, mirror finish. However, Jon had somehow managed to dip into deeper waters to stir up the emotions that rested like silt at the bottom. What had surfaced had changed him. Like happiness. Baltsaros could truly say that having both Tom and Jon in his life made him *happy*.

Unfortunately, the chain reaction catalyzed by Jon had made Baltsaros rather susceptible to the emperor's device. It had churned up everything that Baltsaros was, leaving only turbulence and ruin behind.

Baltsaros pressed his lips together and straightened. Normally, the thought of his torture brought with it sharp, hot spikes of anger that he fought to control. However, as he stood still in the early morning light, waiting for the fury to overwhelm him, he found that he was able to address it with some detachment, thanks—at least in part, he figured—to the rough play with Tom.

Am I just suppressing my anger? he wondered as his heart rate slowed and his good humour returned.

With eyes narrowed at the bloodstained rug, he wondered whether Abetha was right about how to approach the repercussions of his ordeal. His ex-wife was convinced that having iron control over his emotions was deleterious to his recovery. That to feel *less* would somehow continue to cripple him.

His mind on the interesting conundrum, Baltsaros left the room and started down the stairs. Before Jon, there had been satisfaction. Contentment. Peace. If suppressing his emotions would bring him back to that, would that be so bad? He'd be giving up the happiness he had found, but he'd also be losing the simmering rage that constantly set his blood to boiling over the smallest things. He'd no longer be robbed of coherent thought as he was torn apart by furious emotion.

Brow furrowed, he turned down the corridor and headed towards the rear of the castle. Maybe keeping his emotions buried *was* best for him. Who was to say which path was right when it all felt so labyrinthine? He passed through the big glass doors and into the topiary garden. The late-morning sun was hot, and Baltsaros ducked beneath one of the orange trees that shaded the garden. Reaching up, he quickly found a ripe fruit and then sat down with it on the marble bench.

Smirking, he wondered if it were even possible to keep his feelings bottled up given that he would never let Jon go. He also had to admit to himself that he didn't *want* to give up what he was feeling for the boys, whatever it was. But did that spell a life of constantly shifting waters for him?

Baltsaros let the orange peels fall between his bare feet and breathed in the sweet, tangy smell. As he chewed on a juicy slice, he mulled over his dilemma and waited for Abetha to join him with a mug of coffee in each hand, just as she had most mornings since his arrival.

～

*J*on cracked an eye open and saw that Baltsaros had gone. His bladder was full, and he was groggy and sweaty, but his hangover seemed to have peaked, and he felt better for sleeping. Judging by the slant of the sun outside the leaded-glass windows, it was past noon. When he tried to lift the first mate's arm away, Tom moved against him and let out a little rumbled growl.

"Where d'ye think yer goin'?"

"I'm overheating and I have to pee," complained Jon, giving the burly man's arm another shove. "Get yer bleedin' carcass off o' me."

Tom laughed low at Jon's imitation and released him with a dramatic sigh.

Jon slid off the bed and made his way to the small door that led to the water closet beyond. When he was done, he walked back into the bedchamber and saw that Tom sat on the edge of the bed with a pained look on his face. Jon raised his eyebrows. In addition to the tattoos, the first mate's chest sported fresh, mottled bruising, and he winced as he prodded at his ribs.

"Fucker knows how to land a punch," he muttered when he saw Jon watching him. There was a painful-looking cut on one of his cheeks, and he let out a low grunt as he flexed his hands. The knuckles of his right hand were torn up.

Jon smiled at him.

"Was it worth it?" he asked as Tom tried to peer over one big shoulder to see the damage on his back.

Tom laughed and nodded, his green-blue eyes amused. However, when he went to push himself up, he grimaced and stood slightly hunched. Forehead creased, he looked sheepishly at Jon and held out his hand. There was a bloody, jagged slice across his palm.

"Can ye take a look at this, love?" asked the big man. "Think there's glass in there. I'd be obliged if ye got it out."

Jon grinned wider and teasingly clucked his tongue before taking Tom's hand in his to see if he could find the sliver.

*A*fter squeezing lemon over what Abetha had called *harira*, Jon stirred the thick soup and ate a spoonful of the chickpeas and chicken. It was delicious and savory, and the meat was extremely tender. Across the table, Tom dunked a piece of flatbread into his bowl with his bandaged hand, a frown on his battered face. Abetha watched the first mate for a moment, her nose slightly lifted, and turned her attention back to Jon. Her eyes, so like Tom's, regarded him coolly for a moment.

"No, I'm sorry, Jon," she finally answered him. "Baltsaros won't be joining us. He has decided to take the noon meal in his rooms. He was unduly stressed by your arrival, and we believe that a quiet afternoon to himself is what is needed."

Jon's eyes widened and he glanced at Tom. The first mate's scowl had deepened as he attacked his soup with more bread.

The moment they had sat down, Abetha had coldly upbraided

Tom for his lack of shirt—something that Jon could sort of understand; they were eating in a lavish dining room, and that *did* call for a slight bit of decorum. In return, Tom had just curled his lip and had basically turned into a sulky child with shoulders high and eyes focused on the table in front of him. The queen had then proceeded to belittle the first mate every chance she got—using polite terms of course—but Jon couldn't ignore the rancour that poured from her. It made no sense, given the deep well of pain that he saw in her. Or did it? She had pulled the same sort of thing with Baltsaros, hadn't she?

Jon spooned up more soup and tried to come up with something to say that would diffuse the tension a little. Maybe he could find some common ground to get the two of them talking. However, Tom pushed his bowl away and locked eyes with his mother before Jon had a chance.

"Ye mean *you* think a quiet day is the right fuckin' way, aye?" he growled. "Ye meddlin' old cunt. Ye can't bloody keep Da from me, ye know."

The queen's eyebrows shot up and bright spots appeared on her pale cheeks.

"The language on you... And when will you desist in calling him that? Do you know how *sick* that makes you sound?" she shot back in venomous tones. "No, Thomas. Baltsaros was in on the decision."

Jon's senses told him that she was telling the truth and felt a small pang of disappointment. Baltsaros had taken a different route back to his tower, and they'd missed him by mere minutes; it would have been nice to confirm for a fact what the queen was saying.

She ripped off a tiny piece of bread and chewed it slowly before continuing in a low voice.

"You and Jon can work out whatever arrangement suits you concerning your sleeping quarters; I have no desire to know more about that." Abetha flared her nostrils and shook her head. "However, you will *not* go to Baltsaros whenever you feel like it."

"Like hells, I won't," spat Tom, lurching to his feet.

"Thomas, I swear that if you take a step near that tower, I'll have you put under lock and key."

Jon's eyes went to Saban, and he saw that he was shaking his head slowly at Tom.

The first mate pointed at Abetha, his bright eyes snapping with fury.

"Ye'd like that, ye bloody witch. Lockin' up yer son like an animal? I hope ye choke on this crap." Tom backhanded the bowl of *harira* and sent it flying to the floor. He turned to go but not before meeting Jon's eyes. The creases deepened further on his forehead, and Jon saw something like confusion cross his rugged face before he stormed off. Surprisingly, he went in the opposite direction from Baltsaros's rooms.

Abetha pushed her chair back.

"Please excuse me," she said in a faint voice and left.

Saban let out a long sigh and scraped the bottom of his bowl, spooning up the last of his soup with a grimace.

"Well... That was awkward," he muttered after he'd swallowed. "I have half a mind to put the both of them in a small room and not let them out until they resolve whatever it is that makes them so awful to each other. However, it would probably end in murder."

"Whose?" asked Jon with a smile.

"That, I am not sure of," replied Saban, grinning as he tore off another piece of flatbread to mop up any remaining liquid in his bowl.

Jon glanced down the corridor where Tom had disappeared.

"The weirdest thing is that I think he's actually going to obey his mother," he said with a headshake. "But I wonder where he went."

"Easy. What does our laconic first mate do when he's pissed off? He drinks or he gets into a fight, or both," said Saban, shrugging. He stood up. "Shall we go see if he's already ripping into some poor fool at Maya's?"

Jon nodded and pushed away from the table, following the taller man out of the dining room.

~

*B*altsaros sat in the comfortable chair in his study with his feet up on the cushioned stool as he watched the maid scrub the bloodstain on the rug. On his knee was the copy of *Standard Parables* that he was translating into Common—an activity suggested by Abetha—but the monotonous task had turned into an irritation. All the passages seemed insufferably bromidic to him suddenly, and he found himself skimming and unable to give a shit about any of it.

With head tilted, he narrowed his eyes at the young woman on the floor. She was not yet twenty, he guessed, and had a pleasing figure that ran to plump. As she worked on her knees, he was given an excellent view of her heart-shaped backside straining against the stiff, dark material of her uniform. He let his lips curl into a hungry smile. She was pretty and probably would not mind it if he took liberties with her.

Hands folded in his lap, Baltsaros imagined himself standing up and closing the distance before falling to his knees behind the girl. Then he thought about pulling up the maid's skirt, freeing his cock, and taking her quickly and roughly from behind. He pictured her cheeks and neck going pink as he'd labour over her like a beast, with no tenderness or mercy to his thrusts.

Maybe she would even enjoy it.

Baltsaros cupped his hand over his hardened length.

Ok. Good, he thought.

She would then have to say something to trigger him. It was always deep ignorance that made the bloodlust sing in his ears, so he imagined her making some sort of crass, small-minded comment about the relationship with his boys. Baltsaros watched her working for another long moment before leaning his head back against the chair with his eyes closed.

He thought about flipping her over forcefully, his knife cutting away the material of her uniform to bare her breasts as she lay supine beneath him. Baltsaros's breath became a touch laboured as he imagined her eyes bugging out in fright, her rosebud lips squashing beneath his palm against the hardness of her teeth... The vibrations of her terrified scream would be felt in the small bones of his hand.

Baltsaros squeezed his cock gently through his pants and let out a slow sigh. He'd taken Tom twice in rapid succession the day before and once more upon waking. Though the semi-serious brawl between them had granted him the lustiness and recuperative powers of a much younger man, he was a touch tender. Regardless, his erection throbbed hard and willing against his fingers at his little fantasy.

He took a deep breath and imagined that, as the maid struggled, he would press the tip of the knife against her soft skin and then push it in so slowly that he could feel the beat of her heart shiver the blade as it slid home. Jaw clenched, Baltsaros thought about the blood that would well up almost black, but that would taste so rich and *red*.

"Sir?"

Baltsaros opened his eyes. The young maid was less pretty than the one that still lay beneath him in his mind. Her cheeks were flushed with embarrassment, but he didn't care that she was witness to his blatant arousal.

"Yes?"

"That's the best I can do for now," she nearly whispered, her eyes darting down to the hand in his lap.

Baltsaros looked past her to the rug. It would have to be replaced.

He thought for a moment about asking her questions to unearth any slight bigotry she had. It would be just a test to see whether he could keep from killing so as to honour his promise. Otherwise, he would have to start hiding his hunts from both Jon and Tom; Baltsaros knew the first mate was no longer his ally in that regard.

"Thank you, my dear," he said instead and dismissed her. After she had gone, Baltsaros leaned back again in his chair and thought some more about blood and promises.

❧

*O*n the way to the *Grog Blossom*, Saban brought Jon up to speed on a number of things. The first made him pause in his tracks and stare at the Balorian in disbelief for a moment. Ceara had been given the repainted *Saber* and had set sail on a mission for Baltsaros. She had been sent to strike a deal with the masters of the mainland iron holdings and the silk producers of the southern peninsula in regard to continued trade with Ereme'ia Balor. She was also to spread rumours of a navy ketch seen sinking off the midland isles during a bad storm. The rationale behind this was to keep the king from sending an armada to the rift; if the ketch had simply sunk due to bad weather and dumb luck, there was no burning need for retaliation.

Jon agreed that it made sense, but he wondered what would happen when Ah'puch's ship missed the next rendezvous. Would the navy simply give up and turn around, or were the citizens of Balor going to get an unpleasant visit? Saban pointed out that the latter was highly doubtful, as they almost certainly had no map to get through the winding mountain pass.

As Saban talked about Ceara, Jon kept glancing at him. The way he spoke of her made him think that there was more there but before he could ask, Saban switched to Baltsaros and his "treatments".

On their arrival, the deposed captain of the *Heart* had had one of his crazed spells that had resulted in him barricading himself in his rooms. When they'd finally been able to get to Baltsaros, he had been covered in his own blood but calm. After that he had just gone along almost meekly with whatever Abetha came up with:

quiet walks, something called *meditation*, and a cocktail of medicines to lessen the opiate addiction he had developed from being drugged so often on the trip back from Balor.

"So, all these things helped?" Jon asked as they walked side by side down the steep, cobbled road.

Saban nodded slowly, his eyes on the cobbled road ahead of them.

"I've also been helping out with the mind-strengthening activities that worked with my father," the big man said, then frowned. "Though if you want the honest truth, I think that his recovery was beginning to stagnate."

"Meaning, you think that Tom's presence helps?" asked Jon.

"And yours," said Saban with a glance at Jon. His green-brown eyes were warm. "It seemed that he was just going through the motions after a while. Baltsaros cares for the two of you very much; your arrival has reminded him of that. I think it's a good thing. Maybe. Though who really knows what goes on in that man's mind? Maybe he opted for seclusion today because it really was too much for him all at once."

"Or he could be testing himself to see what the effects of our arrival have had on him," offered Jon.

"You know him better than I do," replied Saban with a shrug.

"And Tom knows him the best," affirmed Jon. "You know, Tom stalking off like a wounded panther might have nothing to do with him obeying Abetha. If the captain decided he needed space, and I do believe the queen was speaking the truth, then Tom would be the first to give him that. I think."

Saban's face creased into a soft smile.

"I think you might be right."

"Saban, I know how much you like Tom," said Jon to the man at his side as they neared the *Blossom*. Saban stopped walking and turned to stare at Jon, his hazel eyes wary. Jon chewed the inside of his cheek and tried set aside his jealousy; the look on Saban's face had just confirmed his suspicions.

"I just meant that I can count on you to help me help Tom,

right?" Jon asked lightly with a friendly smile that hoped hid his discomfort.

"Of course, Jon," came the quiet reply. "I promise to do whatever is in my power."

Jon nodded up at Saban and then pushed the tavern door open.

18

THE WRONG PEG

*T*om watched the bottle bob in the water in front of him, lost in thought. He was kneeling in the shallow surf with the warm water up to his chest as he scooped up handfuls of fine sand from the bottom. Occasionally, little schools of transparent fish with black eyes would surround him, and he would try to catch them, but they always eluded his grasp. The salt in the water stung his wounded palm, but he knew he would heal all the faster for it. Tom grabbed the bottle, pulled the cork, and took a deep swallow of the rum within. His eyes caught movement below the surface, and he recorked the bottle, setting it to floating again as he watched the crab make its sideways journey towards deeper water.

"Tom?"

At the sound of Jon's voice, Tom smiled to himself. He turned around and saw him standing at the shoreline, accompanied by Saban.

"What are you doing?" asked Jon, shielding his eyes against the glare that came off the water.

"Thinkin'," replied the first mate. He plucked the bottle from the water again. "Drinkin'."

"Kat gave me your message," said Jon. "It said you'd gone for a swim."

"Didn't get to swimmin'," replied Tom, licking saltwater and rum from his lips. He'd intended to swim out past the land bridge but instead had found himself dawdling in the shallows. While waiting for Jon to find him—lords knew, the lad was predictable and would come running the minute he could—he had forced himself to really *think* about his anger. Not to drown it completely in liquor or violence for once. Not to shove it into a dark corner until it grew like a poison in his blood.

The truth was that all the evil bitterness he had inside him was over something *already done*. It was over the actions of family that he hadn't even known when he *was* there—hells, he'd called Polly the wet nurse "ma" when he was a wee tyke. This hatred of a woman whom he had never really known was bloody stupid, and it shamed him that it had taken seeing the look on Jon's face earlier to finally realize he was acting like a crybaby over milk that had been spilled a long fucking time ago.

He had to stop hating the family who had lost him and concentrate on the family who had found him.

Jon watched him for a few seconds, a concerned look on his handsome face, and Tom felt his cheeks dimple in a broad, saucy grin.

"Drop yer shorts an' come for a dip? Water's lovely," he said, swishing his hand beneath the crystal-clear surface. Then he lifted his dripping fist and pointed to Saban. "Yer welcome to join, fella."

The tall Balorian grinned and started to strip. If there was one thing that being a slave taught a man, it was how to be unashamed of nakedness. Jon on the other hand… He stood with his hands on his belt, but from the look on his face, he was going to need a little more coaxing.

"C'mon, lovey. Don't be such a fuckin' prude," chided Tom with a laugh. " 'Sides, Saban's already seen yer damn cock. What's the bloody harm?"

Even from this distance he saw the colour rise in Jon's face, and he wondered if reminding him of that night was a mistake. However, Jon just pressed his lips together with a tight nod before pulling his tunic over his head to drop it and his shortened, black linen pants to the white sand. The sight of the ugly, twisted scar on Jon's chest always made Tom feel guilty for not being there for him when the shit went down with his crazy, bloodthirsty step-da. He sighed and turned to watch Saban enter the water.

As Saban walk towards him, Tom admired the well-defined, flat muscles of his stomach and the alluring V of his pelvis. Then, more than a little astonished, Tom saw that the man's cock, cut like his own, sported a shiny silver ring at its head. He squinted, trying to tell where it went in and where it came out. When he glanced up, he saw that the Balorian looked amused at the scrutiny.

Jon splashed through the shallow water quickly, passing Saban, and sank down onto his knees next to Tom with a small smile. Jon took the bottle of rum from him.

Tom watched Jon take two long swallows, his Adam's apple working below the trim black beard, before handing it to Saban who had crouched nearby in the warm water.

"I thought you'd be drunk as a skunk or brawling by now," said Jon, his dark brows high.

Tom just shook his head.

"But, what are you going to do about your mother?"

"Don't bloody care," replied Tom. He scrunched up his eyes in the direction of the castle and lifted his shoulders. "She ain't my ma. Just some old queen. Never really knew 'er. Not sure why I should be dinin' at a queen's table, anyway. No place fer the like o' me. Her little boy, the one who got nicked in the middle o' the night?" Tom scowled and shook his head. "He's dead. Gone. So who the fuck cares whose bloody fault it was?" He felt an unexpected lump form in his throat and took the bottle from Saban to take another few swallows. It was good rum, nice and dark with molasses sweetness to it, and it worked well at washing away some of his bitterness. Or so he told himself.

"Tom, I'm not sure that's the best—" Jon started.

"It'll do for now," growled Tom. He let out a slow breath and then smiled at Jon. "Just… Lemme work on it, lad."

There was a deep crease between Jon's brows; he was obviously skeptical, but he dipped his chin in a small nod. The sunlight glinting off the water made bright ripples over his skin as a small wave passed. Jon's nipples were puckered, and Tom watched a drop make its way down his chest to fall from one of them. With a growl, Tom reached for Jon and pulled him in close; he weighed next to nothing in the water. With a nervous laugh, Jon pushed at Tom with a look at Saban, but Tom wouldn't let him go.

When Jon felt Tom's growing erection against him, his eyes widened a touch.

"Oh."

Tom laughed and quested forward to capture Jon's lips with his own in a brief but heated kiss before releasing him. What was it about water that always made him so horny?

When he glanced over his shoulder, he saw Saban turn his head away quickly, and Tom felt his pulse kick up a notch.

Just as he was about to kiss Jon again, Saban let out a yell, and Tom turned in time to see the big man rise quickly to his feet and fall backwards with a big splash. Saban flailed for a second and regained his footing as he backed into deeper water. He looked like he was in some amount of pain.

"I think something bit my… uh," said Saban, wincing.

Tom burst out laughing.

"That bit o' shine on the end of that long cock o' yers is like to have made an ol' robber crab greedy, mate," he said. "Are ye bleedin'?"

Saban hunched his shoulders and peered down into the clear water, inspecting himself.

"Want me to take a closer look, lad?" asked Tom, grinning. "It'd be my pleasure."

Jon smirked and splashed water at the first mate.

"I… think it's fine. Mostly took me by surprise. Are you sure there's nothing that could have bit me?" grimaced Saban.

"Could be a peckerfish lookin' for a mate," joked Tom. "Though their bite's a fair bit toxic. If that's the case, me and Jon can take turns suckin' the poison out."

This time Saban let out a bark of laughter, and he sent a volley of water at Tom's head.

Tom yelled and dove forward to duck into water that came up to his shoulders. He wiped seawater out of his eyes and Jon laughed. The mood had gone to playful, and he was damn glad for it.

"Bring the bottle here, love," he beckoned to Jon. "An' come wrap those skinny legs o' yers around me." Jon gave him a mock scowl and drank some rum, but with nothing more than a quick, backwards glance at Saban, he came closer and hooked his legs around the first mate's hips. Tom let out a little growl of pleasure and grasped the moons of Jon's ass, leaning forward to plant a kiss on the corner of Jon's mouth. When he pulled back, he saw that Jon's blue eyes had gone dark with lust. Tom moved one of his hands so that he could stroke a fingertip over Jon's pucker softly. Jon started, his sphincter contracting at Tom's touch.

"Tom…" he warned.

Tom grinned, his heart hammering and cock getting harder with every beat. He glanced over at Saban. The Balorian raised a quizzical eyebrow, but there was something in his face that said he knew exactly what Tom was about.

"He can't see," he murmured close to Jon. "I could push ye down and fill ye right up with my cock, and he wouldn't see." He tested Jon's opening with his finger, feeling Jon's pulse as he breached it slowly. "That is… if ye weren't as tight as a vestal bloody virgin."

Jon flushed dark at Tom's words and surprised him by suddenly shoving him backwards, sending Tom over the ledge of the seabed so that he had to tread water.

Tom laughed and ducked below the surface, swimming along

the sandy bottom until he reached Jon. He turned over onto his back and could see a wavy version of Jon looking down at him, framed by a sky of purest blue. He noticed that the lad's cock was as stiff as his, and as Tom surfaced, he made a point of stroking it with his fingers. Jon scowled at him, but between the rum and the water, and the gorgeous bloody sunshine, there didn't seem to be much real reproach. Tom picked the bottle out of the water and drank some more.

"Saban!" He flipped the corked bottle into the air, and the tall man caught it easily. Tom swam closer, wishing he could think of a way to... *something*. He was starting to feel reckless.

Saban took a sip of rum, looking a little nervous. He met Tom's eyes but turned away almost immediately.

Tom felt Jon's hands on him, and he smiled as he was pulled backwards and dunked in the water again. He popped up, shaking salt water from his face and then sent a wave over Jon's head. Saban let out a yell as Jon barrelled backwards into him. To Tom's amazement, the big man picked Jon up out of the water and sent him flying over his shoulder.

The first mate grinned wide at Saban.

Soon it was an epic battle to drown the other as the three splashed and wrestled in the chest-deep water. They all laughed breathlessly as alliances forged and changed on a dime. However, this was innocent play only on the surface, and the tension in the air was so thick it seemed to gain real weight. Tom's body felt tight and sensitive to every touch—wet skin sliding over wet skin to ostensibly throw the other when, in reality, hands had begun to wander. The first mate let out a little, barely voiced groan when Jon's fingers encircled his stiff cock for a quick squeeze before pushing him below the surface. A moment later a hand too big to be Jon's touched his ass and lingered. Tom was panting, but it had little to do with boys' horseplay.

He moved into deeper water with a grin, crazy lust painting a wonderful and terribly bloody stupid idea in his head.

"Catch me if ye can, ye bloody landlubbers!" He laughed and

turned, swimming out with broad strokes towards the *Heart* anchored not far away. When he heard splashing behind him, he glanced over his shoulder and saw that the others were gaining on him. He made himself go even faster, strong arms propelling him forward through the cooler deep water until he got to the ship. He reached up and grabbed hold of the bottom rung of the Jacob's ladder, climbing quickly. When he got to the top, he felt the rope ladder jerk and saw that Saban was hot on his trail. After jumping down to the deck, Tom started jogging sternward.

He knew he was being feckless, but he was so horny he could barely contain himself. Two sets of thudding footfalls behind him meant that Jon had made it, so Tom slowed his pace. Grinning like a loon, he wrenched open the door to the captain's quarters and let himself into the cool shade. Tom's eyes adjusted in moments, and he turned when the others entered the stateroom. The tension had turned into a high keening noise just beyond hearing, and Tom felt as if he would burst from it.

He grabbed Jon by the arm, dragging him roughly to the table. Breathing heavily, Jon stared at Tom, looking unsure but just as excited as he was. Brow furrowed, Jon licked his lips then let out a small moan as Tom pressed his pelvis against him, drawing him in for a kiss. Cock to cock, they strained against each other, Jon's mouth tasting of rum and seawater. When Tom broke away, he took a handful of Jon's dripping black curls.

"I want you," he murmured, leaning in to press another kiss to Jon's open lips. "Right now. Right here."

Jon's eyes darted to where Saban stood frozen to the spot. Tom could feel Jon's heartbeat against his chest; it sped as fast as his own in the few seconds that it took for him to make up his mind. When Jon looked again at Tom, he nodded once.

With a pleased growl, Tom butted himself harder against Jon, his cock wet and almost hurting as he kissed him deep. Then he stepped back and forced Jon to turn around and lean over the table, his chest to the cold, hard wood. Hand on the back of Jon's neck, he cast about for something to use as lubrication and spotted the small bottle of oil on the armoire.

Tom contemplated Saban who continued to stare mutely at them; the muscles twitched in his strong jaw as he met Tom's gaze.

"Tom… This isn't going to… I am not…" whispered Saban, letting his eyes drop to Tom's stiff cock. However, his arousal was blatant in the dark, veiny staff that curved up proud from a nest of crinkled black hair.

"Be a love and get me that?" said Tom, pointing to the oil.

Saban's eyes widened, but he went quickly to fetch it, his long cock bobbing with his strides. When he handed the little bottle to Tom, he held onto the first mate's hand for the span of a breath, and his eyes were so tragic that Tom felt a small pain erupt deep in his chest. Saban shook his head. There was a war going on in the big man that Tom didn't envy one bit… one that he realized wouldn't be solved in one sunny afternoon in a darkened stateroom.

"Tom, I can't…" Saban whispered, watching Tom smear oil on his cock and push some into Jon.

"But ye wanna watch, don't ye?" murmured Tom, his heart pounding; Jon's body quivered, and he let out a soft groan as Tom's finger quested deeper into him. "No harm in watchin', mate."

Saban didn't reply, but his eyes stayed locked on Tom's oiled finger slowly fucking Jon's tight hole.

Tom swallowed hard, watching the bead of perspiration making its way down the Balorian's neck. He was fucking gorgeous and so obviously turned-on by what he was seeing that it made Tom's cock throb hard in his fist. Eyes on Saban, Tom pulled his finger out of Jon and placed his cockhead against the greased opening. As slow as he could, he pushed himself into Jon's slick heat and gasped both at the feeling and at the way Saban's brow furrowed as if in deep pain, his mouth open in a soft pant.

However, Saban stumbled backwards a moment later and was gone before Tom could say anything.

Tom reined in his disappointment and pressed his lips together, turning away to concentrate on what he was doing to Jon instead. Hands on Jon's hips, he fucked him with slow strokes and let out a soft sound when Jon began pushing back against him. Fucking Jon was a glorious bloody thing; he responded with such enthusiasm and with all these gorgeous little needy noises. Tom knew for sure that Jon was stiff and drooling clear drops onto the carpet below, needing nothing more than a cock in his ass. It always fucking amazed him.

Eyes closed and cheek pressed against the mahogany, Jon began to whimper in time to Tom's thrusts.

"Ye like that, love? Ye feel so good," murmured Tom.

Jon's groan had a desperate edge to it, and Tom began to pound into him, driving himself quickly to the edge. Jon cried out and tensed with a shudder, his ass almost too tight on Tom's shaft for a second. Tom closed his eyes with a growl and let himself go, every cum-slippery thrust pulling a grunt out of him as he rode out his climax, his jerking cock buried deep in Jon. Finally, he slowed and then stopped, leaning forward over Jon to place his forehead against his shoulder as he panted. He rested there a moment, catching his breath, until his softening cock slid out of Jon's body. Jon let out a little gasp and Tom pressed his lips to Jon's sweat-covered back.

When Tom could stand again, Jon pushed himself off the tabletop and turned, looking a little dazed. He shoved back his damp tangle of curls and rubbed his face.

Saban was nowhere to be seen. Tom figured he probably wasn't even on the ship anymore.

"Tom... What were you trying to pull with Saban?" Jon said quietly. He didn't look happy.

Tom groaned and ran a hand over the top of his head, his eyes lowered to the rug beneath his feet. Jon had said yes, hadn't he?

In the heat of the bloody moment.

After a few breaths, he looked up and saw that Jon was watching him, his grey-blue eyes cautious.

"Ye sore at me, lad?" Tom asked with a grimace.

Jon responded with a shrug and came forward to wrap his arms around Tom, burying his face in the crook of the first mate's neck.

"Yeah. Maybe a little," came the mumbled reply.

With a deep frown, Tom stroked down the curve of Jon's spine as he stared out the open door at the blue sky beyond, feeling like a bloody arse. Now that it was over, fucking around with Saban seemed like such an idiotic thing to do. What had he been thinking?

"I'm sorry," he rumbled, feeling ashamed.

"S'ok," sighed Jon. "Forget about it."

Tom knew that Jon was more hurt than he was letting on; he didn't even want to touch on what the captain would say when he found out that he had tried to add a third without his permission. One thing was for certain: he had to get Saban out of his head for good. Nothing right would come of it. He was thoroughly disgusted with himself for letting an idea get him all fired up.

As he led Jon to the bed, he tried to come up with a way to fix things. Jon curled up quietly against his shoulder and draped one leg over Tom's thighs. The breeze that came in from the windows felt nice, and though Jon was lying directly on some rather tender ribs, Tom didn't want him to move.

When Tom was very young, he had stolen one of his mother's scented silk handkerchiefs—a small square of royal blue—because he had been obsessed by the colour and the softness of it. He'd kept it hidden in his room, a cherished secret that he would rub between his fingers or against his face as he lay in his little bed. It had been so damned pretty. Then, one day, he noticed that the silk was getting worn in places, and he'd somehow managed to get it dirty. There was even a little blood on it from a cut on his finger.

He had *ruined* it.

That horrible realization was the closest thing he could think of for how weighted his heart felt when he thought of what had just happened... Well, what had *nearly* happened with Saban.

"I'm sorry," he said again, whispering the word into Jon's hair.

"Tom, I want to let this *go*... But you can't do that again," said Jon slowly after a few breaths. He played gently with Tom's nipple ring. "I don't want either of us to."

"Aye," murmured Tom. "Don't bloody know why I was thinkin' with my fuckin' cock. Ain't like me. I love ye, Jon. Never again."

Jon nodded against him, and Tom felt a little better.

"You're not the only one to blame, remember?" said Jon. "You know, you and I haven't exactly been doing very well. I think it's ok to admit that."

Tom grunted in agreement. It was true. With the captain's malady, something had broken between them.

"We been tryin' to plug a hole with the wrong-shaped peg," muttered the first mate.

Jon laughed.

"Well, that's one way of putting it."

"Mm." Tom smiled then winced a little as Jon shifted against his bruises. "Da's better. He'll be back behind the wheel before too long... keep us both in fuckin' line, aye?"

Jon just chuckled in response and kissed the side of Tom's neck.

Tom tightened his hold on Jon and shut his eyes.

*A*s he felt slumber creep up to him like a cat on silent, furred feet, Tom thought about the look in Saban's eyes that had been so at odds with his impressive erection, and a memory filtered through that image. It was one of Jon lying in the washtub when he first came aboard.

Unaware that Tom had returned to fetch the captain for something, Jon's face had been twisted in the heat of desire as he jerked off slowly in the warm bath water. Tom had stood, transfixed and breathlessly hard, watching the dripping pink head of the boy's cock emerge from the water, the pads of Jon's fingers teasing at its plump crown before it submerged again with the motion of his hips.

It had been a maddeningly gorgeous sight, one that conflicted with all the rancour and betrayal he had felt over the captain's ridiculous mooning about over the pale, skittery whelp. Once more, Jon's cock had broken the surface, and Tom had nearly let escape a groan as Jon's fingers squeezed and pulled at the taut flesh. Tom's hand had gone to his own straining erection, squeezing hard when Jon let out a soft cry as he covered his jerking cock to catch his seed in the washcloth he held in the other hand. However, when the boy's face had fallen a moment later, Tom's hand had stilled and he had taken a quick, silent step back through the door.

He stroked his fingers sleepily through Jon's hair, remembering how he had felt sudden shame at witnessing such an unguarded moment. Tom had been oddly torn between laughing off his own discomfort and going back into the room to take Jon in his arms to soothe away the same tormented look that had been on Saban's face before he had fled.

Tom's folly had probably cost him the friendship.
He hoped not.

19

A THIRD BOND

*J*on started awake when he heard a thump. Lifting his head, he squinted at the open door. The wind had died down while Tom and he had slept; despite the wide-open portholes, the room was like an oven. When he peeled himself away from Tom's side, Jon felt a little nauseous from the heat. The first mate groaned, rolling over on the sweat-soaked sheets just as Baltsaros ducked into the room with a wry grin on his face.

"You do know that there's a room at the castle for each of you to use, don't you?" he said, chuckling.

Jon blinked slowly, trying to get his cooked brain to work. When he pushed himself to standing, his legs felt weak.

"Yeah... So I hear," he muttered. His head spun.

"How'd ye find us?" asked the first mate in a hoarse voice.

"I didn't think you'd be wandering around town naked," Baltsaros replied, holding up the clothing they'd abandoned on the beach.

"Ah. Right," Jon said and took his tunic and shortened pants with a crooked smile. Teetering on one leg to get dressed, he watched the first mate get out of bed, scratching himself as he blinked sleepily.

"I thought ye needed an afternoon to yerself?" Tom mumbled as he accepted his pants from Baltsaros.

"I thought I did," admitted the captain, hooking his thumbs into the red sash around his waist. "Then I found myself unable to stop thinking about the two of you and said *scupper that…* So I flew the coop."

Baltsaros's white smile was wide in his tanned face, and his dark eyes crinkled at the corners; Jon thought he looked happier than he'd seen him in a long time.

Wrinkling his nose, the captain looked around.

"Yea gods, I leave you alone for a few weeks, and you manage to make my quarters smell like a barn." He scratched at something that had spilled on the table, curling his lip in disgust.

Jon glanced at Tom and grinned.

$\sim$

*B*altsaros watched Tom deftly peel a mango then cut thick slices away from the fibrous pit as juice ran down his arm. Jon accepted a piece with a grin and offered the plate of cheeses to the first mate. Tom chose some hard-rind cheddar from the midlands and held it between his teeth while he poured himself and Jon some more of the strong black coffee from the golden ewer at the centre of the table. They were completely in sync with each other, and it made Baltsaros smile.

"Saban told me about Ceara," Jon said, munching on some toasted currant bread. "You really trust her? What happens if she decides to just go to the navy and collect the bounty on our heads?"

The captain shook his head.

"She won't. What motivates Ceara isn't money, Jon. It's power and knowledge. I've put her in a position where she has both, and I think it will be enough to keep her loyal. Besides, I told her that if she crosses me, I will have Saban flayed alive in front of her," he said and bit into a ripe *gessal*. The fruit's sweet skin was a nice complement to the tart flesh inside, and he chewed it slowly to savour the taste.

Jon's eyes widened.

"I was kidding," Baltsaros laughed. "Jon, relax."

"Wait... Why Saban?" asked Tom with a frown.

"Didn't he tell you?" asked the captain, surprised. "The two of them were married a few weeks ago."

Tom and Jon glanced at each other, and Baltsaros felt something kindle deep in his chest at the looks on their faces. Tom's green-blue eyes were the first to turn back to the captain, and Baltsaros didn't like the bland expression in them. The fact that Jon stared down at his plate before meeting his eyes made it worse. It seemed that the boys were hiding something from him.

"Excuse me," said Jon, getting to his feet. "I need to use the facilities."

Baltsaros watched him go, tapping his bottom lip with the side of his finger.

"Tom... Do I want to know?" he asked finally. He turned to the first mate and saw that Tom's gaze was trained on nothing. The big man's forehead wrinkled as he rubbed the coarse dark-blond stubble of his jaw. After a few seconds, he focused on the captain, grimaced, and shook his head.

"You instigated?"

The first mate gave a terse nod but then frowned and shook his head.

The possessive spark took flame, and Baltsaros felt heat course through him. How dare Saban think he could—

"Was Jon's idea," Tom broke in gruffly. "At least the first time."

The *first* time? Baltsaros took a deep breath and closed his eyes. He was incredulous, angry, curious, and jealous at once. The emotions simmered just below the surface, fighting to break through.

Calm yourself.

"Is it likely to happen again?" asked Baltsaros, trying to keep emotion from his voice. He looked again at the big man across the table.

A firm headshake.

"You are certain?"

This time it was a tiny scowl followed by a nod.

The captain tilted his head and stared hard at Tom. The first mate stared back, unblinking.

"Ok," Baltsaros said... and simply let go of his anger.

It almost startled him how easily he did it. Just like dropping a pebble over the side of a ship, it faded from sight as it sank beneath deep waters. Oddly, he didn't *feel* less. It was just tempered with something he was only beginning to understand: trust.

Tom's eyes widened for a brief instant, suspicion flaring only to be extinguished by astonishment. When Baltsaros gave a reassuring nod to show he was serious, the first mate's face creased into a relieved grin. After he ate another piece of mango off the end of his knife, Tom chuckled.

"Yer a changed man, Da."

Baltsaros smiled and turned his head when he felt the breeze on his cheek; scented with fruit, flowers, and the tang of the sea, it cooled the skin at the open collar of his shirt. The sky was cloudless, and the palm fronds swished over the sound of the surf below. A perfect day.

After a moment, Baltsaros thought of something and narrowed his eyes at Tom.

"What did you do to the figurehead on the *Heart*?" he said, changing the subject. "It looks completely insane. I hope to hells that's not some kind of commentary on my mental acuity."

Tom began to laugh.

. . .

*a*s they waited for Jon to join them again, Baltsaros leaned back in his chair and crossed his arms as Tom began to describe the fight aboard the *Sabre*. The first mate's hair was a little too short for his liking, and the bruising on his face had started to go an unattractive shade of olive, but his ocean eyes were lively and the way the light caught them caused Baltsaros to ache a little. In a good way.

"You're beautiful," he murmured.

Tom choked on his words, his hands stopping in mid-gesticulation.

"You're beautiful, Tom," the captain repeated, "but... so much more than that. I am a very lucky man to have found you... I am incredibly thankful for everything you've done for me."

"Da, stop—" growled Tom, hunching his shoulders.

"Son, I just want you know how *much* you mean to me. You make me very happy. *Do you understand me?*"

The first mate quickly looked down to stare at the table, blinking fast; Baltsaros could see the play of muscle in his jaw.

"Tom?" asked the captain, leaning forward.

Tom nodded slowly. When he glanced up, there was a shimmer to his eyes.

"Aye, Da," he said in a hoarse voice. "I understand."

Baltsaros rose to his feet and rounded the table to sit in Jon's departed chair.

"I need you to do something for me."

"Always, Da. Anythin'," swore Tom.

The captain reached out and curled his hand behind Tom's big neck, watching the tropical ocean hues of his eyes shift as they widened slightly. Slowly Baltsaros leaned in to kiss Tom's full lips and tasted mango when he bit down softly on the lower one. Baltsaros's pulse skittered and went wild as he gently investigated Tom's mouth. Dipping his tongue between Tom's open lips to taste more sweetness, he wrapped his other hand around him to deepen the kiss. When Baltsaros finally pulled away, Tom's eyes stayed closed for a moment. Looking a little flushed when he opened them, Tom's gaze darted over the captain's face.

"I don't know why it took me so long to realize you were such an incredible kisser," said Baltsaros. "And that you needed a bit of tenderness once in a while."

Tom chuckled and looked down at his hands, his face reddening further.

"Now *that*," laughed the captain, squeezing the back of Tom's neck, "is a blush worthy of Jon."

"Oh bugger off, ye ol' fiend," said Tom with a grin. Then his forehead creased in confusion as he appraised Baltsaros. "That's what ye needed me to do for ye?"

"No. Give me your knife."

Baltsaros ignored the flash of concern that passed over the first mate's features as he handed over the long, bone-handled dagger. Knowing that he'd probably have to treat the two of them for infection afterwards, he pressed the blade to his forearm and mirrored the healed scar he'd made with Jon on the other arm. Tom watched him with a deep comma between his sandy brows and let out a small grunt when Baltsaros took his thickly muscled arm in hand.

There were no words spoken between them as Baltsaros sliced into Tom's skin, nor were there any when they pressed their bleeding forearms together. They weren't needed. Tom bent forward and placed his forehead against the captain's shoulder with a long sigh, and Baltsaros pressed his cheek to Tom's cropped hair, wrapping his free arm around his broad, scarred back.

～

*J*on washed his hands slowly and carefully. Aware that he was stalling, he wiped his fingers on the square of white cloth that hung above the pitcher and basin and straightened his sweat-stained black tunic. Wishing that there was a mirror in the little alcove where he stood, Jon smoothed back his hair and took a few calming breaths. Every time he thought about what had happened with Saban, Jon's pulse sped, and he felt a pit open in his stomach.

Mouth a little dry, he rubbed his face hard to try to snap himself out of it. Baltsaros would no doubt be furious when he found out... That, or he would see it as an excuse to break his promise and try to add a fourth—or more—to their bed. Jon groaned inwardly as he made his way back down the hallway to the patio where they had been eating lunch. The problem was... Jon was confused. He'd been excited knowing he was being watched by Saban—incredibly, unbelievably, agonizingly turned-on. Then it had turned to deep shame and... fear? Anger? He realized that the only reason he wasn't incredibly pissed off at Tom was because Jon knew he had planted the idea in the first mate's head. It wasn't an excuse. It just wasn't, but he knew that Tom understood that too.

Jon just wanted to leave the whole fucking mess behind them and chalk up the morning to a lapse in judgment. With shoulders squared, he pushed open the glass door and stepped out into the bright sunshine.

*W*hen Jon saw Baltsaros and Tom in their quiet embrace, he stopped. More than a little uncertain, he stood just watching them for a moment. However, when the captain lifted his head and looked at him with nothing but open affection, Jon's jittering pulse began to slow. He stepped forward, and Tom turned to watch him approach. He nodded at Jon with an encouraging smile.

Everything will be all right.

It seemed that the first mate had decided to trust Baltsaros with what had occurred earlier, and there would be few or no repercussions. Something had... changed.

Jon noticed the blood on Tom's knife and their clasped arms

and let out a small noise, realizing what it meant. There were no feelings of betrayal, no sense of exclusion. No... It was as if something had finally been fixed, a hole patched. The old woman's orphic words about mending the tapestry came back to him but he quashed the tiny trill of horror that rose up in him at the memory. While there were things in the world he didn't or couldn't understand, here was something before him that he *did*.

Their relationship would continue to grow, to change. There would always be pain, and they would be tested... Their triad had the shakiest of foundations, based as it was on mistrust, jealousy, and deception. But *ships* didn't need pillars pounded into the earth; no, they needed strong, protective hulls that could carry them over the ever-changing waves of an uncaring sea. With trust, hope... love—all things they had built *together*—they could weather anything.

Jon closed his eyes and folded himself into the three-sided embrace, no longer adrift.

2 0

DIVINE TORTURE

*J*on took a breath and as he let it out slowly, squeezed the trigger. The flintlock jumped in his hand, and the bottle on the pile of driftwood exploded in a shower of brown glass.

"That-a boy, Jonny!" whooped Katherine and lifted the flask of whiskey to her lips. "Now let's see if you can do that again."

With a wry headshake, Jon pulled the other pistol from the holster at his hip and pointed it, left-handed, at the beer bottle's twin. He moved the cock to full and fired. This time, the lead shot hit the bottle's thick bottom and sent it flying into the air.

"I never thought I'd see the day," said Katherine, grinning. "With a little more practice, I think I'll make a crack shot of you yet."

"Uh huh," smirked Jon. He was able to hit a target if it was both inanimate and close by. He doubted that he'd ever be a great marksman. He started to unbuckle the belts, but Katherine stopped him.

"Keep 'em," she said.

Jon looked at the beautiful pistols and shook his head.

"Kat… I couldn't—"

"You can and you shall," said Katherine, sobering. She lifted her hook to eye level and sighed. "They're a matched pair, kiddo. A lotta good they do me. Go on, keep 'em."

Smiling a little sadly, Jon slid them both back into the tooled leather belts.

"Ok fine, but let me give you something in return." Jon thought for a moment but couldn't come up with anything on the spot. "When I think of something suitable."

"I won't argue with that," said Katherine with a grin.

Jon looked at the sun. It was not yet midday. The item he had commissioned from the blacksmith wouldn't be ready until that afternoon, so he had time to kill.

"I'm hungry. You hungry? Want to check out that new place?"

Since their arrival, a pair of ambitious ex-Balorians had set up shop selling something they called *fish cutters*—pieces of battered fish in a salt bread roll—and Jon hadn't had the opportunity to try them yet. With a nod, Katherine wedged the flask at her belt and made towards the crumbling staircase that led to the cobbled road above.

The small structure had been quickly built from odds and ends and decorated with old fishing nets and glass buoys. It housed a stone fire pit with a cast-iron shelf above it. At the small counter leaned the proprietress, a slightly hunchbacked older woman wearing colourful silks. At their approach, she straightened and smiled wide.

"We are just having the fire lit! Come, come," she said, gesturing to the tiny eating area in front of the shack.

Jon and Katherine sat down on old crates to either side of a table made of a barrel and a few boards nailed together. Katherine looked at Jon in amusement and wrinkled her nose.

"You take me to the fanciest places," she teased.

Jon shrugged just as the woman came out the side of the shack and set down two mugs in front of them.

"First customers will always be having free drinks to start," said the woman happily. "Two cutters?"

"Yes, please," replied Jon.

"With pepper sauce?"

"Sure... Why not. Kat?" Katherine nodded, and the woman hollered in a dialect of Balorian that Jon couldn't understand. The woman's partner, a much younger man from the fisherfolk tribes, peered out from the ramshackle hut and yelled something back.

"Will be soon," said the proprietress and turned to greet some more customers who had just arrived.

Jon lifted his mug and took a swig. He recognized Maya's brown mild and sighed happily. If there was one thing that Katherine's wife excelled at, it was brewing beer. He wondered if she had ever thought of exporting some to the *Jewel*. With a frown, he remembered the strange conversation he'd had there with the old seer woman over a pint of beer.

"Kat... Do you believe in fate?"

*K*atherine devoured her fish cutter and ordered a second while Jon told her of the woman's fortune-telling. When he was done, she shook her head at him.

"You know how I hate to agree with Tom, but he's right, Jon. It's just total bullshit."

"Then why didn't she take my money?"

"Because she's a loony old bint? I don't know. It doesn't even make any sense," replied Katherine, shrugging. "Like the tapestry thing. So your family crest is a wolf and Baltsaros's a lion. Big fucking deal. Do you know how many families have the same? Hells, I think Maya's got one of each on hers. And Tom's crest isn't even a cat. I think it's some kind of fish. If this were some magical fucking card, don't you think there would have been a fish instead of a cat?"

"Well. The captain calls Tom his tomcat all the time..."

Katherine nearly choked on her beer and started laughing.

"He does? Hells, that is funny. I didn't realize they were into pet names. Hmm... I like 'kitten' for Tom. What do you think?"

"Kat, don't you say one word that I told you!" he said, aghast. "It's just that... Well, ever since I came aboard, I've had dreams about a black lion and a wildcat. I know that they represent Baltsaros and Tom..."

"And she made a card suddenly appear that fit?"

"Well..."

"I think maybe Tom just interrupted before she could fleece you."

"But... the moon boy. The way I see things."

"I'd hardly call a knack for body language 'visions', but that's just me."

"And the coincidences..."

"Pure bunk," insisted Katherine. "Listen... When you're looking for accidents of chance, you see them all around. Trust me."

Jon was about to point out that they predated his encounter with the woman, but Katherine narrowed her eyes at him.

"Speaking of trust... How's it going with the captain and Tom? You know I worry about you with those two."

"It's going well, actually. Really well. There's no need to worry about me. Baltsaros is leaps and bounds better than he was just a few weeks ago. Tom and I are still keeping a close eye on him just in case, but I really believe that he's almost recovered," Jon said, handing their plates over to the proprietress of the fish shack. "You know, you're wrong to despise Tom so much. He's not like what you think."

"So you keep saying. But I've known him longer than you. That boy is nothing but trouble with a troubled past."

"*You've* got a troubled past," Jon pointed out. Katherine didn't talk much about her life before she went pirate, but Jon knew she had been a prostitute from a young age in a brothel that catered to men with "exotic" tastes.

"Yeah well, I don't get off on being tortured. There's liking a little pain... and then there's Tom. He's unhinged."

"It's not torture. It's... I can't explain it, but it's ok."

"And you like torturing him? See, that's the thing that bothers me the most."

Jon laughed.

"It's *not* torture," he repeated. "And yes... I like it. And so does he. And so does Baltsaros. It just seems to work between the three of us. Trust *me*. I'm happy... Happier than I've ever been in my whole life."

"Fine. You know what's best!" Katherine chuckled and lifted her hands in defeat.

Jon averted his eyes from the dented hook. If only there were something that would serve her better. Looking skyward, he was startled to see that the sun was on the downswing; it was later than he thought. After brushing crumbs from his shirt, Jon stood and dropped some coins on the table.

"Thanks for eating with me," he said. "Now, I have to go pick up something from the blacksmith and head back to the castle. Do you want to meet on the beach for more target practice tomorrow morning? See if I can hit something a little more challenging?"

Katherine grinned and nodded before downing the rest of her beer.

*J*on looked at the hoop of metal, testing the hinge. Doug folded his arms across his leather apron.

"I had to outsource the clasp to Tegan the jeweller because she's so much better at the small stuff than I am, but she promised me it would hold up to quite a bit of force," said the huge blacksmith and handed over a pair of small, silver keys.

Nodding, Jon opened and closed the clasp a few times.

"Perfect," he said with a smile. "It's exactly what I asked for. How much do I owe you?"

"Why don't you consider it a gift for giving me some ideas?"

said Doug with a smile. The blacksmith scratched the back of his neck, and Jon saw that he had reddened slightly. "I'm thinking of making one that'll fit me. You know… for the missus."

With a laugh, Jon pressed a few coins on him anyway and thanked him again.

⁓

*T*om glanced up when Jon came through the door and saw that he looked as chuffed as a dog with a bone, a cheeky smile stretching from ear to ear.

"Why are ye lookin' so pleased with yerself, lad?" the first mate asked with a grin. Baltsaros put down the book he'd been reading and raised his brows at Jon as the younger man crossed the room.

"I have a gift for you," replied Jon, reaching into the cloth pouch he carried. "Since we had to cut the last two off of you, I thought you might like something a little more lasting." He pulled out a silver circle of metal and handed it to Tom.

Tom's heart began to pound faster as he turned the slave collar over in his hands. It was fitted with a little hinge and what looked like a lockable clasp. It was lovely little bit of craftsmanship. He swallowed thickly; the air in the room had gotten thin.

"I had two keys made. One for me, one for Baltsaros," said Jon quietly. "Do you like it?"

Tom ground his teeth together and looked up. Jon's storm-grey eyes were on him, curious. Baltsaros had risen from his seat and looked on with the hint of a smile on his gracefully curved lips.

"Tom?" asked Jon, the tiniest touch of concern in his voice.

With a shiver of excitement, Tom licked his lips and tried to find his voice. How in hells could he explain what it meant to him that Jon had done this?

"Aye," he rasped finally. "Like nothin' else."

"Would you like us to put it on you?" Baltsaros reached out

and accepted one of the little silver keys with a smile before stepping to Tom's side.

Instead of answering, Tom just slid off the small, cushioned stool and knelt on the carpet. He closed his eyes and waited.

Two sets of hands touched him, gentle and sure. The metal was cold around his neck, and he let out a shuddering sigh as it closed with a sharp *click*.

"Come," murmured Baltsaros, helping him to stand. "That's not the only metal I want you wearing." Jon tilted his head at the captain, but he nodded in understanding a moment later.

Tom was led to the bed, and when he lay back, the captain deftly undid his pants and lowered his trousers. Jon appeared with something in his hand. As the captain claimed Tom's mouth, Jon slipped something cool around Tom's hardening cock, snapping it closed carefully behind his balls. With a little moan, Tom recognized the cock ring. It was one that wasn't particularly tight to begin with but would get almost painful the longer he was kept hard. When Jon's hot mouth sucked in the head of his cock, Tom let out a groan.

Baltsaros pulled back.

"How long has it been?" The captain's fingers closed over Tom's nipple and pinched.

Tom closed his eyes with a sigh as Jon's hand gently stroked the inside of his thigh.

"Three days," he replied and gasped when Baltsaros squeezed his nipple harder.

"That's not a very long time. Jon, is that a long time?"

Jon chuckled and licked around the crown of Tom's cockhead.

"No. Not very long at all."

Tom let out a sound that could only be called a whimper. Yes, three days didn't sound like a lot unless your balls were aching day and night and you couldn't think of anything but cumming; since the incident with Saban, they'd begun to regularly take him to a state of hyper arousal to keep him there for long stretches of time without any relief.

It was divine torture.

～

*J*on smiled as Tom let out a soft groan, muffled by the red silk of his gag. The first mate was kneeling on the bed, thighs wide and pelvis forward, with his wrists secured tightly to his ankles behind him. This had the effect of bowing his back in such a way that his ribs were starkly outlined and the thick tendons in his neck stuck out as he held up his head, blue-green eyes fixed on Jon. He trembled from the strain of keeping the uncomfortable pose, but Jon had told him if he let himself sink down onto his calves, he would be denied release again.

With a pleased sigh, Jon leaned forward to lick another slow line down Tom's chest before closing his lips over a nipple to worry the bud with his teeth. Despite how the first mate's muscles bulged and strained against his bindings, he didn't struggle. Jutting from the thatch of dark-blond hair at his groin was the reason why; Tom's cock was a thick, hard, upward curve that jumped up every time Jon bit down harder.

This was the first mate's idea of a good time.

Jon chuckled against Tom's skin, almost lazily stroking his hands down the big man's sides to grasp his muscular buttocks before biting him again. This time he took the metal ring between his teeth and tugged on it. In response, Tom's cock grazed Jon's bare stomach and left behind a slick streak. Jon grinned and sat back on his own heels, grasping his cock in one hand to rub it against the head of Tom's. The first mate let out another low sound, closing his eyes as he thrust his hips further forward. Jon obliged him for a moment; taking the wide head in one hand, he thumbed along the underside, teasing Tom as he stroked his own cock. They'd been at this for the better part of an hour.

"Do you want it?" asked Jon with a wolfish grin.

Tom nodded quickly, a plea in his eyes. Jon reached for his jaw and tugged down the gag.

"Let me hear you say it," said Jon softly. His fingers stroked along the edge of the slave collar Tom wore. The first mate's skin was hot and wet to the touch, and his pulse thumped against the tips of Jon's fingers.

"I want yer cock," rasped Tom. Another drop of arousal slipped from the slit of his cockhead and perched there for a moment, shiny and clear, before sliding down along the thick vein and over the smaller metal circlet that he wore tight around the root of his cock. "Please, Jon. I want ye to fuck me. Hard. Please. I'll do anythin' ye want. Just… please."

Jon patted Tom's cheek lightly with a smile and looked up. The captain's tanned face was creased in amusement as he lounged behind Tom on the bed stroking his own cock and watching Jon taunt the big man. At Jon's nod, Baltsaros sat up and moved forward to quickly free Tom's wrists. Jon watched the captain narrow his eyes in concentration as he undid the knots.

Jon smiled softly. For the past week, Baltsaros's eyes had been clear and his strange turns had all but vanished. That the captain felt "sane" enough to participate in some slightly rougher play with him and Tom gave Jon hope that things would soon return to normal.

Whatever that is, he thought.

He turned back to Tom and saw that the first mate was looking at him with pupils blown out from lust and *char*, completely oblivious and lost in the moment. He was absolutely gorgeous like this, willing to do almost anything for the sake of pleasing him… a living plaything, but so much more.

Someone to cherish.

Jon widened his grin and ducked his head to cover Tom's lips with his own, nudging them open to begin kissing him slow and deep. When Tom's arms finally came free of the rope, he curled them around Jon's waist and surrendered to the embrace, his chest rumbling with small growls of pleasure. Then Tom tensed suddenly against Jon, breathing a gasp into the kiss. Curious, Jon slid his hand down Tom's hard stomach, past his cock and sensitive sack, to discover that the captain had slid two fingers into the first mate. Baltsaros let out a slow breath when he felt Jon's tentative touch and leaned over Tom's shoulder to press his lips to Jon's cheek.

Jon broke the kiss to share breath with Baltsaros for a moment. Smiling against his lips, he slid his own finger next to the captain's and into Tom. The first mate trembled between them as they fucked him using their fingers, opening him up, their hands slick with oil. Soon Tom's normally gruff voice broke on a whimper as he begged.

"Please, Jon... Da. For love's sake," said the first mate. "I've been good, aye?"

Jon laughed, breathless and wild with desire, and he shared a look with Baltsaros. It was tempting to make the first mate wait longer, just to hear how desperate he could sound, but instead he grabbed the back of Tom's head and kissed him again.

"Yes, you've been a good lad, Tom," murmured the captain. His long-fingered hand stroked up Jon's arm, the touch gentle. "How would you like to take the both of us? Hm? Would that make you happy?"

Tom pulled away from Jon, his eyes glazed and fervid, lips parted on a slow pant.

"Oh... fuck yes, Da."

Jon's heart pounded, and his cock throbbed in his hand as he watched Tom straddle Baltsaros and then lay back against the man's chest, bracing himself on his heels. The captain cushioned the big man's weight with one hand, moving to push his thick cockhead against Tom's puckered opening with the other. Jon licked his lips, an involuntary moan expelled with a hitched breath at the sight of Baltsaros's cock stretching Tom open and sliding deep into him. Tom let out a shallow grunt and closed his big fist over his own length. Jon watched hungrily as the captain fucked the first mate slowly for a few thrusts.

With a crease between his brows, Jon climbed back up on the bed and stroked himself, unsure about how to approach. Tom's eyes were closed, but when Jon made no further move, the first mate lifted his head and frowned at him. Tom held out his hand.

"Come," he said with a smile that faltered into a grimace of pleasure as Baltsaros's cock thrust deep again. "You can't hurt me, lovey."

Jon nodded weakly. Dizzy and excited, and a touch nervous, he found a place for his legs, straddling the captain, and leaned forwards over Tom. The first mate's legs hooked over Jon's hips as he stroked the head of his cock over the captain's thrusting length and then eased in slowly when the man paused. He pushed hard, and Tom's eyes closed once more. It was tight, almost too much. When Tom let out a pained breath, Jon stopped, but the first mate just chuckled a shaky laugh.

"Don't ye dare stop, Jon. Don't ye stop..." Tom groaned and let his head fall back over Baltsaros's shoulder. Jon's fervour took over. He plunged his cock into Tom's ass, sliding tight against the captain's length. It was glorious, and he found himself teetering on the edge of climax quickly. He paused, eyes closed and so sensitive that he was almost in pain. For a moment Jon just held back, waited, and relished the feeling of the captain's cock sliding against his before resuming. However, it wasn't long before he couldn't stop himself from spilling over, the swell of pleasure breaking out into molten waves of intensity that tore the voice from his throat and left him breathless and weak. When the liquid pulses that rocked him slowed, then stopped, he leaned his head against Tom's furry chest and eased out slowly, wincing as he did so.

Tom let out a grunt of surprise a moment later when Jon moved over to begin working his mouth over Tom's cock. The first mate buried his shaking hands in Jon's dark curls as Jon gagged trying to take all of Tom in. Jon swallowed and tried again, keenly wanting to reward Tom. He relaxed his throat, shifted his position, and lapped at the head of Tom's cock before sliding it back into his throat.

With Baltsaros thrusting into him from below and Jon gorging himself on his cock, Tom soon started breathing through clenched teeth with a low, rumbling moan that Jon knew meant he was close. Jon curled his fingers around the base of Tom's cock and tightened his lips, spit running down the sides of the big man's shaft and over Jon's fingers.

Suddenly Baltsaros let out a low growl, fucking Tom faster with his arms tight around the first mate's chest, the muscles taut and twitching as his body rocked beneath him, caught in the feverish, frantic surge of orgasm. Then, with a strangled cry, Tom finally let himself cum, his bitter seed gushing over Jon's tongue as his body shuddered and hands clutched at him before falling limp to his sides.

Jon almost laughed with giddiness. With a grin he came forward to press kisses to Tom's sweat-slick skin when the captain rolled the first mate gently to his side and began murmuring soft praises.

"Good boy."

*J*on woke a few hours later, curled against Tom's side. Tom slept soundly, his broad chest rising and falling with every deep breath. On his other side, the bed was empty. Jon frowned and sat up. The early-morning light streamed in through the curtains and painted the room in a hazy, golden hue. After climbing out of the huge four-poster bed, Jon padded quietly to the front room to see where Baltsaros was. When he saw that this room too was empty, a finger of worry stole into his heart. Then he saw the note. He picked it up from the big desk and peered at it.

J & T,

All hands needed to stock up and ready the ship. We leave tomorrow at noon. Meet me below when you wake.

— B.

*J*on pulled the thick velvet curtain aside and squinted at the beach. Sure enough, there was a bustle of activity. He could see a jolly boat making its way to the ship with a load of supplies. Confused, he turned back to the desk. There he spotted a letter written in the spiky alphabet of the northerners. He snatched it up and ran back to the bed, shaking Tom from his slumber.

Tom rubbed his face blearily, blinking around him in confusion with eyes tinged in red before he scowled in annoyance.

"What?" he rumbled.

Jon shoved the letter into his hand.

"The captain is down at the ship, getting her ready to leave tomorrow," he said, his heart skipping in his chest. "Does this have anything to do with it?"

After swiping at his face again, Tom focused on the letter. A deep crease formed in his forehead, and when he looked back up at him, Jon saw deep concern.

"Aye, lad," said Tom quietly. "Seems we're headed north. Far north."

Tom sat up and read the letter out loud, translating as he went. Written by someone called Sister Iezabel, it described a barbarian raid that had destroyed a nearby settlement. The letter was addressed to Baltsaros, and the wording suggested that they had known each other for a long time. However, it was the first that Tom had heard of a friendship with some nun.

Jon sat down on the bed next to him looking worried.

"You mean where the captain's from?"

"Aye," muttered Tom. "Bloody hells, I hate fuckin' snow."

21

FIRST BLOOD

Monsters are real, and ghosts are real too. They live
inside us, and sometimes, they win.

— STEPHEN KING

Captain Baltsaros pointed to the trapdoor, and the young
deckhand made his way belowdecks with the bag of
supplies over his shoulder.

"I don't understand," Jon said. "That letter has to be months
old. Why are we going now? Isn't it a little after the fact?"

Tom was cleaning his nails with his knife while he lounged on
the stairs. Though he seemed concentrated on his task, he lifted
his eyes to the captain's, an expression of disapproval on his
rugged face.

"Aye," said the first mate. "We only bloody just got here, Da.
What is the fuckin' rush? Are ye havin' a turn?"

"I'm fine. And the letter is at least a year old."

"Then why are we leaving *now*?" asked Jon, his eyes round in
confusion.

Baltsaros reached out and clasped him on the shoulder with a smile before directing another load of supplies. He then gestured to Jon and Tom and led them to the captain's quarters.

"Sit," he said and pointed to the table, closing the door behind him. He walked to the crate next to the empty fridge and pulled out two bottles of Maya's strong beer. They were warm because that month's ice shipment had not come in yet, but he didn't think the boys would mind too much. He felt his pulse get a little faster, and it felt like there was a hand in his chest squeezing his heart. With a deep breath, he placed the bottles in front them and sat down. Tom grabbed one bottle, untwisted the wire and pulled the cork out with his teeth. He handed it to Jon and did the same for his own; the first mate's forehead wrinkled as he watched the captain mutely.

"What's going on?" whispered Jon.

Baltsaros took another long breath and steepled his fingers, staring at the space between them as he tried to gather his thoughts.

Just speak.

The captain closed his eyes and swallowed in the stillness.

With eyes shut, Baltsaros began to unwind the memories that sat coiled and cold in the space between his soul and heart. When he spoke, his voice was steady and calm.

"The place I was born is called Heaven's Gate, or *Sormaheine* in my native tongue. It is an ancient city built high on a steep mountain, protected from raids by barbarian tribes by a massive gate at its base. One day, in a fit of childish rage, I led monsters through the gate and then helped them to slaughter my family."

~

*A*fter escaping past the gate guards, Baltsaros ran across the ice, furious tears freezing on his cheeks. They would pay. *All of them.* His skinny legs were a blur and his breath heaved in his bony chest. It wasn't *fair* that he had to wait another year to apprentice. He'd been counting on his father's approval. He had been *so* sure of it that he had secretly spent his coins on an alchemist's vest. If he had to wait another year, the vest would be too small! It was a *waste*! Baltsaros had never been so angry before. He wanted to hurt someone.

Suddenly, he tripped over a chunk of ice and went sprawling. With a cry, he pulled himself to sitting and wrapped his thin arms around his knee; he rocked as he sobbed. There was blood on the ice. He had torn open his knee, and Mother would be furious about the rip in his pants. Weeping like a stupid baby, he didn't see the men until they were nearly upon him.

Baltsaros's stomach dropped, and he froze in terror when the leader pointed to him; the huge stranger's hand was bare despite the cold, and he could clearly see that the palm of it was blood red.

Blood ogres from the northern hill! The rhyming song about them was in his head as he stared slack-jawed at the fur-covered strangers.

One, two, they're coming for you...

Before Baltsaros had a chance to get to his feet, one of them grabbed him by the front of his parka and lifted him straight into the air. With a scream, he struggled and kicked in the man's hold; he tried to dig his nails into the stained fist, but it was as if it were made of stone.

Three, four, always wanting for more...

Baltsaros let out another shriek as he was tossed in the air. A second man caught him and turned him around; he whimpered when he saw the sharpened teeth. The man's breath was foul, and when he smiled wider, Baltsaros felt his bladder give out.

Five, six, seven, the red hands, they beckon...

Baltsaros was shaken roughly, and the laughing man who held him said a few words in a strange tongue to the others. The sound of their laughter surrounded Baltsaros. He began to cry harder.

Eight, nine, ten, slaughtered now, feast on men...

His school friend Kyrillosr had made fun of him when he had said they were real ogres like in the fairy tales. Kyr had told him that his father said they were just brutal barbarians from far, far in the north where there was no break from the cold in summer.

Saros, don't be stupid. People just call them ogres because they eat human flesh.

"Child of Sormaheine," growled the man holding him. He had horns on his leather helm, and around his shoulders he wore a great black musk-bear pelt; the reek of it was heavy in the air. "What are you doing so far away from home? Don't you know there are bad men who would do bad things to you?"

Baltsaros's sobs had turned to high wails, and his whole body heaved and trembled. He barely heard the words.

"What should we do with you, hm? Roast you over a fire and pick your bones clean? Or... Should we have a little fun with you first?" said the huge, grinning cannibal.

The men tied him to the saddle of a shaggy, four legged creature. Head hanging over the side of it, he thought that when it glanced back at him, it looked a little sad. Baltsaros's crying had stopped. He just felt numb like his heart or his mind had been frostbitten; he barely understood what was happening to him.

After a long, cold, bumpy ride he was taken into a tent and forced to drink something bitter. At first he was nauseous, and then it was like he was watching the world from one end of a paper tube. The blood ogres had stripped out of their furs. Baltsaros could see their red-stained feet and hands, and for some reason it made him laugh. Kyr had said it was something called *pigment*. Baltsaros had no idea what that was. Did it come off with water? Did they wear it for fashion, like his mother wore colour on her eyelids?

Baltsaros was hot. However, once he had wiggled out of his parka, he felt too light as if he would float away. The men laughed at him, and he scowled. He couldn't understand their words... and then he could. They were speaking of ransoming him. Or eating him.

But, it didn't matter. He was no longer afraid of them.

With a smile, Baltsaros sat down on the piled furs. Then he had an idea and pulled off his shirt to feel the softness against his skin. He squirmed and sighed. A man reached for him and pulled him up. Again the language was gibberish. He laughed and copied them. The giant men found it funny and gave him another bitter drink. His head began to spin again, and the next few hours were just moments that jumped faster and faster towards him:

Telling the leader of the ogres that he knew how to get them into the city.

A cold ride in the dark.

Stairs and great splashes of blood on the wall from the dead guard.

A woman crying for help.

A headless man.

An ogre grunting between the legs of another woman as she stared blankly at Baltsaros.

His father lying in a puddle of blood with his head caved in.

Then, his mother picked him up and for a moment, a tiny moment, he knew fear again as she ran with him in her arms. Blood was everywhere—in his mouth, in his hair. He whimpered when he saw that his hands were red like the ogres' hands. Then more red hands took him from his mother, and she fell, a great wound in her chest. A barbarian worked at her with a knife and pulled her heart from her chest. Had Baltsaros also taken a bite? Was he crying or laughing? Vomit on the ground. His grandmother dead. The neighbour's wife stripped naked and on her hands and knees, screaming as an ogre did something to her. Baltsaros shook his head when the flask was pressed to his lips, but a third time he was given the potion. Everything was jumbled in his head. The barbarians turned to true ogres, carving up the living. Stacks of bodies. His little sister found in the closet crying. A knife thrust into Baltsaros's hand. Laughter.

Do it, do it, do it! Were they chanting? Was he screaming? Excitement. Horror.

He stabbed Cassia so many times that she no longer looked like a person.

The night became grotesque tintype stills in black and white, and minutes were preserved as hours.

He remembered wondering why, when he'd had the knife clutched in his little fist, he had not stabbed one of the men instead of Cassia... And then there was nothing.

~

"*I* must have passed out from exhaustion or from shock, I don't know which," said the captain softly. His voice had not once wavered in his narrative. He'd already told the tale to Abetha, and this second time around was much easier. "Sister Iezabel found me under a bed. The citadel's guards had finally arrived on the scene some time earlier and had dispatched only a few of the attackers. Seems like most of the barbarians had abandoned their revelries and left with their *meat*. I don't know if they meant to leave me behind or if they had simply forgotten about me." He rubbed his forehead and closed his eyes. "It gets a little fuzzy after that," he said, sighing. "I remember that I was mute for the first six months I was in the orphanage. A year and a half later, shortly after my ninth birthday, my uncle came to get me, and you both know the rest."

"Bloody hells, Da," said Tom in a hoarse voice. Baltsaros opened his eyes and smiled wanly.

"That memory has been locked away for a long time."

The captain looked at Jon. The young man was staring at the table, pale with shock. When he raised his head, Baltsaros was alarmed by the fury in his eyes.

"What kind of monsters would do that to a *child*?" he choked out. Baltsaros glanced at Tom and they shared a long look. The first mate's face was drawn with sympathy, remembering his own monsters. For a moment no one spoke.

"Did they do anything else to you?" whispered Jon. Baltsaros frowned at him, trying to keep from feeling or thinking too much about that long, bloody night.

"There is a lot that I don't remember, and I am glad for it. I've only told you because it may shed some light on some of my behaviour… my buried guilt over what happened."

"How can you possibly think you're guilty for *any* of it? They drugged you!" Jon exclaimed.

"I was, as you pointed out, a child. What child could possibly understand the logistics of blame in that situation? I suppressed the memory, either on purpose or as a result of shock; I have no way of knowing. Since I never spoke of it to anyone, no one knew that it was me that distracted the guards, or that it was my hand that ended by sister's life, so no one helped me. They treated me like a victim without knowing that I blamed myself. It's like I've been harbouring a terrible secret—one that I wasn't even privy to myself until my mind recently vomited forth everything in luminous detail."

"But… You have to know now that you're not to blame!"

Baltsaros lifted his hand.

"I *do* know that, Jon. Trying to convince my psyche of that fact is specifically what I've been doing since the memory resurfaced," he said grimly. "And that is the *last* I would like to speak of it."

"That's not—"

"Jon. I am in control of myself, now more than ever. I may be a broken thing, but I understand *how* I am broken. I don't need to rehash the past," he reached out and covered Jon's hand with his.

"Why're we goin' north then, Da?" asked Tom in a quiet voice.

"Sister Iezabel, in all her letters, never once mentioned a word of what had happened to me. I think she feared reminding me would revive my trauma. Then about year back, when her letter arrived with the news of a barbarian attack, I honestly thought nothing of it. This morning, there was a new letter from her—

nothing out of the usual with this one—but when I put it away with the rest, I saw the previous one and suddenly understood the significance of what she had written. Though we are too late to save those lost in that attack, Sister Iezabel's description of the barbarians closely matches that of the ones that took me as a child. I want to attempt to track them down."

"To what end?" asked Jon softly.

"To kill every last one of them."

22

FATE'S FOOLS

*J*on held onto the ratlines with his eyes closed, happy to feel the sun and salt spray on his bare chest as the ship cut through the water at full speed. They had been at sea for nearly three weeks and with only one planned stop to resupply along the way, they would continue to sail day and night until they reached the northern continent. Jon was excited, worried, nervous... He breathed in deep the buffeting wind and let it out as a long sigh. He was trying to keep himself from over-thinking things.

Deeply disturbed by the horror of the captain's story, Jon had felt nothing but a rousing thrill when Baltsaros had revealed his motives for going north. Jon's blood had sung at the words, as if they were nobly setting off for battle. It was only when the adrenaline had worn off that Jon wondered if retribution could ever be called *noble*.

He looked back at the straining sails. It would take them two more months to get to Sormaheine—*if* they weren't becalmed by a lack of wind like Captain Romas had. He jumped down from the gunwale and walked slowly sternward, trying to turn his mind away from heavy thoughts. If he let worry gnaw away at him this early in their journey, Jon would be a wreck by the time they landed at the northern coast.

Jon smiled to himself. No, for the moment the most he had to worry about was making sure that he lived up to his new position as quartermaster. Jon was still surprised and humbled that the crew had voted in agreement to the captain promoting him; times really had changed. Now he was the second only to Baltsaros, ranking even above Tom, and his job was to counterbalance all of the captain's orders—to keep him in check. It was a daunting honour; Jon didn't look forward to the time he had to veto something. He could just imagine the furious spark in the captain's eyes as he stared down at Jon, the beast forged inside his mind by blood and terror trying to convince him that Jon was a nuisance that needed to be removed. However, Baltsaros was confident that Jon was safe from him. Jon just had to trust that he was right about that.

Tom sat cross-legged on top of a large crate with a book open in his lap. His forehead was creased in concentration, and his lips moved ever so slightly as he read. It was a peculiar sight. Jon approached and grinned up at the first mate.

"You're reading."

Tom marked his spot with a finger and glanced over at Jon.

"Aye. What of it?" asked Tom with a frown.

"You're reading out in the open… I thought you revelled in your reputation as an uncultured lout."

Tom snorted in amusement.

"Ye know I don't give a rat's arse," he said. He lifted the book so Jon could see the cover. It was one of Baltsaros's surgery books. "Just doin' some thinkin' about the little project ye gave me."

Jon felt a touch of alarm.

"I didn't mean to do anything drastic. Nothing invasive… Just something simple."

With a chuckle, Tom nodded.

"Don't ye worry, Jonny-boy. I ain't goin' to be butcherin'… I think ye'll be happy with what I got planned."

"I hope so," said Jon with a grin and thumped the side of the crate with his fist. "Hey, I still need you to get that gun hoisted back into its moorings."

"Anythin' fer you, big brother."

Jon scowled and shook his head.

"Don't you start on that again unless you want to see how long it takes before your balls actually turn blue."

Tom just winked and looked back down at his book to continue reading.

Amused, Jon thought about the first mate's peculiar ideas about family as he went belowdecks to find something to eat.

∾

*J*on took his chair at the long table in the palace dining room and looked at those seated across from him. The captain was in quiet conversation with the queen, their heads tilted towards each other. Saban was conspicuously absent; the man had been so more often than not after that confusing day aboard the *Heart*. Jon's face felt hot at the memory of what Saban had been witness to.

Since being made so acutely aware of Saban's confusion, Jon had begun to ponder his own experiences and wondered why there had been so little inner struggle for him in comparison... Was he open like the captain in his preferences, or was he like Tom, who always said that he'd take "cock over cunt" if given the choice?

As if his thoughts had summoned the man, Jon raised his eyes at the sound of a cleared throat and was surprised to see the first mate in the doorway. Despite what Tom had said about not being suited for the queen's table, it seemed that he had finally decided to make a concession; it was obvious to Jon that the belted tunic Tom wore was a peace offering. Jon nodded at him with a tense smile, thinking that the first mate looked both nervous and a little hostile. This could go very badly if Abetha chose to be on the defensive.

"Thomas," said the queen quietly. "Please join us."

The crease between Tom's brows deepened, and Jon held his breath.

"*Tom*," corrected the first mate. For a moment it looked like the queen was going to retort with her usual vitriol, but then she just inclined her head graciously.

"Tom," she conceded and gestured to the empty chair next to Jon with a delicate, pale hand.

Jon hid his smile by wiping his mouth with the napkin from his lap.

Well... It's a start.

"Good for you," he said quietly when Tom had settled. The first mate just grunted noncommittally, but he squeezed back when Jon reached under the table and took his hand.

*T*he conversation circled around trade; Ceara would be back soon, and the queen would be responsible for keeping track of everything. It still bewildered Jon that the captain felt confident enough about the ex-spymaster to give her such an important role. However, he had begun to realize that Baltsaros was much better at using people's skills than he was. Jon frowned and wondered if his overdeveloped sense of empathy kept him from seeing people as tools like Baltsaros did. Or maybe it was the captain's *under*developed sense that made him better at it?

The queen's voice interrupted his thoughts.

"It's peculiar, Jon. With that beard, you remind me of a young man I used to know."

Jon smiled politely.

"Yes?"

"His father was employed as my father's stableman," she continued after taking a sip of wine from her fluted glass. "Yes, there's something about the lines of your face. Richard was the same age as me... We grew up together."

A prickle went up the back of Jon's neck, and he swallowed his mouthful, staring at the queen.

"My father's name was Richard," he said softly. "He was also a stable master."

The queen's eyes widened a touch, but her lips slid into an indulgent curve.

"It *is* a common enough name," she pointed out. "Was your father from the midlands isles too?"

"No, Your Majesty," Jon replied; he heard a note of something approaching fear in his voice. "He was actually a mainlander. His father was a stable master somewhere in the northern area... near the lakes."

"How... amazing! What are the chances? That is exactly where my family hails from," laughed the queen. "Your father must be the Richard I knew!"

Jon could feel his pulse stuttering as he contemplated the incredible coincidence.

Do fluke and fortuity court you like lovers? He could almost hear the old woman laughing.

"No, it's impossible," he said, groping for a solid reason. "It can't be the same man... Reginald told me that my father had been expelled from the household he grew up in because he was caught in an indiscretion with the lord's daughter... Oh." As the words left his mouth, he saw bright spots appear in the queen's cheeks, and she dropped her eyes.

Tom barked out a laugh.

Aghast, Jon desperately tried to think of something else to say as Abetha started to push her chair back; Baltsaros quickly caught her hand and stopped her.

"Abetha, we were all young once," he said with a gracious smile devoid of any reproach. "No one at this table would judge you for a maiden's tryst." The queen stared at him for a long moment, her bright blue-green eyes unsure. Jon elbowed Tom to try to stop his chuckling, but all it did was make him laugh louder.

"Holy hells, Jon!" he whooped and slapped the tabletop. "We're bloody brothers!"

"You most certainly are *not!*" exclaimed the queen, drawing herself up. Her face was almost crimson, and Jon thought he could see a glimmer of embarrassed tears.

"Lookit you! Dickin' about with the help!" Tom said with a grin, but Jon caught something surprising. The first mate was amused, yes, but there was nothing malicious about his tone for once. In fact, he seemed almost impressed.

Abetha flared her nostrils and raised her chin a notch.

Tom held up his hands, his expression quickly falling serious.

"Naw, listen... Peace. Really. I'm just glad to see you've got blood runnin' through your veins like the rest of us." Tom's accent had shifted ever so slightly—an echo of what it must have been like when he was a boy. "I'm sorry. Please?"

The queen lips worked together for a moment.

"Ye know, if this bonny Richard of yers was half as good-lookin' as Jon here, ye didn't stand a bloody chance..." continued the first mate with the first friendly grin Jon had ever seen him give the queen.

Abetha's cheeks flushed even darker, and her neck was mottled; Jon was worried for a second that she would storm off, but instead she surprised him by smiling a little sheepishly.

"Yes. And he was as young and foolish as I was," she muttered, and Jon suddenly saw her as she had been then. Headstrong, somewhat brash, a little wild... Jon glanced at Tom; the apple did not fall far from the tree.

Abetha cleared her throat and stopped fiddling with the cloth napkin, her cool composure returning to her.

"Now, if we've finished discussing my lapse in judgment, I would like to get back to the business of trade, if you will?" said the queen.

Mother and son stared at each other for a few beats. Jon

sensed something pass between them. The beginning of an understanding? Tom finally nodded and went back to his meal.
However, Jon could see that his posture was much more relaxed.

"Yer thinkin' it's a hell of a coincidence 'bout yer da, aint'cha?"
murmured Tom a few minutes later when he had finished his
curried goat and couscous. "Mind's on the ol' fortune-teller
again?"

Jon nodded slowly. He had just been replaying in his head the
encounter with the old woman.

"Well, ye can stop," said the first mate. "It's not even—"

"Tom, I can't... Everything she said is true!" Jon exclaimed.
Tom stared hard at him as though he were sizing him up; not for
the first time, Jon wished he could read him better. At last a sly
grin stretched Tom's lips, and he winked.

"All the bloody coincidences happened to me too, ye know," he
said, reaching for his wine. "Hey, what if I'm the one who's causin'
them, and yer just along for the ride?"

Jon blinked. It hadn't occurred to him. The first mate *had* been
part of every twist of fate. Or... Had he? But then so had the
captain. Jon scratched at his beard, feeling a little flustered.

Tom leaned closer and tapped his callused forefinger against
the glossy pale wood. He narrowed his eyes.

"Ye know... Maybe when that witch was lookin' in her crystal
ball—"

"They were cards."

"Fine. Cards. Maybe..." Tom moved even closer, his voice
dipping to a hush. "Maybe she could see that fate..."

"See that fate what?" whispered Jon, his heart skipping.

"Maybe she could see that fate's chosen us special because
we're brothers," said Tom with a little waggle of his eyebrows.

"What?" Jon couldn't help laughing at the impish look on the
first mate's face. "Ok, it is *literally* impossible that we're brothers,
given that I'm older than you. My father married my mother, and
I came about less than a year later. He died four months after
that."

"He could-a paid a wee visit to my ma and done 'er somewhere between then?"

"Oh, for fuck's sake, will you stop it?" said Jon with another laugh.

"Well. It's *like* we're brothers, aye? Seein' as our da's both dipped in the same waters?" Tom's grin had a coy edge to it.

"You worry me, you know that?"

~

*J*on had just finished up changing the duty roster for the coming weeks—Baltsaros believed in altering it a bit every month to keep the men interested in their work—when Tom came up the stairs to sit next to him at the helm. The big man stretched his arms out with a groan and then took a thin cheroot out from behind his ear. As he lit it, he looked around with a peaceful expression on his face. Jon smiled. The first mate's cheek was smeared with something black, and he smelled of clean sweat and salt air.

"I sometimes find it hard to believe that you weren't born to this," Jon said.

Tom laughed and flicked away some ash from the end of his smoke as he contemplated Jon.

"Why d'ye say that?"

"You just seem so much more at home... happier? I don't know. It's like you were meant to be a pirate."

"Oh, I was a bloody piss-poor sailor for a long bloody while, love," said Tom, the slim cigar jammed in the corner of his mouth. "But if ye really want somethin', ye gotta work for it."

Jon nodded and watched the smoke curl from Tom's nostrils as he squinted into the distance.

They sat in silence, watching the sun set slowly to the west.

The pink sky was hung with small clouds that seemed blue in comparison. When Jon raised his eyes to the darkening canopy above, he saw a few bright stars.

Looking to the stars is a better means of finding your way...

"Do you think going north is foolish?" he asked, turning to Tom.

Tom thought for a moment. When he took a drag of his smoke, Jon could see his eyes were narrowed shrewdly.

"I tend to think most o' life is foolish, lovey," he muttered after a while with a little shrug. "But... If we can grant a little peace to Da by goin' on what I figure is a bloody wild goose chase—" He turned at the soft footfall on the quarterdeck staircase.

The captain looked down at the two of them.

"Wild goose chase, hm? Why don't you continue, Tom?"

The first mate looked a bit self-conscious and grimaced.

"I was gonna say that it was bloody worth it to me," he pointed out.

"It just makes me happy to hear you say it," replied the captain with a smile. He walked over to the side of the quarterdeck and leaned on the railing, watching the sky for a moment. "However, I do hope you're wrong."

23

BAD LUCK

*J*on watched Katherine lift the musket and rest the long barrel on her hook as she aimed at the target—a dummy made of an old leather coat stuffed with sailcloth on a frame of wood. The shot she fired went over the side of the ship, but she was definitely improving.

"Fucking hells," she growled. "I'm worse than you are. Talk about luck... Why couldn't the fucking cannonball take my other fucking arm?"

"I wish it hadn't taken your arm at all," said Jon with a sad smile. Katherine huffed out a little laugh and passed the musket over to Jon so that he could reload it.

"I used to be great marksman," she sighed. "The captain used to say that I was a better shot than Peter, and that man was well known for his skill with a pistol."

Jon made sure the wadding was tamped firmly and handed the musket back to Katherine.

"The captain's mentioned him before. What happened to him?"

Katherine poured the fine powder, pulled the hammer to full cock, aimed, and fired again. This time she had better results—the lead ball actually grazed the target. She shook her head in disgust and walked up to the dummy to lean the long gun against it, obviously done for the day.

"Peter?" she asked. "He was first mate when I joined the crew. Had been since the mutiny. When the captain brought Tom aboard, it never sat well with Peter. I overheard a few arguments, and it wasn't pretty. Then, when the captain and Tom started to, well... When things changed between them, Peter was *extremely* vocal about his disapproval. He had religion and was a bit of a holy joe—didn't stop him from sleeping with whores or slitting throats, mind you—but he took exception to what went on behind the captain's doors. He criticized the captain in front of the crew, and that was it."

"Baltsaros killed him," murmured Jon with a nod.

Katherine's dark brows rose up.

"Uh, no," she replied, sounding confused. "The captain can be cold-blooded, sure, but why would he kill Peter? No... He just gave him a fair amount of coin—enough to buy himself a ship should he like to—and we dropped him off at the next port."

"You saw this with your own eyes?" asked Jon.

"Jon, what are you on about?"

"Never mind," he replied, spying Tom coming towards them. The first mate held a bundle in his hands. Excited, Jon smiled.

Tom stopped before them and creased his forehead at Katherine after a quick glance at Jon.

"I only did it because Jon asked," he muttered and held out the lumpy sack to Katherine.

Her eyes widened, and she opened it awkwardly, pulling out what Tom had made for her.

Jon grinned wide. It wasn't pretty, but it was definitely an arm. It had a long leather tube with buckled straps on one end, a jointed elbow, and wooden forearm that ended in a lifelike carved hand. Jon could see a leather thong running along its side that disappeared into a hole in the wrist.

Katherine seemed not to understand what she was looking at, so Tom took it back and held it up.

"This," he said impatiently, squeezing the leather cuff, "fits over yer damn stump. It'll probably be needin' somethin' to pad it, but... Do ye need me to put it on ye, or do ye think ye can handle that yerself?"

Katherine hastily pulled up her sleeve and undid the buckles that held her hook in place. It thumped to the deck, and Jon had to avert his eyes, sickened slightly by the sight of her stump. When he heard Tom swearing under his breath, he chanced a look and saw that he was adjusting the prosthetic. Mute, Katherine just watched as Tom lifted her arm to tighten the straps. Her eyes were bright, and her expression was one of sheer amazement.

"All righty... See this?" Tom said, tapping a bolt on the outside of the hinged wooden elbow. "This'll tighten or loosen the joint here. Ye can keep it bent, or ye can keep it straight. Whatever yer little heart desires." The first mate crooked the elbow and twisted the bolt so that it stayed bent. Then he showed them that the wrist swivelled a few degrees. Finally, Katherine's grin widened in disbelief when he demonstrated that the fingers were jointed and that pulling the leather thong would curl them in.

Jon whistled under his breath.

"Tom, that is fantastic," he said. Tom's eyes flicked to him, and Jon could see that beneath his gruff, impatient demeanour, he seemed a little flustered.

"Uh... And ye'll have to hold the end of the cord with yer teeth for a sec—bloody sorry 'bout that, couldn't think of better—and so when ye push in this here"—he pointed to a metal clasp on the outside of the wrist—"it'll keep the grip locked in. So ye can hold... somethin'."

Blinking rapidly to try to dry the tears that rose in her eyes, Katherine let out a small, choked laugh and threw her good arm around Tom to pull him in for a tight hug.

Jon swiped at his own eyes, laughing at the look on Tom's face. The first mate looked startled, and there was a flush in his tanned face. He patted Katherine's back hesitantly a few times and glanced at Jon.

Bloody hells.

"Weren't my idea, love," Tom mumbled. "Was Jon that asked fer it."

Katherine pulled back, her dark eyes amused. Before the scowling first mate had a chance to step away, she pecked a quick kiss on his cheek.

"Thank you," she said, smiling. "Really. Thank you for putting so much thought into it. I didn't realize you were so talented. It's really amazing… I've never seen anything like it."

Tom grunted and looked down, scratching the back of his neck.

"You really outdid yourself," said Jon before turning to Katherine. "Seriously, I asked him for something simple. He designed it himself."

"All right!" growled the first mate, crossing his arms. "Enough already. So I'm the cock of the bloody walk. I get it." Despite his words, Jon had never seen him look so proud of himself.

"Come on, lads," said Katherine with a laugh. "Let's go see if I can hold a tankard of ale in this thing!"

She took off towards the hatch with a strut in her step that Jon hadn't seen in a while.

Finally letting his face settle into a cocky grin, Tom slung his arm over Jon's shoulder.

"Ye heard the wench," he said with a wink. "I got a mighty thirst."

～

Tom leaned back against Jon's legs, a mug of slightly warm beer in his hand. They had taken out one of the low brass braziers and formed a circle around it with crates and barrels to sit on. Tom sat cross-legged on the deck, gazing into the fire. Soon they would have to light braziers all the bloody time to keep from freezing; thankfully, this night only needed a little warming, and the fire was there mostly for cheer. According to

Baltsaros, the north wasn't as brutally cold as the trip to the spires, but Tom would be happy if he never saw another fucking iceberg for the rest of his natural life.

He took another sip of beer and looked at Katherine sitting across the fire on the now-empty barrel of beer. She was holding a tankard awkwardly in her carved hand, but she was bloody holding it. Thinking about a jointed toy soldier he'd had as a boy, Tom saw how he could improve his design by making the wrist move in the other direction. When he lifted his eyes, he saw that Katherine was watching him. She held the mug a little higher and nodded to him with a tight-lipped smile. Hells, it looked like she was a little dewy in the eye region again. Tom just grinned and raised his own beer in salute. He had a feeling that they'd go back to razzing each other in the morning, but could be that a knife-edge would no longer be hidden in their taunts.

Bloody kind-hearted Jon, he thought with a smile.

"So the mate's talkin' nineteen t' the bloody dozen so's I can't understand a bloody word 'e's sayin'," laughed Harris, his face glowing in the firelight as he told his story. "Well, 'e's jus' pointin' to the bloody thing like 'e's wantin' it fer 'is own, but ev'ry time I ask t' see 'is bloody—"

"Shut it!" growled Tom, cutting Harris off. On alert, he held out his hand and sat up. He could have sworn he'd just heard something off port. Everyone was quiet as he listened hard. After a minute of not hearing anything further, Tom frowned. He looked across the fire at Baltsaros and saw that the man's hooded eyes were trained off in the same direction as the noise he'd heard. The captain turned back to him, concern etched on his face. Baltsaros rose to his feet and left the warm circle of light to peer off the port side.

"What is it?" whispered Jon.

"Thought I heard somethin' creak," Tom replied, getting to his knees. He'd had a fair bit to drink, and his balance was off as he lurched to his feet. He used Jon's shoulder to support himself.

"Stay here, love. Could be nothin'." He patted Jon's shoulder before making his way through the dark to the captain's side.

"I heard it too," said Baltsaros quietly when Tom stepped up.

Tom squinted into the distance, night-blind from staring into the fire. It hardly mattered though; there was only the barest sliver of a moon left, and with the scattering of clouds above, the night was rendered almost pitch-black. A few minutes passed, and Tom was about to return to Jon's side when he caught sight of something darker than the sky around it. A second later, he heard another creak. There was a ship sailing less than a quarter league away from them.

"Cock and bloody fuckin' balls, where in the bloody hells did that come from?" he said, pointing. The captain followed the first mate's finger and leaned further over the gunwale, looking at the ship.

"It's completely dark," murmured Baltsaros. "Could be abandoned, just moving along in the same wind as us. You and I both have seen that happen in the past."

"Aye, and could be that they've snuck up on us," rumbled Tom. He had to hold onto a line of rigging to keep from swaying from drink. Great bloody time to run into trouble.

"I'm going up top to take a better look," said the captain. Tom nodded and followed him up the port staircase to the quarterdeck. Malik was behind the wheel, looking a little sleepy and bored in the lantern light.

"What's going on?" he asked with a yawn.

"We're being shadowed by a ship," replied the captain, taking his binoculars from the shipwright.

"What? Where?" asked Malik, glancing around.

"Port. Look between the shrouds and the last gun," said Tom, pointing.

Malik peered off into the night.

"I don't see anything."

"It's there," said the captain in a quiet voice. "Three masts. I'd say twice the size of us. Looks like a frigate." He passed the binoculars over to Tom.

Tom lifted them to his eyes and nodded. He could just make out the masts by starlight.

"Shit. If they ain't friendly, we're in a lick o' trouble, I'd say," he muttered.

"That's if it's not a ghost ship."

Tom was about to lower the binoculars when he saw a glint of light from the other ship. At first he took it to be a window-glass reflection of their own burning brazier, but when he saw the flicker again, he recognized it for what it was.

"*Guns!*" he roared. He grabbed the captain's arm to pull him away from the side and throw him to the deck. The double boom of cannons rang out only a breath before the ship shuddered and the air exploded in a shower of wood splinters. Below, the men yelled out in surprise. Tom didn't hear any shrieks of agony—that was a good sign. Buzzing adrenaline had wiped the alcohol out of his system; his mind was racing but clear. When he got up on one knee, he saw that a cannonball had taken out part of the railing that ringed the quarterdeck. Another volley could hit them at any moment. Tom glanced at the captain who had also risen to his knees. With a tight nod to his first mate, Baltsaros got to his feet and ran towards the wheel; Tom knew what to do. He skipped the stairs, jumping over the railing to land easily on the deck below.

"Douse the lights! Brace hard to port!" he shouted and then pointed to the metal fire pit as a few men sprinted quickly to extinguish lanterns. "Harris! Give a hand." Harris bent low with Tom, and they each grabbed a side of the brazier. The first mate gasped as the handle seared his flesh, but they both ran the few steps to the side of the ship to toss it overboard. They couldn't take a chance that the bucket of water they kept at the fire's side would be ample enough to put it out immediately, and the resulting smoke billowing above them was sure to catch what little moonlight there was.

Blowing on his smarting hand, Tom glanced up at the captain

just as the lantern above him was extinguished. The last image he had of Baltsaros was of teeth bared and eyes wild, straining hard to port to turn the ship starboard. He hoped that with the lads hauling the yard round to match, they'd turn smartly. The wind wasn't blowing hard, but it just might be enough.

Where is Jon?

As the thought crossed his mind, he heard the double boom again, but this time with a slight pause and the hint of a whistling before the deck bucked beneath his feet. He heard the crunch of wood and a scream. Praying that they hadn't been hit badly, he jogged towards the sound of mayhem.

Please, brothers of the sea and lords of the light and devils of the underworld, if you let us survive this bloody mess, I will be a better man and never steal from a temple again, and I'm sorry for some of the folks I've killed...

When Tom reached the bow, he could see nothing but dark shapes. He smelled blood.

"What happened?" he growled, pushing his way through the crowd.

"There be a hole, sir," said someone to his right. Tom recognized Hitch's voice. "Next to th' capstan. Ye'll be mindin' yer step. What I be thinkin' were a chain-shot aimed t' cripple us took a mate's leg clear off, poor craiter, before holin' the deck."

"Holed right through, ye think?" Tom asked, falling to his knees to search for the edges of the jagged breach in the wooden planks. He could hear someone moaning softly and wondered who had lost his leg.

It can't be Jon. He forced himself to pay attention to Hitch.

"Canae rightly say, sir," said the scrappy pirate, crouching next to Tom, "but it be darker than th' black hells, be damned. No hearin' any water below, though, and no leanin' yet. Feck... It'd be the luck o' the gods if we be spared."

Tom pressed his ear to the boards and listened for the telltale gurgle and surging sound of a ship pierced through. He heard nothing and heaved a quiet sigh. However, as he lifted his head, he heard another double cannon blast.

All the men seemed to hold their breath in the heartbeats that followed. Then, off the port side, they heard a loud splash and then another. Tom heard a few whispered prayers and some relieved laughter. They might be out of range, but they were far from safe. He slapped Hitch on the back, gave permission for light belowdecks as long as the portholes had their blackers on, and turned his attention to the man groaning on the deck. As he crawled to the side, his hand came down in what could only be blood.

Please don't be Jon.

He reached out and felt for the man's leg. When he touched the sharp edges of bone, he moved his hand higher.

"Mate?" he asked, wondering if the man was conscious; he'd gone quiet. A moment later, a moving light shone up from the hole in the deck—which was thankfully smaller than what he had feared—and was relieved to see that the man wasn't Jon but one of the new deckhands from Ereme'ia Balor. He was pale and sweaty in the dim light, and his eyes wandered as if he had lost his senses. Tom squinted at the wound. What was left of the man's calf was a mess of shattered bone fragments and clumps of flesh. He was bleeding badly; there was a steady torrent of red pouring into the hole made by the chain-shot.

"Someone get Cook," he shouted, pulling off his belt so he could make a tourniquet. However, as the words left his mouth, the skinny Balorian's breath started hitching in his chest, and he stared at the first mate with wide eyes. Tom recognized the look; Cook was a decent surgeon, but the lad was past saving.

The dying man clutched at the first mate's hand, and Tom squeezed back reassuringly.

"I'm sorry, mate," said Tom, shaking his head. "Ye weren't a pirate long, but ye did yer job well. I remember ye, and I'll find out what words to say over ye from yer friends so that yer gods can find ye—the good ones, anyway. Make yer peace, but don't go scared, mate. I'm here with ye." Tom had no idea whether the young man could hear him or even understand him, but he felt like someone should witness his passing. The poor bugger had come from a world away, only to die a bloody, dark, and grue-some death. After a few more gasps, each more ragged than the last, his hand went limp in Tom's. The first mate closed the young man's eyes and stood just as Cook came running.

"He died well," said Tom, wiping his bloody hands on his trousers. "Now get him out o' the fuckin' way, and be prepared for more o' the same if we can't outrun the bloody scoundrels before the sun comes up."

Cook nodded and gestured for the kitchen boy to help him haul the body out of the way.

With a look to the east where the sun would be rising in a few hours, Tom ran through the dark to aft and took the steps two at a time. There was a faint glow from a covered lantern set on the wooden boards by the captain's feet, and Tom was glad to see Jon standing by his side.

"Bloody hells, Da," swore Tom, his heart finally beginning to slow. Jon turned and gave Tom a quick hug.

"Oh gods, I am glad you're ok," said Jon. The back of the slighter man's shirt was damp with what Tom assumed was nervous sweat.

"Damage report," murmured Baltsaros, his eyes on the blind darkness ahead of them.

"Not much. Near the bow, we got a hole big enough to swallow a barrel sideways but doesn't look like we're takin' on water. Got the boys lookin' into it. One man down... one o' them lads from Balor," Tom replied.

The captain just nodded. Lit from below by the lantern, his face was all angles and planes. He resembled nothing so much as a demon from a fairy tale.

"Who are they?" asked Jon. "That was no warning shot across the bow."

"Blasted if I know, love," said Tom, looking over his shoulder as if the ship were looming right there in the dark. "There's no tellin'. With a frigate that size… could be navy or could be pirates. All's I know is that they're bloody sneaks and yellow curs to be firin' at us from the dark."

"Like you wouldn't do the same, given the chance."

Tom frowned at Jon. To his amazement, Jon winked.

"All righty, lad. Yer right," he smirked. However, he quickly sobered when he heard a shout. When it turned out only to be an update on the state of the hull—intact, thank the gods—he took a deep, calming breath. *Baal's Heart* could weather this if they managed to get far enough from their attackers, but they had to assume that the other ship had turned as well.

"Do we tack back to port, Da?" he asked quietly. Changing their course would help them lose the tail; the frigate was faster than they were and every effort counted.

The captain frowned in thought.

"We'll wait a little while before resuming our original course. At least then if we do run into them again, we'll still be under cover of night. Keep the lights low or covered for now, Tom. I'll let you know when to have the men square sails."

"Aye, Da."

As his sweat cooled and the adrenaline left his system, he realized he was holding his hand curled into a claw. When he closed his fist, he understood why. He squatted next to the lantern and held his palm out to the light. Under the dried blood there was a blister in the shape of the brazier's handle raised on both the heel of his hand and across his fingers. Tom swore under his breath; it wasn't bad, but he'd be favouring the other hand. Not great if they were boarded and had to fight.

Tom heard Jon let out a shaky breath and glanced up. The lad rubbed his face, looking weary and pale in the wan light. When a shudder ran through his slight frame, Tom stood in alarm.

"Are ye ok, love?" he asked, curling his good hand around the back of Jon's neck. His hair was wet, and Tom's hand came away bloody. "Bloody hells, yer hurt!"

"Hurt?" asked Jon, his voice vague. "I'm just a little cold. Unh

—" He teetered and collapsed against Tom. The first mate's pulse jumped and his guts twisted as Jon shivered. "I feel weird."

"What's wrong?" The captain's voice held a tinge of fear. Tom looked up and shook his head. Carefully, he examined Jon's neck and shoulders looking for a wound. When he found nothing, he slid his fingers along Jon's scalp.

"Why am I bleeding?" asked Jon, sounding a little scared. Tom's fingers came into contact with something small and hard sticking out of the back of Jon's head. "Ow! What is it?"

Tom frowned and felt around the edges of what he thought was a big splinter of wood embedded in Jon's scalp.

"Sliver o' wood, Jon. Ain't nothin'," he said lightly, dismayed by how much blood he felt in Jon's hair. Scalp wounds bled like the black devils; Tom didn't dare pull the splinter out. He lifted his eyes and met Baltsaros's.

"I'm gonna take him to Cook," he said quietly, knowing that the captain would want to stitch Jon up himself. However, the crew needed their captain, and Tom hoped that Baltsaros wouldn't let his fragile emotions get the better of him. He saw something cross the captain's stark face, but he just nodded quickly.

"Tell the men to square," said Baltsaros, his voice calm. "And return to me."

~

*J*on held his breath as the needle poked into him again. He could feel the catgut pull his skin, and it made his nausea from blood loss worse; he was afraid he was going to be sick. However, he closed his eyes tighter and took a few quick breaths through his nose, waiting for the next stitch to be tied.

Cook's hands smelled of onions, but he was gentle as he worked on Jon's wound.

"You are lucky, my boy," said Cook with a smile in his voice. "Any deeper and you might not have made it."

"Thanks, but I'd rather not think about that," muttered Jon. He couldn't help but let out a pained sound as the needle pierced him again.

"You should, Jon," replied the ship's cook. Jon felt the tension of the thread break when the catgut was cut with a knife. "You should take the time to really think about the near misses."

"I'd rather not dwell on my mortality, if it's all the same to you," replied Jon as he sat up slowly. The back of his head throbbed and the room spun in a lazy circle. He swallowed hard.

"Not *dwell*," said the Cook, his midlander accent so similar to Jon's. "But *face* them. It makes life that much more precious to know how close to death you've been. This is the third time, isn't it?"

"Third?"

"Third time you've been close to death... Hey, you know three's a special number, right?"

Jon's head swam.

Three is a magic number. Did you know that, Jon?

He licked his lips and tried to find his voice.

"Did you just hear a woman laughing?" he whispered, blinking at Cook. The tall, bald man shook his head, a worried look on his homely face. When he lifted a hand to touch Jon's forehead, Jon noticed the tattooed ring of stars around the man's wrist. The sound of his pulse was like a deep drum in his ears. He slid off the counter and stood shakily for a moment.

"Thank you," he said hoarsely. "I have to get back to the captain."

"Are you sure, Jon? Why don't you have a lie down?"

Jon pressed his lips together and shook his head before stumbling out of the room.

. . .

*C*ook frowned at the door, looking a little concerned that Jon wouldn't make it up the stairs by himself. With a shake of his head, he took up his knife and needle to dump them in the cleaning basin. As he was washing the blood from his hands, he paused as if in deep thought.

"Oh, that's right… It was four times, not three," he muttered to himself with a nod. "Poor kid's got the worst luck."

24

DEATH'S REAPER

We don't beat the reaper by living longer, we beat
the reaper by living well and living fully.

— RANDY PAUSCH

om eyed Jon and rolled his cheroot slowly between
thumb and finger before taking another deep drag on
it. The lad was pale and bug-eyed like he'd seen a ghost, and he
hugged himself so tight that his fingers dug into his biceps. Tom
didn't like the way his knuckles were turning white.

"Go lie down, Jon," he said quietly. "Yer hurt, and we ain't in
any pressin' danger. There ain't much ye can offer right now, 'cept
give me cause to worry about ye. Go on now while ye can."

Jon's lips were in a straight, bloodless line, and he shook his
head, strong jaw jutted slightly forward. However, he didn't offer
any explanation; he just stood there with a half-crazed look in
eyes gone to storm-grey in the lantern's meek glow. With a long
sigh, Tom gave up. He turned and lifted the lid to the bench and
dug around for the thick blanket they kept there. Jon let himself

be bundled up and pushed down on the wooden seat. Tom was a little unnerved by the tremble he felt go through Jon's body.

"What is it, love?"

Jon's gaze darted away.

"I know you don't believe in fate, but—" Jon answered at long last.

"Bloody hells! Yer on about this again?" groaned Tom. Jon was going to drive him crazy with all this blasted talk of fate. He wished he'd never let Jon out of his sight at the *Jewel*.

"On about what?" asked Baltsaros, returning from the stern with binoculars in hand.

"Jonny-boy here got his fortunes told by an old witch, and now he's seein' chance like it were writ in celestial bloody stone," replied Tom.

The captain's eyes widened ever so slightly, and he looked hard at Jon.

"Why didn't you mention this before?"

"Because everyone's been telling me that I'm stupid for believing it, but... it's... there's just too much... coincidence," replied Jon in a small voice. "Too much she said was true."

"Did she give you a dark prophesy of some sort?" asked Baltsaros with a tilt of his head.

Jon's forehead furrowed as he thought, his black brows pinched together over distant eyes.

"Not... no, not really. It was more that she knew my mind."

"There was no instruction in her words? No hint of what's to come?"

"Oh bloody hells, Da. Don't encourage him. Ye can't bloody *believe* in this malarkey?" growled Tom. Astounded by the sincere curiosity he heard in Baltsaros's voice, he looked from the captain to Jon and back. They ignored him.

"No. Just that I was at the centre of forces... And that we needed to mend the tapestry, which we *did*—" replied Jon.

"Tapestry?" Tom asked, confused. He rubbed a hand over his cropped hair.

"Well, not an *actual* tapestry... Fuck, it sounds so stupid to say it out loud." Jon hitched the blanket higher over his shoulder, looking uncomfortable. "Baltsaros, what are your thoughts on fate?"

The first mate watched the captain's face grow still, his eyes just shadows in his face. After a short silence, he spoke.

"Do you remember the conversation about fate we once had?" he said softly to Jon. "It feels like an eternity has passed since we sat at my table, and I offered you a place aboard my ship. I said you were a man unhappy with the cards fate had dealt to him, and you literally sneered at my use of the word."

Jon's brows quirked up at the memory, and Tom winced. *Cards.* Like Jon needed any more fodder for his fixation. However, Jon just let out a hoarse little laugh and nodded.

"Honestly, I can't tell you what my thoughts are on fate, Jon. I find it a strange, untenable theory that we are all on predetermined paths towards a fixed point. I don't like the thought of it; it *chafes*. However, at times, my mind is unsettled by chance and consequence that seem too fortuitous... And I find myself turning the idea of fate around in my head like a well-worn river rock between fingers," confessed the captain. He glanced at Tom and smiled at the look on his face. "But, one thing that I know is that it's not healthy to drive oneself to distraction with concepts that are beyond the reach of logic." The captain's tone took on a teasing edge. "It doesn't hurt to have an open mind, however."

With a grimace, Tom shook his head. Jon stared off to the side, seemingly lost in thought, but he seemed less troubled by whatever it is that had set him off earlier.

"I don't hold with none o' that shite," Tom muttered.

"I know you don't, which means you're the voice of reason right now," said Baltsaros, grinning.

Tom wrinkled his nose and let out a plume of cigar smoke before putting out his hand for the binoculars.

"I'll go see if we shook the scourge from our wake," he said, made uncomfortable by this talk of fate. He looked over his shoulder. "Sun's peepin' up." The night had lost its true darkness, and Tom could just make out the damaged quarterdeck railing to his left. The captain pressed the double-spyglass into his hand, and Tom left the others at the helm to go peer about in the early-morning gloom. He could hear Baltsaros and Jon talking quietly behind him as he swept the barely visible horizon. A haze of fog that came off the water obscured the line between sky and sea.

Tom didn't like the idea of fate... or religion for that matter. Then he thought of the little prayer he had uttered earlier and smirked. Well, he obviously didn't like religion until it suited him. He made another sweep of the water and pulled the binoculars away from his eyes when he saw nothing. The problem he had with fate was that it hinted of *something*, be it force or spirit, which had made the decision to rob him of his boyhood. That somehow he had been predestined to grow up a damaged man with strange desires. He ground his teeth together.

Fuck fate—he froze when he spotted something in the fog. Pulse skipping a frantic beat, Tom lifted the binoculars again and saw the prow of a ship emerge from the fog like a knife.

"Da!" he yelled. "We got trouble!"

The approach angle of the other ship meant that they had tacked towards them recently. They had probably changed course once they were too long in coming up to the *Heart*; they'd soon be in cannon range again. Tom heard Baltsaros's orders followed by Katherine's fainter shouts as she relayed them to the crew. It was all hands on deck to ready for attack as they turned starboard.

Tom wondered for the hundredth time why they had never built an aft gun deck below the captain's quarters. At least then they could fire at their pursuers without showing their flank to the fuckers. Going broadside was near suicide.

He stared hard at the approaching frigate and tried to make out their flag. When he saw the long, fanged skull with crossed cutlasses, he swore under his breath and ran back to the captain.

"It's Kriegaard and his Hounds," he spat. "Where he got his fuckin' hands on a fuckin' frigate..."

"Ah... damn," said Baltsaros softly. "I was hoping he was dead."

Jon's blue-grey eyes were wide in his pale face.

"Who's Kriegaard, and why does he want to kill us?"

"A bit o' bad business there, love," muttered Tom, locking eyes with the captain. "A year or so before you came aboard."

With a shake of his head, Baltsaros grimaced as he turned the wheel hard to port.

"He was a... ah... well, sort of a partner for a while, you could say; at the very least, we had regular dealings with him. I thought he had cheated us on a job, and I lost three men in the resulting knife fight aboard the *Heart*," said the captain quickly, holding the wheel steady. Tom glanced at the frigate that loomed large as they swung starboard. "We won the fight. I had his ship sunk in front of him and then threw him and his men overboard. Turns out that I had been wrong about the swindle, which is why we came looking for you and your talent, Jon. I really hate being wrong."

Tom smirked.

"Ye were wrong too about Kriegaard's visit to Davy Jones, it seems."

"Yes, well. Obviously, they were resourceful... that or we're facing a crew of demons. That's all I need: more blasted demons."

"We're about to be killed, and you're making jokes?" The blanket had dropped from around Jon's shoulders. Tom almost laughed at the look on Jon's face.

"Who says we're to be killed, lad? Have ye so little faith in our wee ship's guns?" said Tom with a grin.

However, as if fate had decided to make Tom eat his words, Katherine came running up the stairs just then, stopping halfway to shout that one of the starboard guns was cracked. Tom's guts twisted; they'd been meaning to replace the old cannon for a while. Why didn't anyone notice until they were about to be blown to smithereens that the damn thing was cracked and useless?

"Bloody... Fuck!" growled Tom through clenched teeth, all humour drained and replaced by a bleak anger. Or was it fear? He grabbed the nearest object, a metal cup, and threw it as far as he could. "Everythin' on this fuckin' old tub of a... Fuck! Why does everythin' have to fuckin' fall apart at the last bloody fuckin' cock-suckin' godsdamned—"

He was startled when Baltsaros grabbed him and pulled him so close their noses almost touched. Over Baltsaros's shoulder, Tom saw that Jon held the wheel, deep lines of worry on his face. The captain's fingers were cool on the back of Tom's neck, and his thumbs bracketed the first mate's cheeks; the chaos inside him stilled as Tom stared wide-eyed into Baltsaros's dark, unblinking gaze.

"Hush," murmured Baltsaros, his lips barely moving. "Stop your foolishness, my tomcat. Won't have you scaring the boy, or I'll have you over my knee." The captain's lips stretched into a slow grin, and Tom let out a huff of breath ending on a chuckle.

"Sorry, Da," he replied, the black waves receding in the distance. He found that the brown eyes he stared into held nothing but unguarded affection... and complete trust. The captain's smile softened as Tom straightened his shoulders and let the fear drain away. He could do this... He always had.

"There. That's better. Keep your head. Now, go!" Baltsaros pressed his lips to Tom's in a hard kiss before releasing him.

"Aye, aye, Captain!" shouted Tom, stepping back and offering a cheeky salute. Oh, they would probably die, but he'd die knowing Baltsaros's heart, and that warmed him like nothing else.

He grabbed Jon's arm and pulled him in for a quick hug.

"C'mon, love," he rumbled. "We've got a ship to sink."

～

*B*altsaros kept an eye on the frigate, pleased to see that with the jibs let out, the *Heart* had made a lot of headway while turning. If there was one thing he loved about the old ship, it was that though she would never be great in a storm, she came about swiftly and handled like a dream in calm waters.

Below him, the deck thrummed with activity as everyone made ready. The *Heart* had been in two battles under Romas and another two during Baltsaros's time as captain. The ship bore as many scars as he did. He smiled grimly. Was this the last one?

A fitting end to a turbulent history, he thought.

He heard the boom of one of the frigate's forward guns and watched as some chain-shot came spinning towards them, aimed high; the two half-balls connected by a length of chain was designed to take out masts and would cripple them if it hit true. However, it fell short of its mark and splashed into the sea. He heard Tom's bellow and felt the ship shudder with a twin thunderclap as they let loose with the two starboard 16-pounders, their only hope in reaching the other ship at this distance... A distance that was closing fast. A cheer went up when one of the cannonballs hit their mark. From this far away, it probably wouldn't punch through the deck, but it would bounce and wreak havoc as it made its way sternward. The captain hoped it would find flesh.

"Get some chain-shot in that beast's gullet, matey!" barked Tom above the shouts, pointing to one of the squat 8-pounders. As the *Heart* came broadside to the approaching ship, the cannon would be well placed to take down the foremast. The first mate turned and glanced back at the captain high on the quarterdeck. Baltsaros smiled and nodded once in approval.

"Let's give 'em all we got, lads!" roared the first mate, slapping the shoulder of the man next to him. With his earlier outburst quieted by Baltsaros's own sang-froid, Tom had recovered his usual mix of cockiness and equanimity in the face of danger. When he heard Tom let out a hearty laugh, Baltsaros chuckled to himself; he didn't doubt that the first mate's cock would be primed with lust from the excessive—and spectacularly diverting —addiction to adrenaline he suffered from.

The captain let out a slow breath and realized he was feeling more confident than he had any right to. They might fare badly in this, but it was no guarantee; the sea was a fickle mistress that could change the rules on them at a whim. He smiled; at least their speed was good.

Baltsaros corrected his course slightly, his hands tight on wooden handles worn with age. The one benefit of going broadside with the approaching ship was that they could fire all four guns at once.

Make that three guns, he corrected himself with a frown as he watched the other ship get closer.

Baltsaros scanned the deck quickly and saw that Jon was helping Katherine to preload muskets and pistols, including a few of the new blunderbusses they had found in the *Sabre's* holds. Jon lifted his eyes and looked at Baltsaros. The boy was pale and wide-eyed, but there was a resolute set to his jaw and his shoulders were squared. The captain nodded to him.

Good luck, Jon.

Then the young man he had kidnapped turned and yelled the order to take arms. Baltsaros felt his chest ache and his throat constrict strangely, but there was a smile on his lips. Perhaps he had lied to Jon about something after all.

❧

It was utter chaos as the dawn sky swirled with gun smoke, the air throbbing with cannon fire and the screams of the dying. A lucky shot had taken out the mainmast of the frigate, crippling her, but she had retaliated by punching holes in the side of the sleek corvette. *Baal's Heart* shuddered and creaked as she came about to try firing upon the other ship again.

Katherine reassured Jon that the hits to the hull had to be above water or else they would be listing by now, and Jon just nodded slowly, staring at the frigate with his heart pounding and throat dry. He could see part of the name painted on the side of it in big curling letters: *Reaper.* There had been something before that, but a cannonball had taken out most of the lettering when it had blasted through the hull.

D... Dead Reaper? Day Reaper? No... Day Reaper makes no sense.

"Jon?" Katherine smacked his shoulder, and he blinked, feeling dazed.

"What?"

"Give me a hand with these," she growled, pointing to the stack of grenadoes they were readying.

"A hand?" Jon's laugh had a hysterical edge to it as he looked at her wooden hand. They were all going to die.

He let out a yelp as Katherine grabbed him by the ear and twisted.

"Snap the fuck out of it, Jon!"

"I feel like I'm in a bad dream," he said, shoving her away. He rubbed his ear, wincing. The whole back of his head was throbbing. Jon turned his eyes back to the *Reaper*. It looked like they were turning to meet the frigate head-on. Orders were shouted; cannons belched fire, iron, and lead. Men cried out as pieces of them were torn away... It all came to Jon through a haze. Nothing felt quite real. The sea around the warring ships was full of floating debris, and Jon made himself stare at the arm that floated serenely between a barrel and a broken piece of wood. The wind shifted, and the grisly sight was obscured by grey, nostril-stinging smoke.

"I'm not made for this," he said. He glanced back at a sharp laugh from Katherine.

"No, you're not," she said with a kind smile and handed him one of the hollow iron spheres. She had a smear on one cheek, and escaped tendrils of dark hair played across her forehead, but her almond eyes were calm. "I don't think anyone is, Jon. You just have to grab whatever stones the gods granted you and try not to lose your fucking head. That's it. Now quit being a moon boy and fill those smokepots with shot."

Jon's hand stilled as he reached for the pouch of lead shot.

One eye open for visions. One eye closed for dreams.

"Moon boy?" he shouted over the salvo of cannon blast. He felt like he was going both crazy *and* deaf.

Katherine jammed the wooden fuse into the filled grenadoe held between her knees and nodded.

"Mooning about! Now get that filled and get ready to start lighting and tossing them as we come alongside that bitch!"

Jon felt the *Heart* lurch under his feet and swung around in time to see a second cannonball fly over the deck and bounce twice, leaving chewed up deck boards in its wake before blasting through the door to the captain's quarters.

"Fuck!" he yelled, scrambling to his feet. "Shouldn't we be raising the white flag now? Kat, why isn't the captain surrendering?"

"Ain't gonna happen, Jon," said Tom, clapping him hard in the centre of his back.

Jon spun and stared at the first mate. Tom had a cheroot wedged in the corner of his mouth, and his eyes were bright spots against his smoke-darkened face. There was a dripping line of red across one big pectoral, and the lower part of his right arm was dark with blood, but he was grinning.

"We're never going to win," stammered Jon, his guts turning to water. "Surely if we surrender…"

"They'll serve us tea an' bloody crumpets?" chuckled Tom grimly. "No. Ye never parlay when yer on the back foot, lovey."

Jon felt the boards beneath him shudder again. He thought he was going to be sick.

"I want ye to fire the smokepots quick as a wink and lob 'em over when we scrape by," said Tom with a glance at Baltsaros fighting with the wheel high on the quarterdeck. The first mate's expression faltered a moment, but he found his smile again as he looked at Jon. A big, rough hand squeezed Jon's shoulder. Though his lips were curved, there was deep sadness in Tom's ocean eyes.

"I bloody love ye, Jon," said the first mate.

Jon forced himself to laugh.

"Ok. Now you're *really* scaring me," he said. He'd meant it to sound bluff, but his voice sounded thin.

"Shit! Get down!" yelled Katherine, and Jon heard the belch of a cannon followed by a rapid *thwack thwack thwack* against the hull. More grapeshot. Not fired high enough to pass over top the gunwale nor hard enough to pierce through, thank the gods. Or so he thought until he turned and saw that Tom was staring down at a perfect, round hole in his side. Jon let out a devastated cry as it began to weep a thick fall of blood that followed the curve of Tom's hip and pooled along the waistband of his pants. Eyes wide, Tom clapped a hand over his wound.

"Fuck," he muttered to himself. "Bastards."

"Jon!" shouted Katherine. Jon turned in a daze and watched her pull in the leather cord to curl the fingers of her wooden hand around a burning brand. She held the cord in her teeth and jammed the clasp to keep the grasp in place before stooping to pick up one of the grenadoes. The wooden wick caught easily, and she awkwardly tossed the metal sphere left-handed. Jon blinked. The other ship was so close he thought he could reach over the side and touch it.

Tom let out a pained grunt beside him. He saw that the first mate held another grenadoe out. Things slowed to a crawl in his mind as he stared at the hollow iron ball filled with gunpowder and shot. Even terribly wounded, Tom held it together better than Jon did.

If you assume that you will die today, you drag death to you as a cold, unforgiving stranger. Instead, embrace death like an old friend, for you will fight side by side with her; and, if death decides to choose you as her champion, you may yet live to fight, and love, another day.

Jon blinked again. Suddenly the panic let go of his limbs, and he stooped to grab a smokepot of his own in one hand and a burning brand from the brazier in the other. Quickly, he lit both his and Tom's grenadoes and they threw them hard. Jon watched the arc of the two hand-bombs, Tom's flying a little lower than his, and smiled when they exploded on the deck of the *Reaper*.

A moment later, his world erupted in fire and splinters.

∼

*T*he four port cannons thundered one after the other. Baltsaros strained hard on the wheel, and men pulled at the braces to try to keep them from crashing into the *Reaper's* side as they passed so close. The captain could almost feel the cannon-balls punching through the hull of the other ship in the deafening sound of wood cracking. Above the roar, Baltsaros could hear men screaming. It was chaos aboard the frigate as explosion after explosion rocked the massive, crippled ship... Yet she still did not sink.

He glanced down at his own deck. Barely visible through the rising haze of smoke, he saw that every man not working a rope was lobbing grenadoes and firing flintlocks.

Or dragging away the dead. There were red streaks of blood across the worn boards to where bodies were piled up. Just dead things pushed to the side so they wouldn't get in the way of the living. He frowned and looked away. A cold hand wrapped its fingers around his heart at what he had glimpsed in the stack of corpses.

A tattooed arm. A mop of dark curls.

Baltsaros realized he was breathing quickly through his nose. Frigid seawater flooded his veins, and he smelled the tang of blood. Nothing could make him take a closer look at the bodies thrown aside on the deck. Water shimmered in his eyes as his jaw clenched; his hands had turned to claws on the wheel.

Weak, hissed the beast over his shoulder. He felt the leathery skin graze his back, cold as death through his coat as the beast curled around him. Baltsaros ignored it. Baring his teeth in a rictus of effort, he kept his footing and twisted the wheel further to counter the swell of waves buffeting the *Heart*.

Lost, it taunted him.

"Shut up," growled the captain under his breath. He had to remain in control.

"It's nice to see you're planning on returning my ship to me, nephew," said another voice to his left.

"*My* ship," Baltsaros whispered to the ghost at his side. He felt the familiar flutters of madness clouding his mind, and he shook his head to clear his vision.

"Don't you want to look below again? See what your folly has caused you?" chuckled Romas, his fleshy face pale as milk in the corner of the captain's eye. "Ah. I see. You want to hide from the fact that you've killed those poor lost boys. Oh, how they loved you! But that's what happens to those who do... You know that now don't you, Saros? Your parents. Your grandparents. Poor little Cassia! The way you carved her up. *Tsk.* Even Ol' Calum's gone because of you. They all die in your wake. Just like those boys below."

"Stop," mumbled the captain; his eyes closed for a moment before he remembered where he was. The yard swung, and he yelled out in a strangled voice for more slack in the jib.

"They loved you, and now they're dead," sneered Romas, his words finding all the little, stinging cracks in Baltsaros's stone heart. "How many more will die following you and your foolish crusades?"

"You died too, you bastard," growled Baltsaros, keeping his gaze focused on the choppy water ahead of the bow. They would come about and fire again at the now-listing frigate. "You held no love for me, only some sense of twisted *duty*, and I certainly held no love for you."

"Then why did you get on your knees and open your mouth so eagerly to me?" Romas paced behind him. Baltsaros could hear the way that the dead man's waterlogged boots squished as he walked.

"Fuck you," he whispered, shoving the loathsome memory aside. "Get off my ship."

"You'll be coming to see me soon enough, Saros," said his uncle, wet hands on Baltsaros's shoulders. He could hear the beast's hissing laugh. "You've doomed your entire crew..."

Baltsaros barely heard the cheer when it went up. He glanced around him in a daze, the ghost of Captain Romas gone. At first he thought the sounds of jubilation came from the other ship and that they had been holed through, but more happy shouts broke out and his brain finally registered that they came from *Baal's Heart*. When he saw who mounted the steps, he leaned his weight against the wheel, weak with relief.

"They've surrendered, Captain," said Jon, smiling. There was a cut under one eye that would need seeing to, and he was absolutely filthy, but he seemed intact. Jon's grin slowly faded. "Baltsaros?"

With a dry lick of his lips, the captain nodded.

"Tom is…?" Baltsaros asked, voice tight in his throat.

"Tom managed to attract a stray shot, but he's being a bull-headed idiot and acting like it's no worse than a hangnail," said Jon with a shrug. "You know, the usual. Kat says that he got lucky, and it went straight through. He also somehow managed to burn his hand pretty badly. Cook's patched him up for now, but I'm sure you're going to want to take a look after Tom's satisfied that the other ship's not just going to cut and run."

A parched swallow and another nod. Baltsaros lurched away from the wheel.

"Good," he muttered. "Jon, take the helm for the moment please. I have something to attend to in my quarters. Thank you."

He left Jon staring at him and nearly stumbled down the stairs in his haste to get to the stateroom. When he was confronted with the destroyed door, he stepped over it, scraping his hands on the jagged wood that jutted from the frame.

He nearly didn't make it to the basin before his stomach emptied itself. Leaning over the porcelain bowl, he shut his eyes and made himself breathe slowly lest he throw up a second time. Baltsaros waited until his shaking had subsided somewhat before straightening, and he pulled a handkerchief out of his pocket to wipe at his lips.

Jon and Tom were alive. The ship had not sunk.

Disquieted by his body's reaction to those two facts, he threw the embroidered hemp square over the mess in the basin to clean up later and rooted around in the bottom of the armoire for the bottle of aged rum he kept there. Eschewing a glass, he turned to sit and noticed for the first time that the long mahogany table lay in pieces on the hand-knotted silk carpet. He glanced around and spotted a hole at the back of the room. After taking a swig of rum, he squatted and peered through the hole. It seemed a cannonball had come in through the door and had taken out both the table and one of the chairs before exiting through the far wall. He sighed and stroked the worn boards.

"I'm sorry," he whispered. "I've not been very kind to you, have I?" Romas was right. Everything he held dear got hurt, including the old ship. With a sigh, he straightened and dragged a chair through the rubble so he could sit on it with his feet up on another. The second swallow of rum brought with it a delicious warmth as it settled his belly. After a moment, he furrowed his brow and lifted a hand to his cheek. It was wet.

"Da?" Tom's voice was hushed in worry.

"Baltsaros, are you ok?" asked Jon, stepping over the mess as he followed the first mate across the room.

The captain grimaced a little and lifted the bottle to his lips again.

"I don't know," he said finally. He looked up into two sets of blue eyes—one dark, one bright—and smiled sadly.

Tom crouched next to him with a low painful sound, his hand shielding the bandages on his side. Baltsaros reached out and ran his thumb over Tom's bottom lip. The first mate opened his mouth and licked at the wide pad. It was a sweet display of submission, and it made the captain smile. However, the concern in Tom's upturned eyes hadn't broken at the touch. Jon's hand came down gently on his shoulder and stroked to the crook of his neck. Baltsaros closed his eyes and sighed at the caress.

"As soon as we deal with all of this mess, I want you both aboard a jolly boat—Katherine too—and away from me. You can make it to the *Jewel* in less than three days from here and arrange passage back to Madierus. I've decided I won't be stopping at the southern peninsula to resupply; I'm sure there's enough in that bastard's hold to keep us in provisions for—"

"No," said Jon quietly. Baltsaros opened his eyes and looked up at the sombre young man.

"Jon, it's not up for discussion. I nearly led the two of you to your deaths before, and it looks like I'm doing it once again. I… just can't stomach the thought of it," he said wearily. Tom rubbed his stubbled cheek against Baltsaros's knuckles, and something twinged inside him at the thought of never seeing the clever, gorgeous brute again. He took a long pull from the bottle. Shouts came from outside the room as the pirates secured their prisoners. They would tether the ships together if the other one wasn't sinking.

"You don't get to make that decision," replied Jon, his fingers massaging the captain's shoulder softly. "I nearly lost my head out there today; I was absolutely terrified. Then something reminded me why I am here. This is my home, Baltsaros. *You* are my home. I've thought this many times, but *there is nowhere I would rather be.* It's here or nowhere. I think I'm speaking for the both of us."

Tom nodded mutely. Baltsaros could see the strain of his injury in the lines of the first mate's rugged face, but his eyes were wide and clear.

"I don't want to put you in danger," the captain said softly.

"Too late, old man," said Tom, smiling wide. He winced as he shifted his position slightly, and Baltsaros realized that he should really be seen to.

"Yeah, loving you is a real godsdamned hazard," Jon said, grinning. The cut beneath his eye had opened back up, and he bled freely.

Love.

Somewhere in the back of his mind, the beast chortled.

"You're going to follow a madman to your deaths," Baltsaros stated, but the rum had warmed his blood and he knew he had lost the argument.

"I'd rather die followin' a bleedin' madman than die a sad ol' bugger without ye," said Tom. "But"—he gasped in pain as he stood slowly—"please tell me ye'll hold onto yer senses long enough to stitch me up?"

Baltsaros laughed and nodded. He glanced around. They would need to use Cook's counter for a flat surface… if the galley had survived better than the stateroom.

"Oh, and, Da?"

The captain looked over at Tom. The first mate's face had gone grey, and Jon was holding him up. Barely.

"Yes?"

"Pass the rum?"

With a throaty chuckle, the captain passed the bottle over and helped Jon support Tom as they made their way out the destroyed door.

25

DEAD MEN TELL NO TALES

*T*he captain ran his hand along the banister as he made his way down the stairs, happy to see the crew busy with repairs. The results wouldn't be pretty, but hopefully the makeshift patches would hold until they made their way to a decent port where Malik could hire a few shipwrights to help finish the job. Baltsaros narrowed his eyes in thought. It definitely wouldn't hurt to careen her too so they could take a measure of the hull. The *Heart* hadn't been taken out of the water in years; there was no doubt that there was plenty to scrape from her bottom. Hells, maybe once they were shipshape, he would forget his foolish pursuit of vengeance. They could turn back south, and he would just try harder to embrace happiness and make himself learn to accept the peace that Jon and Tom had bought with blood and trust.

And love. Yes, he was a man loved, wasn't he?

The captain frowned at the men waiting for him on the deck. The four of them kneeled with their arms bound behind them, expressions ranging from outrage to terror. Kriegaard was on the far left, his one good eye watching Baltsaros warily as he stepped towards him. The northlander was almost as broad as he was tall, and though he was bald as a priest, a thick red beard fell halfway down his chest. Baltsaros could see the small bird skulls Kriegaard liked to braid into it and smiled; some things didn't change. When the captive pirate captain swivelled his head to watch him approach, Baltsaros saw that the dog-skull-with-cutlasses that flew aboard the *Death's Reaper* was embossed on his leather eye patch.

Baltsaros came to a stop in front of Kriegaard and stared hard at him. As he had told Jon, they had once been partners, often teaming up to take down the massive merchant galleons that came through the trade passage. However, when part of some treasure had come up missing, and Baltsaros had blamed Kriegaard, their partnership had ended.

Badly.

As it turned out, a week prior, half the valuables had been unloaded from the target ship in preparation for taking on some passengers midjourney—a change in cargo that had eluded the pirates' information source. No one, in the end, had been to blame.

"You tried to sink my ship," Baltsaros said softly.

Kriegaard laughed, the sound hollow.

"You sunk mine," growled the red-bearded pirate.

Baltsaros lifted his eyes to the frigate listing slightly to port off the bow. Kriegaard's previous ship had been a sloop of war, not that dissimilar to Baltsaros's corvette. It had sunk in only a few minutes.

"Where did you get your new one?" he asked. He was honestly curious.

"In a sea battle," replied the thickset captain. "Easy pickings."

Baltsaros's brows rose, and he turned to Jon.

"He's lying," said Jon with a small tilt of his head. In the bright sunlight, the swelling under his eye was mottled and ugly. Baltsaros had been as careful as he could with his stitching, but he knew Jon would always bear a scar. For that alone, Kriegaard would die.

"This again?" asked the bearded pirate, incredulous. "I'm not lying! You almost killed me over a mistake before. Don't you think you should—"

"Where did you get the ship?"

"Why in the hells do you care? But if you want the bleeding truth, I found it. All right?" huffed Kriegaard. "It was abandoned about a day's sail east from Sormaheine... along the rocky coast."

Baltsaros glanced at Jon who stood watching with deep creases between his dark brows. When he saw the captain's look, Jon pressed his lips together and nodded his head.

"That's better," said the captain, smiling.

"Now, will you let me and my men go? Let bygones be bygones? Come on, old friend," said Kriegaard, revealing a gold-capped front tooth as he grinned; the smile didn't touch his eyes. "For old times..."

"You tried to sink my ship," Baltsaros reiterated. "You *killed my men*. I should skin you alive for that." He placed a booted foot on Kriegaard's shoulder and shoved hard. The man landed on his side with a grunt, and as he squirmed on the floor trying to right himself, Baltsaros saw something around the pirate's wrist that strangled the breath from him. He stared at the jewelled cuff for a moment, then grabbed his sword. Pulse racing, he leaned over and severed the rope binding the man. He pulled Kriegaard's arm towards him, his fingers digging hard into the captive pirate's forearm.

"Where did you get this?" asked Baltsaros. The words were said very slowly, making absolutely sure that the man did not mishear him.

Kriegaard's eye went wide.

"It was on board the frigate," he replied. Perspiration beaded on his forehead, and his face grew red. "Really... It was just lying there. In a huge heap of treasure. Ow! Fucking hells, Saros!"

One glance at Jon showed the man was telling the truth; Baltsaros ignored the questioning look in Jon's eyes and turned back to his captive.

"Was there another one?" growled the captain. He twisted Kriegaard's wrist and was rewarded with a grunt of pain. "Was it a matched pair? Tell me."

"Why... Augh! Yes, godsdamnit!"

"Where is the other one now?"

"I don't know... Ow! Fuck!" howled Kriegaard. "I must have sold it with all the rest, you fucking lunatic!"

Baltsaros pulled hard on the man's wrist and twisted as he brought his curved sword down in a full swing. A shriek burst out of the bearded pirate as his arm was severed midforearm.

The captain stepped quickly back to avoid the arc of blood and stared down at what he held in his hands. There was nothing but stillness in Baltsaros for a moment, and then memories flooded through a breach caused by the sight of the big red jewel embedded in the bronze. He slid the bracelet off the limb and dropped the arm to the deck, barely registering Jon's nervous jump to avoid it.

In the background someone gibbered and wailed, but it was quiet in his mind.

"This was my father's," he said, turning the marriage band around in his hands. "See?" He lifted it up to the sun and pointed to the silhouette of a lion etched in the red spinel stone.

Jon nodded quickly, but his eyes returned to the man who bled and writhed on the deck. His face was pale behind the bruising.

"Oh, for..." Baltsaros muttered. He reached out and plucked one of the pistols from Jon's belt. He quickly cocked it to full, pointed it at Kriegaard's head, and fired. Baltsaros then handed the flintlock back to Jon and squeezed his shoulder gently. "Better?"

Jon stared at him in shock.

Such a soft touch.

"This was my father's," Baltsaros repeated with a frown. "My mother had a matching one."

Jon hesitantly accepted the bronze cuff and held it carefully as if it were the most precious of things. He was a little glassy-eyed and looked utterly confused.

"Oh, it's not worth anything to me, Jon. Maybe a little sentiment... But that's not what's important," the captain said, his excitement building. "My parents were wearing these marriage bands when they were killed... Don't you see: *these are trophies.* They have to be. Why else would they be kept in a set?" His mind reeled with theories and possibilities as he paced back and forth in front of his captives.

"You," he said, pointing to a dark-skinned man with a dirty bandana on his head. "Kriegaard said the ship was abandoned. For how long?" The man's eyes bugged, and he shook his head quickly.

"Sir, I don't know, sir," he stammered. He let out a long, burbling croak as Baltsaros's sword opened his throat. The next captive over was much more keen to find immediate answers to the captain's questions.

"No more than a day, Captain!" offered the young man. He had long, messy blond hair and dark-green eyes that sat a tiny bit too close together over a hawk nose. The effect was that it gave him a slightly birdlike cast. He looked up at Baltsaros eagerly, and the captain could see his pulse in the vein throbbing on his otherwise smooth forehead.

"How do you know that?"

"Perishables ain't had time to rot. I found a half-eaten bone that weren't covered in flies," chirped the young pirate, gaining confidence. "If you pardon my opinion, I think it were left guarded by a man or two and them were taken unawares-like."

Baltsaros reached out and stroked the boy's hair out of his eyes. The young captive didn't flinch from the captain's touch, choosing instead to lean into it. Baltsaros caught Jon's frown in his peripheral.

"What's your name, son?" he asked, letting his lips bow up slightly.

"Sten, sir," replied the blond boy with an overly friendly smile.

He was a canary trapped in a lion's claws, singing prettily in hopes of being let go.

"Well, Sten, you can tell me all about your theories," said the captain, his voice low and kind. "I'm interested."

Sten's eyes lit up, and he began to tell them about the burned and gutted villages they had encountered along the coast, about the signs of encampments that pointed to a roving band of barbarians, and about the giant musk bear tracks that were found all around the area where the ship was anchored. While he talked, Baltsaros gently smoothed back the boy's hair.

"So you think that the men guarding the ship went off to hunt the bear?" he asked quietly when Sten had finished speaking.

The blond boy nodded brightly, but his green eyes, despite being held wide in the semblance of innocence, were cagey.

"You're from the tiny islands near the mountain range in the north, are you not?" he asked Sten, guessing from his accent. The young pirate nodded again. "Do the children there sing songs about the blood ogres and their red hands?"

This time, Sten's smile held a touch of mockery. Baltsaros glanced over at Jon who was watching the exchange closely.

"You think them barbarians are the cannibals in the fairy-songs?" laughed Sten. He then winced as Baltsaros's fingers closed in a fist in his blond locks.

"I do. Now, since you've been so helpful, I will kill you swiftly and with little pain," said Baltsaros, baring his teeth as he raised his blade.

Sten went rigid in his grasp, his dark-green eyes so wide it was almost comical. Again, Baltsaros spared Jon a look and waited a moment.

"But–but I told you all I knows, Captain!" Sten stuttered, trying to pull his head free. "I can be more help to you. I swear it! I'll... I'll keep double watch... and watch you while you're sleeping. And... uh... and I'm a damned good cocksucker, sir. If you like that, I mean..." When he saw that his words had no effect on the captain, he tried to shift closer, licking his lips. "I'll show you. I'll suck your man's cock too, if it were to your like—"

Baltsaros's blade quickly severed his vocal chords, and there was an odd little warbling hiccup and a hiss before his neck was sliced far enough to end his life. At the moment of death, Sten had that startled, glazed look of stuffed birds with glass eyes. He let the boy fall to the boards and quickly dispatched the next man without a word.

Curious, he looked at Jon. His face was still pallid, but there was no recrimination in his eyes.

"Not angry at me?" asked Baltsaros.

Jon took a deep breath and glanced down at Sten's corpse.

"No," he said quietly as he watched two deckhands begin to drag the dead away.

Baltsaros approached Jon and reached down to tilt his head up.

"Why?" he asked with a smile.

"If we had spared his life and kept him aboard, he would have killed us in our sleep," replied Jon with the hint of a shrug. Then he curled his lip. "Or, if we had spared him to go free—" Jon rubbed at his mouth as if disgusted by the words he had to speak. "Baltsaros, that boy was a murderer and a rapist." The captain saw a shudder go through Jon's body, and he pulled him into a warm embrace. Jon's lips touched Baltsaros's neck as the older man buried his hands in his ebony curls.

"How do you know that, my clever boy?" he murmured, happy with the outcome of his demonstration.

"The way he talked about the corpses in the burned villages. The women... He got pleasure from seeing them... that way. What had been done to them. Baltsaros, I could *see* it in his words," said Jon, his warm breath rising to tickle Baltsaros's earlobe.

The captain nodded and held on tighter to Jon's slight frame.

"Did you believe me, my love, when I said that I was done killing the innocent?" he asked, resting his cheek on the crown of Jon's head.

"I think so," came the slow reply. A long pause. "If I had told you to spare that boy's life, would you have?"

"Yes," replied Baltsaros truthfully.

Jon pulled away to stare up into the captain's eyes, his expression serious.

"So I'm to be your moral compass?" he said after a few breaths. At the captain's nod, one corner of Jon's mouth quirked up momentarily, just a twitch. "And if I can't stop you?"

"That's what Tom is for," answered the captain, tugging gently on Jon's curls.

Jon's storm-grey eyes bore into Baltsaros a moment longer before he nodded once. He seemed sufficiently satisfied with the captain's answer.

Oh how you've changed, Baltsaros thought. But somehow, remarkably, Jon had retained much of his innocence; it had simply been altered a little to fit into the world he now lived. The captain wondered whether Jon realized that he had adapted without losing himself as he always feared.

Baltsaros stroked Jon's cheek with the ball of his thumb gently and returned his soft smile. Then he pulled away and looked down at his father's marriage band held tight by Jon.

"So you think the roving barbarians he described are the same bastards who destroyed your family?" asked Jon, handing it over.

"Oh, yes," breathed Baltsaros, his heart a steady thrum in his broad chest. He lifted the gem up to the sun again and stared at the etched lion. "We will find them, Jon. I can feel it."

∼

Jon supervised the loading of valuables from the *Reaper* into their own hold. True to the captain's word, there would be more than enough to sustain them for the trip north, so no stop would have to be made. Malik was busy repairing the hull as best as he could with some help, but all told, the *Heart* had fared reasonably well in the battle. The few holes here and there had been patched, and they would just make do where furnishings had been destroyed. He thought of the broken table in the captain's quarters. They had propped the pieces up on crates, and Jon was sure that Baltsaros was suffering a little due to the disorder in his normally elegantly appointed quarters. He smiled.

After waving at Harris to let the man know that they were done and he could start placing the charges around the frigate, Jon busied himself by tidying some newly acquired rope and waited for his crewmates.

When everyone was back aboard, and he felt had done his duty, Jon stood in the dying light of day and watched the lit grenadoes arc through the sky and explode on the *Reaper*'s deck. Within minutes, there was a lively fire burning. Then, as the fire began licking the kegs of gunpowder, Jon turned and walked away. A thunderous blast was followed by a second and then a third; even from this distance, Jon could feel the heat at his back. Jaw clenched, he made his way aft to the captain's quarters and tried to push from his mind the image of Kriegaard's men locked in the belly of the frigate, doomed to share the fiery fate of the blood ogres' ship.

2 6

TIED DOWN

om threw up his hands in frustration and lay back down on the bed as he was told, despite the fact that he thought Jon was being completely and totally fucking ridiculous.

"Bloody hells, Jon, I'm all right!" he groused. Being kept immobile was starting to make him downright tetchy.

"A metal ball went right through you. Don't act like it's nothing," said Jon, scowling as he dropped the cloth in the cooling bowl of water and deposited both on the sundered table.

"I've had worse, lad," said Tom, trying not to wince as he shifted to get more comfortable against the pillows propped up on the headboard. The wound had closed well, but it would take longer for his muscles to mend fully. He crossed his arms over his chest, and grey-blue eyes regarded him solemnly.

"How does that make *this* any better? You're still recovering, Tom. Stay the fuck in bed, or I will tie you to it," said Jon.

Tom let himself smile. It had been nearly three weeks since they had defeated that bilge rat Kriegaard, and he had seen very little in the way of action since then.

Jon saw the look on his face and shook his head.

"Don't be an idiot."

"Don't yerself, lovey. Shite... If Da says I'm fine, ain't that enough for ye? It's barely a flesh wound—no rot and pain's just fine. Ye don't need to be nursemaidin' me to bloody death, darlin'... I'm as right as rain," he laughed. "Bloody relax, Jon. Really. Yer scowl's gonna stick to ye."

With a sigh, Jon sat back down on the edge of the bed. He looked at his hands for a moment.

"I'm just... nervous," he said.

Tom sobered. They would be in Sormaheine in less than a week, and despite his assurances to Jon, Tom didn't know how well he would fare in a fight with bloody ogres. However, there was no point in worrying over it now. Could be they'd never find the bastards.

"Come 'ere," he said, crooking his finger at Jon. Jon hesitated for a second, but after a playful moue from Tom, he struck sails and gave in. He crawled further onto the bed and curled up against Tom's uninjured side.

Wrapping his arm around Jon's shoulder, Tom closed his eyes.

"Honestly, though, Jon..." he said quietly, trying to keep the smile out of his voice. "What's hurtin' me more than my bloody side are my balls. My hand to the gods."

Jon's laugh made Tom grin wider.

"You can't go more than a day without thinking of your cock, can you?"

Tom furrowed his brow and shook his head.

Another chuckle came from Jon, and to Tom's surprise, his fingers came skating over the first mate's stomach, featherlight. His fingertips skimmed the edge of the sheet that covered Tom from hip down before returning to tease at the fur line below his navel.

From weeks of doing nothing more than lying around, Tom felt as soft as milk pudding. He tensed his abdomen under Jon's touch a little, but it hurt like hells, so he let out a slow breath and willed himself to still and relax under the caress.

Tom had the same sort of pain when he tried to jerk off; he'd discovered that he couldn't keep from tensing right before he came, and it was driving him crazy. It wasn't the sort of pain he liked, and it stole the thunder right out of his pleasure every time. He felt like he hadn't had proper release since his injury.

As Jon's hand moved lower, Tom's abs tightened, almost of their own accord, and he grimaced again. Jon saw the look on his face and shook his head.

"Relax yourself completely," murmured Jon, sending little vibrations into Tom's cock as he scratched lightly at the sheet covering it. "Don't force it... Just let it happen."

"Mmm," said Tom with a smile, trying to hide his frustration. His cock throbbed as it swelled fuller, making the sheet dance under Jon's palm. He moved his hips a tad for more contact. However, the motion hurt, and he must have winced, because Jon noticed and took his hand away.

"I said relax, not 'hump my hand,'" said Jon, laughing.

Tom opened his eyes and wrinkled his brow.

"Love, I'm hurtin' here," he pleaded. "Don't stop."

"I'm going to stop every time you try to move. I want you relaxed. Completely limp," replied Jon. His hand hovered over the sheet.

With a cheeky grin, Tom put his arms behind his head and sank further down into the cushions carefully, spreading his legs a little wider.

"Oh, I don't think ye want me completely *limp*, ducky," he said with a wink. "Where's the bloody fun in that?"

Tom heard Baltsaros's boots, and he turned his head. The pirate captain's cheeks were ruddy with the chill night air, and his ashen hair was windswept. Tom smiled serenely when Baltsaros's dark eyes homed in on the outline of his erection.

"Am I interrupting something?" he asked, pulling the scarf from around his neck.

Tom looked to Jon. It was amazing that the lad had the capacity to blush after everything they'd been through.

"I'm trying to help Tom with his ridiculous needs," said Jon, trying to sound annoyed as he rested his hand on Tom's hard length. "His bellyaching is driving me crazy."

"It has been bad as of late, hasn't it?" said Baltsaros with a smile as he rid himself of his coat. He slung it over the back of one of the undamaged chairs before taking a seat on the mattress by Tom's side. "Still having the muscle pain issue?"

"Yes, but nothing I'm doing helps, it seems. He just ruts against my hand and hurts himself, then complains when I stop even though he's going to curse and swear when he's cumming in agony."

"He's too worked up to be patient and then tenses because it gives him some amount of control over his orgasm. I don't think it's entirely voluntary though. I could be wrong. If we had any *char* left, I would suggest using that to help him relax, but since we don't, we'll have to rely on other means of providing Tom with some pain-free release…"

Tom's cock pushed at Jon's hand again as they continued discussing him. For some reason, he liked it when they talked about him as if he wasn't there. It didn't make him feel invisible… No, it was more like he was a cherished belonging that they took great pains to care for. He closed his eyes again and breathed deep through his nose, startling when Baltsaros's mouth touched the rim of his ear.

"Lie down flat, Tom," said the captain, his voice soft.

Tom winced as he wriggled down further on the bed, but he made it onto his back and let out another slow breath. Despite all the kidding around, he really was trying to do what he was told and relax every muscle in his body.

Jon's hand touched his cock, and Tom concentrated on keeping still; he let out a little humming sound of pleasure as Jon squeezed and stroked him through the sheet. However, it wasn't long before he strained up and sent pain knifing through his side again. Jon's hand stilled.

"Fucking hells," griped Tom. The captain's fingers slipped

under his jaw and turned his head. Baltsaros's eyes were an opaque black, and he stared silently at Tom for a moment.

"If you can't be still on your own, I will force you to be still," he said softly. Baltsaros stood and walked to the foot of the bed to begin rummaging through the chest there. When he came back, he held a bundle of black rope in one hand.

"I was waiting for a special occasion," said Baltsaros as he placed the items on the bed. "But I suppose now is as good a time as any."

Tom felt a tingle of apprehension as he heard the undercurrent of the captain's words: they were close to their goal... How many special occasions did they have left to them with their fate unknown? With jaw clenched, Tom tried to settle his mind as he watched Baltsaros tug his shirt over his head. The sight of the captain's broad, furry chest made him grin however, and he threw his dark thoughts overboard.

Baltsaros sat back down next to Tom and showed him the rope. It was thinner than the red hemp one that Baltsaros normally used, and it had different texture to it.

"Silk. Strong and beautiful... I think you'll appreciate how it warms to the touch, almost like it's a living thing. Feel how soft it is." Baltsaros slowly swept the rope up Tom's chest and teased his nipples with the bundle. Tom let out an appreciative sigh as he felt his nipples harden, and Jon gave his cock a little squeeze. A moment later the sheet was folded back, exposing him to the cool air, and he shivered as two sets of hands stroked the length of his body slowly. He licked his lips and shut his eyes, letting himself float with the sensation. He was almost deliriously excited, and his heartbeat was a quick, hushed tempo in his ears.

Then, with extreme care, Jon helped Baltsaros to bind him.

Tom had always found it a mesmerising process. Baltsaros would first stroke the area he wished to cover softly with his palm or the pads of his fingers, as if to wake the skin and prepare it to take the rope. After he was satisfied with the placement, he would twist a knot and double back the length to begin anew. Sometimes, when Baltsaros was at his most cruel, he would place the knots directly over painful pressure spots. Other times, he would weave and wind the ropes around Tom in complex patterns, seemingly satisfied with just the aesthetic effect. He was usually bound in ways that exposed him entirely to Baltsaros's desires and for some reason that always calmed him completely. His rebellious soul, the true pain he rarely let surface, the memories that burned like a poison in his heart—all of it fell away when Baltsaros stripped him of control. It was like losing the fight but winning the battle; it was defeat and love and courage and *need*... Tom felt himself relax into it.

Binding was always done very quietly—the captain's voice only breaking the silence now and then to coax Tom into position or to soothe him into submission—but this time Baltsaros murmured of the past to Jon as he tied knots and slid the soft black rope over the first mate's sensitive skin.

~

*B*altsaros wiped a hand across his mouth and winced when his knuckles came away bloodied. Tom crouched, panting and sweaty, against the back wall, green fire in his eyes. It seemed that they had arrived at an impasse; submission didn't come easily to the ex-slave.

"Need I remind you that you came to *me*?" Baltsaros said, keeping his voice even.

"Aye," growled Tom. "But I ain't bloody doin' *that*." His hands were balled into fists, and every muscle in his naked body was tense. He looked furious... and terrified.

Baltsaros had had the younger man pinned against the wall, trembling and whimpering in conflicted pleasure as the captain alternated between choking and biting him. He'd been growling his own desires, driven mad by the ex-slave's rock hard erection against his own as he pressed himself against him. It had been going so well... until he forced Tom to face the wall and began to slide his cock against the younger man's ass.

Then the hells had completely broken loose.

Tom had effortlessly pulled out of the captain's grasp with a choked shout—his strength completely dwarfing Baltsaros's—and lashed out, leaving him reeling from a blow to the jaw.

Nostrils flared and eyes wide like a cornered cat, Tom waited for Baltsaros to retaliate. However, when the captain raised his hands and took a step back, Tom's brow creased in confusion.

"I'm not looking to harm you, Tom," Baltsaros said gently.

"Bullshite," spat Tom.

"You let me beat you, tear your flesh, make you bleed... Yet when I coax you to accept something that will bring you at least some measure of enjoyment, you run scared."

"Ain't scared." Tom's expression had gone sullen, but his eyes were guarded and closed off to the captain.

"Then submit to me."

"Listen, Captain... I'll suck yer fuckin' cock all nice, but yer never gonna stick it into me. Never," promised Tom. He straightened from his crouch, but his hands were still fisted, and he came no closer. Despite being free from his cage for well over half a year, Tom was still like a wild animal at times.

The thought gave Baltsaros an idea. He remembered the wild foal with the broken leg he had discovered in the woods behind the orphanage. Baltsaros had made it his goal to use the horse to practice his bone-setting and plastering skills. However, despite all of Baltsaros's best efforts, the wounded horse had reacted almost violently to his touch, hurting itself further. Sister Iezabel had witnessed his frustration and had suggested that he bind the creature up so it couldn't move. When Baltsaros did, he witnessed an incredible change in the foal as it was rendered completely immobile. At first, Baltsaros had wondered if it was frozen in terror, but when he saw that its breathing had slowed, and it looked at him with nothing but curiosity, he realized that binding the young horse had calmed it. It made some sense, given that was essentially what the nuns did by swaddling crying newborns.

Tom, however, was not a horse. It would have to be done with a little more consideration.

"Go on," he said to the naked young man. "I'm done with you. You're to spend the day helping the workers. I want this palace near finished before we set sail."

Before Tom stooped to retrieve his clothes, Baltsaros caught a glimmer of something in his eyes. He looked either bewildered or disappointed, but he couldn't be sure. It was frustrating being so inept at reading the emotions of others, and Baltsaros wished it were a skill he could learn. He feared it was simply beyond him; sometimes even the most blatant shifts of temperament managed to catch him completely by surprise. His relationship with the boy's mother was a good measure of that deficit.

He rubbed his sore jaw and turned away, deciding to give the youth some privacy and time to get himself back in hand. As he stepped through the outer door of his chambers, Baltsaros began to form a simple plan in his mind. First, he needed rope…

*T*wo weeks later, Baltsaros stood supervising the final pieces of the arched walkway being put into place. The graceful, fluted columns had been designed to resemble the architecture of his homelands, but he wondered if that had been a mistake. When he looked at them, it was like something scratched around inside his head. Memories. Memories of…

"They're gonna put water in the fountain this afternoon," said Tom. "I think that's the last thing. Well, that and the bloody fish."

Baltsaros laughed and nodded, the strange tickle in his mind gone. He reached out and rested his hand on Tom's broad shoulder. Pleased that Tom didn't shy from his touch, he gave a gentle squeeze.

"You did well, Tom," he said, trying to ignore the prickling sensation radiating down from his nape caused by the contact.

"Come have a drink with me? As a thank you?" He felt Tom's muscles tense under his palm at the words, and the burly young man looked at him apprehensively. Baltsaros hadn't pursued any sort of physical intimacy with Tom since the day he had taken a blow to the jaw—avoiding him altogether when he could—so he didn't blame him for being suspicious of his motives. However, after a moment, Tom bobbed his head and followed the captain to his tower.

When they stepped into Baltsaros's sitting room, Tom declined a seat with a gruff noise. Eyeing Tom thoughtfully, the captain handed him a cut-crystal tumbler of aged rum and watched as he mechanically lifted it to his lips. Baltsaros grinned wide as Tom's brows shot up. With a dazed expression, the ex-slave held up the rum to the light.

"That's bloody good, mate," breathed Tom, and he took another sip.

"I thought you'd like it," said Baltsaros. He settled back in his chair and put his feet up on the stool, crossing them at the ankle. "Feel free to have as much as you'd like."

The guarded look returned to Tom's eyes, but the captain left his expression neutral and looked away. Swirling his glass, he watched the dark amber liquid coat the inside of it. After a long stretch of silence, he heard Tom pour himself another measure of rum and sit down on a chair. At the creak of wood, Baltsaros lifted his head.

Tom's blue-green eyes regarded him shrewdly. He rubbed the side of his thumb along the line of his jaw slowly; Baltsaros could hear the scratch of his stubble.

"What are ye playin' at, Captain?" Tom asked finally, his voice a low rumble in his broad chest. "One day yer all grab-hands and wantin' to impale me on yer cock, the next yer treatin' me like I ain't nothin' but a bloody builder."

"I want you, Tom," said Baltsaros with a shrug. "And you're going to submit to me."

Tom barked out a humourless laugh before knocking back his

rum in one motion. He reached down, and Baltsaros saw that he had placed the bottle of dark rum on the carpet between his feet. After sloshing more into his glass, he held up the bottle with a quirk of one sandy eyebrow. The captain shook his head.

"So it's that simple, aye?" said Tom after he'd downed more rum.

Baltsaros nodded and took a small sip.

"And if I say no?"

"That's your prerogative. However, judging by the way you're burning through my rum, I would say that you're conflicted about your own desires."

Tom looked nervous, and he let out another hoarse laugh. But were the nerves tempered by excitement?

You're nowhere near as skittish as a colt...

"What do *you* want, Tom?" asked Baltsaros, watching him closely.

A look of pain flashed over the young man's face.

"Want?" Tom scrubbed the top of his head. "Ye know... Yer the first bloody person to ask me that question in a long fuckin' time."

Baltsaros waited.

Tom frowned into his glass. The captain thought he could detect a flush in his cheeks, but whether from drink or from something deeper, he couldn't tell. He tilted his head and decided to take a different approach.

"*Tell* me what you want." It was a command.

Ocean eyes narrowed, Tom stared at a spot over Baltsaros's shoulder for a moment.

"I ain't got a bloody clue what I want," he confessed.

Baltsaros changed tactics again.

"If I asked you to strip naked for me, would you do it knowing that it pleases me?"

There was the slightest hesitation before a mumbled reply.

"Aye, Cap'n."

"Good. Now... Do you *want* to strip naked for me?"

Tom's eyes darted to Baltsaros's. The captain remembered how hard it had been for Tom to admit to desire that very first time. The ex-slave licked his lips once, and Baltsaros realized that Tom was perspiring. He was sure that if he put his hand to Tom's chest, he would feel the heart racing beneath the thick slabs of muscle.

"Yes." It was barely a whisper.

"Then do it."

Over the next half hour, he asked Tom questions. Each one was answered with a quiet *yes* until the boy was kneeling, his lips red and wet from having Baltsaros's cock so far down his throat that he had choked tears. However, not once had he tried to pull away. Not once had he refused. Baltsaros smiled down at Tom and wiped at his bruised cheek with this thumb. Tom closed his eyes, his swollen cock held firmly in one scarred fist as he leaned into the moment of gentleness.

"If I asked to fuck you, would you do it knowing that it would greatly please me?"

"Not that."

"Why not, if you give the rest to me?"

"Can't," mumbled Tom.

"Because you're afraid I'm going to hurt you?"

Tom's eyes snapped open, and he stared up at Baltsaros, his brow wrinkled.

"Ye can't hurt me," he replied.

"Then why are you afraid?"

Instead of a response, Tom just gave a little headshake.

"So this is the only thing you won't do for me?"

Tom thought for a moment.

"Aye, Cap'n."

Baltsaros smiled.

"Ok. Come with me," he said and walked to the door to his bedchamber. Tom followed obediently.

"On the bed," said the captain, pointing. He rid himself of the rest of his clothing as he watched Tom climb hesitantly onto the bed to kneel near the close edge. Then Baltsaros took up the bundle of red hempen rope that he had dyed and braided with his own hands, and Tom's eyes went wide at the sight.

"Now wait a bloody second, mate," he said, backing up as Baltsaros approached.

"Trust me, Tom," murmured Baltsaros. "Lie down on your stomach and put your arms behind you."

"Like hells I will," growled Tom, but he didn't move away. Baltsaros quickly grabbed him by the throat and brought his lips close to Tom's.

"What? Is this another thing you won't do for me?"

Tom grunted when Baltsaros curled his hand around his cock and squeezed hard. The captain then traced the edge of the flared head with this thumb, letting the nail drag on the hot skin. It was enough to pull a hoarse moan from the big man's trapped throat. His cock wept a slick trail across Baltsaros's palm.

"Trust me."

He stroked Tom a few times and then reached for his testicles. Tom's eyes closed and a deep V appeared between his brows as Baltsaros fondled him gently.

"Obey me," he said in a soft voice and released Tom.

The sound that came from the naked young brute was barely a whimper. He looked so tormented that Baltsaros feared that he wouldn't submit. However, Tom dropped his shoulders in defeat and threw himself down on the bed. As he turned his face away from Baltsaros, he clasped his hands behind his back.

Baltsaros pressed his lips tightly together as his eyes swept over the twisting map of scars that covered Tom from shoulder to below his buttocks. It was a testament to his inner strength that he had made it out of slavery alive. He crawled onto the bed and stroked Tom's back softly. The thick ridges of scar tissue were a living landscape under Baltsaros's hand, and he frowned to himself.

He needed to secure the ex-slave's absolute trust; it had

become curiously important to him that he be the first man not to take Tom in rape.

To start, he simply wrapped the rope around Tom's wrists, not tying a knot just yet. Tom held himself rigid; Baltsaros could feel a tiny tremor go through his body as he looped another length of rope higher up his arms.

"You'll submit to me, Tom. Of your own free will."

Tom's noncommittal noise made Baltsaros shake his head. He reached between Tom's thighs, coaxing him to spread his legs so he could fondle his sack.

"Do you like that?"

Silence. He tightened his grip until he heard Tom's muffled cry.

"Do you like that?" he repeated a little louder.

Tom just nodded, and his back rose and fell with his rapid breathing.

Baltsaros then wove a few quick hitch knots to secure the loops in place and pulled, tightening the whole. Tom grunted, and Baltsaros realized how hard the first mate was trying to stay still and obey. Another slow stroke of Tom's sweat-damp skin was followed by a loop worked underneath Tom's chest to bind his arms in place.

Soon he had woven a net that extended from Tom's shoulders to his waist. It was tight but not enough to constrict Tom's lungs. In fact, as he worked, he noticed that Tom's breathing had slowed and he no longer held himself so stiffly.

However, when he moved down the bed to secure his ankles to the bedposts, Tom raised his head in alarm.

"What are ye doin'?" Tom's voice was strangled, and his cheeks were pink.

"I'm going to tie your legs open so that I have access to you without worrying that you're going to kick me in the head.

"Fuck you!" growled Tom, wresting his ankle out of Baltsaros's grasp.

The captain raised his hands in a gesture of surrender, hoping to calm Tom somewhat.

"I'm not taking anything from you that you won't freely give me," he said.

Tom dropped his head back down on the bed, and Baltsaros could hear a hissing sound as if Tom were breathing quickly through clenched teeth.

Brow furrowed, Baltsaros waited a moment.

"Tom? Do you trust me?"

"No. Fuck... yes? I don't bloody know, mate," grumbled Tom.

"What do you *want*?" Baltsaros reached again for Tom's ankle but just held it in his hand. "Tell me."

"To kick yer bloody teeth in," replied Tom, but he made no move to pull his leg away when Baltsaros slipped the rope around his ankle and bound it securely to the partially carved post.

"Really?" Baltsaros stroked his hand all the way up the back of Tom's thigh and then delivered a hard smack to his ass. "I don't think so."

Tom's breathing stilled for half a heartbeat, and Baltsaros smiled. He smacked him again, harder this time, and left his palm against the warming skin.

"That," whispered Tom raggedly against the coverlet.

"Hm?"

"I... I want *that*," replied Tom. Oh, what did it cost him to admit to these things?

"You want me to spank you?"

Nothing at first but then a stiff nod from Tom.

"Will you let me tie your other leg?"

Another nod and an audible sigh when Baltsaros pulled the rope tight and knotted it off. He slipped off the mattress and stood back to admire his work.

Tom lay in the center of the bed on his stomach, his arms bound to his torso, hands clasped above the cleft of his ass, and his legs spread wide. It was an impossibly delicious sight. He stroked his cock back to fullness, enjoying just looking at the immobilized young man on his bed.

"Where d'ye go?" asked Tom after a moment, lifting his head. When he saw that Baltsaros was touching himself, he let out a barely heard groan.

"Tell me what you want."

"Ye know that. Just said it, didnt'cha?"

"I just want to make absolutely sure," purred Baltsaros, taking a step closer regardless. There was a play of muscles in Tom's jaw and a deep frown before he let his head sink back down.

"I want ye to come lay yer bloody hands on me. Spank me if ye like… but make me *feel* somethin', Da."

Baltsaros nearly laughed with astonishment at being called "Da", but the gruff honesty of Tom's words merited a more composed reaction. He climbed up onto the bed again and began to strategically lay down strikes across the back of Tom's thighs and buttocks, making sure to cover the same areas again and again. Tom writhed against the bed, his groans getting louder the longer Baltsaros hit him. By the time the captain tired, Tom had almost dissolved into the mattress; there wasn't a shred of tension left in his body.

The captain stroked Tom's heated skin and let his fingers slide along Tom's softly furred cleft. Unfortunately, this had him go rigid once more, and Baltsaros stilled his hand. His brows rose in surprise when Tom shook his head.

"No… Don't stop," Tom said with a tight smile as he looked over his shoulder. "This is fuckin' stupid, but I wanna trust ye."

"Good," Baltsaros replied and moved his fingers lower, ghosting Tom's hole before he began a slow massage of the area between it and his testicles. The other hand he worked beneath Tom's body and found his cock hard and leaking. It was frankly astonishing how much pleasure Tom derived from pain.

"Don't!" gasped Tom, trying to move out of his grasp. "Too close."

Chuckling, Baltsaros just tightened his hold but didn't move his hand. The first night Tom had stolen into his bed, the boy had ejaculated almost as soon as he was touched. Tom would need to learn a little discipline, but for the moment the captain felt charmed that he could bring him so close so quickly. He brought the fingers of his other hand to his mouth and wet two of them. He gently worked them into Tom and his gasp brought more blood to Baltsaros's cock. As he began to steadily stroke his fingers over Tom's prostate, the sounds that came out of the bound man became shamelessly eager.

He closed his eyes, relishing the subtle movements of Tom's hips as he fucked him with his fingers. Tom let out a long, low moan and Baltsaros stopped and pulled away.

"Not yet. Soon, but not yet. I want to fuck you first," he murmured with a little smile. "You're going to let me fuck you now, aren't you?" He saw that Tom's face was completely flushed, and his brows were pinched together. Breath hitching in his throat, Tom licked his lips.

"Fuck," he croaked. "Gods."

Baltsaros left Tom on the bed to grab the bottle of oil off the nearby table.

"Yer a right bastard, ye know that?" Tom laughed breathlessly. "Ye've got me near beggin' for yer cock in my arse when I said ye'd never have me."

"I've been told I can be rather persuasive."

"Bloody hells," swore Tom as Baltsaros slid his oiled fingers back into his ass. He was panting like he had run a mile.

When Baltsaros had finished slicking his cock and began to rub the head of it slowly over Tom's puckered hole, Tom tensed again with a whimper. The captain stopped moving.

"No. No, don't fuckin' stop, ye bastard. Don't ye fuckin' stop," growled Tom through clenched teeth.

"You want this?" asked the captain, his own breathing a little uneven.

"Yes, fuck," snarled Tom.

Baltsaros pushed against Tom, not hard enough to penetrate,

just to tease. Tom's buttocks flexed, and he let out a soft cry, shifting his hips. Smiling, Baltsaros realized that Tom was trying to move towards him, not away. Then, a string of choked, frustrated-sounding curses burst from Tom, followed by a harsh laugh.

"Fine. Ye bloody win, Da. *Fuck me*. Is that what yer waitin' to hear?" he said, twisting his head to look back at Baltsaros. "Just bloody fuck me. *Please*." The captain was almost startled by the fervid, furious passion he saw in Tom's gorgeous eyes. He didn't hesitate or tease, but obeyed Tom immediately and slid himself deep, groaning when Tom's body yielded to him so easily.

⁓

"That's definitely not how I imagined it happening," murmured Jon. His heart was forcing a stutter in his breathing, and the blood pounded in his ears. Tom and Baltsaros shared a look before turning to Jon; they both looked a little amused.

"How so?" asked Baltsaros, sitting back on his heels. His hand strayed, as if of its own volition, to rest on Tom's thigh.

Jon scratched the back of his head and lifted one shoulder in a shrug.

"I... thought it would be more... I mean, I didn't think it would be so..." He stumbled over the words he wanted to say: *I thought it would be more like abuse*. Instead, the scene that Baltsaros had described surprised him with its warmth of mutual desire, acted out under a guise of unwilling submission to allow Tom to confront his own fears.

"So considerate?" said the captain, his stark brow held high. "What kind of a monster do you think I am?" The last was said a little playfully, and Jon felt his face get hot.

"Like I said, Tom is not a horse. However, he did need a little... ah... *gentle* breaking," said Baltsaros, looking over fondly at his first mate.

Tom smirked and rolled his eyes.

"Right, right... enough about what a fuckin' bleedin' heart Da is. My cock's feelin' slighted, Jon. I think ye might just be able to make it up by givin' it a kiss."

Jon glanced at Baltsaros and the captain gave him a little nod. Tom was trussed up on his back with his arms over his head and secured to a pin in the carved headboard. His chest was bound by a radiating pattern of knots that avoided the healing wound at his side, and one leg was straight with the ankle of the other leg tied to the knee. What Jon had realized as the captain wound the rope around Tom, sharing the origins of their relationship, was that when he had said he would *force* Tom to be still, it had little to do with how immobilised the first mate actually was. Tom could still move if he wanted to; it wasn't as if he was tied down to the mattress. It was just a symbol... a way for Tom to release control of his body. Jon smiled and leaned forward to place kisses on Tom's inner thigh between the lengths of rope.

The first mate remained completely still, held that way by nothing more than Baltsaros's will. When Jon licked gently at the root of his cock, Tom gave a muffled groan. Looking up, he saw that Baltsaros was kissing Tom with gentle passion. Jon let out a soft sigh... No, he was no longer jealous nor did he feel like an intruder. They had needed him to get to this point in their relationship; in a way, Jon was responsible for this.

It made him happy.

Opening his lips over Tom's cockhead, he closed his eyes, working his tongue in lazy circles and prodding the tip of it against the bundle of nerves beneath the smooth, swollen glans. Despite the low noises that seemed to sigh out of Tom with every slow breath, the captain stopped Jon every time Tom started to tense up. The first mate's cock throbbed taut and hard in Jon's mouth; the constant slow seep of precum was testament to how close he was to release, kept on the edge by his body's inability to remain limp. At one point, Jon heard Baltsaros whisper "breathe" and Tom let out what sounded like a sob. Jon reached up and rested his hand against the first mate's chest—just a reassuring touch as he worked his mouth faster over Tom's cock. The first mate's balls were huddled tight against his palm.

So close. Just fall into it, he thought. Tom exhaled a shuddering sigh. *You can do it.*

Then, Tom let out a startled-sounding cry and his cock bucked in Jon's mouth. As the first surge of cum hit the back of Jon's throat, Tom's moan grew louder as if he were pouring all the pent-up energy from keeping his muscles loose into his voice. Jon swallowed, milking Tom's cock quickly with the other hand. When Tom finally let out one last hoarse groan, his cock spent, Jon lifted his head. The first mate's eyes were closed, and he breathed jaggedly, but his lips were curled in a serene, blissed-out smile.

"That wasn't so hard, was it?" said Jon, grinning.

A soft *Mmm* was the only reply.

Jon turned in time to see Baltsaros's bleak look before his features composed themselves. Ever since the discovery of the bracelet, the captain's mood had been odd, and it made Jon worry about what would happen if they found no trace of the barbarian horde. Would he be able to let go?

Baltsaros gestured to Jon to help him untie Tom, and Jon set to work, praying to fate that whatever they found in Sormaheine would give the captain piece of mind.

At the expense of yours? asked a dark little voice in his head. With a frown, Jon pulled another knot loose and tried not to think of sacrifice.

27

BROKEN THINGS

Do not be too hard, lest you be broken; do not be
too soft, lest you be squeezed.

— ALI IBN ABI TALIB

*J*on stared up at the rolling green hills to either side of
the ship as they sailed slowly into the natural
harbour. He'd been expecting snow, not short scrub
grass dotted with black boulders and long-stemmed pink wild-
flowers blowing in the chilly breeze.

It was summertime in Sormaheine.

With a hand on the wheel, Jon watched the crew heave to in
preparation for dropping anchor. When the mainsails and fore-
sails were pulled in opposite positions to counter the drive of the
wind, Jon lashed the wheel in place. A flock of gulls arrived to
dive and whirl above the ship, crying their harsh calls to one
another as they searched for something to eat. They were almost
twice the size of gulls from the midland isles, and despite the
overall bleakness of his time there, the sight treated him to some
unexpected nostalgia about growing up in a port town.

A memory came to him, and he quickly searched the coast, curious to see who was watching the ship approach. High above on the hill to his left stood a young man tending a small herd of broad-antlered deer. With his arms crossed over his slim chest and his dark hair blowing in the wind, he could have been Jon that day on the hillside, looking down at the sleek pirate ship docking in the Portsmouth harbour.

He startled at a touch on his shoulder and looked over at the captain.

"Is something wrong?" Baltsaros asked, concern narrowing his dark-brown eyes; Jon could see the flecks of gold in them that only made an appearance when the sun was bright.

He shook his head with a wry smile.

"Nah. I was just remembering the first time I saw you," he replied.

"Oh?" Baltsaros's gaze softened in amusement. "At the brothel?"

"No, before. When I watched the ship come in. You know, I could swear that you looked straight up at me that day," said Jon. After his capture, knowing that he'd been the sole purpose for the pirate ship's stop in Portsmouth, he'd often wondered whether the captain had actually seen and recognized him that day. "Did you know it was me?"

Baltsaros's smooth brow crinkled.

"How would I know it was you? I didn't have a description of your appearance, only of your talents of observation." He finished wrapping up his binoculars and placed them in the leather sack he had been filling.

"Oh," Jon said. He pulled the neck of the dark-grey coat closed and shivered a little. Despite the dazzling sunshine and green hills, it felt barely above freezing. He frowned.

"What is it?" asked Baltsaros.

"It's just… I don't know how it is you knew of me." Jon glanced over at the captain. "It's not as if I was written about outside of Portsmouth… Was I?"

Baltsaros tilted his head; he looked startled.

"Tom never told you?" he asked.

"No," replied Jon. "He wouldn't give me a straight answer when I first came aboard, and it just sort of became unimportant." He laughed. "Fuck, bringing it up with him now would probably just get him teasing me about how it was fated because we're *brothers*. I know I'm seeing coincidences everywhere I look, but the fact that his mother knew my father... That one takes the cake."

"Jon," said Baltsaros with a smile. "Where do you think I got the information about you? Abetha knowing your father is no coincidence."

Jon's eyes widened.

"Wait, what? But the queen said it was," he said, confused.

"The queen also calls all of her maids Pesha because she can't be bothered to remember their names," replied Baltsaros, shaking his head. "Despite her efforts to appear sensitive to the needs of her servants, she is still the daughter of a lord who has been surrounded by these 'invisible' people her whole life. I'd be surprised if she even knew a single concrete detail about their private lives."

"And you do?"

"I listen," said the captain. He furrowed his brow at Jon. "A few months before I came looking for you, I was getting a horse saddled and overheard an interesting conversation between the old stable master and one of the grooms. It was about a boy who could see a lie in a man's words as easy as reading a book. Because of what happened with Kriegaard, it piqued my interest, so I asked a few questions.

"Jon, when Richard left, he kept correspondence with his father, Duncan—the old stable master that Abetha inherited from her father's estate. After your father's death, your mother wrote to Duncan to tell him of your birth. Because the old man liked hearing of you so much, they kept writing, and when your mother passed, her handmaiden kept it up, sending him news from time to time of your accomplishments and talents."

"Handmaiden?" Reeling from the news, Jon tried to think of who this handmaiden was. He could remember no one taking an avid interest in him.

Baltsaros frowned, thinking to himself.

"I believe she stayed on and became Lord Barton's cook," he said after a moment.

"Cook?" Jon asked numbly. The fat old woman with the checked apron was a far cry from what he imagined a hand-maiden to look like. Cook… who had always kept little things on the side for Jon, like apples and the mince tarts he liked so much. He breathed out slowly, trying to curb his mind's breakneck speed as it pulled up his every memory of the old woman at once. It was true—out of everyone in Barton's employ, Cook had always been the kindest to him. Regret flooded through Jon for never taking the time to get to know her better before… before…

Jon sat down hard on the bench. He was nauseous.

Before she was killed in the fire.

"Shit," he whispered.

"Jon?"

Jon looked up at the captain; his throat was completely dry.

"You killed her."

"Me?" Baltsaros looked confused. He sat down next to Jon, but made no attempt to reach for him.

"In the fire. She burned alive. Oh gods…"

"No one was in the fire that night save Reginald, a handful of guards, and Lord Barton," replied the captain with a slow shake of his head.

Jon stared at the captain, his mind stumbling over itself; he wasn't lying.

"You didn't kill them all?"

"Why in the name of the gods would I kill them all? What purpose would that have served?" Baltsaros asked. "Don't you remember me telling you that my men emptied the servants' hall?"

"I thought you were lying," Jon said in a weak voice. "I was sure of it."

"As I recall you weren't exactly at your best that day," said the captain with the hint of a smile. "And on top of what was a harrowing, exhausting day, I woke you up in the middle of the night to dazzle you with a rather grisly display of devotion. It doesn't surprise me that you assumed I was lying."

Jon slowly stroked the hollow of his cheek, absorbing this new information.

"Though I have to say, what I *am* surprised about is that you didn't make more of it, if you thought I murdered all those people," continued Baltsaros. He reached out and touched Jon's arm, and Jon moved to curl his fingers into the captain's hand. His soul felt a little lighter.

"You know strange things happen to my head when I'm with you," Jon said softly.

"And I've given you cause to doubt me, time and time again," said Baltsaros with a small nod. He squeezed Jon's hand. "All I can think of saying is that I'm sorry."

Feeling foolish, relieved, and bewildered all at once, Jon blew out his cheeks and sat back. In silence, the two of them watched the jolly boat being lowered over the side.

Something occurred to Jon and he turned to Baltsaros.

"I have a grandfather?" he asked hopefully.

"I'm afraid you don't," replied the captain, a tiny comma between his brows. "He died weeks before we even left the island. Nothing tragic… just old age. But, I can show you where he's buried if you'd like."

"Yeah. I'd like that," he replied. "But… Why didn't you think to tell me about him before?"

"What would you gain from learning you had yet another dead relative?"

The question was asked so guilelessly that Jon had to laugh despite everything.

"You know, sometimes I think you're not even a real human being... just a close approximation," he mused. "When you ask me questions like that, I begin to really question why you care so much about this vendetta you have."

~

"Why *do* you care, Baltsaros?" asked Abetha, leaning towards him in the shade of the orange trees.

The captain looked away from the steady blue-green eyes that reminded him so much of Tom and watched a pair of goldfinches play a sort of aerial leapfrog through the branches of a nearby tree. The story of his childhood trauma was now laid out end to end and made real by telling it out loud; it no longer burrowed like a poisonous black worm in his brain and for the first time since he had recalled that blood-soaked day, Baltsaros felt like he could take a step back from the events. It amazed him how much and how little he felt about it.

"Baltsaros?" Abetha thought she could help him, but even with all of her intelligence and the mounds of books she devoured on the subject of the human mind, Baltsaros knew there was a limit to what she could do for him. Healing would have to come from within; in the meantime he would humour her and wait for his boys to return to him. He pinched the bridge of his nose and turned back to the queen.

"Why do I care? My family was murdered. I was mentally and perhaps physically tortured. I let down my city," he said tiredly. "I murdered my sibling..."

"Yes, but you and I both know that you only care about one of those things."

Baltsaros let out a small laugh. Perhaps he had underestimated the queen's ability to see into him.

"Which do you think it is?" he asked, sitting back on the stone bench.

"When I look at you, I don't see sadness. I don't see shame. I don't see horror. I see *anger*," Abetha said, her voice hardened by her words. "Because they made you weak, didn't they? And you don't like being weak."

"No," agreed Baltsaros, feeling the heat of his temper swell. "I don't like being weak."

~

"Why do I care?" said Baltsaros. "I could tell you that I want retribution for the wrongs done to my family and countrymen because a 'real human being' would want that, correct?"

Jon nodded, simultaneously fascinated and a little unnerved by the captain's complete candour. The mask had dropped, and Baltsaros's face was smooth and expressionless. He eyed Jon thoughtfully, studying his reaction to his words.

"I would be lying to you if I claimed those were my motivations, and I don't lie to you, Jon," said the captain. "No... I'm simply seeking redemption for the evils I have committed because of what was done to me. Those savages took something away from me that day and made me an accomplice to their depravity, then and during the life that I've led. I am done being a subordinate to this *canker* in my past. With their deaths, I take back what was stolen from me."

Baltsaros's dark eyes burned with emotion, and for one startling moment, Jon saw the man that lived within the beast. He blinked and the vision was gone, replaced by the charming smile Baltsaros wore to hide the broken things inside him. If anything, the captain looked a little rattled beneath his composed façade, and his hand trembled in Jon's.

"It's ok to be afraid," said Jon quietly, speaking to the lost soul within the broken man beside him.

"I'm not, Jon," replied Baltsaros, his voice a little curt.

Jon wanted to shake him, but instead he fisted a handful of the captain's coat and pulled him closer so he could put his arms around him. Baltsaros stiffened immediately from the abrupt contact but relaxed slowly as Jon's fingers threaded through his hair and tugged softly. The captain's lips found Jon's neck, and he breathed warm against his skin.

"It's ok to be scared," repeated Jon.

Baltsaros curled his arms around Jon, and he let out a long sigh as he hugged him tight.

Jon closed his eyes, praying that Baltsaros would find whatever it was that he was looking for and that it didn't cost them too much.

~

Tom mounted the stairs a little stiffly. The wound on his side was still raw-looking, both front and back, but he was already regaining muscle strength. However, it would be a while before he was completely healed. Baltsaros had voiced his concerns that he might have permanently lost some flexibility on that side, and he was still in some amount of pain, but he shrugged it off like he did most injuries. If fate was kind and he made it to old age, there would be plenty of time to complain then. The image of himself as a broken, crotchety old man made Tom smirk.

At the top of the quarterdeck staircase, he paused, dismayed by the fact that he was interrupting what looked like a quiet, private moment between Jon and the captain. On hearing Tom's tread, Jon lifted his head, and the first mate frowned at the worry in his storm-grey eyes. However, Jon simply nodded at him.

It's ok.

Tom stepped forward as the captain pulled away from Jon. He wondered what he had missed; Baltsaros's smile was a little strained.

"Da, there's folks linin' up on the beach," said the first mate. He looked over his shoulder. "Friend or foe, I can't tell." A few minutes prior, the usual fishermen and beggarly idlers that seemed to be universal fixtures at harbours the world over had been joined by a group of officials protected by men holding pikes.

"Most likely they're just being cautious," said the captain, standing up. He reached for the leather sack he'd been packing and motioned for the two of them to follow. "They saw us coming from a long way off. You know, it's the same feature that drew me to Madierus when I found it: a natural harbour with the backdrop of a high hill so that intruders could be seen at least two leagues away. It's nice not to be caught unawares."

Tom quirked an eyebrow at Jon behind the captain's back. Baltsaros sounded odd, and he was worried that it meant the captain was on his way off the deep end again. The look Jon gave Tom in return pulled at his heartstrings; he seemed so afraid. Tom wished he could shield him from his own fears.

However, he had no time to lend Jon a little courage by giving him a quick cuddle or a teasing word. The captain, having regained his composure, ushered them with a brisk step to the ladder so they could board the jolly boat. As Tom carefully sat down on one of the planks that made up the seating, he scowled at the crewmen at the oars. Baltsaros had forbidden Tom from rowing until he was completely healed, and it made him feel like a bloody milksop.

"Stop making that face, Tom," laughed the captain. "You'll be back to yourself soon enough."

"Aye, Da," Tom muttered. He clasped his hands loosely between his knees and watched the shore approach. While normally the promise of a brutal fight got him raring to go, Tom felt nothing but the dull ache in his side and a deep weariness. He realized that, for the first time in his life, he'd rather let someone else do the fighting.

~

*T*om watched Baltsaros from the bed, legs crossed and elbows on his knees. He was still sore in a few places from a sparring-match-turned-fuck-session with the captain, and he tried not to wince as he shifted slightly. Across the room, Baltsaros was packing the cedar chest that contained the bulk of their clothing as well as a number of sundry personal items. When he saw the captain place a bundle of letters into the chest, Tom frowned.

"Why d'ye never tell me ye wrote to yer nun friend?" he asked.

Baltsaros gave Tom an amused look.

"I wouldn't count her as a friend, per se," he replied. "But why should you be privy to my correspondence? What, pray tell, could you possibly want with that information?"

Tom scratched at his stubble, slightly put out by the captain's teasing tone.

"I dunno. Just, dont'cha think it's somethin' ye could've mentioned? Like 'Hey, Tom, ye might not know this, but I been writin' to the woman who raised me, and oh, by the bloody way, I been also sendin' her a part o' my pay every year.' Aye?"

The captain smirked with a little headshake before he resumed his packing.

"Is it really that interesting? Do you want to know that I also hold correspondence with a number of others? Let's see... the management from the *Jewel*, certain merchants, the harbourmasters from the various ports we stop in every year, an ambassador from the lands to the east..."

"Yer not makin' yer bloody point, Da," replied Tom. "Ye've been writin' back to and fundin' yer homelands when I didn't even know ye had anyone there."

Baltsaros glanced over at Tom and an odd flicker of emotion passed over his face before he straightened.

"Speaking of mother figures..." He walked out of the room,

and Tom could hear him pulling open drawers. A moment later he came back and held a small packet out to Tom.

"What's this, then?" asked the first mate. The only thing on the brown wrapping was his name written in a neat hand.

"Your mother gave it to me to give to you. She apologizes for not being able to see us off today but offered no excuse."

Brow creased, Tom turned the package over and pulled apart the twine holding it together. Inside was a piece of folded paper, and his mother's perfume drifted off of it, giving Tom an unexpected pang. It was made worse when, on unfolding the paper, something dropped in his lap. Astounded, Tom picked it up and looked at it. Though carefully mended in a few places and obviously washed and ironed, it was the royal-blue silk handkerchief that he had stolen from his mother as a child. For a moment, he couldn't swallow for the thick lump in his throat.

"What is that?" asked Baltsaros, curious.

Tom crushed the handkerchief in his palm and lifted one shoulder in a shrug.

"Nothin' important," he lied. That Abetha had kept and clearly cherished the little square of silk… He blinked a few times and was glad when the captain went back to filling the chest. He flattened the note against his knee and read it.

Tom,

Here is something that I hope will make you realize how very difficult it has been for me to face the emotions and memories I had to bury deep in the heartrending months following your abduction. Please accept it as a peace offering and understand that I desire nothing more than to stop this fighting and find common ground with you. Maybe then, when we have trust between us, I will have earned the right to call you son.

— ABETHA

325

*J*aw clenched, Tom pushed himself off the bed, his vision a little blurred. Before the captain could ask him anything further, he shoved the note and the handkerchief into his trouser pocket and left the room quickly.

Bloody hells, he fumed, angry with himself for nearly breaking down over some sodding words. Walking fast with no destination in mind, Tom made his way through the palace and out through the garden exit, trying to get his heart to stop trying to squeeze itself to a pulp in his chest. After he turned past a shrub tortured into a wedge shape, he came to a stop suddenly at the sight of Saban sitting on one of the marble benches that seemed to litter the grounds like some form of infestation.

Startled by Tom's sudden appearance, Saban lurched to his feet. He wore a pair of dark-blue pants turned up at the calf and nothing else but a long, knotted strand of leather around his neck. From his time on the island, his already-dark skin had gone a deeper shade, and as he looked nervously at the first mate, Tom couldn't help but notice how the tan set off the green in his hazel eyes.

"Sorry, mate, I didn't mean to intrude," Tom said gruffly. They hadn't spoken a word since he'd fucked Jon in front of him.

"I was just leaving," replied Saban, looking away. He started to walk back towards the palace, but Tom grabbed his arm, wanting to try patching things up between them before he left. Baltsaros had mentioned Saban's request to join the crew of the *Sabre* in lieu of serving on the *Heart*; this was the last that they would see of each other for a long time, if ever. However, at Tom's touch, Saban swung around with a snarl and landed a punch to the first mate's solar plexus, knocking the wind out of him. As Tom struggled to breath, Saban stared at him, the savagery of his emotions distorting his handsome features.

"Don't you touch me!" he growled.

Tom coughed and managed to take in some air. He held his hand out, trying to shake off the pain.

"Fer bloody sakes, lad," he said hoarsely. "Why the fuck did ye hit me? I thought we were mates?"

"We're not. You're not very good at taking a hint, are you? I have no interest in continuing whatever the hells you think we were doing." There was no trace of the quiet self-assurance that normally radiated from the big man.

"Hey... Saban, yer overreacting, lovey," said Tom with a frown.

"How many times do I have to say it? We're not friends," said Saban, balling his hands into hard fists. "And stay the *fuck* away from me."

Tom started to get angry.

"What the fuck bit yer ass?" Saban took a step towards him, but Tom held his ground. "Listen, I'm fuckin' sorry 'bout what happened. Ok? But ye gotta admit that—"

"I don't have to admit to *anything*!" yelled Saban, jabbing at Tom's chest with his forefinger. "I told you! I am *not like you*. I don't like to fuck men. For Bal's sake... Get it through your thick skull! I am *nothing* like you, you fucking degenerate. In fact, you make me sick to my stomach." With the last of his words, he spat on the ground in front of Tom and said a few words that sounded like a curse in Balorian. Too dumbfounded by Saban's reaction to do anything but stare, he watched the big man stalk off angrily out of the garden.

A little while later, Baltsaros found Tom in the garden sitting on the stone bench Saban had vacated.

"There you are. I've been looking for you. It's time to leave," said the captain as he eyed the shrub that had been ripped from the ground. "Are you ok?"

"Aye," replied Tom, standing up. He curled his hands into fists so Baltsaros couldn't see his shredded palms.

"Are you sure?" asked Baltsaros.

Tom nodded.

"Let's get the fuck outta here, Da," he said with a forced smile. "I've had enough of this bloody depressin' place."

~

From his seat in the jolly boat, Tom watched the shore approach. As they neared the armed guards and the grim-faced looking bunch of officials, he groaned inwardly. He had the feeling that, seeing as Sormaheine was half-governed by a religious order, they'd have to play chaste, and he'd have to keep his hands off Jon. Burned him to no end what some folks thought was proper and not.

After rising to his feet with a small grimace of pain, Tom sighed and straightened his shoulders, hoping that whatever they found in Sormaheine, it didn't break things further.

28

SORMAHEINE

*J*on stood uncertainly on a beach made of round stones, trying to make out what was being said as Tom and the captain spoke rapidly with the delegation that had been sent to meet them. In front of a cadre of guards armed with tall bladed weapons, there were three men and two women dressed in tunics with geometric designs like the ones that Baltsaros sometimes wore. While they seemed friendly enough, so far the tenor of the exchange felt strained. With a silent sigh, Jon wished that he understood more than just the basics of the northern tongue; he let his eyes roam over the features of the strangers instead, hoping that he could pick up their intentions at the very least.

The Sormet, as the citizens were called, were very tall, men and women alike. They had the same sharp cheekbones and smooth, high forehead as the captain, as well as the slightly dusky cast to his skin. However, unlike the Balorian fisherfolk who all seemed to share the same hair and eye colour, the Sormet were as varied as any mid- or mainlander.

The woman at the centre of the group eyed Jon curiously as she spoke. She wore her silver hair pulled back tightly, making the planes of her face even more severe. It was impossible to tell how old she was; save for the silvered hair and the lines at the corner of her thin lips, she looked ageless.

Jon saw that others deferred to her, so he assumed that she was someone of authority. He chanced a polite smile at her and was startled when a friendly grin creased her face in return.

"Come now. Don't look so worried," she said to him in Common. "Baltsaros, I take it your young friend here doesn't understand us, otherwise he wouldn't look as if we were about to toss him to the bears."

Baltsaros laughed.

"No. Unfortunately Jon has had difficulty learning the language," he replied.

The woman's eyebrows rose and Jon saw a spark of indignity in her icy blue eyes.

"The failure of the student speaks to the failure of the teacher," she said in a disapproving voice.

To Jon's utter surprise, the captain's smile disappeared and he ducked his head slightly like a chastised schoolboy.

"Yes, ma'am," he said softly.

With a little nod, the woman turned back to Jon, the warmth restored to her expression.

"Now, I know of Tom from the captain's letters," she said, glancing over at Tom who looked like he was having trouble keeping a straight face. "A ruffian if there ever was one, but you look like a proper young man, Jon."

Jon realized he was unconsciously straightening his posture under the woman's scrutiny and just shrugged a little, not knowing exactly what a proper young man's response should be. When her eyes shifted down to where Jon was fiddling with a button on his coat, he shoved his hands into the deep pockets and offered a sheepish grin.

"Jon... Tom, this is Sister Iezabel," said Baltsaros, saving Jon from doing anything else that might make him seem completely inept. "Sister Iezabel, Jon and Tom are my"—there was the slightest hesitation before the captain finished with a smile—"life mates."

Almost choking from Baltsaros's choice of words, Jon nearly didn't take the nun's hand when she held it out with a cordial welcome. Then, as soon as she and the captain started up the beach towards a path visible between the great pines, Jon turned to Tom and saw that the first mate's expression hovered somewhere between amusement and awe.

Tom just shook his head slowly.

"I'm as gobsmacked as you, ducky," he said quietly.

When Tom began to grin, Jon had to look away or else the crazed laughter he was keeping in check would bubble to the surface, and he would completely lose it. Feeling a little dazed and absurdly overjoyed, Jon slung his arm through Tom's and followed the group with the armed guard taking up the rear.

∽

*T*om climbed up into the simple wagon and settled in next to Jon. They had walked only a short distance through the dark woods, but they were both covered in red welts from being feasted on by the black flies. Tom grimaced and rubbed the back of his arm.

Bloody hells.

He looked to the front of the open wagon as it started bumping up the crushed-stone road and saw that Baltsaros and the nun were deep in conversation. Sister Iezabel was nothing like he'd imagined. For starters, she was wearing pants. Tom couldn't remember ever seeing a nun wear pants. No, he'd been picturing the round-bottomed, kindly sort of nuns who wore black or grey habits and collected money for the poor at every temple in town —not this towering mast of a woman who shook hands like she meant business and stared down at him like he was a wee nipper with a dirty face. With a frown, he lifted his hand to his cheek and rubbed at it, wondering if he'd missed a spot when Baltsaros made him wash up earlier. Jon smirked at him, so he dropped his hand and twined fingers with him. Tom hated to admit it, but Sister Iezabel was one intimidating nun.

Tom winked to reassure Jon and turned again to study the woman who had managed to cow Baltsaros with a handful of words; that alone made him intensely curious. It was obvious that Tom would be expected to keep his language clean, and he was sure that the old broad probably wouldn't take kindly to a missed *please* or *thank you* either.

On the plus side, however, she hadn't looked the least bit put off by the captain's introduction. Apart from a slight widening of her eyes that spoke of surprise rather than shock, she had taken the news as nonchalantly as if Baltsaros had said they were his drinking buddies. Aye, she was like no nun he'd ever met.

Life mates. Tom gave a little headshake at that new development. Said out loud, the words sounded ridiculous. However, it was all that he could do to keep grinning like a gormless twit every time he thought about just how much he'd liked hearing them.

The lot of saplings that fashioned themselves guards and jogged along with the wagon on either side seemed like a bunch of amateurs by the way they held their pikes. Tom would be surprised if any of them had been in a real fight. The rest of the uppity-looking folk failing to hide their curious stares were a bunch of bureaucrats. Tom could smell it on them.

Jon bumped his shoulder, and he started, then craned his head back to see what had the lad's eyes so wide. Through a break in the trees, Tom saw a city perched atop a high mountain; all gleaming domes and pointed spires, Sormaheine looked like it was part of the heavens.

It was bloody beautiful.

Baltsaros caught Tom's eye and flashed his sharp teeth in a wide smile. It must have been a trick of the sunlight stuttering through the tall pines as they made their way towards the mountain, but Tom could have sworn that for a moment he had seen a dark, horned shadow rise up behind the captain. The first mate smiled back but squeezed Jon's hand until he felt the shiver of dread pass.

*T*he only access to the lofty city of Sormaheine was through a single set of gates in each wall that ringed the mountain. Every time they stopped at one, a complicated series of passphrases and counters were shouted between one of the men on the wagon and the guards who stood atop the parapet. Baltsaros had made mention of only one wall when he had told the grisly story of his past, and Tom wondered whether those events from so long ago are what had prompted an increase in defenses.

As the horses pulled the wagon higher up the mountainside, Tom was surprised that there were no buildings to be seen in the spaces between the gates, only narrow tiered fields of the same scrub grass he'd noticed on their way into the harbour. Here and there were herds of animals being tended to, but the lean-tos and shacks of the poor that were usually relegated to the outer rings of a walled city were nowhere to be seen. It meant either the leaders of the city cared enough to protect their poor or the poor buggers had to live somewhere else. Something told him it was the former.

As they passed through the third and final gate, Tom found himself nodding along mutely as the captain and Sister Iezabel started to identify the buildings that rose up to either side of the well-paved road. The big building with the peaked roof and columns was a bank. The sprawling multistory one was one of the four academies in the city. What Tom took for a temple of some sort turned out to be a hospital, and the tall building with a domed roof that they passed a moment later was something called a *planetarium*. It was no wonder that stories out of the north always sounded so outlandish; Tom had never been in a city with so much bloody stone dedicated to learning. It made more sense to him now why Baltsaros had decided to gift the city with one of the emperor's electricity generators. It also shed some light as to why the captain was so damned learned—it had to be bloody hard to grow up in a place like Sormaheine and not pick up some wisdom just from walking down the street.

As they passed the hall of the alchemist's guild, Tom saw Balt-saros's jaw tighten and he remembered that being barred from joining it was what had him out so far from the city as a boy. The captain remained silent as they continued on, but the nun kept up a steady narrative of what had been built in the city since the captain's uncle had taken him away. When Tom glanced over at Jon, he chuckled at the look of concentrated awe on his face.

"Close yer mouth, lovey," he teased. "Ye look like yer tryin' to catch flies."

Jon blinked as though coming out of a trance and shook his head in amazement.

"Holy hells, Tom. This place… Just imagine how many books there must be here!" he said excitedly.

"I'll thank you to keep a civil tongue in your head, young man," warned the nun though she looked amused. "Don't make me rethink my impression of you." She pointed to a huge structure with four domes and a steep stone staircase leading up to a pair of massive doors. "That is the library, Jon. In it are upwards of forty thousand unique works in scroll, tablet, and bound book. You are very welcome to take advantage of it during your stay here."

"Thank you," Jon breathed.

Then Sister Iezabel turned her ice-blue gaze to the captain, and a few lines appeared on her high forehead as she stared at him.

"Why *are* you here, Baltsaros? After all these years, why have you come home?"

The captain's lips twitched into a humourless curve, and his dark eyes swept over the passing city.

"Home? Not *home*, Sister. This stopped being my home the moment I let those monsters through the gate," he said in a tight voice.

Sister Iezabel stared at him, blank incomprehension on her angular face.

"I will tell you all of it when we've settled in," said the captain, a crease between his brows. "Let's just say that I have a lot to atone for."

The nun accepted Baltsaros's words with a tiny nod. Though she seemed somewhat shaken, she regained her composure enough to continue pointing out details about the city. A few minutes later, they pulled up to a squat building fronted by a covered, arched walkway that Tom immediately recognized from the palace in Madierus. The sight of something so familiar in the midst of the strange city took the edge off of his apprehension, and he grinned at Sister Iezabel.

"Lords help me, but please let there be some grub waitin' for us at the end of the tour?" he said hopefully. He was quickly going from peckish to starved, and his stomach would soon be grumbling loud enough to drown out the details of any more damned buildings.

With a short laugh, the nun stood to disembark.

"Yes, Tom, in just a moment. We've arrived at our destination. You'll be staying in the men's wing of the cloister if that suits you? Yes?" At Baltsaros's nod, she smiled and then put her hand out to the strong-looking middle-aged man who had come up to the side of the wagon. The man, either her servant or something more (did nuns take vows of chastity here too?), peered at the new arrivals with shrewd black eyes before helping the woman descend; he couldn't put a finger on what it was, but the man's scrutiny made the first mate uncomfortable. He scowled at the servant and was unnerved when the man just stared back, his face blank, before turning away slowly to his task.

Bold fucker, he thought. There was definitely something vaguely repellent about the man.

Sister Iezabel stepped down to the paving stones, and when Tom saw the wince of pain, he remembered that despite her spry appearance, the woman had to be in her sixties at the very least. She saw him watching and twisted her lips into a smirk.

"Getting old is no fun," she said and surprised the first mate with a wink, something that immediately bolstered Tom's opinion of the woman, as did what followed. "I take it I should arrange for one room for the three of you to share? We'll have to push a few beds together, but it should do."

As the three of them followed the tall woman up the stairs to the cloister, the wagon continuing on its way with the others, Tom leaned close to Jon's ear.

"Never thought I'd say it, but if this is religion here, it ain't half bad," he murmured. "In fact, I may even be doin' a little prayin' once my belly's full... Do ye wanna hear my sins, Jon?" Jon laughed and playfully shoved Tom away. However, this caught the attention of Sister Iezabel, and when she levelled a disapproving look at the two of them, Tom and Jon both dropped their eyes and continued to tail along after her, meek as lambs.

~

*J*on stood at the window, lost in thought as he watched the play of moonlight on the stark landscape beyond the city. After a simple yet filling meal, the captain and nun had excused themselves to discuss their unexpected arrival. Jon was glad that he wasn't asked to join them—he wouldn't want to be part of that exchange for all the gold in the world. Behind him on the makeshift bed made of three narrow cots, Tom lay on his back, snoring loudly. He'd partaken of the abbey beer brewed on the premises and, pronouncing it to be one of the best he'd ever tasted, Tom had proceeded to drink himself into a stupor with the monks who had made it cheering him on.

Jon looked over his shoulder and smiled at the sprawled-out first mate, thinking he should get to bed too; he wanted to get to the central library early. However, something was keeping him awake.

Returning to the bleak view, Jon's brows met over his eyes in a deep frown, trying to figure out what it was that was bothering him so much. He felt as if something were out of place, and his brain itched as he tried to reconcile his sense of confusion.

It's the lack of snow, he finally determined. Scratching at a bug bite on his neck, he squinted at the tundra beyond. It was all wrong. In his dreams of the north—the ones that left behind a strange sense of portent upon waking—there had been snow on the ground. He shook his head over the weird disappointment he felt. More than ever, Jon knew that he should admit to himself that everyone was right in mocking him for believing the old woman when she said he had some special sight.

Hells, it's not like she said anything like that outright, you idiot. He grimaced. She had merely put the idea in his head, and it was time to let it go once and for all. Besides, all of those dreams had felt ominous; he should be happy that he wasn't predicting their doom.

He turned his back to the window and made his way to the bed. Stripping down to his skin, Jon wondered how in the black hells he was going to get to sleep with Tom making so much noise. With a sigh, Jon began to shove Tom, trying to get him to roll onto his side so he could make a little room for himself and maybe even stop Tom's snoring. If Baltsaros joined them he'd have to find his own space on the bed, but Jon had little doubt that it would be morning before the captain returned.

29

SICK

$\mathcal{T}$he night had been long and difficult, but ultimately had brought Baltsaros some unexpected peace. Sister Iezabel had surprised him with her tears at the end of his confession, and as he had held her gently in his arms, he had been made to understand that she was not crying for the lives that had been lost. No, her sadness was for the little boy who had been twisted and used for evil against his will; there was no recrimination there. The immediate relief he had felt over that realization had startled Baltsaros. Attended only by her somewhat taciturn manservant, they had spent the rest of the night together in quiet conversation, discussing everything—with certain omissions— that had happened to him since.

Then, in the morning, after sending Tom to supervise the transportation of the generator and seeing Jon off to the central library, Baltsaros had returned to their room with the intention of resting. However, as he had lain there, a thought had occurred to him that set his mind ablaze. Despite not having slept yet, he'd suddenly felt anything but tired.

The captain walked quickly down the echoing hallway, remembering his time there as a boy. The building that served as both orphanage and children's hospital was the north wing of the cloister, and he had often wandered into the other wings to escape the bedlam created by the two dozen or so rambunctious boys and girls that called the orphanage their home. As Baltsaros made his way to the cloister's modest library, he passed his favourite of the five small chapels that were placed throughout the sprawling building and smiled. He had spent what felt like hours contemplating the figures carved into the misericords by pagan craftsmen before taking up a knife and chisel himself to see if he could reproduce the fanciful creatures found there. They had sparked a creative urge in him, one that he had kept up over the years in his drawings and carvings.

Frowning, Baltsaros realized that he couldn't remember the last time he had *created* something. Had the emperor burned that out of him, or had he done that to himself? Disturbed by the thought, he turned his mind to the flipside of his desire to create.

Even more interesting to the boy he had been were the surgeries he had watched performed in the tiny operating theatre. Where carving had brought a steady calm, the sight of blood and bone had excited him like nothing before. Held in thrall by what was happening below, Baltsaros had desperately wanted to know what it felt like to run the wickedly sharp scalpel along unresisting flesh. However, the doctors were too smart to leave the tools of their trade lying around for curious boys to steal, so he'd had to content himself with helping the nurses change bandages and remove sutures in the hopes that one day he would be the one holding the scalpel. At night, he had read by candlelight anything he could get his hands on for as long as he could keep his eyes open. Medical books, surgery diagrams, old crumbling scrolls that held nuggets of wisdom alongside blatant quackery—they all had held a deep fascination for him.

Stepping over the library's threshold, Baltsaros wondered whether, had he become a doctor as he had wished, his desire for blood would have been quenched. More likely, training and experience in surgery would have elevated his penchant for murder to a grisly art form. The captain smirked at the morbid thoughts.

Perhaps the only reason you haven't put charcoal to paper lately is because you've been so damn busy, he mused. Busy recovering, busy discovering what truly mattered to him... busy trying to find peace. The last one made him pause. It was true; he was trying to find peace by waging war, but he had no choice. The anger would grow until it tore him apart, taking Tom and Jon with it.

So ready to die? asked the beast.

"I'd rather die than lose control of myself," he fired back at it, annoyed at the intrusion into his thoughts. "If I could cut you out of my head and survive, I would, but it seems that fate has given me another option."

He pulled down a few leather tubes, looking for the map that Sister Iezabel had mentioned. When he found it, he unrolled it on one of the tables and held down the corners with heavy books. Tracing his finger along the box ravine northeast of Sormaheine, he found the tiny village that the nun had mentioned in her letter. Then, he followed the river that started there and continued until it hit the sea. He tapped the spot. That was where Kriegaard had found the frigate loaded down with treasure. Back west along the coast, he came to the villages that had been beset by barbarians, prompting Romas's unsuccessful trip north years after the attack on Sormaheine that had put Baltsaros in the orphanage.

The captain slowly stroked his stubbled cheek, deep in thought. The impetus for Romas's actions had been of a religious matter, having heard that men and women were being forced into rituals venerating the old bloodthirsty pagan gods. Could these barbarians have been the same ones who had taken him as a boy?

If so...

He stared hard at the map, wishing he had more information to confirm his theory, but all he had were decades-old memories and a second-hand account of an attack that had happened over a year ago. He had to believe it was possible that the barbarians were close, returning time and time again to what they considered their favourite hunting grounds. There were so many small villages along the coast and up along the rivers that could easily be wiped out with none the wiser; the boy Sten's account had described exactly that. For a moment Baltsaros's anger blossomed bright. Sormaheine, bastion of civilization, had done nothing but put up walls to block out the threat. As far as he knew, no one from the city had spared a moment's thought about going after the bastards. He rolled the map up, crushing it slightly in his fist as he made his way out of the library.

$\approx$

*J*on walked slowly through Sormaheine's colossal library, his mind reeling with the sheer amount of words that existed between these marble walls. It was absolutely incredible. He passed through a small room where visitors could sit in snug, green velvet armchairs and stepped into what had to be the central room of the building. From floor to ceiling were shelves that held bound books. It was a fortune in leather and paper, not to mention what they contained. Jon remembered how awed he had been over the captain's meagre collection aboard the *Heart* and again when he had gone to a real bookstore in one of the bigger port towns they had stopped at. This? This was a hundred times that feeling. A thousand.

Nearing one of the shelves hesitantly, Jon's heart sank a little when he spied the spiky writing of the northerners. If all of these books were written in their tongue, they were absolutely useless to him. He swallowed back the bitterness he felt over his mind's lack of flexibility. Where Baltsaros and even Tom could pick up a new language with what seemed like preternatural ease, Jon floundered miserably with even the simplest of words. With an ironic grin, he thought about how he'd always remember the Sormet word for *cat*; that one was burned into his brain, alongside the image of Tom kneeling between his thighs, lips and tongue teasing him mercilessly as he looked up at Jon with blue-green eyes narrowed in amusement. Jon felt his cheeks get a little hot, and his heart sped, but he knit his brows when a little faintness washed over him.

That's weird, he thought, breathing deeply through his nose. Despite how easily he blushed, he was no fainting damsel. When the feeling passed, Jon continued on his way, searching for someone who could tell him if there were books written in a language he could understand.

Distracted by the sight of a larger-than-life sculpture of a warrior in the next room, Jon didn't notice that he was scratching hard at the bites on the back of his neck.

*A*n hour later, ensconced in the corner of a small room that held a treasure's worth of bound books and scrolls written in Common, Jon flipped happily through a selection of short biographies of the men who had ruled when the world had been split into numerous small kingdoms. It was fascinating.

When he tired of history, Jon looked for a volume of fairy tales to see if he could find the ones his mother used to tell him as a child. He could barely remember them, but one had featured a man who could fly with wings given to him by an ancient wizard, and another had been about a blue dragon that befriended the knight who tried to kill him. As he searched the titles on a low shelf, he came across a small, thin black book with no writing on the spine. Curious, he pulled it out and nearly dropped it in shock at what it contained. Then Jon glanced over his shoulder to see if anyone was watching and turned the page.

In what Jon immediately assumed were descriptions of torture techniques, naked men and women were bound in numerous poses with the details of their anatomy rendered in stark black-and-white illustrations.

However, by the third and fourth pages, he realized that—whether for titillation or instructional purposes—what he held was an explicit guide on sexual practices. Jon felt a drip of sweat make its way down behind his ear and into his collar, and he wiped at the moisture on his forehead. He felt hot and a little dizzy, the erotic illustrations obviously doing something to him. As he scratched at the back of his neck, he made a small noise at the picture on the next page. A woman with bare breasts looked like she was wearing some sort of belt with a fake phallus attached, and she was penetrating a man bound to a cross. In her hand, she held what looked like a small whip, and Jon breathed hard, wondering if she was alternating between fucking the man and—

"Did you find what you were looking for?"

Jon slammed the book shut and thrust it back between the other volumes. It didn't fit all the way, sticking on something, so he fished around in the gap and found a folded bit of parchment that he pocketed before wedging the book of nude pictures back into place. When he realized the boy was still standing there, just watching Jon flail, he turned and stood. Perspiring as he tugged his tunic lower to hide his erection, Jon licked his lips and cleared his throat before answer.

"Yes. I mean, no. Yes, I am looking, but no I haven't found it. Yet," he said, flustered.

The boy, a gawky teen with unfortunately large ears, peered at him curiously.

"Are you ok?" he asked, his limpid blue eyes concerned.

"Yes!" choked Jon, wondering why his heart was beating so fast. "Thank you. Really." It wasn't as if the boy had caught him doing anything wrong. If that book was here, it was meant to be, no? Jon wiped his sweaty palms on his thighs and watched the boy turn and leave him. A moment later, a shiver went through him, and he wished he had something warmer than his long-sleeved tunic to wear.

. . .

*B*y the time Baltsaros arrived to claim him, Jon could barely lift his head from the table. His skin ached, and every tiny sound made him want to weep. Clutching to Baltsaros, he felt himself lifted into the air, and he burrowed his face against the captain's coat, desperate to block out the light.

~

*B*altsaros closed his eyes as he felt Jon's forehead. The boy was hot but not dangerously so.

"What the fuck's the matter with him?" asked Tom. The first mate was crouched near the head of the hospital cot, his hands clasped between his knees as he stared disconsolately at the wan, sweaty figure of Jon.

"It's just a small sickness that comes with the black fly bites. Nothing serious," said Baltsaros, checking the glands in Jon's neck. Jon's eyelids fluttered for a moment, and he pushed weakly at Baltsaros's hand. "It never once occurred to me. The Sormet have a natural immunity to the sickness."

"Shit," swore Tom. "I'm gonna get it too? I got bit."

Baltsaros glanced over at the first mate. Other than his blood-shot eyes and dark shadows beneath them—both results of overindulgence—Tom looked as hale and hearty as usual. However, there was a visible bite at the edge of his scalp, and he was scratching at a second one on his wrist.

"Stand up," the captain said, gesturing. Tom rose to his feet stiffly, still pained by the healing wound in his side, and the lines across his forehead deepened. Baltsaros took his temperature and felt his neck. "If you're not presenting any symptoms yet, I'd say that you won't get it. Not all strangers do." He turned back to Jon and frowned to himself. Jon being sick would mean they would have to postpone the hunt for the blood ogres until he was better. Even if the fly sickness was usually mild, there sometimes arose complications, and Baltsaros wanted to be there if that happened.

He couldn't leave Jon without knowing he would recover completely.

Weak, hissed the beast, and Baltsaros curled his lip.

"This is more important!" he growled and started when Tom's warm hand closed over his forearm.

"Da?" The first mate looked concerned.

Baltsaros shook his head slowly.

"Sorry, Tom," he muttered. "I was just thinking to myself that Jon's health was more important than our search."

"But, he's gonna be all right… Right?"

Grinning at the big man's wide-eyed worry, Baltsaros patted Tom's cheek.

"He's going to be just fine. A little fever and some disorientation, but he should be right as rain in a couple of days," he replied. "I promise."

The first mate visibly relaxed, nodded, and went back to Jon's side.

With a resigned sigh, Baltsaros glanced around; Tom would need a chair if he was planning on holding vigil. Across the big room, he spotted Sister Iezabel's attendant and beckoned him over with a hand. However, the man just stared at him a few seconds longer, his expression unreadable, before he turned and left. The captain watched him go, unsettled by his reaction.

When Jon was lucid again, he would ask him what he thought of the man and see whether the malice he detected in those dark eyes was just his imagination.

His feet thudded on the packed snow, claws barely making a dent in the hard surface. Ahead of him the wild cat chased the black lion between high white mounds that sparkled in the moonlight. Their shadows were long, reaching back throughout time. Jon should have been cold, but he wasn't. His shaggy grey fur kept him warm. Above, the stars were so numerous that it seemed the firmament would crumble from being so

pierced through. Jon stopped running after the other two and sat back on his haunches. When he lifted his nose to the sky, a mournful howl echoed through the stark landscape. They were going the wrong way! The lion had to chase the cat. Jon let out another cry. Cracks appeared beneath him and the world rumbled. He was going to fall! Jon struggled, trying to free himself from the thing that wrapped around him, confused by the sound of a child crying...

~

*J*on jerked awake, tangled in the blankets and sweating profusely. He had no idea where he was. Light filtered in through windows set high in the walls, and he could see he was in a long hall filled with narrow beds. Breathing hard, he wiped his face and tried to remember how he got there. The library... faint memories of being uncomfortably warm. Or was it cold? There had been a cart. Baltsaros's greatcoat. He licked his cracked lips, bewildered by how parched he was, and sat up slowly. Near him, a skinny child lay crying in a bed, a woman in a white smock holding its hand. When Jon swung his legs over the side of the bed, the nurse looked up at him but said nothing when he got to his feet.

Have to tell Baltsaros... he thought and stopped, not knowing what it was that was so important. His head was muddled as he sat down in the empty chair beside the bed and started tugging on his clothes. Couldn't remember what it was, but he had to go. The nurse frowned at him and that was all.

[...]

When he remembered the parchment in his pocket, Jon flattened it out on the stone wall and peered at it. There were stars, patterns of stars, and here and there a word.

It must mean *something*, he thought, hunching his shoulders when the guards passed by again. He was in a building, but he didn't recognize where he was. A door opened and he saw the covered walkway with the fluted columns, and he smiled because it meant he was still in the palace. Had to get to Baltsaros. Tom too. They were going the wrong way.

Wrong way to what? he asked himself, doubt flooding his mind. He stumbled a little as he made his way to the walkway. Didn't matter. He just had to get to Baltsaros's tower and then everything would be ok.

~

*B*altsaros looked up from his maps and stared at Tom for a moment, trying to make sense of his words.

"What the hells do you mean Jon is nowhere to be found?"

30

LOST AND FOUND

*J*on winced and hugged himself tighter. He was freezing and whatever he lay on was cold and lumpy, and it jostled to and fro. Cracking open one eye, he was immediately confused by his surroundings. Stacked in front of his nose were a half-dozen or so dirty sacks filled with something that smelled like earth. He knuckled his eyes and blinked, the minute details of the burlap coming into sharp focus in the crisp grey light. As he lifted his head and peered around, Jon realized that he was on the back of a wagon travelling through the woods. His brain slowly unfolded memories of being beset upon by children in the streets who emptied his pockets and kicked him in the side when he wouldn't let go of the creased parchment in his hand. Then there was a kindly old woman. And a... man?

Jon pulled himself to sitting and regretted it almost immediately when his head spun and blackness threatened.

"Awake at last," said a deep voice. "Do not worry. I will have you back to your ship soon."

"My ship?" Jon blinked slowly at the hooded man driving the wagon. He had huge red hands and a black beard that took up most of his face.

"In your fever… You said that you wanted to see your captain," said the man in accented Common. "You're from that ship that arrived? The *Heart of Baal?*"

"Oh gods. Wait no… The captain is in the city! Stop, I have to go back," Jon said, alarmed. He held onto the side of the wagon as it swayed and shimmied over the crushed-stone road.

"Well, you cannot go back to the city yourself, little man," said the wagon driver with a furrowed brow. He scratched at the leather hood he wore and stared at Jon over his shoulder for a few seconds. "Are you certain? I can still take you to your ship. It is not far now. You can then figure out where you want to be from there—"

"I have to get back to the city!" insisted Jon, his heart thudding hard. He had to tell Baltsaros about his dream… about… how they were lost. He closed his eyes and let his head loll forward as another wave of dizziness overtook him.

"You were in the city and my mother-in-law found you on a street corner. That is certainly no place for the likes of you! Wandering by yourself in the market. Tsk. The street rats had already picked you clean," the man rumbled on cheerfully as the wagon made its way over the bumpy terrain. "If you still want to go back, I can take you when I'm done delivering these potatoes to the harbour warehouse. You need the passphrases to get through the gates."

"Please…" Jon rasped. "I don't feel so well."

"I can see that. You have the fever. It will pass. It is not serious," said the farmer with a firm nod. He clucked his tongue at the antlered animals pulling the wagon to speed them on before twisting again on the hard bench to look back at Jon.

Jon stared blearily at the man with the reins for a moment and then down at his hands. The parchment was twisted and sweat stained, and he could see that he had gotten ink on his fingers. *Think about the dream… about the stars…*

He unfolded the map in his lap as the curious farmer looked on. Jon had very nearly ruined it; the drawn stars were smeared and blurred. However, there was one word that remained legible, penned in the spiky writing of the Sormet.

"This…" he whispered, holding it up to the bearded man. "What constellation is this?"

The man reached for the star map, but when Jon wouldn't surrender it to him, he squinted hard. After a moment he said a word that made Jon's pulse race and his stomach drop.

"Cat," the man said in the northern tongue.

Out of all the words… the only northern word he knew well.

Follow the cat, Jon.

Without another thought, Jon rolled off the wagon, landing painfully on the hard-packed stone. However, before the man in the wagon could stop and grab him, Jon had picked himself up and darted into the deep woods at the side of the road.

Jon had mended the tapestry. He had to look up at the stars.

He had to find the cat.

~

*B*altsaros pinched the bridge of his nose and forced himself to think.

"I said I was fuckin' sorry, Da," growled Tom. "I was gone for all o' five minutes. Did ye want me to just piss myself?"

"No. Of course not," said the captain softly. He wanted nothing more than to strike the first mate for leaving Jon alone, but Tom was not to blame, and the first mate was beside himself with worry and guilt.

"I just can't believe the nurse just let him walk out in his condition," said Katherine, shaking her head.

"They're understaffed. Overworked. It's a hospital for orphans and the poor. I can't put any blame on them." Despite his words, he was seething on the inside.

He pressed his knuckles hard on the mahogany and took a deep, calming breath. When the heat of his anger had died down a little, he ventured a look at Tom. He stood in the middle of the captain's quarters, his arms down at his sides and hands curled into hard-knuckled fists. Staring at Baltsaros in anguish, Tom bared his teeth and let out a frustrated sound.

"Da, what if he's hurt? Fuckin' hells. Fuckin' bloody gods-damned mother-whorin' hells," he groaned. "Bloody Jon…"

"You said that the guard is scouring the city?"

"Aye. Yer nun lady made 'em hop the second I seen he was gone," said Tom, looking like he would either start cursing again or break something.

More like Tom will break down in tears, thought the captain.

"Da, I came here as fast as I could. Thinkin' maybe he was tryin' to get home to the *Heart*."

Baltsaros sighed and rounded the patched-together table and pulled Tom to his chest.

"You did good, Tom. It's all right. We'll find him. Just let me grab my things, and we'll head back to the city," he said, resting his cheek on Tom's rough-shorn hair for a moment before he stepped back. "I'm sure he hasn't gotten very far."

Tom cleared his throat and straightened his shoulders with a little nod. Baltsaros was a little surprised when Katherine slung an arm around Tom's waist and offered him a quick hug and a few quiet words the captain couldn't make out. The sight brought a smile to his face. That Jon had managed to forge a path to friendship between the pirates was amazing; the two of them had been at loggerheads since day one. He shook his head and turned away. They *had* to find Jon.

*A*s Baltsaros was closing the bag of warm clothes they'd need for the expedition, Hitch popped his head around the door.

"Cap'n, sir," said the scraggy pirate, tugging on his forelock. "There be a tater farmer 'ere says 'e seen yun' Jon."

"Oh, thank the bloody gods," breathed Tom loudly as he and Katherine followed Hitch out of the room with a quick step. Baltsaros slung the bag over his shoulder and made his way with them towards a dark-haired man standing nervously at the bow. Tuvi and Tuli loomed to either side of him, watching him suspiciously, and it was obvious that the man had come aboard with them. Baltsaros waved the twins off with a smile and stepped closer. Over the stranger's shoulder, the captain could see a wagon hitched to a pair of reindeer on the shore.

"You've seen my missing man?" he said, trying to keep the urgency out of his voice.

"Yes, sir," said the farmer, his mouth almost completely concealed by a bushy black beard. He held a hat or a hood in his hands, creasing the leather in his big, red-knuckled hands "My wife's mother found him passed out under the archways of the marketplace. Some street urchins had already turned his pockets, but he was holding onto some old star map like it was made of gold."

"Star map?"

"Yes, sir. He wouldn't let go of it. He was feverish with fly sickness and kept saying he had to speak to his captain. That's how I knew he arrived with your ship. I was coming this way anyway, so I loaded him onto my wagon but"—the man twisted the leather harder, and his black brows pinched together high in the middle of his forehead—"it was the damnedest thing... He asked about the little otter constellation and then just jumped off and ran into the forest! I'm sorry, but he was away before I could catch him. I looked in the woods for a while, sir. No trace of him. But I'm no woodsman, sir. I know fields..." The man seemed so wretched that Baltsaros put a hand on his big shoulder.

"You did well in coming to tell me," he said reassuringly. He glanced to the side and saw that Tom was already pulling together a search team of their best hunters. The first mate turned to the captain, his bright eyes full of fear but jaw set in determination.

We'll find him.

"Katherine, you are in charge. Send runners if there are new developments."

"Aye, Captain!"

Baltsaros turned back to the farmer.

"You'll show us where he jumped off?" he asked.

"Of course, sir," the man nodded, placing the mangled hood back over his wild hair.

Yes, gods... We'll find you, Jon, promised the captain and tried to ignore the malevolent laughter of the ghosts in his head.

~

*J*on marched through the underbrush, his eyes narrowed against the prickly needles of the pines reaching for him from either side of the winding track. Though his arms were crossed over his chest and hands jammed into the opposite armpit, Jon was growing colder the longer he walked. Breath pluming with every step, he fought the urge to just find somewhere to hole up until it got warmer.

Warmer... Jon laughed to himself. He doubted that it got much above freezing this far north, especially as the sun went down. It just baffled him why there was no snow on the ground. It made no sense.

All of his dreams had shown him snow... He huffed and panted as he broke through between the trees, still unable to see past the branches above his head.

The constellation couldn't be just a coincidence. It *had* to mean something. Of all the creatures it could have been named after, it ended up being a *cat*. Like Tom. Like his dream. He had to find and follow it to get... to get...

Jon stamped his feet hard as he walked, forcing the feeling back into them.

What are ye lookin' for, Jon? There was a mocking quality to Tom's voice.

"You're going to laugh at me," murmured Jon through numb lips. "I'm tired of you teasing me for this." A root hidden beneath the thick, almost spongy blanket of rust-coloured pine needles nearly succeeded in tripping him. There *had* to be a way out of these woods. Then, when he could see the stars, he would follow the cat, just like in his dream. It would take him to... take him to... Baltsaros? No. Wait... Something that would *help* Baltsaros?

Puzzled, Jon paused almost midstride, trying to remember exactly what it was that the cat would bring him to, but came up blank. It had been so clear to him just a moment earlier. Would it bring him to the blood ogres? The thought made him resume his pace.

No, that can't be it, he thought with a frown. The wolf and the lion needed to follow the cat. But to what end? Up ahead in the dying light, there seemed to be a break in the trees, and he anxiously picked up his pace.

Dont'cha want my help? laughed the first mate.

"Not unless you can part the trees so I can see the *fucking sky!*" Jon shouted in tearful frustration as what he thought was a clearing turned out to be just a dense copse of white-barked trees. He slumped against one of the strange trees, his forehead pressed to the peeling bark, just breathing deep for a moment.

"What am I doing?" he muttered. It had all made absolute sense to him before: his dream, finding the map and constellation, striking out on his own... Jon closed his eyes and swallowed thickly.

Are ye ok, love? rumbled Tom.

"No," whispered Jon to the ghost in his head. "I'm not. I'm lost and I'm cold, and I swear to fucking gods that I am going as crazy as Baltsaros."

Why don't ye tell ol' Tom about it?

Jon pushed himself away from the tree trunk and peered around in the deepening gloom. After a moment, he slid down to the small hassock at the tree's base and pulled the calfskin map out from the neck of his shirt. He unrolled it, laid it across his knees, and then blew into his cupped hands.

"I'm looking for a fucking cat," he muttered, but it didn't make much sense anymore. Jon couldn't even remember which constellation was the cat. He should have stayed in the hospital.

Hospital? Jon covered his ears with his hands, the latter only slightly warmer than the former.

You're lookin' for me, love? We're lookin' for you...

"I wish you really were," mumbled Jon. "I should have stayed on that fucking cart. Then at least I would have made it to the *Heart*. Now you'll never know where to look. Tom, what have I done?"

When Tom didn't answer, Jon let out a shuddering sigh and wiped at his leaking nose with the edge of his sleeve.

Move or die, he thought grimly as he stood. His feet were nerveless blocks of ice, but he forced himself to start trudging forward again. Night was coming and it sure as hells wouldn't get warmer once the sun went down. If he had any chance at all in finding a way out of the woods, it wouldn't be by sitting and feeling sorry for himself.

~

om let loose with another stream of curses under his breath as he kept close to Rémi, stamping flat ferns and saplings with his big boots as he went. They'd been searching for nearly two hours in these godsforsaken fucking woods, following what the southlander pirate swore were Jon's tracks until, suddenly, they'd lost sight of them near a bunch of paper birches.

Baltsaros walked alongside him, his head swivelling from side to side as they made their way deeper into the woods.

"How are we supposed to hear Jon if you won't cease your endless profanity," admonished the captain quietly.

Tom glanced over at Baltsaros and clenched his jaw. The captain frowned at him from beneath his sailor's tuque but said nothing else. Behind them, trailing to either side, were a few more men that swore up and down to the blue heavens that they knew their way around a forest.

Bloody good it'll do us in the stone dark.

"Tom, you're doing it again."

With a scowl, Tom picked up his pace, overtaking Rémi. He could swear that they had passed this exact same spot twice now. If they were going in circles, he would personally tie the good-for-nothing southlander to the mast and whip him raw himself.

You're going the wrong way.

"Am I, Jon?" whispered Tom, his nerves obviously beginning to wear thin.

Glancing over his shoulder, Tom realized he was alone. However, he could hear the others nearby, so he stopped walking and rubbed his face as he waited for them to catch up. Jon was lost somewhere in these woods, and from what the farmer had said, he hadn't been wearing nearly enough clothes to be out in temperatures that were dropping the longer they searched.

They *had* to find him.

Tom stuck the black cheroot between his teeth before patting his pouch for a match, thinking about what Baltsaros had said when they set off. Jon was probably delirious with fever, which could be why he broke away from the farmer like a blasted madman, but it didn't explain where in the hells Jon had found a fucking star map.

Tom, really, you're going the wrong way.

"Completely barmy," he grumbled, but he couldn't shake the feeling that they were indeed heading in the wrong direction. Tom struck the match against the tree and lifted it to the slender cigar. As he puffed a few times against the flickering flame, something caught his eye off to the left. It was a glimmer... Tom squinted into the shadowed dusk and lifted the match above his head. There it was again. A light.

And then it blinked.

Tom's eyes widened when he saw the grey wolf emerge from between two ground-hugging spruces. It stood appraising him for a long moment, the flame reflected in its eyes. The same cold gust that played in the wolf's thick ruff sent the match's fire back against Tom's fingers, and he dropped it with a curse. The wolf, startled by the sudden motion, turned and darted back under the tree cover. When the trees swung with its passing, Tom saw something and his heart began to box a merry beat against his ribs —there were branches broken at man-height above where the wolf had gone. Hope rekindled, Tom set off after the wolf. At the sight of more freshly torn foliage just beyond the broken twigs and then an obvious boot print in a bed of moss, Tom stopped in his tracks.

"We're going the wrong bloody way!" he bellowed. "Follow me. I think I found where he went."

⤳

*B*altsaros sank down to his knees and reached for Jon, afraid of what he would discover. However, when a branch cracked loud beneath his boot, the younger man started awake. Jon looked blearily around, clearly disoriented. Tom let out a relieved laugh and squatted next to the captain.

"Jon?" murmured Baltsaros. Jon was lying on his side in a small depression at the base of a red pine, his arms tight around his torso and knees nearly to his chin. He uncurled himself with a pained expression and groaned softly.

"Fucking hells, am I glad to see you," Jon said in a hoarse voice and winced as Tom helped him all the way to sitting.

Baltsaros pulled the wool blanket he had brought out from his pack and quickly wrapped Jon up. He was shivering, but apart from a few scratches on his face, he seemed unharmed.

"Fuck, I'm cold," mumbled Jon, burrowing into the blanket. Tom curled around him from behind and buried his face in Jon's neck. From the way Jon's brow creased in chagrin at Tom's rough whispers, Baltsaros guessed that the first mate was scolding him.

"I'm sorry," said Jon. "I am so sorry." His blue-grey eyes lifted to the captain's, and Baltsaros forced a calm smile onto his face.

"We found you. That's all that counts, my love," he replied. "That's all that counts."

"I don't know what happened," Jon said quietly. "It's all muddled in my head. I woke up in a hospital, but I don't know why I was there. And then there was a man with a wagon. And... a map, but I lost it when I rolled down a hill. I walked and walked, but then I just couldn't anymore. I... I needed to sleep a little to regain my strength, and I was going to set out again." His confusion seemed to have a cleared completely. The captain guessed that the frigid temperatures had brought down Jon's fever enough to stop the delirium that had caused him to wander off to begin with.

"Well, I'm glad we found you before you slept too deeply," said Baltsaros. Tom lifted his head and frowned at the captain. The first mate gave a tiny headshake; there was no need to continue that train of thought.

"Ye had a fever, lovey," rumbled Tom. "Nothin' terrible, just a bit o' sickness. But, I'm the one who's bloody sorry. I went for a leak and left my post. Ye were gone when I—"

"Yes, you're all very, very sorry," said a new voice. "It's unexpectedly sweet coming from the lot of you, I must say."

Startled, Baltsaros looked up and saw a few men standing by a group of pines. In the faded light, he couldn't make them out clearly, but by the tongue spoken, they were obvious natives of Sormaheine.

"Who are you?" he asked, rising to his feet.

"Oh, you know who I am... But now I know who you *really* are," said one of the men, but Baltsaros barely heard his words because as the speaker stepped forward, the captain recognized the middle-aged attendant that served as Sister Iezabel's manservant.

Baltsaros then felt a conflicting mix of relief at seeing a would-be rescuer and confusion as his brain finally registered the malice in the man's tone. At a shout from Tom, the captain turned to see the first mate and Jon struggling with more men. Nearby, the body of Rémi lay in a mess of pine needles slicked with red, steam rising slowly from it in the deep cold. This was not a rescue.

Before Baltsaros had time to dodge the big man who grabbed at him, he felt something hard hit the back of his skull. The last thing he saw was Tom with his arm around Jon, his wrist bent at an impossible angle, as he tried to fight off their assailants with his long, bone-handled knife clutched in the other hand.

Then the world went black.

31

THE DEAD

Whoever fights monsters should see to it that in the
process he does not become a monster. And if
you gaze long enough into an abyss, the abyss
will gaze back into you.

— FRIEDRICH NIETZSCHE

Tom fingered the raised calluses on his chest, twisting
his lips in disgust at how pale and sensitive the skin
was beside them. How long had it been since his master had put
that fucking harness on him? Now, it was gone, cut off by an
oddly genteel pirate captain and his sour-faced first mate. The
latter, a son-of-a-fucking-whore if there ever was one, had just
thrown him back in the tiny cage in the captain's quarters with
nary a word before he stormed off, leaving Tom in the bloody
dark by himself.

With a sigh, he sat down gingerly, still sore from being abused
and then doctored on, and wondered what in the black hells was
expected of him. Three days aboard the bloody ship, and Tom had
done almost nothing but sit in his gods-be-damned cage like a

fucking animal. Hands curled to fists in his lap, he bared his teeth in a frustrated grimace and thought about the shard of pottery he had hidden beneath the thin mattress.

Soon.

It had taken most of the previous afternoon tossing the tied strips he'd made of his shirt at the jug on the table before the loop had caught the lip. A quick jerk had brought the jug down to the floor, but it had survived the fall, landing unharmed on the thick carpet below. Tom had had to strain through the bars to reach the jug and then dash it a few times against the wall of his prison to get it to break.

As luck of bloody fucking luck would have it, Peter had been on his way into the room when he heard the pottery break, and then all hells had broken loose of course, with the surly first mate cursing and hollering while he and two others had tackled Tom to the floor. He'd nearly broken his wrist trying to jam the jagged splinter of pottery under the bed while being pinned by the fuckers.

Tom rubbed his wrist with a scowl. Being forced to scrub the deck for three hours as punishment certainly hadn't helped his sprain or his mood. As he was debating whether he should try to get some sleep or do some more sit-ups, he saw something that made his heart falter and his hackles rise. There, on the little crate that served as a table within the small jail cell, was the shard he'd thought hidden away. Just sitting there, plain as fucking day. Tom blinked slowly at it, wondering what it meant. It seemed like a big *fuck you*—like they were laughing at him and his puny excuse for a weapon—and it sat there mocking him.

See how easily I found your sad little secret? See how I let you keep it?

Aye, it bloody reeked of that poncy fucker in the greatcoat with the peculiar fucking name. The one who stared at him with those pitchy eyes of his, lips all curled and pleased with how he thought he'd bested Tom.

Tom.

The ex-slave closed his eyes with a smile and rolled the name around in his mind before giving it breath.

"Tom," he murmured. It was the first thing that was truly his. Not *Thomas*. Nay, Thomas was a little boy dressed in silks and crying as the men—

"If you learn how to behave like a human being, you'll have much more than just a name, Tom," came the voice from the darkness.

Tom leapt to his feet, hands tight around the bars as the captain's words split the silence. Furious at having such a pathetic little private moment witnessed, he hunched his shoulders and let out a low growl at the man reclining on the bed across the room. When the captain chuckled and sat up, Tom thought he would break his jaw, his teeth were clenched so tight.

"Not tonight, then, I take it?" asked Baltsaros. He slipped off the bed and, dressed only in tight black leather trousers, padded barefoot across the rug to the front of the cage. The captain's hair was loose and a little dishevelled and made him look as if he had just now woken. It hung down past his powerful shoulders, a tress of it straying against the broad pectoral generously furred with dark hair. As the captain crossed his arms, Tom's eyes were drawn to the way the moonbeam from the porthole played on the sculpted, hard muscle of his forearm, sun-dark skin turned pale in the cold light.

Strong. He felt a flutter of dread as the captain continued to watch him silently. Though rigid with apprehension, Tom leaned harder into the bars and sneered at the man.

"Fuck ye lookin' at?" he growled.

"And so it can speak," said the captain, his tone playful.

Tom's fear turned again to fury at being mocked, and he lunged out quickly to grab his tormenter. However, the captain was too quick for him and simply stepped out of reach.

"You want to kill me. That much you've made blatantly clear, Tom," said Baltsaros with a little tilt of his head. The captain's accent gave his words a clipped quality that accentuated the aura of good breeding that he perpetuated with his manners and dress.

All it did was remind Tom of those who had given up on him; shoulders hitched up further, he let out another low animal noise as he watched the captain walk to an armoire. When Baltsaros returned to the cage, he held up a long, bone-handled knife in a leather sheath. Tom's pulse sped, and he felt the familiar cool surge of adrenaline tighten his loins in preparation for a fight. However, Baltsaros merely shook his head at Tom's desperate display.

"The day you prove to me that you are more than *that*," the captain said, pointing to the slave collar that Tom still wore, "is the day I will give you *this*." He unsheathed the knife and turned it for Tom to see. "Prove to me that you're worth as much as I think you are, Tom, and you'll know what freedom means again."

Tom breathed quickly through his nose, eyes on the fine blade, then hawked and spat at the captain.

Quick as a snake, the man jumped forward and punched Tom hard through the bars. Pain exploded in Tom's face as he felt his nose break and again when he fell back and landed hard on his sprained wrist. With another derisive laugh, the captain turned away, leaving Tom to lick his wounds.

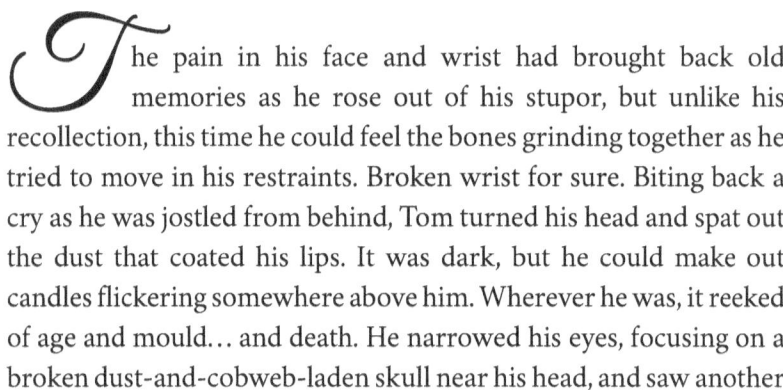

The pain in his face and wrist had brought back old memories as he rose out of his stupor, but unlike his recollection, this time he could feel the bones grinding together as he tried to move in his restraints. Broken wrist for sure. Biting back a cry as he was jostled from behind, Tom turned his head and spat out the dust that coated his lips. It was dark, but he could make out candles flickering somewhere above him. Wherever he was, it reeked of age and mould... and death. He narrowed his eyes, focusing on a broken dust-and-cobweb-laden skull near his head, and saw another one lying right behind it. Judging by the roughness of the ground beneath him and what looked like a stone sarcophagus to his left, he was in some sort of crypt. It was only when he was nudged again that he realized that whoever was tied up with him was waking up.

"Jon? Da?" he whispered.

There was a weak moan behind him, and he tried to lift his head to see if Jon was all right, but all he did was twist his wrist further. It also felt like he had ripped something inside the healing wound at his side, and Tom felt nauseous from the pain.

"Jon?" he tried again.

"Huh fuck," coughed Jon, sounding muffled. "What...?" When he shifted against Tom, the first mate let out a pained grunt.

"Stop movin', Jon," he rasped. "Yer hurtin' me."

Instantly Jon stopped squirming and lay still.

"Where are we?"

"I don't fuckin' know, love," said Tom with a grimace. "Do ye see Da?"

"No." Jon's voice sounded small, like he was terrified.

"Don't worry, love," murmured the first mate. "We'll figure it out. Keep yer head."

However, when the fall of boots sounded loud on the stones a moment later, heralding the approach of a group of men, Tom began to feel his own panic. Their captors had hit the bottle hard; Tom's nose burned with the smell of rotgut when one of them bent low to peer at him with a malicious grin.

It was always worse when they had been drinking...

∼

*B*altsaros woke in a dimly lit room with hewn stone walls, his head throbbing in a nauseating tempo of agony. After licking his lips with a nearly dry tongue, he found he could barely swallow for the dust in his throat. Despite how disoriented he felt, it only took him a few seconds to place the smell of powdered bone and mildew that assailed his nose with every breath.

The catacombs.

Short of aboveground land to bury the dead, a sprawling necropolis undercut the mountaintop city of Sormaheine. Miles of narrow, sarcophagus-lined tunnels looped beneath the streets, sometimes doubling back on themselves—like a giant spiral maze fashioned to keep the spirits of the dead from ever finding their way to the surface. There were entrances to the catacombs all over the city, but Baltsaros knew one of them very well; the children of the orphanage would often sneak into the cloister's cellar and dare each other to climb through the trap door to the crypts below with nothing but a bit of pilfered candle to keep the ghosts at bay. Baltsaros, smaller and deemed strange by the other boys, had been forced down there alone many times, made to wander for hours until he found an alternate way out.

"Ah, you've returned to us," said a voice, and Baltsaros lifted his head to squint at the figure before him. It was the middle-aged man from the woods, the attendant that always seemed no further than Sister Iezabel's elbow, always at the ready with a steadying hand or a cup of the mulled wine the old nun liked to drink. There was no mistaking him. The man had been there with the captain and Sister Iezabel the whole long night they had spoken of times past; Baltsaros had memorized the slant of his dark eyes and the way his greying hair curled across his high forehead.

"What do you want from me?" asked the captain hoarsely.

"To the point. I do like that. I was told you were a man who understood the value of succinctness in the face of death," replied the man with a smile.

"I apologize if you think I've wronged you in some way," said Baltsaros, wishing he could touch the back of his head to assess the damage. However, his hands were useless to him as they were bound to the arms of an old wooden chair. "You and I don't know each other. I have no conflict with you, so I ask again: what do you want from me?"

"Oh, yes, we do know each other. Though you've only just become aware of my existence, I've known of yours for a very long time," said the man, his voice growing quieter. "A long fucking time."

As he gazed at the captain, his lip twitched up slightly in what looked like a nervous tic.

"Let me and my men go, and I will make you a rich man," said Baltsaros, working his fingers around the seam where the chair arm was joined.

"You want to pay me to let you go? No, Captain. You owe me *far* more than that, it seems," the man said, pushing his face close to Baltsaros's. His breath was rank, and the captain nearly gagged from it. Then, after his wide-eyed stare ended with a humourless chuckle, the man tutted and shook his head in disappointment.

He had to be mad.

Trying to keep his breathing steady, Baltsaros pressed back against the chair, testing the state of the wood, and was pleased when he heard a creak. Instantly his head was flung back when the man punched him, forcing his damaged skull against the hard surface with a painful rap and causing him to see bright lights behind his eyelids. The candlelit room shimmered strangely when he opened his eyes.

"None of that, now! You're my prisoner, and you'll die by my hands... you and the two you seem to hold so dear. That is, when we're finished with you of course. It's been a while since my men have had a little reward for loyalty, and they're not especially choosy as long as they each get a turn."

Baltsaros panted quickly against the rising faintness, disturbed by the sound of a struggle somewhere behind him. He heard Tom cry out in pain, followed by a surge of ugly laughter. Then, heart in his throat, Baltsaros heard Jon's whimper, and he gnashed his teeth in anguish. Tied as he was to the chair, he couldn't see behind him and trying to twist around brought with it another wave of cold nausea.

"You bastard," he growled. "Let them go."

"Or what? You're going to scowl me to death?" taunted the man as he pulled up another mouldy-looking chair to sit on. "You're right, you know," he continued quietly. "I'm a bastard... And now I know *you* are the reason why that is." He leaned forward in his seat with hands clasped together and stared again at Baltsaros with a curious blankness in his dark eyes.

"Growing up in an orphanage isn't easy. Something you're well acquainted with, I know. The teasing, the bullying... Lords, I'm sure they even made you come down here by yourself..."

Jon let out a low moan, and there was a string of curses from Tom that led to a thud and a grunt of pain. Baltsaros let out his own strangled yell when the man in front of him rose out of his chair and slapped him hard across the face.

"Pay attention to me when I'm talking to you. I'm *saying* that you and I are not that different," said his captor calmly and reclaimed his seat. "We *both* grew up in that godsforsaken fucking cloister, Captain. So I'm *also* acquainted with what it's like to be terribly scarred and bullied for it. The barbarians... the blood ogres... Those monsters took our families away from us. See, your family and my family were neighbours, and they killed my mother just as surely as they killed yours, except mine"—the man laughed a little jerkily; his hands twisting together, white-knuckled, were the only indication that he was struggling with extreme emotion —"mine took another nine months to die. They tell me she died screaming as they pulled out the baby those monsters put in her belly."

Baltsaros didn't need Jon to see from the man's vehemence where this tale was going. Behind him he heard Jon's voice again, muffled and in pain. He scratched at the chair arms, desperate to free himself.

"Do you have any idea how much fucking harder it is to grow up among those fucking brats when you're the son of a faceless rapist *monster*? Do you have any idea what that was like? But you... You were the boy that survived! Sure, they all whispered that you were cursed, or you did horrible, perverted things with them so they would let you go, but it couldn't possibly have been as bad as being the *get* of those bloody savages."

Nostrils flaring, the captain tried to chase from his mind the memories of those taunts; he remembered all too well those accusations. He was in agony, madness only a step away as he heard Jon whimper again.

"I started to help Sister Iezabel because she was kind, and because I knew she had been kind to you. Lords, you probably have no idea how happy she was when you sent that very first letter, do you? And it made me happy too. Here was another scarred, damaged boy... And he had escaped! Lords, and he was making something of himself... a true survivor. Gods, I wanted to be you, Baltsaros. Waiting each year for that single, dry, impersonal letter you sent Sister Iezabel out of some strange sense of duty... and all that coin! Do you know I travelled out to the midlands to see you? I had some notion of becoming part of your crew. Perhaps becoming friends because we shared our terrible beginnings. But you wouldn't even see me. No! That miserable animal you call a first mate... *He* turned me away. Said that you didn't need another land-grubbing sailor to dilute the ranks. And then I heard *stories* about you..."

Tom cursed again, and Baltsaros closed his eyes as the first mate began to beg, not for himself but for Jon.

You made this happen, snickered the beast from somewhere. It was too crowded in Baltsaros's head. He could hear Jon's cry of pain, and his whole body trembled from the sound of it.

"So I began to practice pillage and plunder on my own. Then, I found others who *understood* the power behind fear, like you do. And we started taking settlements, villages—small at first, then bigger. Oh... We've gotten very good, Baltsaros."

The words finally caught fire in the captain's brain and started burning through the threatening madness. He stared hard at the man, comprehension finally dawning on him.

"*You* are the barbarian raiders," Baltsaros said. His hands were claws on the chair's arms.

"Yes. But that's not what I'm—"

"You have been raping and destroying, emulating the blood ogre tribe."

"The blood ogres? The blood ogres are *nothing*, Baltsaros. *Nothing*. I was not much past twenty when we hunted them down and killed every last one of them. I was emulating *you*, you dim fuck! And then, during your sob session with that old cunt, I discovered that my idol, the man that I'd been striving to be all these years, is the *one who let those monsters into the city*. *You* are the reason I suffered all of those years. You. Do you have any idea how hard it was for me not to just slit your throat right then and there? No, I had to keep playing my part until I could get you alone. How fortuitous is it that Sister Iezabel sent me to help you, and that you and your men were as easy to track as musk bears crashing through the woods?" The man's chuckle was bitter, and though the fervour in his voice had grown, there was little rebuke in his expression. He remained an unremarkable man in his middle age with a solicitous smile and an almost kindly manner. It was as if he could not rid himself of the mask he wore day to day. However, the twitch in his lip returned as he leaned far forward again to peer almost curiously at the captain. "Baltsaros, *you* are the monster. By killing you, I redeem myself, don't I? Take back what you've stolen from me? Yes… I'm going to put an end to you and take your ship. We are very much alike, aren't we? Both dark-eyed northerners… Why I could even take your name, couldn't I? How many would realize before it's too late? Oh, I am so very thankful for whatever gods or devils it was that brought you to me… like fate itself blessed me to take your place…"

The captain's head spun, trying to put together the pieces.

Look behind you, said Romas with a truculent laugh. *Look what your stupid quest is doing to those dear boys of yours. Can't you hear Jon sobbing? Oh, Tom will never cry. He'll just take it, but you know what it'll do to him…*

Something clear and painful cut through Baltsaros, and he grasped at it, feeling like he was opening his eyes for the first time.

Before Romas could say another word, Baltsaros simply dismissed him and narrowed his focus down to a needle's width.

"—finally found my own ship to get away from this—"

"The ship. The frigate... It was yours," Baltsaros whispered.

His captor sneered at him.

"Yes, and it was stolen from me. Along with—"

"All the treasure you stole from these crypts. My parents' wedding cuffs weren't trophies kept by the ogres, they were burial items taken by you and your *pathetic little band of savages.*"

The man's eyes bulged and he stood, taking a swift step backwards when the rotting wood of the chair finally gave way beneath Baltsaros's wrist. It was as if he was held in thrall by the captain's unblinking gaze and, complexion waxy, he gaped as Baltsaros quickly freed his other arm.

Baltsaros smiled grimly. Was it fate or uncaring gods or even fucking devils that forced him to use to his advantage the harrowing abuse taking place just paces away? The men were so distracted with their beastly sport that they didn't realize their leader was in trouble.

"Let me guess... You don't have enough men to sail that frigate, so you needed the riches of our dead to fund your cause of murder and mayhem. Oh, you *are* right, you know. We are both murderers, you and I," purred Baltsaros. He felt a little faint as he stood there, but the tremor that went through the snivelling traitor before him bolstered his step. "I wish I could honestly say I was sorry for your beginnings, but I am not. I don't care."

Baltsaros couldn't help but risk a glance back across the chamber. Jon's face was wet with furious tears as the man behind him grunted and thrust. Tom's eyes were closed.

The claws that had held the beast to the captain for so long could find no purchase in what that sight had unleashed within him, and the phantom howled as it was torn loose. This would end here and *now*. No more madness feeding on madness. Nothing but the future... and only if he managed to mend it after this night.

Time stopped as Baltsaros reached for the man who had captured them, twisting his head so violently that he felt his jaw dislocate before the crack of broken bone jolted his palms. The man, unnamed and rendered meaningless, fell in a heap. Quickly, Baltsaros dug into the corpse's belt to retrieve Tom's blade.

Startled into action by the captain's shout of rage, two men then set upon him as the others abandoned Jon and Tom on the dirty floor. The long knife, always kept razor sharp by the first mate, sliced through jugular and tendon, scraping against bone as the captain wielded it furiously. Tom, up onto his feet in a flash, looped his bound arms over the head of one of the attackers and bit deep into the side of the man's neck. Though it must have been agony on his broken wrist, he fought the man to the floor and finished him off with a knee to the back of the head, snapping his neck.

As Baltsaros took on a third and then a fourth, he saw Jon cut Tom's bindings. Then, freed from his own ropes, Jon set about hacking and slashing with a dagger taken from one of the dead men.

The captain let out a cry as the man he was fighting managed to cut his arm, but he retaliated and, changing his grip on the long knife, managed to sink the blade deep into his attacker's eye.

The triumphant bellow that burst from Jon nearly startled Baltsaros into dropping his weapon, and he turned in time to see him slice through his opponent's neck with a bright arc of blood. Eyes wide and crazed, Jon then jumped to the first mate's aid.

In less than a minute, it was over.

The three of them stood panting in the dusty mausoleum, surrounded by the bodies of their abductors and covered in blood. Tom held his wrist to his chest, and his face was pale beneath the streaks of dirt and gore. Even so, he cracked a grim smile at the captain who was putting pressure on the deep cut in his arm.

Jon looked dazed, his grey-blue eyes huge and lost. Apart from a dark bruise on one cheek, he seemed relatively unharmed.

"Did they hurt you?" Baltsaros asked softly, reaching for him.

However, Jon shied away from the captain's touch like a skittish colt and wouldn't meet his eye.

"I'm fine," said Jon, his voice tight. "I'll… be fine. Just…" Jon wiped the back of his hand across his mouth and then looked around. He walked away from the captain and stood staring down at one of the bodies for a long time in silence. Tom leaned with a gasp against Baltsaros as the last of his strength ebbed. The captain looped his arm around the first mate's waist to support him and watched as Jon kicked the corpse as hard as he could in the side. When Jon turned back to the others, his face was blank of expression, but he wouldn't lift his eyes.

"Are we going after the blood ogres?" he asked.

"No. No, the blood ogres are dead," Baltsaros said, shaking his head. "The last one died here tonight."

Not seeming to care enough to ask why that was, Jon just nodded once. With a sigh, he ran a bloody hand through his curls and finally met the captain's gaze. His eyes were red-rimmed, but if there was pain there, it was locked away. Baltsaros thought he heard a ghostly chuckle from within.

"Then are you satisfied?" Jon asked. "Is there enough redemption in this for you?" It was an accusation.

The captain's guts twisted at the hollow sound of Jon's voice.

"Yes, Jon. We're done," Baltsaros replied. "We're going home."

32

THE LIVING

ONE MONTH LATER

fter we found our way to the surface following our ordeal, we were tended to in the small hospital by Sister Iezabel's staff. My injuries were minor, but Tom suffered a bad break in his right wrist as well as some tearing in the healing wound in his side. He's still on the mend and not happy about it. While I think we managed to isolate the bones as best as possible, I'm afraid he'll lose some mobility when using his dominant hand.

As for Jon, I don't know the extent of the physical damage he sustained; he refused treatment, assuring me he was fine, and I chose not to press the issue. My general observations over the last month have led me to conclude that the physical trauma he suffered was minimal.

Sister Iezabel was devastated that she had failed to notice the monster in their midst. It seems that he was able to commit his barbarity undiscovered by first telling her of raids that had not yet happened then attacking the villages or settlements when Sister Iezabel sent him with relief funds and supplies. She blames herself for not seeing him for what he was, but I assured her that his disguise had fooled everyone.

When the man's quarters were searched, they found all the letters I had sent to Sister Iezabel along with never-sent missives penned by his hand and addressed to me. All of them described brutal acts that he thought we both could partake in, growing ever more cruel and sadistic with each consecutive letter. It seems his obsession was complete, and I was gleefully painted such a monster in his eyes that I felt strangely lacking in comparison upon reading the letters.

On top of his depraved ramblings, a cache of bones was found beneath a loose flagstone in his room. These grisly trophies seem to span as far back as his childhood—so clearly his appetite for murder was not, in fact, born of being spurned from my ship by Tom (or Peter?).

One thing I find most fascinating is that he didn't seem capable of reconciling his "positive" view of me with the "negative" truth of what I had done to cause the death of our families and his subsequent suffering at the hands of his fellow orphans. What makes a monster? A small, selfish part of me wishes I had not ended his life so quickly, for when I looked into his eyes, I saw a deformed reflection of myself.

I could have studied him.

However, I am honestly glad that I did dispatch him as I did. And, though I did indeed learn the man's name from Sister Iezabel, I won't give it form here. Let him be forgotten so that his legacy is nothing but dust.

This is the last I will touch on the subject.

After the startling and rather abrupt end to our purpose in Sorma-heine, we left almost immediately, and I do not think that a return trip will be in our future. Though I will maintain my yearly letters to the good sister until her death, and a portion of my wealth will continue to make its way to the coffers of the cloister beyond that time, there is nothing left for me in the north. However, it was not—as Jon claims—all for nothing. What I took away from our time there was an under-standing that I cannot find redemption through vengeance. When I was robbed of my chance to hunt down the men who abused me and that failed to wound me as I thought it would, I realized something:

My past is unimportant. It is what the future holds for me that will be my salvation—and that is the love of two broken creatures that I cherish more than life itself.

I truly believe that there is no cure for what causes my deficiency of emotion or my inability to empathize with my fellow man. I am simply what I am: a cultured monster. I have finally made peace with that fact. What I can and will do is stop putting my needs and desires at the forefront.

I have lost that privilege.

Instead, I will devote myself to making sure that my boys never suffer harm through my influence again. It is a worthy cause, and I can only hope that whatever damage I have caused so far will truly be forgiven in time.

After we set sail from Sormaheine, it troubled me deeply that Jon chose to sleep apart. My instinct was to pull him to me, but I held back and said nothing as he retired, alone, to Tom's tiny cupboard of a room belowdecks night after night.

Tom, on the other hand, acted like he always has: gruff and dismissive of his own abuse. It is an admirable quality in him, and though I recognize the selfishness of this, I was thankful for his ability to bury pain. I have no shame in admitting this now, but I desperately needed him to be there in the face of Jon's desertion. In return for his generous loyalty, I have started to frequently offer Tom tenderness in what we do, knowing that though he desires it from me, he would never ask on his own.

After all, I desire it too.

With Jon, things soon started to improve on the surface. I recognized that his friendship with Katherine gives him something that neither Tom nor I can, so I began to nurture it as much as possible. Then, one night, Jon crept into my quarters and slipped between the sheets without a word of explanation. That he stayed there all night, pressed to my side... I cannot amply describe the relief I felt.

We have not slept apart since.

However, all is not right with Jon. Not yet. Jon has always been prone to a solemnity bordering on the morose, and what happened to him in Sormaheine only served to worsen that predilection. Day by day, I see changes in him, some good, some bad, some simply... incomprehensible to me. While he is decidedly more confident about what he wants and does not, both in his work aboard the ship and in my quarters, he maintains this ridiculous guilt over our abduction. As far as I can understand it, he blames himself and his fixation on the tarot card reading for the capture and subsequent abuse he, and especially Tom, suffered. He believes that it was the reading of signs in everything that made us fall prey. I don't pretend to understand it, and I have tried to turn his mind away from such thoughts, but it is like a burr within him.

Fate may no longer be a topic of interest for Jon, but I have found myself mulling over what happened with a strangely indulgent mind. While he did not lead us to the blood ogres by following the stars (I am a little unclear about the link), Jon did lead us to their proxy, did he not? Simply put, I do not feel I can dismiss the fortuity of what happened so easily.

Now, despite all the strides made towards recovery, there is one change that frustrates me beyond reason at times:

I no longer have full access to Jon's body. He sleeps with me, lets me kiss him and stroke him to completion, but the moment I try for anything more, he rebuffs me—politely and respectfully done, but still a rejection. I understand that he needs to heal and that the best thing I can offer him is time and patience, but it distresses me that he no longer submits willingly. It is made worse by the fact that I know he lies with Tom in private. It is no secret kept, and they are not going behind my back, but it weighs heavily on me. Tom assures me that things will resume their course one day, and I have learned that trust is something worthy to uphold, so I bide my time and accept Tom's word. What choice do I have?

We will be arriving at the southern peninsula in a few days. The men are restless and the pleasures of the Jewel will provide them with ample divertissement in preparation for our long journey south to Madierus. I have planned to seek out the vile old woman who put such foolishness in Jon's head and—

.   .   .

"*D*a, will ye quit yer fuckin' scritch-scratchin' and come to bed?" groaned Tom from across the room.

Baltsaros looked up from his writing and saw that the candle had burned down quite a bit. The hour was later than he had thought, so wrapped up as he was in updating his neglected journal. He dropped his pen in the inkwell, and, leaving the leather-bound book open to dry, he stood with a crackling of tendons.

Tom lay on the bed on his stomach, one beefy forearm supporting his cheek while the other, still sporting a stiff bracing bandage around the wrist, rested on the mattress beside him. Other than the bandage, the first mate was completely naked. Beside him, dressed only in a pair of loose silk pants, Jon scowled at small book he held in one hand while his fingers idly played over Tom's back. The sight made Baltsaros chuckle, and Jon looked up from his book with a frown.

"What?"

"I like looking at the both of you together like this. Just… simple and comforting is all," he replied, ridding himself of his shirt.

Jon's expression softened, and he gave a tiny nod. When the captain finished unlacing the front of his pants and pulled them down, a crease appeared between Jon's dark brows, and he stared at Baltsaros a moment before shifting over.

"Put out the candle and come here," said Jon, gesturing to the space between him and the first mate.

Curious, Baltsaros snuffed the flame and crawled onto the low mattress, settling himself on his back between Tom and Jon. Though it was dark in the stateroom, the sky outside was clear; both star and moonlight made their way through the stained-glass windows above and cast the three of them in a ghostly light.

Tom rolled over onto his side and draped his bandaged arm across Baltsaros's chest as he moved closer. With a smile Jon clasped Tom's hand and bent down to press a kiss to the captain's lips. However, when Baltsaros lifted his hand to cup the back of Jon's head, Jon pulled away. Baltsaros furrowed his brow, questioning the way that Jon's eyes seemed to narrow at him, but the younger man just leaned in for another quick, almost chaste kiss before he undid the drawstring of his pants and pushed them away.

"Turn onto your side," said Jon, lying down beside Baltsaros.

The captain made to turn towards Jon, but when Jon shook his head, he realized that he had meant towards Tom. He turned over and saw Tom's grin stretch as they faced each other, and he found himself smiling back. Gently, he placed his hand on the first mate's warm side and felt the scar left behind by the stray shot that had holed him through. Slowly, he trailed his fingers up over Tom's ribs, turning the first mate's skin to gooseflesh, and settled his hand behind Tom's neck.

Tom's eyes closed at the touch, and he let out a low, appreciative noise.

Behind Baltsaros, Jon slowly stretched out with his chest to the captain's back and the knobs of his hips touching Baltsaros's buttocks.

He was astonished and intrigued when the younger man began to move against him—he registered the soft, crinkled hair at Jon's groin tickling the cleft of his buttocks only moments before he felt the firm push of Jon's cock getting hard.

Breath turned unsteady, he clasped the back of Tom's neck a little harder, wondering what Jon's intention was.

"Kiss him," whispered Jon in Baltsaros's ear, nudging his hips harder into him.

The captain frowned. His natural inclination was to refuse the softly spoken command, the third of which Jon had uttered in the last few minutes. He was all for indulging Jon's desire for a little control, but the hard cock butting against him suggested that he was aiming for more than what was reasonable.

Or *was* it unreasonable? It wasn't like Jon hadn't taken him before in the past. Once at the *Jewel*, and a second time when they first arrived in Madierus. When Tom's eyes opened and he watched the captain quietly, Baltsaros realized what it was that was bothering him about Jon's forwardness: he had never submitted to Jon in front of the first mate.

Does that matter?

"Kiss him," repeated Jon, his tone patient but firm.

Brow still creased, Baltsaros moved forward on the pillow and claimed Tom's mouth in a soft kiss. The first mate's lips were supple and warm against his for only a heartbeat before the small groan of pleasure from Tom turned Baltsaros's kiss greedy and he deepened it, his mouth wide to devour Tom's needy rumbles that urged him on. Eyes closed, he breathed into the heat of the kiss, fingers digging gently into Tom's scalp as he let out his own quiet moan. Already his cock was a thick hardness against his thigh, and he wanted to feel Tom against him. However, Jon held onto his hip, stopping him from shifting forward for contact.

He gasped in startled pain when Jon's teeth closed hard on his shoulder, and he pulled away from Tom, breathing hard. Jon slipped his arm around Baltsaros's waist and used his knee to push the captain's thighs forward a touch so that he would lay with his legs bent. He resisted for a moment, but then Jon bit him again, a little harder this time, and he relented.

Conflicted, Baltsaros let himself be moved so that Jon could rub the swollen head of his cock over the captain's sensitive opening.

Do I want this? Tom quested forward to kiss him again, and Baltsaros let the first mate's soft lips take his, passionate and slow. Jon shuddered behind him, his cock stroking over Baltsaros's pucker again, a little teasing push, then away, so slippery that the captain thought Jon must have slicked his cock with oil while he lay kissing Tom. Another pass of Jon's cockhead caused Baltsaros to push back, losing himself in the first mate's embrace, their mouths locked and tongues seeking. Yes, he did want this. If Jon needed to use him to reclaim the sense of control he had lost, so be it.

Jon finally stopped his slow tease, and he forced his cock into Baltsaros, slow and hard until his hips were flush against the captain.

When Baltsaros tensed and gave a small, pained grunt as Jon opened him up, Tom drew back, his eyes wide. His hand slid down from where it rested on Baltsaros's side to his hips. Understanding dawned on his face as he realized exactly what was happening. With a raw-sounding moan, he shifted close enough that their cocks touched and pulled the captain's leg up onto his thigh. Baltsaros's pulse soared, and he felt a surge of lust from the naked desire in Tom's eyes as the first mate held onto him while Jon fucked him slowly from behind.

Jon's teeth closed on skin again—there was no doubt in the captain's mind that he would be marked and sore, but it made him groan in encouragement. With panted grunts, Jon fucked into him faster, more frantic, and Tom and Jon's hands clawed lines of pain over his skin as he was savaged by the first mate's fevered kiss. Then Jon let out a strangled cry and buried his face into the back of the captain's neck as his thrusts went erratic, a few deep plunges followed by a series of shallow strokes that sent a sweet pulse into Baltsaros's core.

Lungs heaving, Jon lay still for only a moment before he pulled out of Baltsaros. Hand on the captain's shoulder, he roughly turned him onto his back. Jon's eyes were dark as he leaned over him.

"It's Tom's turn now," he said quietly, his breathing ragged.

Baltsaros frowned, wondering if he had misheard.

"Jon?" said Tom. He sounded more confused than aroused.

"It's ok, Tom," said Jon, gaze locked on Baltsaros. There was power there. A challenge... and yet, affection. "He'll submit because I want him to and because he loves you. And... He loves me." He stroked the side of Baltsaros's face, lips barely moving as he spoke in a hush. "Baltsaros, I want to watch Tom take you."

Baltsaros winced and made a small sound in the back of his throat; he was so tense that a tremor went through him. He didn't know how to voice what he felt at Jon's words. Heart thundering and breathing made difficult, he hesitated only a moment longer before turning on his side. Baltsaros lay there, amazed at how easy it was to obey Jon. Without quite knowing why he did, Baltsaros realized that he completely trusted him.

"Tom, this isn't always. This is just right now," said Jon. "Just for me."

Eventually, there was a small grunt of assent from Tom, and he curled his warm body behind Baltsaros's. With a gentle hand, he carefully manoeuvred Baltsaros into a suitable position so he could penetrate him. Though he couldn't see Tom, the captain could tell how apprehensive he was.

The captain had to laugh.

"I'm not made of glass," he said, opening his eyes. Jon's cheek dimpled in the briefest of smiles.

Tom mumbled something against his skin; though he didn't catch what it was, it sounded like either a prayer or a curse.

Or, he thought with a smile, *it could be both.* However, his levity was broken a moment later when Tom's cockhead pushed hard against his opening and began to slide tight into his body.

~

*B*altsaros let out a sudden sharp breath and his brow furrowed, eyes locked on Jon's. Tom had obviously found the nerve to do as he was asked and let out a soft grunt as he thrust his hips forward slowly against the captain.

A sound caught in Jon's throat, and he nodded quickly.

"That's it," he whispered. "Fuck him deep, Tom." Jon couldn't explain to himself why he needed to make them do this, only that it ate up some of the anger and shame that he was carrying around like lead in his belly. It was as if he needed to restore some of the power and control that had been ripped from him. He lifted himself up on one elbow to watch Tom and Baltsaros; the first mate's side glistened with sweat as he fucked the captain slowly with brows pinched together and eyes closed with his efforts.

Jon reached out and placed a hand on Tom's ass, coaxing him to move faster.

"This is for you, not for him," he said, and found that though he was sated, the sight of Tom ploughing into Baltsaros had his cock again at half-mast. "Gods, that's gorgeous. Don't hold back... Do you like fucking him? Do you like having your cock in his ass?"

Tom let out a small moan and fucked the captain harder, curling his arm around Baltsaros's chest possessively; though he didn't reply, he sighed a word.

"Da."

Jon touched himself, teasing the head of his cock as Tom worked himself closer using Baltsaros's body. He lay back down and saw that Baltsaros had closed his eyes.

"Don't... I want you looking at me," he said softly, kissing the older man's bottom lip. Baltsaros opened his eyes, and when Jon reached down to begin stroking the captain's cock, the hoarse groan that burst from him sounded raw. Baltsaros kept his eyes on Jon's, desire and devotion giving him an almost pained expression as he breathed heavily in time to Tom's thrusts.

Behind Baltsaros, the first mate's grunts began to be punctuated by broken, sobbing sighs, and Jon voiced a soft moan of his own.

"Don't hold back."

In response, Tom let out a growl, a deep, desperate thing that sounded like it was torn from his chest, and Baltsaros bucked hard against Jon as the first mate came inside him. Jon waited until Tom had stilled, panting loudly, before he pushed him away from the captain.

"Fuck..." panted Tom.

Jon shifted lower on the mattress and quickly took Baltsaros's cock nearly to the root into his mouth. It was only a matter of seconds before he swallowed down the captain's salty-bitter cum with Baltsaros's fingers twisting almost cruelly in his hair as he cried out in pleasure.

~

*T*he captain cleaned up as best as he could, postponing a full bath until daylight, and returned to the bed. Tom was fast asleep, but Jon watched Baltsaros silently as he climbed around the first mate and between the sheets. He sighed at the feeling of Jon's naked skin against his as he gathered the younger man to him.

"Are you all right?" he asked quietly.

Jon laughed and nuzzled against the captain's neck.

"I was actually going to ask you the same thing," Jon replied. "And apologize if I was out of line."

"No apologies necessary," said Baltsaros with a smile. "That's not something I would like to repeat any time soon, but... I understood it." Baltsaros felt Jon tense at his word choice. He couldn't tell him that he had *enjoyed* it, because enjoyment had little to do with the complex and strangely tender emotions that the act had brought him. He stroked Jon's dark-brown curls, thinking about how to reword what he'd said when Jon spoke up.

"I'm hurt," he confessed.

For a moment, Baltsaros thought he was talking about physical pain, and he stopped his hand, startled.

"I'm hurt," repeated Jon, his voice a little rough with emotion. "I've been feeling so fucking *raw*, but I'm getting better." He sighed. "I also feel like I'm overreacting because, shit, that was nothing compared to what Tom and you have been through."

Baltsaros shook his head, tugging softly on Jon's hair.

"Rid yourself of those thoughts immediately, Jon. Take the time you need to heal and know that Tom and I will always be here for you."

"I know," whispered Jon. "And we'll live happily ever after..."

With a chuckle, Baltsaros nodded.

"Indeed we will."

*T*he captain had thought for certain that Jon had fallen asleep as they lay entwined on the cool sheets. However, Jon lifted his head a few minutes later and peered thoughtfully at Baltsaros.

"I've been having dreams," he said, sounding hesitant. "The kind that feel, um, *important.*"

Baltsaros's brows rose. It was the first time Jon had voiced anything of that nature since leaving Sormaheine.

"Oh?" he said, trying not to let his curiosity make him sound too eager lest he deter Jon from telling him of it.

Jon's forehead creased, and he turned his head away, thinking.

"Yeah. A few times a week… the same dream," he said.

"What happens in the dream?"

"We sail east," replied Jon.

"Ah," said Baltsaros. "Would you like to go east?"

With a little laugh, Jon lay his head back down, twining his fingers with the captain's.

"Maybe, but let's just spend a long, *long* fucking time doing nothing but sitting on the beach first, ok? Maybe build that shack you talked about?"

Baltsaros laughed and closed his eyes.

"That sounds perfect."

"Aye, it does," muttered Tom sleepily. "Now quit yer jawin' and let me get some bloody sleep."

Despite the annoyance in his voice, the first mate's hand crept over Baltsaros's hip, pulling himself closer, and the three remained that way, with tangled limbs and quiet hearts, as sleep finally lay claim to them.

WANT TO KNOW MORE?

See maps, a pirate glossary, diagrams and details of *Baal's Heart* at
<u>baals-heart.com</u>.

—Bey

FATED AUDIOBOOK - NARRATED BY MICHAEL FERRAIUOLO

Fated is now available for the first time ever in audiobook format (*whispersync* ready).
Relive the adventures of Jon, Tom, and Baltsaros, now exquisitely narrated by the very talented Michael Ferraiuolo.

Find it here: http://geni.us/pageFated

BOOKS BY BEY DECKARD

FOR AN UP-TO-DATE LIST OF TITLES, VISIT:

https://beydeckard.com/blog/buy-my-books/

MAX, THE SERIES

Max

Max, the Sequel

BAAL'S HEART SERIES

Caged: Love and Treachery on the High Seas

Sacrificed: Heart Beyond the Spires

Fated: Blood and Redemption

Careened: Winter Solstice in Madierus

F.I.S.T.S

Sarge

Murphy

F.I.S.T.S. Handbook For Individual Survival in Hostile Environments

THE ACTOR'S CIRCLE

The Complications of T

The Last Nights of The Frangipani Hotel

THE STONEWATCHERS

Kestrel's Talon

STANDALONE BOOKS

Better the Devil You Know

Exposed

ABOUT THE AUTHOR

Artist, Writer, Dog Lover

Bey Deckard is the author of a number of novels including the *Baal's Heart books, Max, Beauty and His Beast,* and *Better the Devil You Know.*

Bey lives in Montréal, Canada where he spends most of his time writing, doing graphic work, painting portraits, speaking French, cooking tasty vegetarian eats, or watching more movies than is good for him. If you're the curious type, www.beydeckard.com is where you'll find art and free stories by Bey as well as information on his published works.

bey.deckard@gmail.com
Look for Deckard's Diablerie on Facebook

facebook.com/authorbeydeckard
twitter.com/BeyDeckard
instagram.com/beydeckard
goodreads.com/beydeckard
bookbub.com/authors/bey-deckard
pettingzoo.co/@Beybey